The

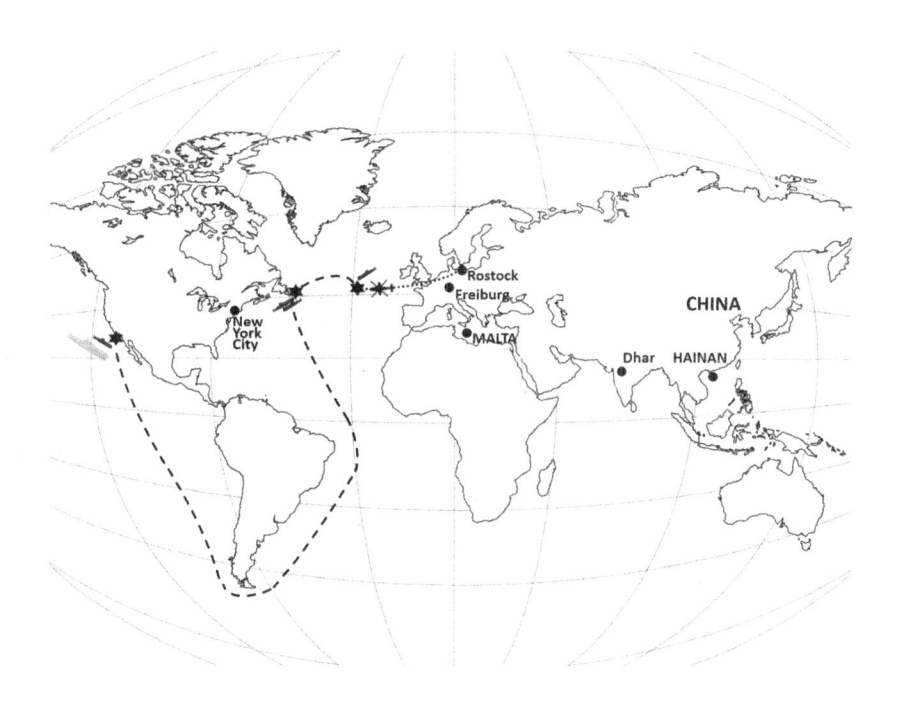

Rostock
Freiburg
New York City
MALTA
CHINA
Dhar HAINAN

The appendix contains an index of persons. Some terms are *italicized* in case there is an explanation in the glossary. When based on facts, sources are also mentioned there.

For eBook formats: The *italicized* terms are linked to the glossary.

Karsten Lehmann

The Sound Trap

Techno Thriller

Bibliographic information of the Deutsche Nationalbibliothek (German National Library): The Deutsche Nationalbibliothek lists this publication in the Deutsche Nationalbibliografie (German National Bibliography); detailed bibliographic data are available on the Internet: www.dnb.de/EN

First English Edition 2022
Copyright © 2022 by Karsten Lehmann
Based on German Edition "Z-ALPHA"
Editing: Elke Harms
Translation: Ron McKinney
Cover design: Karsten Lehmann

www.karsten-lehmann-books.de

Printed and published by: BoD - Books on Demand GmbH, Norderstedt/Germany
ISBN 978-3-7562-4874-2

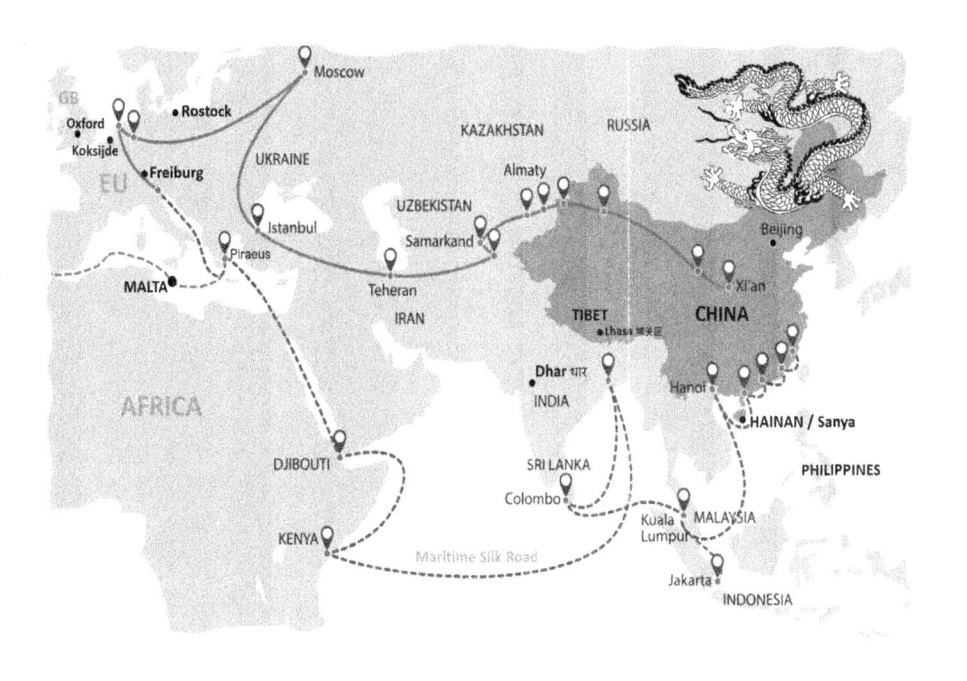

CHAPTER 1	7
CHAPTER 2	25
CHAPTER 3	36
CHAPTER 4	59
CHAPTER 5	83
CHAPTER 6	96
CHAPTER 7	120
CHAPTER 8	159
CHAPTER 9	197
CHAPTER 10	225
CHAPTER 11	261
CHAPTER 12	280
CHAPTER 13	301
CHAPTER 14	315
CHAPTER 15	336
CHAPTER 16	351
CHAPTER 17	381
EPILOG	402
AUTHOR'S MESSAGE	406
PERSONS IN THE BOOK	412
GLOSSARY	416

*The truth is a mixture
of facts and assumptions,
but is sometimes difficult to see.
Prejudices are no good as visual aids
because whoever takes them off,
can look much further.*

(Indian lore, about 800 BC)

CHAPTER 1

"What a shit!" Brian heard cursing from down the hall. That must have been Olaf, known for his tantrums. It was annoying, but by now, most were already ignoring him. Few understood it as a cry for help, and hardly anyone knew how to act. Since conversations in the office were already problematic, hardly anyone dared to talk to him about private matters. It was like a solid wall that grew higher and higher over time. Finally, one after the other had given up. It was an open secret that the poor guy had been pushed into this thankless position shortly before his retirement. He could work out his frustrations alone at the end of a long staff building.

Something else was on Brian's mind from the moment he got up; one thought stuck in his head like gum on the sole of a shoe. It was the book just read, the autobiography of a former professional basketball player. In it, he movingly described very intimate things. Especially when it came to sexual fantasies, Brian experienced people usually being a little communicative. Although he generally poured out his heart openly, this did not apply to such topics. Reading this, he realized that perhaps the athlete had opened a door for many. A door through which Brian would not walk at the moment. Conversely, it was his job to use all communication channels to penetrate the most hidden regions of other brains.

With other cultures, he learned about significant differences. Intimate topics were handled very differently and sometimes not discussed publicly at all. Nevertheless, Brian knew that most would gladly confide in someone if only there were opportunities. However, Brian also found widespread knowledge about sexuality was still severely limited. It bothered him that young people still didn't easily find practical, age-appropriate information on the Internet. As in Brian's family, it was often not the parents who provided practical sex education at the right age.

The fact that he was so agitated that day could have been due to a small passage in the book. To his knowledge, no one had ever dared to do such a thing. And now it's simply in the autobiography of a celebrity.

Specific fantasies also occupied Brian since childhood. At that time, he thought it was because he was not quite normal in other respects. It didn't bother him much when he was sometimes called a freak. But he was offended when rumors about his psychic abilities circulated at school, which someone must have made up. Although the teachers at the time did a lot to clear things up, he still felt the unease of some parents when he visited school friends.

This basketball player described how he could get into a mental coupling with his partner. They developed their fantasies together before physical contact occurred. Things got even crazier when he claimed to have had sex with an angel in this way before. Brian knew most people would dismiss it as a description of fanciful dreams. He read between the lines that there were possibly actual events described. He suspected it might be a special distress call or warning. Certainly, a strange thought, at least at the first moment.

By half past three that morning, the book's last page had been devoured. When the radio alarm reminded him of real life, fatigue set in, and, once back at his office, so did the inability to concentrate on work.

For the past six months, he had been assigned to a special command that, among other things, coordinated operational plans for naval vessels operating worldwide at the Rostock site. The newly built Maritime Operations Center (*MOC*) complex was occupied only a few years ago. Before that, the location on the German Baltic coast moved from Glücksburg to Rostock. Brian got his own office in the four-story building. He wasn't used to that and didn't like being there alone. Working in teams was essential to him because, as a language expert, he preferred to use all his senses in communication. When he began serving in the military, he was offered the opportunity to work more intensively with computational linguistics. This was a means of filtering out emotions in texts or synthetic languages.

During the pandemic of the early twenties, people inevitably moved apart. The lack of physical contact meant that Brian, too, spoke to others mainly by electronic means. It was hard for him because he had learned to use his entire body to convey words and feelings all his life. Isolating people meant a dramatic change for him. However, he also heard other things. After all, many contemporaries had already become accustomed to communicating mainly via digital media.

His employer, the US Navy, had sent him to Germany for a particular NATO project. Although it involved an exciting topic, he would have liked to stay back in the States for the time being. It was, therefore, increasingly difficult to meet up with old friends. As a result, these relationships became increasingly superficial.

Since he was fluent in several languages, he was sent around the globe immediately after joining the navy. That was probably one of the reasons his ex had broken up with him after months of long-distance dating. She also made no secret that she was now living with one of her former co-students.

There was something about the way staff officers often requested Brian's presence when negotiating with international parties to a conflict. During his primary studies at the University of North Carolina at Greensboro, he learned about Tibetan Buddhism and various types of meditation, as well as Egyptian alchemy and shamanism.

Before joining the navy, he had spent time in Germany several times, taking special courses at the University of Freiburg. There he could meet other people with paranormal abilities and expand his knowledge of telepathic communication. He also learned ancient Greek and Sanskrit there. These languages allowed him to read the writings of the ancient philosophers and the Indian *Vedas* in the original. He remembered this time in southern Germany fondly. Someone had arranged for him to stay in a student flat-sharing community for the first few days. Initially skeptical about whether he could cope with his mania for order, he liked it so much that he moved again into a larger shared flat.

At the university and in his living environment, he met the most exciting friends of his life. Communicating with them was always something special. One of the unusual kinds of people was Anna. He dealt with her during training, in particular techniques in telepathy. As a lecturer, Anna taught even more advanced ancient methods of this communication. While his friends found Anna attractive, Brian didn't feel that way. Somehow, he thought she would treat him dismissively, too. As soon as he drifted into a private conversation, she distanced herself. That could be one of her principles to keep some authority as a lecturer. Sometimes she even seemed a bit snippy to him, almost like a pubescent teenager.

In the first weeks, Brian had thought Anna had met many skeptics. Such people sometimes faked their interest, even if there was some curiosity. She used to tell her students how she could test their real interests. It was the way someone dealt with their failures in training. And much of Anna's methods reminded Brian of his experiences with skeptics.

Most people secretly wished they had some supernatural powers. The desire for recognition was part of life, and those who had mastered something special were quicker to take center stage. On the other hand, Brian experienced absolute rejection from those who saw his abilities as a threat to their careers. After all, the ability to lie well is a means of gaining an unfair advantage. In Brian's presence, however, this advantage quickly vanished into thin air.

There was one thing Brian found particularly interesting about Anna. He quickly noticed that she sensed it immediately when he tried to get inside her head. Outside his training group, most people thought it was hocus pocus when he tried to talk to them about telepathy. He was quickly labeled an esoteric crackpot. In any case, his non-verbal communication skills improved every year of his life. Anna undoubtedly contributed to this with her techniques and unconventional teaching methods.

In the meantime, Brian had developed into a tangible medium. He was now able to teach others. When others called him a medium, he was somehow uncomfortable. It brought back unwanted childhood memories. Believing he could read their minds, most people quickly distanced themselves. People with this ability knew very well that many myths circulated around telepathy, but still little enlightenment. Of course, it was also to blame for the fact that the currently available scientific articles could only be found if you knew your way around. The TV stations have also realized there is good money to be made in popular science content. In the meantime, even topics like the UFO phenomenon had become presentable. At that time, Brian was like most people because he still lifted his head towards the starry sky when he dreamed of extraterrestrial life and not human intelligence.

"Brian, wait a minute! Are you coming bowling Thursday night?" Christina approached him from behind. She, too, had not been working on the *MOC* for long. Few things Brian knew about her personal life. This included many friends and the fact that she always wanted to experience something somewhere. Christina didn't seem to be in a committed relationship, however.

Unsure how to answer and to buy a few seconds, Brian asked, "Is the new bowling center open yet?"

"Yes. Although we have only one lane, with you, I would have then anyway only s..., I mean.... we would only be six anyway."

Brian started laughing even before Christina finished the sentence. He apologized for it right away. She had no way of knowing, but it was the case that Brian was already thinking the sentence through before his conversation partner could formulate it. He didn't think it was anything like clairvoyance. He explained it to himself with the fact that he could process body signals simply furiously fast. Besides, it was logical because now only seven people were working on this floor, and six sometimes did something together. As in this case, Brian usually found a reason why he often knew the outcome of a conversation in advance. However, there were sometimes situations when he was surprised when he was right in his foresight. It was uncanny, for example, when he saw an interview on television and had the impression that the interviewee was reading the answer from Brian's brain. Of course, there were various explanations for this, and it didn't have anything to do with paranormal abilities. If there weren't other strange occurrences that his superiors also knew about.

Until recently, Brian had been stationed on a navy frigate, which had lately been in port in Malta for a few days. During shore leave, an accident occurred that also involved his comrade Sean. During questioning, they could only remember some of the details. The captain wanted to send them both on convalescent leave on the doctor's recommendation. Brian, however, had other plans and asked to be allowed to do indoor duty at Rostock Naval Base instead of convalescent leave. The captain granted him this on the condition that he attend psychological care twice a week for as long as the medical staff deemed it necessary.

At the first examination in Rostock, Brian was asked to give details of the incident. Thereupon he described very roughly what had happened but then quickly regretted it. Either the psychotherapist was interested in this story, or someone had asked her to squeeze Brian. Or maybe she was happy to have found an intriguing subject for her research. At first, he only wanted to describe a few sentences. But the therapist was not satisfied with that and insisted on hearing the whole story.

So, Brian began to describe the circumstances of his accident:
"My basic training was just completed when I was transferred to the US Naval Information Service. We call that unit ONI. That was just under six months ago. I was interested in this position because it seemed the most interesting job in the navy. They mainly handle surveillance of other nations' naval forces there. As everywhere, there are also a few special units that deal with counterintelligence tasks. I didn't have much information about this at the beginning …."

After an exercise in the Mediterranean, Brian's ship, a German Saxon-class frigate, was in Malta for a few days. Brian persuaded Sean, with whom he sometimes spent his free time, to visit some archaeological sites. He already had something in mind and now only had to convince his comrade to come along.

"How are we going to get there?" Sean wanted to know.

"I've been looking through the local tourist listings. Look, we could rent an electric quad here. Supposedly you're allowed into the national parks with that thing."

"But only when I'm driving!" Sean wanted to make it clear.

"Looks like we'll have to rent two of these things then. I'm not getting in the back with you," with which Brian made it clear that he found something wrong with his friend's driving style. Sean just returned from his vacation and boarded again two days ago in Malta. Suddenly, he had other doubts and said, "I have a terrible muscle ache in my ass. I wonder if these quads have proper seats?"

"Sore muscles? You never do any sports on vacation, and you can't ride either! At most, it could have been the sports seats in your new Mustang!"

"Haha, admit it already that you are jealous of my car. By the way, it's not just my ass that hurts. I had the shittiest seat on the transport flight from Ramstein to Malta. That won't happen to you, of course. You usually fly with the officers in business class. Someday I'll figure out how you do it."

Eventually, they agreed to each drive their quad and booked a day tour over the Internet.

From books on European antiquity, Brian knew that Malta was one of the most amazing places in Europe and had a lot of archaeological features to offer. Like Sardinia or the Balearic Islands, parts of the Maltese republic hid many mysteries. Therefore, extensive protection measures had been initiated on the wondrous island of Menorca and Malta to protect the unique temples, caves, and structures that still seem strange today.

Brian knew from his student days that many places from ancient writings do not yet appear in modern literature. At least in the official archaeological records. Despite this, more and more laterals were writing about what mysterious things were still to be discovered there. In the writings of the ancient Greeks, there were regular mentions of structural facilities, the purpose of which archaeologists were still puzzling. Since a mystery sounds like something scientists wouldn't know what to do with, many of these discoveries were eventually simply declassified as "cult sites".

People like Brian, however, smelled this rat from afar. One example that immediately came to his mind was the matter of the miles-long, so-called *cart ruts* on the ground-level rocks. With this term, tourists were fooled for a long time, probably to avoid further inquiries. Fortunately, there were also technically versed visitors, who immediately noticed that a cart track running in the ground would always have to run parallel. The wheels would have had to be huge, with indentations up to 27 inches deep. In addition, there are places where the track is interrupted and suddenly continues a little further away. After all, one would hardly have carried the car there. Sometimes the paths even cross each other.

During a lecture in Malta, a lecturer amusedly reminded us of the female Cyclopes from Greek mythology, who might have driven their babies around in gigantic baby carriages. A student had replied that it must have been the cyclopean males who were put on the track by their wives to dutifully drive out the children. And by the way, no one is stupid enough to walk the same path every day without noticing that the wheels are digging deeper and deeper into the rock. Moreover, women would prefer the company of other parents and walking side by side to be able to talk. Then someone went one better and added, "The parents of the baby cyclops must have already owned smartphones. With these 'rails' in the rocks, they could chat with their friends while walking, without paying attention to the path." Eventually, everyone agreed on why the cyclops were extinct. Namely, some of these "tracks" ended in the sea. Consequently, all those smartphone-junkie parents and their offspring probably drowned while walking.

"Well, that should be a warning to all new-age parents!" the lecturer concluded then with approving laughter.

At least such casual incidents at the university showed Brian that there were tendencies in official science to no longer convey nonsense without comment. During this trip, they would finally be able to look at some of the remains of these strangely carved stones. He was not only friends with his comrade Sean, who, as an intelligent technician, often had good ideas when discussing old cultural sites. One thing bothered him, though. Sean often obtained information from the Internet, the originators of which Brian did not consider reputable. When questioned about it, the topics and the way they were disseminated usually matched what he knew about manipulative methods in *social psychology*. But since Sean was still listening to others, Brian didn't think he was a lost cause.

The trip started on an early Sunday morning. Still in the port of Malta, they picked up their reserved electric quads from a rental station. It was apparent from the four-wheeled motorcycles that they were already doing hard labor. The rental station employee pointed out that they could only drive on public roads. Of course, the two only smiled because they could have rented a small car for half the price. They wanted to experience the fun of driving off-road. Sean looked skeptically at the wheel suspensions and suspected that the models were not designed for heavy terrain. Not wanting to worry Brian, he said nothing.

Then they drove off. Sean had brought a military GPS device. It wasn't strictly legal, but there seemed to be a broad interpretation of the regulations for his fellow troopers. With this device, navigation was enjoyable, especially off the roads. The information about the current position, which was accurate to less than one yard, made the map an excellent orientation aid. The satellite images were so detailed that even trees and stone walls could be used for navigation.

The way led across the island in the direction of the south coast. They had first entered the small town of *Dingli* as their destination. Then the software had to calculate a route they could pass with their barely fifty-inch quads. This was not difficult, but they noticed something strange. Some spots on the map had been blurred. While they knew blurring military or other secret installations was standard, the nearby radar station was tiny. That didn't explain why such large portions of the area had been neutralized. Military maps could be cleared of "blurs" using a password, depending on the user's security level. Sean, of course, had not been able to obtain such a password. In any case, it was suspicious and made the two excursionists curious about what to see.

They needed much longer for the route than planned. Sean got stuck in a crevice, and they already had the first breakdown. The search for a stable branch to lever out was finally successful. Shortly after that, both failed on a slope. It was too slippery even for the four-wheel drive vehicles because of the wet green surface. Hence, a detour had to be found.

The next surprise was soon to come. They got a terrible scare when a goat suddenly cried out right in front of them. The quads approached, and the poor creature probably saw its end coming in mortal fear.

"The goat should have heard us coming. Why didn't it flee? Or are the E-quads not easy to hear off-road?" Sean asked while Brian was already formulating his answer, "Maybe the old beast is already deaf, or someone rarely strays here, so the local game feels safe."

"I don't think so. Take a look around. There are remnants of bird-catching nets lying around everywhere. I know that catching wild birds is forbidden here."

"Right. And it won't be the remains of a veil party. So, they're still catching rare birds. And that's why bird catchers will show up regularly."

They stopped their vehicles again a few minutes later to look at the navigation device. Their destination was near. Despite the proximity to the ocean and slightly gusty wind, it was dead quiet. Sean asked, "Can you feel it?"

"Yes, funny. It's not just the goats that seem to go deaf here. It sounds like being in a soundproofed recording studio. And your voice sounds all silenced, too."

"I've seen something like this before, and there are legends about it," Brian spoke very loudly, "In England, there are *Whispering Knights*. They are also called Whispering Stones. They belong to a complex of monuments south of Long Compton. In this, various groups of monoliths are scattered in the area. These were arranged in the landscape following a given system."

"I've heard something like that before. But what did you experience there?"

"This place is haunting, and I didn't feel well afterward."

"What do you mean?"

"This megalithic site seems to have a life of its own. It sounds idiotic, but the stones don't just speak to people. They also speak to each other. If you stay there in certain places and times of the day, there's an effect like this. All the sounds of the surroundings fall silent. At similar sites worldwide, most people don't feel much or only imagine they feel something because they go there with a certain expectation. At the *Whispering Stones*, it's different. There, anyone who spends a little longer among the monoliths gets goosebumps. They say it's the language of the dark side. And although I understand many languages, I couldn't do anything with those creepy sounds."

Sean had listened with interest and replied, "I'm so glad!"

"By the way, the measurements have shown that the stones emit an ultrasound. This is strongest shortly after sunrise. There are also already scientifically confirmed reports for this."

"I'd consider anyone else a nut who told me stuff like that," Sean replied.

"And you don't think I'm crazy?" Brian wanted to know.

"Sometimes I do because you say kinky stuff all the time. But you've also proven a lot of it to me. You always blush when you lie, which makes you trustworthy."

"Yeah, nobody wants me on their team at *rubber bridge*," Brian admitted.

"The honest ones always lose. Sometimes you let others take advantage of you with that, too."

"Maybe, but I feel good the way it is. Even though honesty will probably never make me rich."

Finally, the two decided to stay on the slightly more passable path the rest of the way to *Dingli Cliffs*. Brian rode behind Sean's quad, struggling to keep up with him. His eyes scanned the ground for noticeable structures, hoping to find something unusual. Then he saw something, stopped, and walked back a few feet. Sure enough, across the path ran two plunging grooves that continued left and right of the way in the rocky ground. The two-yard-wide roadway had tracks about fifteen inches deep filled in with concrete. Otherwise, they would have caused an unpleasant drop over the handlebars. Sean saw Brian lagging in the rearview mirror and turned around.

"What's the matter, something broken?"

"No, but I think we found it!"

"You don't mean those grooves in the rock? The stone here was certainly washed out by the water. I thought we'd look at something exciting!"

"No, this has nothing to do with erosion. It's the *cart ruts* I told you about. Let's continue foot from now on. The tracks that cross this path here are mostly overgrown. But I think I know where they lead."

"Do you know, or did you have another one of those visions?"

"I can't tell you. I just know," Brian muttered. The tone of Sean's question annoyed him. For sure, he would have preferred to ride the quad rather than walk now. Brian, on the other hand, was electrified after his discovery. The excitement was evident on his face. Sean finally gave in, but not without grumbling again, "I was looking forward to a breathtaking view at Dingli Rocks. Finally, we jump through the bushes like goats following imaginary tracks."

While Sean finally walked behind him, unmotivated, a thought occurred to Brian. Why had he just remembered the *Whispering Stones* earlier? There were many more striking examples of the hearing loss phenomenon. Now he feared that this might have been one of the suspicions that did not bode well.

Brian was so energized that he missed Sean struggling over the rocks covered with flat shrubs, barely keeping up.

"Be careful; there are crevices and holes here! At this rate, we'll fall in somewhere," he called to his friend from behind.

"What's got into you? Are you trying to show the goats how to long jump? They can do it better with four legs!"

Brian then waited a moment, turned to his gasping comrade, and yelled, "Sorry, I feel we don't have much time left. I'll explain later. Right now, we need to hurry. Just trust me."

When Sean caught up, he muttered, "I am an idiot! What have I gotten myself into here again? One day this madman will kill us."

Less than a minute later, Brian stopped suddenly, but Sean could not control his run so quickly and rammed into the man in front of him. Rowing with his hands, he tried to hold on to the bushes as he fell. But they gave way, and Brian slid headfirst into a hole in the ground. Hanging in the bushes, he tried to bring his body upright. The feet had to get a grip somehow. He succeeded at first, but the branches broke. That's how the slide began. In any movie, the casualty would have screamed to heighten the drama. Brian, however, remained silent. Sean watched helplessly from above as his comrade disappeared into the hole. When the rumbling had subsided, and Sean was staring down in panic, he shouted Brian's name. There was no answer, and the view was blocked by dense bushes. Only a foul stench came out as if stagnant water had been stirred up, in which plant remains had been moldering away for centuries.

"Are you still alive?"

At least Brian was moving because sounds could be heard from below. Then came an answer, "No, I don't think so. But other than that, I'm okay…just gross down here."

"I can't see you. How deep is the hole?"

"Maybe fifteen feet or so. I can't say exactly. There's nothing stable to climb up."

"I'll go back and get the rope. Make yourself comfortable for that long!"

"Thanks for the advice!" Brian replied, but Sean was already returning to the quads where they had left some equipment. While waiting, Brian tried to shimmy his way to the pit's edge. After pushing some plants aside, it became clear the hole had been driven into the rock with tools.

Could this be an old pitfall? Hardly, the inhabitants would have discovered it long ago and filled it in like the many other holes in this area, Brian thought. He also noticed that rainwater could only accumulate in this cavity for a short time. The water edges on the rock indicated a changing water level. It was a very porous sandstone.

Why has this hole been left without a barrier? Something is not right here, Brian pondered while he waited for Sean to return.

After a while, he looked at his watch, which by now showed ten minutes to one, and wondered. Sean should have been back after forty minutes. But an hour had already passed. That he could have gotten lost was very unlikely. He pulled his cell phone out of his leg pocket and was pleased to see that the thing had remained waterproof as promised in the commercials. He dialed Sean's number but got no connection, although a G5 quality reception bar was displayed.

There could be a dozen reasons why someone might be late. Meanwhile, the stinking mud made Brian's body shiver with coldness. It was summer, but the temperature was much lower than outside the hole. The damp rock acted like a wine cooler.

What's this guy doing so long? Hopefully, he didn't fall and is lying around with a sprained ankle. I was so stupid. Why did I run so fast in front, even in this terrain?

Then he heard a rustling sound as if the wind were brushing through leaves. Of course, this was not possible in this hole in the ground, so it had to have another reason. Brian slid his hands along the plants and moved from one spot to another. He searched ceaselessly for a better foothold and a way to free himself from the unpleasant plant mush. Now he noticed that it was getting darker. Was a thundercloud passing by here? The weather forecast had not predicted any rain for this and the next two days. They would never have dared a trip to the cliffs on the coast if a thunderstorm had been announced.

It was getting darker and darker, as if someone was dimming the lights with a switch. Another glance at the clock and ... *Son of a bitch. How can this be?* His smartwatch already showed 17:30. *The damn thing couldn't have changed itself to the wrong time zone*, he thought and pulled out his phone again to see what location it was showing. The circumstances became stranger and stranger. The phone now read 17:50, as did his wristwatch. Time seemed to fly. Had his gaze upward not encountered a starry sky, he would have simply dismissed the mystery with the time as a technical error. But the cell phone display showed a cell phone provider he didn't know, instead of the Maltese provider "GoMobile" as he had expected. With the four-and-a-half-hour time difference, the onset of darkness, and the location of Nandi in the Indian state of Karnataka indicated, it all fell into place. Brian had already experienced a lot of adventures. Some of it, however, he could not tell others just like that. Or only to those who knew his oddities. His comrades had already had fun with him, maybe because he seemed like a weirdo. But this experience here was so absurd that it couldn't even be a prank by his comrades.

I must concentrate now and get my pulse down. Otherwise, the meditation will fail. Without this calm, I won't come up with anything creative, Brian thought and pressed his back against the rock behind him. Now he began his thought exercises to tune the frequencies of several brain regions to each other. A few minutes later, his pulse dropped while, at the same time, his brain's *theta waves* (4-7 hertz) increased. These waves occur when the human subconscious is active, such as during REM sleep, meditation, or hypnosis. In this state, some people could achieve mental coupling with others, provided the interlocutor was familiar with this practice and his brain was in a similar condition.

For Brian, it made no sense to think about whether what was going on in his head now was real. He had learned enough about Asian meditation to know that you must first listen to your thoughts. Only when enough information had been accumulated could the two brain hemispheres weigh logic and emotion against each other and piece together the puzzle of snippets of thought. Brian was able to memorize much faster than most people using this method. What he had found out during years of training was later confirmed for him in Freiburg. Both the instructors there and Anna, with whom Brian had trained frequently, confirmed a long-held suspicion. A person experiences a breakthrough in creativity only when he can tap into the global information fields, also called *morphic fields.*

Maybe today I'll have the improbable luck to succeed without outside assistance, Brian encouraged himself. While trying to sense these information fields, there was an irresistible urge to look at the clock. No matter what time it was, it wouldn't get him any further. With that, the mind won out, and Brian fell into a deep trance. Although this was part of everyday life for a practiced medium, something unexpected happened in his body during this self-hypnosis.

Δ

For the last few yards, Sean sped up his run again before throwing himself at the edge of the hole in the ground and calling down, "I'm back. Are you okay?"
　Even for an athletically built soldier like him, this run across the rocky ground was torture. Despite his increased breathing rate, he held his breath for a moment. It was the only way he could concentrate on what Brian would answer. No answer came, however. Panic set in because that silence down there couldn't mean anything good. Calling down repeatedly, he finally began to look for a solid spot to tie the rope. A few yards away, there was a dry olive tree. Using a flat stone, he exposed a root and tied the rope's end. This root should be able to hold two adult men if necessary. The rope was long enough to wrap the other end around a second tree trunk. This could serve as an improvised pulley if necessary. He hurried back to the hole and threw down the rope's end.
　"Brian! Can you hear me?"
　Still no answer.
　Hopefully, he didn't pass out from the putrid gases. If a poisonous animal bit him, Brian might have fainted and suffocated in the rotten pulp, Sean thought, trying to think of a way to protect himself from an insect bite. But he couldn't think of more than stuffing his pant legs tightly into the lace-up boots. Then he checked the rope several times and descended into the hole. As Sean climbed, his eyes kept a panicked lookout for spiders and snakes.
　If I were better versed in biology, I'd know what to look for. Oh well, those who see a lot worry more, he told himself, trying to stop thinking about the little creepy crawlies that could jump down his neck at any moment. Before he set foot in the stinking mud, he turned around in all directions. There was nothing to be seen of his comrade.

Damn it! He must have gone under. He had no choice but to climb into the wet material. With his arms, he rummaged panic-stricken in the plant mush, trying to feel Brian's body. With his hands, he pulled out branches until he got hold of something that caused another adrenaline rush. It was a piece of cloth. He pulled it out and was relieved to find the remnant of a bird net. After minutes of intense searching, Sean wondered if it could even be that. The hole was perhaps ten feet in diameter. With his body, he was only sunk in above the waist. Brian couldn't be in the mush. There was no room for a second grown man here.

Can this be a stupid joke on his part? That doesn't fit Brian. Maybe the guy had already climbed out, and we missed each other?

Sean decided to climb out again.

"Brian, where are you?" he shouted in all directions after standing upright at the hole's edge.

Where did this guy go? Why didn't he wait for me, he wondered, once it was clear that his comrade could no longer be in the immediate vicinity. Whether he was lying helplessly behind the hills could not be seen from the ground. It was possible, however, that they had passed each other. In any case, help was needed. According to regulation, he dialed the military emergency number. The rope kept attached to the tree hanging down into the hole so it could be rechecked later. The sailor on duty in his unit answered the phone and calmly took the news of Brian's accident. While still on the phone, he reported the incident through the mandatory reporting chain and assured Sean that help was on the way.

Due to a supply mission north of Malta, the only naval helicopter stationed nearby could not be deployed. The German navy, therefore, contacted all nearby ships that had aircraft. Then, in the early afternoon, a helicopter arrived from Sea-Watch 5, patrolling south of Malta. This vessel, which had only recently been commissioned by the sea rescue service of the same name, was able to reach the accident site by helicopter within 30 minutes. As this was a recreational accident and not a military operation, no special permission had to be obtained to call in civilian agencies. The deployed search team found no trace of Brian that evening or the following day.

The story Brian had told his psychologist ended at this point with a mundane abbreviation of what happened. Only the end of the strange tale corresponded to the facts. According to it, Brian woke up in daylight next to the hole in the ground near the Dingli cliffs and was alone. It took him a few minutes to remember that he was on a trip with Sean before disappearing. His cell phone's battery hadn't died yet, but for some reason, it only showed "No service available". Maybe someone had blocked his SIM card. Based on his surroundings, he tried to orient himself. Because of his previous study of Maltese maps, he knew his way around. So, he also knew that the place Dingli was not far away. He set off on foot. Entirely filthy and smelling bad, Brian was looked at skeptically by the village's inhabitants. Eventually, however, someone kindly offered him help and a cell phone. After dialing the military emergency number, which Sean had also used after his disappearance, Brian's trip to Malta ended.

Of course, this was not the end of the matter. The commander wanted to know why he had not been found, even though he woke up very close to where he had last been seen. The search cameras and the helicopter's thermal imaging recordings proved that no human could have been at this spot during the overflight. Brian had no choice but to claim that he did not know what had happened.

Although his life up to this point had been anything else but monotonous, the circumstances of his absence were the most exciting thing he had experienced so far. His task was to find someone he could trust with the actual story without them doubting his sanity. He did not count his superiors among them. The psychologist, to whom he later had to tell this story somewhat involuntarily, was also not one of these trustworthy people. That is why he had not told her that his memories were limited to hours while they had spent four days searching for him in Malta.

CHAPTER 2

Do I hear church bells ringing, or are these the angels at heaven's gate already? Brian did not feel as if he were in a trance. He had the impression of having dozed off for a short time or been entirely unconscious for a moment. He was sure that the self-hypnosis had worked quickly. The longer the ringing continued, the stranger it seemed to him. The bells made of iron or bronze, as they were found in church towers, he had remembered differently. This one had an unmistakable sound, and the different pitches were audible.

These can't be angelic bells. If angels were involved, they would probably keep me away from paradise with wild cries. Maybe the angels are also warned by the guardians of heaven about an idiot like me, Brian thought.

Can the next village be so close that you can hear the bells in this hole in the ground? But now Sean should be back slowly, or did something happen to him? Did someone get me out of the self-hypnosis, or what is going on here? Meditating always brings surprises. Today I guess it didn't work. Instead, the unanswered questions are piling up. Anyway, Anna seems to be unreachable at the moment. It would also be a remarkable coincidence if she had her head free to sense my mental approach. Perhaps I overestimate her, too. She is undoubtedly a brilliant medium but not nearly as well trained as the old priests. Well, in any case, she seems to be more developed than I am. Then the fault may well be mine. I wonder if she knows I don't think she's beautiful, and that's why she sometimes treats me so ... gruffly? Perhaps she can also look deeper into me than I can myself. Indeed, she won't have guessed that I sometimes had erotic thoughts when I saw her in those tight jeans. Although, when erotic thoughts are involved, even advanced people have trouble reading clear emotions in other people. Stupid stuff, I'm thinking here! I need help and can't think of anything better than dealing with my secret fantasies.

When Brian returned from his self-hypnosis and opened his eyes, it was still dark. It seemed to have gotten warmer, and there were drops of sweat on his forehead as if he had a fever. Voices were now approaching. It sounded like one of the fast Asian languages. He guessed Hindi, as he knew it from India. The voices came closer, and the glow of a flashlight hit him from above. Placing his hand protectively in front of his eyes, he asked in English if they could help him out of the hole. Soon a rope ladder dropped, and a piece of wood hit his head. The two rescuers seemed rather excited, telling him to hurry. Brian clumsily put his foot on the first bar. The rope ladder dangled back and forth on the hole's wall, which required strength and body tension to climb. Once he got the hang of it, he noticed something else. All plant growth had disappeared from this hole. There was sticky mud and a lot of debris at the bottom, but nothing that felt alive. It could never be the same hole he had fallen into.

Brian clambered awkwardly up the rope ladder. In his brain, electrons moved through the cerebral cortex at breakneck speed. His mind was trained for such moments of conflict-solving. The result of the training was that the brain areas needed to find solutions had networked together effectively. So this kind of intelligence was not a miracle, as some claim, but the result of hard training and Brian's lifestyle. This and probably a few unknown factors had enabled his brain to react optimally to such demands. It helped him to find a structure in the language of his rescuers within a few minutes.

All who possess this ability should be able to learn a new language within a few weeks. During his language studies, he realized that in the earliest phase of human development, a primordial language must have evolved from which all other languages later descended. The brains of the first humanoids had unique markers, which made them different from animals. It was the ability to perceive time, that is, to put temporal sequences in the correct order. This is one of the prerequisites for understanding logic and the birth of mathematics. At least, that was the opinion of most scientists at that time. However, during his education, Brian also talked to lecturers familiar with the

Vedas from ancient Indian culture. The texts sometimes suggested that artificial intelligence must have known more than logic in the past. However, according to the generally accepted thesis, ancient texts were only religious interpretations, not science. When Brian discussed with his friends, it was sometimes about the question of whether every form of logic could be represented mathematically. In any case, he held this opinion without having found the final proof yet.

In some of the old writings, it is said that this knowledge also comes again from older records. Brian could already find out some things because he had met Anna, an exceptional mathematician.

Anna was told there were places on this planet that could provide answers for Brian. To find those places it would take very little. It is the will to discard old ways of thinking and to open himself to the seemingly impossible. Then his brain would start to see differently. Then his brain would also begin to connect to a much more extensive network. Anna had also promised to tell him more about it when he was ready. But as she pointed out, it was not her job to reveal these things to him. It was all so mysterious that it kept driving Brian crazy because he couldn't get all the answers immediately. Why was Anna so cruel and closed herself to his questions repeatedly at some points? She probably knew secret things she wasn't allowed to discuss with everyone.

It was a mystery, as it often is, why all this was racing through Brian's head at that very moment while he was being rescued from a hole in the ground by strangers. He was supposed to have other problems at that moment. Or was all this no coincidence?

"Why are you so late?" one of the two old men asked in another language, and when Brian didn't answer right away, again in English. Meanwhile, he gathered up the rope ladder. The two flashlights gave enough light to let Brian see that the ladder was just long enough as if it had been made precisely for the depth of this hole.

Surely none of this could be true. The two older men look funny and act strange. I wonder if they are part of a rescue team, constantly waiting to save someone from this hole. Brian was finishing his thought when the other old man surprised him with an answer, "Don't talk nonsense, boy. We've been waiting here for you for a week. What's happened? We're running out of time!"

Brian was sure he had not spoken aloud. Therefore, at least one of the two had to be able to communicate telepathically.

"Thank you for getting me out of the hole. But why do you say you waited? Did you know I would fall into that pit?"

No sooner had Brian asked the question than it struck him as silly. Of course, they knew. He had just said they had been waiting for him for a week. *I'll have to ask them for their names later,* Brian thought.

"My name is Ravi, and this is Kanja," they introduced themselves. The two men ran as if the devil were after them. Although Brian might have been decades younger, his legs seemed to struggle to keep up with the pace. A few minutes later, relieved, he saw a small lighted hut they were heading toward. He hoped that would be the destination of this chase. There was disappointment when Ravi yanked open the wooden door and hurried into a room at the far end of the hut. So without a break in sight, the chase continued. As he did so, he spurred Brian on again, saying, "Now hurry up! We must leave here."

The room was empty. Only a worn coconut carpet lay in the middle. Ravi pulled this aside, and a floor flap appeared.

Instinctively taking a step back to press his back against the wall, wanted Brian to know, "What are you doing?"

"We don't have time to explain now. Just trust us and start opening up to our thoughts. Then we won't have to explain every detail."

While Ravi was saying this, Brian sensed a few snippets of thought from Kanja that sounded like, *"Is he the Messenger, or should we check him out first?"*

Since Kanja was thinking in his language, Brian was unsure if he had translated it correctly. Words in Sanskrit could have different meanings. The "Messenger" was also called "the God Sent".

Brian tried to cheer himself up inwardly: *I don't feel like an angel. Hopefully, there is no confusion with an alien here.*

Then Kanja made it clear with his head that Brian should descend the steps and follow Ravi into the black hole under the floor flap. *Another hole. The last one didn't bring me any luck either,* he thought, but at the same time, he realized that there were more reasons to trust the two older men than to resist their urging.

Brian indulged in these thoughts for another second: *Escape instincts are more substantial than logic. I should instead follow the logic in this case.*

Thought, done. Brian climbed down the steps into the dark.

A stone floor continued under the last step. Brian was good at observing his surroundings. That's why he noticed that the stairs and floor were worn as if people had used them for centuries. You wouldn't expect something like this in a private basement, but rather in an ancient public building. The wear and tear were so severe that he had to weigh every step, while the older men probably knew all the pitfalls of the stairs. Both Kanja and Ravi carried a small LED headlamp. Brian was amused by this sight as he thought, *I wonder if the guys ordered their headlamps on the internet.* The answer came as Ravi replied in spoken English, "Go ahead and make fun of us. You're about to stop laughing."

Brian did not find Ravi's warning worrisome. On the contrary, it reassured him. It would be different for most people in this situation, though. His specialties were linguistics and special communications. To not only hear an expression but also understand it, the listener must absorb all the factors and, at best, the energy being transmitted. He recalled a lecturer at Greensboro University. According to his thesis, spiritually advanced cultures can have a large vocabulary but need only a few words and simple grammar to express complex things. Having lost some of their language capabilities, cultures could communicate only orally or through two-dimensional writing. For this, they had to invent additional characters. Suppose you can sense the feelings of the person you are talking to. In that case, you don't have to struggle with unnecessary formulations. As proof of this thesis, the lecturer brought up Egyptian culture.

According to this, the "kings of the gods" of the pre-dynastic period got by with only a few hieroglyphs. Whereby even these were probably only used for communication with the priests. Also, the Mayas' written language in Central America proves this thesis. Scientists should understand the oldest records best because these should be expectedly the simplest. Precisely the opposite is the case.

In the end, it was still unclear to Brian why Ravi radiated so much optimism as the three traversed a dark underground tunnel.

Even tall people could walk comfortably here. The walls were relatively smooth and regularly carved out of the rock. Some parts of the walls already had signs of abrasion, indicating very long and intensive use. Twice they had turned right into another passage. In addition, all the routes ran with a slight curve. They had walked about 200 yards by now. The path then came across a larger one. It was more like a tube with a diameter of about 18 feet.

"I guess this is where your government wanted to build a subway railroad?" asked Brian, not expecting an answer. He got an explanation that would run through his mind several times over the next few hours, "You're right. Unfortunately, it wasn't the current government, and what you call a subway railroad would rather scare most people these days."

Ravi abruptly stopped speaking. With a wave of his hand, he made it clear that the others should wait while he seemed to listen to some noise with his head raised. Then, turning to Brian, he said, "We'll be right there. Please don't be worried. We're getting on the 'subway' now."

Knowing that Ravi could read his thoughts, he now closed them off to others by operating a locking mechanism in his *neocortex*. This worked quite quickly and was only a short autogenic training. In doing so, he imagined a pyramid hanging upside down in his head and rotating counterclockwise. This exercise worked after only a few seconds and was the quickest way for Brian to stop it from entering his head. Years ago, he was proud when he discovered that this exercise was a variation of another activity practiced by meditation teachers. These taught their students that one should imagine in one's mind a rotating octahedron, which had the shape of two pyramids glued together at the base. The octahedron produced a strong energy field as long as one imagined the geometric form while it was rotating in the head. There was only one crucial difference to Brian's unique method. While the octahedron established a connection from the brain to other fields, the upside-down pyramid prevented this connection.

Brian knew very well that this form of self-hypnosis was a powerful tool for manipulating a brain. A beginner should, therefore, always be supervised by a master. While some were able to achieve unique effects after a short time, they were also able to cause damage to their own or others' brains. A fellow student, with whom both Anna and he were in a training group at a course in Freiburg, had given this warning at the beginning with condescending comments. The consequences for the fellow student, who was eager to experiment, were severe. A self-experiment caused short-lived amnesia. Whether this also left permanent damage, no one probably knew. However, the individual was later implicated in a scandal involving the alleged misappropriation of donations to an American foundation for seriously ill children. At the hearing by American law enforcement authorities, this scoundrel could not remember anything that might have to do with irregular donations. After the business magazine Forbes reported on this, Forbes was added to the list of "fake news sheets" by the family of the person concerned. When this was also a topic in all media, Anna and he gave this kind of memory loss the name Pyramid Syndrome.

However, at that time, very few people besides Anna and Brian knew how correct this name was and what it had to do with how many ancient pyramids worked.

However, Brian knew well that he was not entirely free of narcissistic dispositions. At the moment, though, it was not the right time for remorse. He had to concentrate on what was happening to him here in this underground tunnel.

After a few seconds of concentration on the rotating pyramid, the desired effect occurred: He felt alone in his head again. This brought some relaxation. Soon, however, he began to doubt whether this shielding from the outside world might not be a mistake. Kanja seemed to be busy. He had put both hands on the tunnel wall and closed his eyes.

On the other hand, Ravi's face immediately revealed that he had noticed Brian's shielding. His face radiated a subtle smile as he said, "I understand you very well, but for now, you must trust us. When we reach our destination, you will understand everything."

"How much longer will it take … I mean, when will we get to our destination?"

"You've mastered the most amazing tricks with your brain, but you're missing the point. Look at your wristwatch. Do you notice anything?"

Brian's face must have contorted into a frightened grimace as he read off the time. It was already 9 o'clock the next day after his accident. How could that be? Ravi immediately recognized the shock on his face and said, "Now, maybe you understand why we have to hurry. Your watch should still be showing the time in Malta at the moment. This runs many times faster than here. We can sort this out later, but your return will be harder to explain with every minute of discussion."

That's reassuring. The men probably assume that I will return, Brian thought. A glance at Ravi, who was now smiling at him, immediately made it clear that he probably couldn't prevent the intrusion into his head after all. Before consciousness faded, he could think for a second: *What strong people they must be if my meditation tricks hardly have any effect.*

Regaining consciousness, he lay in a single-axle cart on a quilted blanket. The carriage was pulled by a donkey, whose strong smell of manure could be smelled despite the light breeze. His back and everything he thought belonged to his body ached. Next to the cart walked Kanja, and the donkey did not need any instruction to find its destination.

"Are you all right?" Kanja asked, but he didn't expect an answer and said, "You fainted when we left the tunnel. Don't worry about it. There's nothing wrong with your head. Next time it will be easier for you to go through the gate. You don't need to ask me about it. I don't know much about the principle of operation. You'll have more time to deal with it later."

"Where did Ravi go?"

"He's already gone ahead. We'll be right there, too."

"Oh, I guess he took the subway and rode 1st class?"

"Never heard that there is 1st class on the subway. Although, people can be trusted to do that," Kanja said, and it seemed like he meant it. Brian was unsettled: *Didn't Kanja understand my joke? Sure, he did. He probably wanted to tell me that he may be old but not unworldly.*

The swaying became less because the reddish-brown sandy path ended, and the cart had turned onto an asphalt road. The donkey knew the destination already because it suddenly went faster and faster. They were getting closer to a town, and less than five minutes later, they spotted Ravi standing on the left side of the road next to a minivan waiting for them. He signaled Brian to get in the passenger seat. Before getting in, Brian recognized from the license plate of the fairly new-looking Mitsubishi that they were in the Indian state of Madhya Pradesh. Sitting behind the wheel, Ravi looked completely transformed despite his dirty caftan and worn sandals as he moved the vehicle as if it were the most natural thing in the world. But Ravi's glimpse of the road and the ease with which the car was steered did not reassure Brian. Doubts arose about whether all drivers in this country had been taught that left-hand traffic was the rule. In any case, Ravi sometimes drove on one side and sometimes on the other. Hard to say if it was to avoid the potholes or for different reasons. While Brian clung to each bend in the road in anticipation of oncoming traffic suddenly appearing, Ravi's face beamed as if it were a special blessing to be behind the wheel.

"I guess you thought the old man could only meditate and didn't know anything about technology, huh?" As he said this, he looked at Brian, not the road. Brian was already thinking about whether it would have been safer in the donkey cart. The animal, following its instincts, would dodge any traffic. As if sensing Brian's concerns, Ravi responded again, saying, "You know, it's time you got to know our culture better. We don't just trust ourselves because we've learned that our destiny is already written. If something happens, it was meant to happen."

What he heard caused Brian's adrenaline level to shoot up once again. But to his surprise, Ravi said, "I can see my words aren't reassuring you. From now on, I'll drive as if I had a driver's license. But we'll be right there anyway."

Laughing, he actually kept looking at the road now.

Then Brian remembered the time difference. His smartwatch always showed two times. One was the time in his hometown, and the other was in the current time zone. This made it easier to track the daily rhythm of his friends in Washington. His navigation app showed the ancient, ruined city of Mandu in India as the current location. This was in the Vindhya Mountains, and various points of interest were marked as places to visit. After a few minutes with his mind on Washington, he asked Ravi, "Does the problem with time moving at different speeds still exist here?"

"No. You experience this phenomenon only in the holes in the earth and transport tunnels, with the help of which you came here. And only when they are on the energetic lines of force of the planet. If you move a small distance on it, you can cover a multiple of the distance by trigonometric projection. You must only bring your body into resonance with the rock. That's how it works in the hole in the ground."

Brian doubted that Ravi was familiar with the physics behind this phenomenon and thought: *Probably it only described the myth. His teachers must have shown him how to use the tunnel. Anyway, it sounded like what I've seen in Egyptian depictions. At least with the pyramids and temples, the Egyptians could measure time and precisely determine geological and astronomical distances.*

The stay in Freiburg greatly expanded Brian's basic knowledge about such things. Therefore, he also knew that this once belonged to the understanding of the Freemasons and other organizations.

In him, a little doubt spread whether it could be a coincidence that the truth about the ancient knowledge was sometimes so difficult to prove. By now, he knew that many ancient mysteries had been passed down as secret knowledge until modern times. The best examples are the traditions of the Templars and

Freemasons. Their handed-down sciences were always so isolated that they have since forgotten much of it. Only their symbols for rituals originating from Egypt, such as the rough stone, the eye, the protractor, and compasses, still testify to the origin and the knowledge of that time.

Perhaps the older man was right, and there are still functioning installations from ancient times.

Curiosity gave him a new power. He said to Ravi, "I need some more time to think about it. But how did I get here to India from Malta now?"

Ravi did not take his eyes off the road as he replied, "With your mind, how else?"

Rarely did Brian experience a situation like this. Instead of bringing certainty, every other answer unsettled him. He could think of nothing that could quickly change this circumstance. Instead, he felt a deep dissatisfaction with himself. Ravi's last answer seemed to be the reason. He had asserted that Brian's thoughts had brought him from Malta to India without hesitation and very firmly. Briefly, he mused that it was all in his head after all. The actual impressions, including the pain in his back, made him quickly reject this idea. But he was also concerned about not being able to see inside Ravi to elicit his knowledge. In his life, things went differently otherwise. When someone asked him for help, for example, to "read" people or distinguish truth from lies, it gave him a sense of control. Control over the current situation and other people. It was not like that on this day. He was now slowly becoming aware that he was losing control. Instead of worrying about possible reasons, Brian focused on current events. His mind refused to accept these mysterious circumstances and realized he was at someone else's mercy. Therefore, he decided to take care of the most critical question: *Why India? Who organized this action, and why wasn't I asked?*

There was only one thing that Brian could already answer: they must have believed that he would not have gone voluntarily! And Brian had another certainty as well. He was smart enough to know there is no point in waiting for answers unless you ask the right questions. Here a trusted person could help, and that would be Anna, his meditation teacher in Freiburg.

CHAPTER 3

Listening to music is relaxing. Not everyone would agree with this opinion, especially when rhythmic hammering came from the neighboring apartment for hours.

Anna knew well what music or sounds, in general, could do to the human body. It had been part of her everyday life since childhood in many ways. On the one hand, there was what most people imagined music to be. A melody produced by instruments or solely sung by a human voice. Anna was a blessed singer, and not only her friends claimed that. She also played the piano and keyboard wherever the opportunity arose.

Every ethnologist knew that spoken or sung words had been part of people's lives. Nevertheless, very few thought about why living beings loved music so much. Immersing herself in these mysteries was something Anna occupied herself with every single day of her life. In the past few years, she had already seen more exciting things than others on the couch with a series subscription to a streaming service.

She had her most incredible adventure at the age of sixteen. This was a particular age for those with the necessary physical and spiritual qualities. Anna had to pass her first significant maturity examination, in which her suitability for further spiritual education had to be proven. Why just the sixteenth was related to tradition and physical maturity. In most countries, children begin their schooling at the age of six. Only Anna belonged to the people who genetically brought special conditions for learning. It could not be fully explained why some children were highly gifted even though their ancestors did not have this gift. Anna's parents were also quite ordinary people. She had never liked it when someone said that she was highly gifted. Her younger brother, a very average boy, was neither particularly musical nor could communicate telepathically. Anna had both gifts, but this was only told to acquaintances and family friends until her youth. The family also kept all other paranormal abilities a secret for

Anna's protection. Traditionally, youngsters like Anna were told at a very early age why certain secrecy had been part of the tradition for a very long time.

The last millennium was something scarce not only because of the date. Whether by chance or not, the fact was that more and more highly gifted children were born at the end of the twentieth century. New sociological terms such as millennial children or even Generation Y were coined. Anna was born after the millennium and thus belonged to *Generation Z*. The fact that these children were assigned to the last letter in the alphabet could not be coincident. Even if many older generations see it differently, these offspring heralded the dawn of a new age.

It was no secret that each generation was determined by its behavior and how its descendants would one day think and feel. As everywhere in nature, this seems to happen cyclically. And now, no one could prevent this generation from maturing into the new leadership elite. And like Anna, some incredibly gifted had received special training at the University of Freiburg. Before earning a master's degree in music, she gained experience worldwide. Eventually, she was persuaded to return to Freiburg University to train the best of *Generation Alpha*. They offered her an average lecturer's salary. According to her employment contract, she was a research assistant at the Institute of Psychology in the Faculty of Economics and Behavioral Sciences. In addition, she had a contract as a freelancer at the Institute of Archaeological Sciences. This also included a particular arrangement as a guest lecturer.

The faculty organized scientific exchanges with partner universities and arranged grants from private fundraising organizations for special projects. The latter was necessary because there needed to be more official funding for some research and the individual education of gifted students. In return, research was largely independent of other institutions. Above all, the interference of undesirable lobbyists was to be prevented. The most important principle, however, remained strict secrecy, which meant that strangers were rarely given access to the research content.

Her current project was a collaborative effort between several faculties. It was about educational plans for highly gifted children and adolescents. Since many were taking similar subjects, the university began to merge some faculties. This made it easier for Anna to incorporate ancient musical teaching methods and meditation into her educational plans.

While the world was beginning to become familiar with the term Generation Alpha, few realized what task lay ahead for these children. This is where Anna saw the biggest challenge for her work. Adults have probably always thought teenagers would be difficult. However, it could become hard when teenagers start to educate adults. Anna wanted to help her students understand how they could influence the change-resistant part of the older generation. The whole thing became visible to the outside world when small groups formed themselves into global organizations.

Anna herself had sometimes participated in demos of the student movement Fridays for Future. Soon the first effects of this provocative public relations work became apparent. It began with an adapted language in politics and business after even the unteachable felt that young people were no longer following them. Of course, Anna was not the only one at the university who supported these movements. With her boss, the institute's director, she had the best prerequisites to accommodate new thoughts in the curricula. He was one of those who quickly sensed that something entirely different was happening at some universities around the world.

In China, for example, for a long time, it was good manners for rich people to study in a Western country. Then, with the emergence of the new generations in North America and Europe, China suddenly began to close itself off again. Anna quickly understood that ideological isolation on all sides would lead to new enemy images being burned into her subjects for many years to come.

There have also been movements in other areas of society due to the changing zeitgeist. Initially, Anna believed this had brought about a breakthrough in ecology and sustainability. Disappointment followed on its heels. Resistance from the giants was far from being broken. Those who supplied the software for stock exchanges and digital currencies had yet to play all their cards. Now the age of artificial intelligence has dawned on even better ways to direct people and financial flows. Methods of the regulatory authorities, which were supposed to prevent such things, initially only ever had a defensive character. Here, however, a great opportunity presented itself. Either the authorities procured equally powerful software with artificial intelligence, or humans had to improve their intelligence. Or perhaps both. In any case, Anna was sure of one thing: all of it was being worked on somewhere in the world.

With the sunset, Anna also began to feel hungry. Usually, hunger triggered a signal in her, which initiated the return from a deep meditation. However, this time, she waited a moment before returning from self-hypnosis. Someone was calling out to her. Not like before, when her parents or little brother would barge into the room and call for dinner. No, these comforts no longer existed since she lived in a new shared apartment in the student settlement at the lakeside park in the western part of Freiburg. It wasn't that she didn't feel at home there, but on some days, thoughts of her sheltered childhood also brought up melancholy.

In the meantime, her daily routine had fixed meditation phases equally for relaxation and learning. When the weather permitted, she meditated on her small balcony, which offered a magnificent view of the adjacent lake. In the "StuSie Bar" next door, small and large groups of her students enjoyed communicating. The popularity of this bar was probably not only due to its coziness. There were almost always a few students or faculty members from the campus who had senses similar to Anna's. There, communication was possible on particular channels. Even foreign visitors were said to have been able to sense this atmosphere if they were sensitive enough.

Learning for Anna meant absorbing scientific content and the everyday madness of life and daily events. Meditating also allowed for the exchange of ideas with many people. This made it easier to engage with other opinions. She always tried to use several sources if interested in a topic. This gave her some confidence to talk about it later with enough facts. Since Anna also taught special knowledge to her students, she knew very well how many myths there were about telepathy, for example. If she first questioned new information, it was easier to distinguish between knowledge and wishful thinking. She had always found herself believing in what was closest to her interests. The experts then called the result truth perception.

If only it were that simple, she thought again, before remembering that someone had tried to contact her telepathically earlier. This usually worked by having a familiar person focus on the other person's energy signature in their mind.

It was probably not so important, she thought, because Anna now felt nothing of an attempt at contact.

The roommates in the shared apartment were a lovely student couple who took Anna's courses on *transdimensional* communication. Anna could have afforded a larger apartment long ago. What stopped her was that the closeness of others felt like a warming blanket. That could change once she started a family with a steady partner. Financially, she didn't have to worry about anything, either. Except for a few private trips, she hardly spent any money. A room as a retreat was enough for Anna because her living space was not limited to the apartment and the surrounding area. Most "normal" people could not even imagine that she had access to entirely different worlds with her mind. Those who were open-minded to these things could perhaps imagine this "other world" as an environment in which everything consists only of thoughts. No material things exist there. Those who came from the local world and wanted to find a way had to imagine everything in their fantasy. Only own and foreign thoughts met in this part of the world, which became the term *aka* long ago.

Just imagination was needed to figure out how this works. Everybody could do it, but only in children, it is generally accepted. With adulthood, something manifested in the minds of most children that we call rationality, and that was, after all, an invention of the brain, just of adult brains. So, whoever became "rational" lost contact with that fantastic world. Not so with Anna because her parents had fortunately realized that it was not just a fantasy that allowed their child to speak to others in a particular way. Most parents of such children believed they did not have the children's gift and imagination. But this was not true at all. Let's remember again how our ancient philosophers already defined truth as a mixture of facts and desires. Could wishes influence the truth? Or could wishes also become facts? Anna had a personal goal, namely, to prove that one day. She knew, of course, that this was not suitable for public discussion.

Anna must have been mistaken when she thought someone was trying to contact her telepathically. But she then found another message on her cell phone. After her eyes adjusted to the light, she read it on her desk monitor: "We need you in lab building four. Can you be there before 21:00?"

Δ

Freiburg, university campus, laboratory building no. 4, 20:15

Gregor put down his cell phone. He had briefly interrupted the conversation with his boss to call Anna in. Now he asked: "What do you mean by surveillance?"

"We don't know everything yet. It just seems that Anna has been shadowed for some time. And this time, it's probably not a stalker or a crazed student who fell in love with the youngest lecturer at the university." Answered Sergei, whom they called Prof. He didn't like that nickname but had given up complaining about it. His full name, including the title, was Prof. Dr. habil. Sergei Sergeyevich Fyodorov. One found the academic titles in his presentations only tiny in the imprint. He asked new students to call him Sergei. If one feature of his character was immediately recognizable, it was modesty.

All employees at the institute knew an anecdote about him. Sergei had appeared on a talk show on television. It was about healing through hypnosis. He knew that he had been invited because of his spectacular hypnosis procedures. Indeed the moderator hoped that Fyodorov's critics would be provoked by his recent publications. In them, he recommended the meditation exercises of Tibetan Vajrayana Buddhism as a neurophysiological diagnostic method. Such a thing went too far for some, of course. Sergei told the private television station that he did not want to be addressed by his titles. Nor should explicit reference be made to his education, which began in London after graduating high school at nine. The only thing officially known was that he spent a year enrolled at Yale University in New Haven, Connecticut. At eighteen, he returned to that university as a visiting professor. In the meantime, he stayed several times in Asia to research original ancient texts. More details about his early years were not known. Only his closest confidants knew the reasons for this secrecy. It also had to do with the fact that his grandparents emigrated from the Soviet Union in the 1930s. They belonged to the Russian Freemasons, and this kind of freethinking was not wanted there. In order not to put friends in Russia in danger, old connections with Russian Freemasonry were better kept secret or denied. Whether Sergei still sympathized with the contents of Freemasonry or was even a member of another Order, nobody in his circle of acquaintances knew.

His discussion partners in that talk show were utterly different from Sergei. All of them were in good standing. One repeatedly referred to his generally recognized research results, with which he extensively refuted Sergei's theories. At first, the moderator's plan seemed to work, as a heated atmosphere enlivened the discussion. But the viewers soon realized that the arrogance of the attendees was getting on the moderator's nerves. Since Sergei had hardly defended himself up to that point and listened calmly to the others talk about his work, the moderator wanted to draw him out. He brought up a completely different topic: "Mr. Fyodorov, you told me something about your previous employer before the broadcast. They wanted you to leave this research institution or at least not to do your job at that time."

"That's right," Sergei answered with a serious face.

Waiting for a disarming explanation, the opponents stared spellbound at this scene when the moderator expanded his question, "What exactly didn't your boss like?"

Sergei replied, "Well, my boss probably wanted me to do more for my salary in the future. That's why she advocated my appointment as a chairholder years ago. The faculty should now be able to work more intensively with the Institute of Archaeological Sciences. My current research on paranormal phenomena fits in very well here."

"That's great. Then congratulations on this, Professor Fyodorov!" the moderator concluded this short interlude. Sergei could not enjoy the surprised expression on the face of the most unpleasant adversary. As a professional, he knew very well that an appealing conversation required harmonious vibrations in the room. However, there was no sign of this until the show's end.

21:10

Anna entered the hallway in laboratory building number four, generously furnished with seating. Her colleagues Gregor and Mailly, who had been Sergei's research assistants for many years, were already waiting there. The conversation switched from Russian to German out of politeness as she approached.

"What's so urgent that you're summoning me to the palace at this hour? Unfortunately, it took a little longer because I ran out of air again. On the bike, I mean," Anna said in greeting, seemingly in a good mood despite the circumstances.

Before anyone could say anything, Mailly shot off, "Anna, good that you're here now. We have a problem."

She had gotten into the habit of always adding too much drama to speeches. Anna already knew that from her and therefore didn't necessarily expect to hear anything exciting now. This time, however, she was mistaken. Sergei had previously asked Mailly to gently explain the reason for this meeting to Anna.

"I figured it was important if it couldn't wait until tomorrow. As long as it's not another whacked-out diplomat who sees the world ending because of our research and needs convincing otherwise."

"Anna, it's about two things, and one involves you. At least, that's what we think. The Institute's security service has informed

Sergei that you have been shadowed for at least two weeks. Your 'shadow' has been captured by the surveillance cameras every time you have entered or left the premises. At first, that made us think it wasn't a professional because he didn't spot the cameras. Then we took a closer look at the footage. Look…"

Mailly showed Anna a composite of video footage on her cell phone. She zoomed in with her fingers on the face of a man who looked familiar to Anna.

"Do you recognize him?"

"I can't think of the name, but he looks like that experimental archaeologist from the labs at the institute."

"Exactly. It's the face of Tony Peller. But it's not Tony Peller's body. After matching his work hours and data from access control, he was either at work during the recording or, as in one proven case, with his wife at a birth preparation course."

"So, what does that mean now?"

"Maybe someone wants us to believe that Tony Peller is stalking you," said Sergei, who had also joined the group.

"But that doesn't make any sense. I could meet that Tony by chance at the institute and talk to him, and everything would be blown open," Anna replied.

Gregor worked on improved software that recognizes human behavior patterns through facial expressions and gestures. He immediately saw what might be behind it: "Someone must have hacked our video surveillance system. Even simple editing software can be used for *deepfakes* today."

"You mean those videos where fake speeches by politicians have appeared in the media?"

"Yes. It's effortless to replace a speaker's face or voice in the video. It already works in real-time. You just need a suitable template. In this case, someone misused poor Tony for this. There is enough video material of him on our servers."

"Using this trick, you could easily blame others for your crime. There is video surveillance in public areas all over the world. Cleverly faked, the wrong person could be caught quickly. You may have also heard about the incidents in Hong Kong. Under the 2020 Security Law, Chinese authorities threatened publicly expose dissidents. After they started making good on their threat, the authorities suddenly shut down the entire surveillance system for a few days. This was because someone had hacked the system to get back at the Chinese government. Suddenly, all the cameras showed only two faces in real-time: that of the Chinese president and the face of the head of the government of the Chinese Special Administrative Region. Millions of times. As some footage was leaked, the public could see that any video evidence could be faked. Shortly after the incident, I received a video from friends with funny comments. Although not so common in Hong Kong, lovers were also seen holding hands. This political message was, of course, convenient for the cartoonists. Unfortunately, comedians in these countries often get in trouble for using this humor. In the meantime, however, these fakes can be better analyzed. However, the layman is left to decide for himself what he believes and doesn't."

"Anyway, the motive is still a mystery to me, and as long as it is, we have to be vigilant," Sergei said. After a few seconds of silence, Mailly continued, "But the tailing thing wasn't the only reason we called you in."

"Then I'm glad I didn't pump up my tire twice for nothing," Anna joked, still in a good mood. But when no one said anything, she asked, "So, a wacky diplomat after all?"

"Something like that," Sergei explained, "This time, NATO asked us for help from Brussels. We have not had any contact with the military through this official channel until now."

"Now, don't make it so exciting," Anna urged. But then their eyes met. She was able to capture Sergei's thoughts for a split second. Immediately it had become clear to Anna that Sergei was distraught and was not yet sure whether he would do the right thing now. Anna then asked in spoken words, "Where did it happen?"

"As almost every summer, the usual crop circles in Wiltshire, England. But this time, we find them also in North and South America, Asia and Australia. In the Munich area, as every year, there was again a beautiful specimen. The farmer, the idiot, mowed it down immediately before we could finish all the measurements this afternoon. He probably feared that the many visitors would trample his fields. But since it is the same energy pattern worldwide, we know that the specimen near Munich also represents a *Merkaba*. Even after mowing it down, we could still measure something."

"Show me," Anna urged, and Sergei replied, "Yes, let's go upstairs."

By upstairs, he meant a shielded room on the top floor. This was designed to be tap-proof and had separate Internet access via satellite antenna, which was supposed to protect against hacker attacks with an additional firewall. Sergei took a tablet lying on the conference table. He used it to project a few images onto the monitor on the wall. When the first images appeared, Anna was not yet clear why this should be a big deal. One shot after another showed the same symbol repeatedly in different variations. The size and precision were impressive.

Sergei explained, "I am not so much concerned with the crop circles themselves but with the suspicion that this message could be either a warning or a call for help."

That was also why he had already sought the help of his colleagues. Anna's analytically excellent brain was deeply immersed in her knowledge of what was shown. Then she said to Sergei, "I'm not sure I know enough background about the symbol of the *Merkaba* yet. For example, I know the two superimposed triangles as a symbol from the Jewish religion, right? This is where you guys need to help me out a little bit."

"And that's what we're all about," Sergei replied.

"Make yourself comfortable. I've gathered some data there that we can discuss together."

"But I don't even know how to help you with that yet!"

"At the moment, we don't know anyone who could help us better. In the past, you have sometimes been able to read out things where others have long since given up. I hope you'll come up with something. But for now, let's see what we already know," Mailly said in an almost imploring voice.

It was not the first time Anna's expertise was needed to provide an expert opinion on a phenomenon. Those who knew her knew that she was endowed with a sharp mind and could call on special friends for help. But who would freely admit to being able to communicate with beings that others are also called angels? People who talked seriously about light beings were usually strictly religious or convinced they had been abducted by aliens. Anna found it paradoxical that angels were accepted by the general public only in connection with religion. Yet today's abduction stories resemble the ancient tales in Christian scriptures. Anna saw it as her task to provide people with scientific evidence of what the old stories were about. She closed these thoughts for the time being and said to the others, "Ok, but we get hundreds of messages about crop circles yearly. Why is this particular pattern troubling you?"

Sergei dropped into one of the swivel chairs at the conference table and picked up the tablet again. He then commented on a few film sequences that could be seen on the screen: "About the Merkaba symbols, we know that they are found in all religions. The circle contains a star formed by the two triangles inserted into each other. Mathematically, many constants and units can be derived from it. Unfortunately, spiritual fringe groups also use these symbols and reinterpret them for their messages. Anyone who wants to read the true message must therefore recognize its mathematics. It seems to me that all crop circles point to hidden geometry. Maybe they are also distance indications or… geographical locations? In any case, there are many reasons to take a closer look. We understand many symbols of the Egyptians only since we deal with quantum mechanics and genetic engineering."

"Sergei, we know that. Maybe you can elaborate a little more on the theory we've been developing over the last few days," Gregor asked.

"Yes, you are right. Thousands of years ago, people were given the whole thing as a gift. Because neither paper nor any other material can last that long, it was stored in a special form, in our religious lore."

Then Anna spoke up and asked, "You sometimes talk about the old Bible texts in your lectures. Don't we also find references to the crop circles in it?"

"Yes, there are. But you must be careful with that. One is quickly exposed to the accusation of interpreting the texts in the way that best suits one. In addition, all Bible texts refer to older texts, even older ones. Only… wait a minute. Why don't we look at the Old Testament?"

Sergei typed something on his keyboard, and annotated texts of the prophet Ezekiel appeared on the screen with the heading God's Throne Chariot.

The first chapter describes how the Lord appears to the prophet on his throne chariot. This chariot had the shape of a *Merkaba*. Then Sergei said, "For me, this described passage is interesting. Look..."

> "... a storm wind came from the north, a great cloud with flashing fire and brightness all around it, and something like a glowing alloy out of the fire.
> From within it came the likeness of four living creatures. This was their appearance: they had a likeness of a human, [...]
> The appearance of the wheels and their work was were like unto a beryl: and they four had the one likeness, and their appearance and their work was as it were a wheel within a wheel..."

Mailly laughed and said, "If this isn't a classic UFO sighting. And it also says that several human-like beings came out of that throne. Hallelujah!"

"As you said yourself, Sergei. No one knows what of it is still original text," Gregor said.

"That may be true of many other texts, not this one."

"Why not go for this one?"

"Ezekiel's story appears on all continents. We find it identical in content in the Jewish Kabbalah and various Indian traditions. The Indians called these celestial vehicles of their gods stupa or vimana. The temple towers often have the shape of such stupas. For me, however, the ground plan of the towers is much more exciting. You will find the symbol of the axis of the world wheel with a mandala in the center."

These things were part of Anna's spiritual knowledge. In her mind, she seemed to be somewhere else at that moment. Mailly recognized it by her look because Anna's distorted face did not bode well. She put her hand on Anna's shoulder and addressed her gently, "What is, is something wrong?"

Startled and dazed, Anna replied, "I guess I was too focused on the circle around the hexagonal star. It's true."

"What is true?"

"Until now, I had only heard about it, but now I could experience it myself. We know that the monks use the circle of the world wheel for meditation and that the outer wheel is supposed to evoke visions if you let it spin in your head. I tried it and immediately fell into a light trance. I had a terrible vision."

Tibetan mandala with the symbol of a Merkaba in a circle [11]
On the outer ring of the world wheel are depicted 8 gods with their stupas

Sergei knew all too well what Anna was talking about. In Tibet, he observed the monks sitting in the middle of a mandala and staring at the rings. A few minutes later, they would fall into a trance. Often other monks would sit around them and hum the "Om" typical of meditation. He had then figured out that the outer rings on the edge of the mandala were spinning in the monks' heads. In some temples, these mandalas are made of wood and are movable, so the rings can be turned by hand. This is supposed to help the inexperienced so that they can find their way into meditation more quickly.

"Tell us about your vision. Maybe it has something to do with our problem."

"I guess you could say that." Anna paused while speaking, and the others could see her inner restlessness. The pause was necessary because the pulse had to go down first to talk correctly.

After a suppressed sob, she said, "I don't want to see that again. I was in Yad Vashem, the Holocaust Museum in Jerusalem. It was as if someone was pushing me through the oppressive exhibition rooms. As if I was being led to a specific place in this building. Then the images on the mounted screens. Half-dead, emaciated people with an accusing look into the camera. An indictment without words but with an urgent call to end this madness."

Again, Anna needed a break, and Sergei could empathize with what she might have experienced there. His memories of that memorial never left him. These images do something to a person.

Then Anna could speak again, "I saw a photo in a display case. A Russian newspaper article from August 26, 1903. The newspaper was called Snamja. The article was annotated in English. According to this, it is an extreme right-wing publishing magazine from St. Petersburg. The publisher was known for all kinds of conspiracy theories and the anti-Semitism of its editors. Then I saw the cover of an illustration entitled ANTICHRIST. On it, among other things, a symbol of the Jewish Freemasons. In addition, a braided *Merkaba* and a T in the middle."

"It can't be a coincidence. Again and again, we come across the same message. It's a message, isn't it?" Mailly asked.

"I think it's more than that. Certainly, we are not the only ones dealing with crop circles at the moment either."

Gregor said about it, "We puzzle about the received message. I wonder who is sitting on the sender's side and may now wonder how stupid we humans are getting."

Mailly's response sounded slightly disappointed, "I thought you had an idea how we should proceed now? Maybe based on your spiritual experience and the contact, you know where..."

"I'm sure we'll find the answer. You know that I approach the solution of such problems differently than most," was Anna's answer.

"What do you mean?"

"For an approach to the solution, we all need to find about the same level of discussion. Everything that is said is also simultaneously processed by our subconscious. The brain automatically searches the dusty cells for clues that match the new information. Sometimes you don't come up with the solution until you talk about it with others."

"Or meditate!"

"Yes. Anna is right. We call this swarm intelligence. The term is somewhat misleading because the phenomenon doesn't only occur in creatures that huddle together in large masses. The collective brain power of many individuals also works regardless of where they are. Rarely are great ideas attributable only to individual minds. This is probably why many inventions were made in parallel, even if the inventors were not in contact."

Gregor had been researching this topic for years. He, therefore, wanted to add, "This topic had taken off when science began to look at strange events in social media. As a behavioral scientist and psychologist, I believe animals and humans must have other reasons for swarm intelligence. And that's exactly why we need Anna. She has access to a communication channel most have only read about in science fiction."

Anna commented, "However, I only heard about communication with animals a few years ago in Cairo. A good friend lives there and is an Egyptologist. However, he is no longer allowed to call himself that because he has fallen into disrepute with officials. He claimed that the hieroglyphs of the early Egyptians referred to swarm intelligence in the animal kingdom. In addition, their priests are also said to have spoken with animals. In any case, it is undisputed that the abilities of the animals were revered. The gods were probably therefore depicted with typical features of the animals. Although they were only considered demigods, the later kings copied this. In illustrations, they are often to be seen as mixed beings. Some believe that angels are nothing more than hybrid beings appearing to people during their vision.

The name of this friend is Achmet. I owe him and his friends a lot since I was allowed to take my eleventh-degree exam in Cairo. That was an exciting story, all in the Giza area. Later, by the way, through comparisons with old languages from other continents, Achmet was able to prove that the God-kings, the kings before the first dynasty, communicated with animals. Whether they were indeed animals or alien beings in animal form is unclear. There were also experiments on this, and we could contact the animal world during the meditations in joint sessions. He re-enacted some of the stories that the hieroglyphs tell us. Although there is no animal language we can understand, we can at least measure and evaluate signals from swarm animals. None of this is serious science, say his peers."

Sergei said, "But how can we blame our critical scientist colleagues? We can't prove until now that one can penetrate with thoughts into fields for which there are not even correct names and which we can't measure directly with our technology."

"You also can't prove to your dog that spicy human food harms him. He can't understand it," Mailly said before realizing that the comparison might be arrogant, and she apologized.

"Nevertheless, you are right. The dusty worldview of the dark ages is a consequence of the lost knowledge of our ancestors. More than what is left is needed to open the way to parallel worlds for everyone. Now it is our task to confront the new generations with it."

Sergei looked at the clock and Anna, who had fallen back into a light trance. Then he said, "We digress, and now we should find out why Anna got into this Holocaust Museum."

Even as he spoke, he researched the Internet's Russian newspaper article from 1903. A terrible premonition came true, and he commented on what was simultaneously visible on the monitor, "When I heard Anna's description, I immediately had my suspicions. The memory of what my parents and grandparents told me about their time in Russia put me on this track. It may be about one of the most influential conspiracy myths of the 20th century. From time to time, one hears about the so-called *Protocols of the Wise Men of Zion*.

"You mean this made-up world conspiracy, according to which an elite Jewish group is seeking world domination and is supposed to have put that on record in this secret pamphlet?" Mailly asked.

Anna was suddenly wide awake and seemed to disagree, "No way. I think that we rate these protocols too high. True, the old myths are still invoked when denigrating the Jewish people as the enemy of all other peoples. But I feel like my vision was about something else."

Sergei could feel the inner tension, and he contradicted Anna, "Believe me, my great-grandparents lived in the time of the expulsion. They had to watch how friends became enemies. From one day to the next. And that was simply because those original friends and neighbors blindly followed a spiritual leader. For some, church service was the only political education. There it was enough if the clergyman suddenly preached hatred against a part of the people. Hatred is the end of reason, and one loses his intelligence in anger. Thus began in our village the ideological cleansing and a long flight of my ancestors."

Mailly asked, "How could they suddenly become so hostile to their former fellow villagers?"

"Look at the tenth Christian commandment. There is the reason: 'You shall not covet your neighbor's house, [...] and all that is his!'..."

"You mean it was about the villagers' belongings?"

"My ancestors were respected traders for centuries. The ancient Chinese Silk Road led to the Middle East and Europe via Samarkand and Bukhara. Equestrian peoples ruled the western foothills of the high Asian mountains. Like the Knights Templar in the Middle Ages, some equestrian groups guarded the trade routes and managed financial affairs. The wealthy cities sprang up where there were safe trading places along the route. My ancestors were Jews who emigrated from the Mediterranean, thoroughly honest people to whom the merchants entrusted money and goods for centuries. The trade and the interest brought them prosperity. These Jewish merchants also had a certain political power and were fighting for money and influence. The fact that in every crisis and in times of scarce state coffers, the Jews were blamed was quite understandable. Thus, now and then, a reason was found to limit their power and seize their possessions. This was also the case in the years after the Russian October Revolution. The money no longer flowed into the coffers of the church and the wealth of the popes dwindled. Soon, such reactionary writings were welcome to turn the spear against the Jews. After the expropriation and expulsion, the people had no prosperity, but the money went into new pockets. However, when my ancestors arrived in Western Europe, they soon found that these forged protocols became an export hit. The old fairy tale could be reheated whenever an enemy was needed to inspire the masses to war. The madness of a world conspiracy again fits well into the concept. My family had no choice but to keep their origins and old connections to Russia secret to protect those left behind in the old homeland."

Anna had heard the story with interest but was still determining if that was the reason for her vision. Something was not right. Then she said, "Perhaps we should all think about this again calmly. I suspect you are overwhelmed by your memories at the moment, Sergei. What moves you strongly personally is coming to the fore."

"Maybe you're right. Thank you for your openness. I will think about it."

Anna jumped up from her swivel chair and said, "I want to go home now. There I can concentrate better on meditating, and maybe tomorrow, I will know more about the content of my vision."

Gregor immediately offered to give Anna a ride in his pickup truck, "The bike better stay here. We'll have it repaired in the lab tomorrow. You can stop by Tony's while you're at it."

"We'd better leave Tony out of this," Sergei replied.

"We're not going to tell anyone we know about the *deepfake* yet. Maybe that will put us on another track."

After Gregor dropped Anna off at home, she walked up the stairs to her apartment more slowly than usual. It would have been two steps to get a short workout regularly. At least it soothed her conscience when there was no time for exercise. The mental exertion of the past two hours had drained the last of her strength. With trembling fingers, she typed in the combination code of the door lock to her apartment.

"Code wrong!" she received an error message and repeated the entry; wrong again. After the third attempt, she rang the doorbell, hoping someone from her roommates would be home.

The electronic door locks were installed after the last renovation. They also attached a sticker with an emergency number. There was no alternative but to use it now. After being on hold for several minutes, someone finally answered. However, the friendly voice was just a chatbot. The computer voice took the caller's problem and asked several stupid questions. Maybe the software thought it was helping a drunk homebody looking for his apartment on the wrong floor. Eventually, however, a human voice answered the phone, and the friendly fellow tried his best immediately. After Anna had authenticated herself with her ID via the camera located at the doorbell, the duty officer logged into the locking system. After minutes of keyboard clatter and a few unintelligible murmurs, he finally said that the code to open this door had been changed an hour ago.

"That can't be true. Why changed? There must be some mistake."

"No mistake. A ticket was opened for the change, which documented that a certain Anna Stein had forgotten her access code and therefore had to request a new one."

"Super. It's so easy to get into my apartment!" Anna complained. A few seconds later, she received a new code via cell phone. When the door finally opened, she entered the apartment with a bad feeling. No one from her roommates was there. Before entering her room, she could smell it; a stranger must have been in the apartment.

Is anybody still there? In the bathroom or kitchen?

She turned around in a flash on all sides and flicked on all the light switches she could reach with her arms stretched out long. With her foot, she pushed open the bathroom door. No one was inside. The same action made her realize that no one could be in the tiny kitchen. All that remained was her roommate's big room. It seemed silly, but she turned around for a suitable striking object. The bulky umbrella from the hallway came to her as a possible weapon. No one used this umbrella. It was a giveaway, much too long for going out, and had a tip that could hurt someone. Anna planned to simply thrust the umbrella tip straight into the burglar's body should he approach. A head movie streaked her thoughts as if in fast motion. Anna had often been annoyed by the scenes in crime novels where the threatened person sneaks through her dark house.

Before she pushed down the handle of the room door, she listened. The only sound was the neighbor's flushing toilet. With a kick, she pushed open this door and immediately held the umbrella in attack position. The lightweight door to the room thundered with full force against the gym ball behind it and bounced back with a mighty swing. Anna's horror was enormous when she saw that the umbrella tip was not in the burglar's stomach but now in the door. A one-inch hole decorated the door right next to the handle when the umbrella was pulled out again.

What a shit! They will be happy about this peephole...

After that noise, she didn't need to sneak up on anyone. After a quick look in all the corners and under the bed, it was clear that no one was hiding.

Back in her room, her fine sense of smell could filter out that it must have been two unknown people. In addition, the closet and desk had been rummaged through, and... "What a mess!" she cursed. Now it was clear what had been stolen: her talisman, an ancient engraved egg-shaped stone. She always kept it in her sock basket. The loss hurt because it was a gift from her uncle and a personal object. Several times she had ignored the warning of friends who said that one should not carry around such a prehistoric object or even leave it at home. For others, the stone was just a strange artifact. For Anna, it became a part of life, a spiritual object. She knew for a few years that ancient cultures called such a thing *port stone*. When she learned at sixteen what it was all about, she used it in meditation like a signal amplifier. Since then, she has also been able to make telepathic contact with beings in the *aka*. It was unclear whether it worked only for her and whether the thief knew what to do with the item. The last thought unsettled her even more. She also realized that this could be dangerous.

Just brooding longer didn't help. Anna took her cell phone and thought the burglary should be reported to the police. But what she had learned that evening about the strange tailing and the fake Tony Peller made her dial Sergei's number instead. He was the one she trusted one hundred percent.

"Yes?" she heard.

"Sergei' I've been stolen. I don't want to be more precise on the phone. Can we meet again?"

"Be there in a few minutes! I'm still at the institute anyway."

Twenty minutes later, Sergei rang the doorbell. Anna had just gotten out of the shower and opened the door wrapped in a towel.

"It's not a posh way to order a man's visit," Sergei said before hesitantly entering.

"Sorry, didn't even think about that bothering you."

"Well, what you call disturbing," he replied, sheepishly trying not to look at the bottom of the skimpy towel.

"Why don't you sit in the kitchen for a moment? I'll be done in a minute."

Sergei's gaze fell on the hole in the room's door, and he called out, "Do your roommates ever fight?"

The answer came from Anna's room, "I don't feel like joking. I poked the hole in earlier. By the way, the burglars got a new access code from the emergency key service. They were able to assume my identity just like that. The electronic locks had been sold as an innovation. In the past, students had cheap keys copied at the hardware store. Today, all you need is a cell phone."

"Now, don't exaggerate. We'll take care of this security gap tomorrow. I'll ask Mailly to give the dorm rental a good going over. Today, you can spend the night at the institute. Take a few things with you."

CHAPTER 4

The laboratory building had a few sparsely furnished rooms. Sometimes employees stayed there overnight if they wanted to stay at the institute to supervise test series. A few minutes later, Anna was lying in bed in one of these rooms, trying to fall asleep. A glance at her cell phone showed 2:22. Special combinations of numbers often triggered a signal in her brain to figure out the meaning of the numbers. Although Anna knew it was possible to interpret nonsensical things into them, she regularly fell for this temptation. It was like a gambling addiction and fun because she usually came across intriguing clues.

This time it was different. Lying on the back, she thought about the three trivial numbers 2:22. Finally, she looked at the clock again. It was only 2:04. As it seemed, her tired eyes had been mistaken. Knowing that brooding would only keep her from sleeping, she lay down on her side and fell asleep a short time later. After twenty minutes, she had reached the first short deep sleep phase. After that, her brain became active again to generate the *teta waves* typical of REM sleep. *Alpha waves* were added in parallel, allowing it to see colorful and spatial images. A movie began to play in the dream. Someone held a cell phone in his right hand and began to scroll through a list of stored contacts with his thumb. They were the phone book entries from Anna's cell phone. Her fingernails were always cut short because she had never gotten out of the habit of biting them. No doubt, she saw her own fingers scrolling the cell phone. The thumb stopped at the name Brian Wilson, and the last digits of his number read ...222.

Is that his way of telling me to call him? He could use what he's recently learned for a clumsy approach. *I don't want to think about it. Tired, tired...*

Anna remembered this part of the dream the following day when her first glance again went to the clock radio. This time, the brain had no trouble processing the information analytically, and the result was quickly determined: overslept. At 9 o'clock, she was supposed to pick up a group of students at the main entrance. That was ten minutes ago. There was no gap in her schedule that day. She still needed to look at the self-assessments of the five students, which is what they usually must use to register for classes with her. Instead of jumping up and flying through the bathroom with a cat wash as she often did, she stayed put and started thinking about Brian:

Why is this stupid guy checking in in the middle of the night? Does he think he's so irresistible to think I'd jump at it?

Still, Anna made no move to get up. Why couldn't she get this guy out of her mind?

Without any hurry, she went to the desk and dialed Mailly's number from the institute's internal phone. She answered very formally, probably because the caller was unrecognizable.

"It's me, Anna. There should be a group waiting at the main entrance..."

She didn't need to finish the sentence. Mailly had already taken care of it, "Renaldo will fill in for you today," she said, adding anxiously, "Let's go have breakfast first. Then we can talk about yesterday again in peace."

Shortly after ten, Mailly got a message from Sergei. They should all meet again in the meeting room. On the way there, Anna stopped by her office and scrolled through the institute's internal messenger news. This particular messaging app connected her with all the active and former participants in her courses. This allowed them to share experiences or get help.

But really, Anna was only interested in one thing that morning: had Brian been online the previous night? The app developed at the institute had a unique feature but was still in the testing phase. If the app was active during meditation, brain waves were transmitted to the institute server via the cell phone. The thing wasn't official, though. Moreover, not all users knew how the communication actually worked. Former students from the Massachusetts Institute of Technology (MIT) also collaborated in the development. They were involved in a research project. It was discovered that telephone providers' radio wave networks could transmit certain brain waves.

A few developers in this project were tasked with developing a defense mechanism. This was to prevent unauthorized access to thoughts during transmission. One from that group was Renaldo. Because he had received training from Anna in addition to his studies in Massachusetts, he quickly realized that the Americans' new technology could become a danger. The generation just coming of age was so digitally connected that they would be especially vulnerable to such a security breach. After all, he counted himself among them. What Anna and the other *masters* taught the young people in Freiburg could not be allowed to fall into the wrong hands. Renaldo gained his first experience with the new technology when the most conservative forces in the United States formed a backward-looking government. Their domestic and foreign policy activities awakened many progressive powers in the country, and Renaldo counted himself among them.

Anna could finally answer her question quickly with the help of the app. Brian had been "offline" for more than a day and, therefore, could not have contacted her telepathically last night. The log from the institute server showed that the app had not been turned off manually.

Since his brainwaves could not be recorded via the mobile network, there had been no signal for hours. It could only have three reasons; there was no mobile network nearby, or he was in a permanent deep sleep like in a coma or..., but Anna didn't want to imagine that. In any case, she was now worried that something might have happened to him.

Δ

India, State of Madhya Pradesh

After a long sweeping curve, one could see the first flat huts on the outskirts of the next town. A road sign indicated that it would be another two kilometers to Dhar. Ravi turned left shortly after and said, "Dhar is our destination. My family now lives in Mandu, where we picked you up. But I live most of the time in the temple Lat Masjid. That's where we must go to show you something. It takes too long along the main road. The traffic is getting heavier. We'll take the side roads."

Brian looked at his cell phone. The mobile carrier was displayed, but he couldn't connect to the Internet. Ravi saw it and asked, "Wanna use mine?"

Surprised that the monk owned one, Brian thought: *Hopefully, it's not one from the colonial era.* But to his surprise, he was then given a top-of-the-line model. Via Ravi's cell phone, access to the Internet was instantaneous. Brian now looked at the announced route. The town of Dhar was about forty kilometers north of Mandu. At that moment, he remembered that India used metric measurements. When he had the orientation, he asked Ravi, "Where exactly are we going?"

"To the mosque Lat Masjid. In your language, it is also called the Pillar Mosque. Parts of an older Hindu temple were used to build it. They say the mosque's name probably comes from the hundreds of stone pillars supporting the roof. Each column has a different shape, and many look rather technical."

"But isn't that the mosque where one of the stainless iron columns is located?"

"Indeed. You know your stuff! Maybe, we don't need to explain that much to you. This place dates to when the gods still visited the local palaces. It fell victim to the plundering of the Afghan mercenary leader Mahmud Gazni in 1050 AD. During that time, it was broken into four parts. Our monk brothers were able to bring the most sacred part of the pillar to safety at that time, and for almost a thousand years, it was our duty to protect this artifact."

"Does anyone know why some iron pillars in Indian temples don't rust?"

"Yes. This forged iron owes its stainless properties to a protective film of crystalline phosphate. This requires a complicated manufacturing process. In our time, this was rediscovered very late. For a long time, we monks were not believed. Perhaps because when we meditate, our eyes are closed, as some still believe."

Brian was amused by Ravi's humor and asked, "What do you think this pillar was for?"

Parts of the iron pillar in the exhibition area [54]

"It was a radio mast, antenna, and radio wave amplifier. Originally, you could communicate with the goddess *Shiva*," Ravi replied. It sounded like the most natural thing in the world that an Indian god could communicate in this way.

Brian asked again, "You spoke of a female goddess in your language. In English, Shiva is male. Which is correct?"

"In most depictions, Shiva has a male body. But often, our gods have female facial features. Western literature sometimes says this has something to do with the beauty ideals of the time. This is rather silly because fashion has always been something short-lived. These interpretations probably come from archaeologists from the colonial period. We Indians have other ideas. The forms of Buddhist statues are very detailed, and every detail has its reason. Moreover, the gender of the god is deduced from the stories that have been handed down. Thus, our gods also have partners and children. We interpret the combination of female and male characteristics so that one god always embodies all genders. In addition, the gentle characteristics of the gods tend to be expressed through softer and more friendly facial features. In Shiva's case, you can also see this in other features. Two of her four arms are more delicate and in line with her face. How could it be otherwise if the law of duality is to endure in nature?"

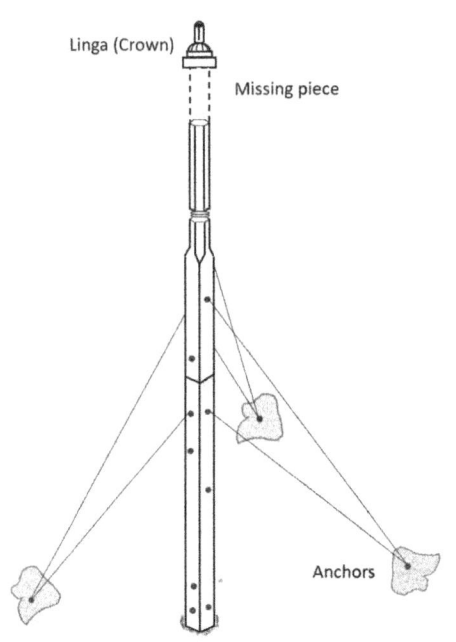

Drawing reconstruction of the iron pillar of Dhar (India) [27]

"Has Shiva always had the same human form?" wanted Brian to know.

"I know Shiva only with a human-like face. But in our culture, she, respectively he, is also known only for a few thousand years. Perhaps he had also given himself other bodies in an earlier epoch."

A little later, the minivan drove onto the grounds of the mosque. After a few steps across the exhibition area, they stood in front of the three pieces of the iron column. Like every visitor, Brian was fascinated by the fact that the iron does not rust. Already in one of his schoolbooks was a picture of the pillar in Delhi. The chemistry teacher had told exciting stories about the reason for the rust resistance. Unfortunately, he said the same thing to all grades. Hence, the younger ones mostly already knew the mystical and spooky tales.

Nevertheless, every student wanted to attend lessons with the old teacher. After all, he knew how to combine fairy tales with material science. Brian remembered every detail told. Some children then passed the stories on to their younger siblings at home. This included that the ore was supposed to come from a magical world whose diminutive wizards later had to turn into humans. They did this so that they would no longer be hunted by humans. At some point, word had gotten around that these wizards could make extraordinary things.

What the pillars were used for, the students did not find out. Even when searching the Internet, Brian only found articles discussing the material composition. He also found only conjecture about how the Asian blacksmiths had made it. To produce the unique lattice structure in the outer protective layer would have required extensive metallurgical processing. But nothing now surprised Brian. The rust-protection mystery would be beside the point if the pillar were a radio mast. It was just noon, and the muggy air made him sweat in his long, completely encrusted pants. The checkered shirt had, in the meantime, also no more recognizable color. Since tourists were already turning around to look at him, and some were probably keeping their distance because of the stench, he approached Ravi, "I'd like to freshen up a bit now. Can you help me?"

"Kanja should be here any moment, too. He will bring you something. Maybe he's already waiting at the entrance. We should also find washrooms there."

Brian didn't have to be told twice and hurried after Ravi towards the temple entrance. Even from a distance, Kanja could be recognized by his eye-catching, colorful earring. Wrapped in an immaculate orange *kesa*, he stood on one leg holding two backpacks covered with thick advertisements. Brian couldn't help but grin because this monk looked like he had just been through a hundred years of time travel. The appearance of the monk in his monk's habit, whose clothes gave off strict abstinence, and the advertising on the backpacks, were absolute contrasts and thus a photo motif for attentive tourists.

On the way there, Brian noticed that also other people seemed to be dressed festively. Kanja guessed his question and said in English, "I once got you two vagabonds appropriate clothes."

Ravi explained to Brian, "Today begins the festival of *Janmashtami* for the Hindus. We Buddhists also pay our respect to this occasion."

Brian remembered that the birth of the god Krishna was celebrated. The Hindus celebrate this for two days. An interesting parallel to Christianity is that, according to Hindu belief, Krishna lived on earth as a human being around 1400 BC. The only difference is that the deities in Asia were usually not the god-begotten children of human mothers but the incarnations of their divine ancestors.

Half an hour later, Ravi was dressed similarly to Kanja. Brian, however, was astonished when he opened his backpack and found complete clothes for a Western tourist inside. Including underwear and brand-new sports shoes. All the correct sizes. Then there was a small cloth bag where he found something that looked like a cell phone. The device had a curved screen and only two buttons. Clothes and curiosity lifted Brian's spirits, and he thought: *These guys are on their toes!* While thinking about what else they would surprise him with, he remembered the iron pillar that was said to have served as an antenna in ancient times. The thing with the pillar had awakened now really his research urge. Which technology would be behind it, and what was sent over this radio network?

With new clothes and freshly washed, Brian suddenly received signals. And relatively mundane signs at that. It was the smell of spicy chickpea porridge, which he hated. By now, however, he was so hungry that he would have loved to buy one of the packed lunches the tourists carried. Fortunately, Kanja remembered that Americans don't get full of meditating alone. The second backpack contained water bottles and real food.

"Before lunch, we should go to the iron pillar. Later the terrain will be crowded with tourists. The exhibition opens to the public during the afternoon of today's holiday. We monks always have access. Arriving there, Brian saw three iron fragments carefully placed on stone pedestals. The pillar must have been over forty-six feet tall, with the missing piece and the crown at the top.

"Can you feel anything when you touch it?"

Indeed, Brian could feel light energy as it flowed over his hand into the body.

"Take the receiver out of the backpack. ...could have already been switched on," Ravi added.

When Brian held the strange device near the iron, a splash screen with a logo appeared on the curved case. It was a *mandala,* and a *Merkaba* was spinning in its center. Brian looked questioningly at Kanja, who waited anxiously to see how Brian would react. When he turned his gaze back to the small screen, the Merkaba began to spin again. Brian tried the game a few times until he realized that the symbol in the center only rotated when he looked at it.

"What kind of cool technique is that?" he asked the monks.

"We don't know everything about it, but sometimes it helps to ask a quantum physicist of modern times. They have copied the device for us after an explanation described in the Indian Vedas. According to this, Shiva is said to have given the people such a device so they could communicate with him when he was not on earth. The legend also says this was only necessary until the people had completely mastered the meditation technique. Our religious teachers have been training this ancient art since that time."

Ravi explained this in more detail: "Indian youth still have something that has been lost to their Western peers. They yet live the traditions of their ancestors, which can protect them from some of the dogmas of materialism. For example, a few scientists at the Bangalore Technology Center managed to identify in the texts of the Vedas not only myths but clear technical descriptions."

"It's all fascinating, but now tell me what you brought me here for!" Brian urged.

"We brought you to Dhar to prove that such iron pillars were once used for communication. Such pillars, like the somewhat smaller specimen in Delhi, can be found all over the country. But these are only receiving antennas. Not so this one. The missing piece in the upper part of the pillar was a transmitter. However, it only worked if you knew the instructions for it."

"And you think I know my way around that?"

"No, but you can help us get the part. And you're not just smug, but also smart."

"Your honesty is truly delightful," Brian replied. Then he paused thoughtfully before asking, "Didn't you say the monks were tasked with protecting this precious item? Don't they have it anymore?"

"They looked after it until the 1930s. Then the Nazis in Germany got wind of it. Some of their scribes found references in the Vedas to strange technical devices related to stainless iron. As a result, they began to search. On behalf of the SS, they organized an expedition to the Himalayas under Ernst Schäfer. This expedition had several goals. Among other things, they searched in Tibet for remnants of an ancient Aryan race. But it was also documented that they brought back an iron statue from Lhasa made of the material of the so-called Chinga meteorite. At that time, the Germans did not know what material the artifact was made of. They were puzzled, just like today's material researchers, about what metallurgical knowledge the makers of this statue must have had. After all, according to legend, the statue was supposed to be several thousand years old. However, iron could officially be processed in such quality only in modern times. So, they continued their research. At some point, they came across the Indian iron pillars, which did not rust despite the humid climate. The column in Delhi was known before. Yet, the Germans now knew that there must be much more interesting specimens."

"Where was the missing piece hidden, from which the small statue was also supposed to come?" Brian wanted to know.

"All parts were in the care of Tibetan monks until 1939. After that, they realized the danger involved if the Nazis came into their possession. The monks sought help so that at least the most important part of the artifact could be brought to safety."

"I still can't see what my role in this story is supposed to be," Brian echoed.

"Be patient! We'll withdraw for now and have something to eat."

The word "eat" had a similar effect as the ringing of the ice cream man in front of the apartment building from childhood. Suddenly, nothing was more important.

His curiosity had made him forget that he was already sick with hunger. He humbly placed his hand on the center iron once again, and then all three of them left the showgrounds for the parking lot where the minivan was waiting. As Brian sat in the back, he pulled the strange radio out of his backpack and asked, "How does the radio know I'm looking at the screen? Because only at that moment does the Merkaba rotate. If I look away, it stops."

Kanja answered that like this, "As I'm sure you know, we don't just communicate via speech, radio waves, and so on, things that we can measure with tools of our physics. You are well-educated in metaphysics and can imagine fields that can leave our material-penetrated space. We enter these fields when we meditate. Telepathy is a good side effect for us. As observed in quantum physics, a defined state, which we want to see or measure, occurs at the moment we measure it. You probably know the physics of this better than I do, but what we know from our ancient writings are the legends about the mysteries of this world. The moment a quantum system is observed from the point of view of the macroscopic world, it no longer changes. It is as if the particles simply remain frozen. At that moment, you can measure them. Therefore, a defined state is only present if we measure it. This is also how thought waves work. Thought is, therefore, a sense that we can use as a measuring tool. Conversely, this means that it can occur if you think something definite in your mind."

"I'm beginning to know what you're trying to tell me. I think of this symbol on the screen, which is why it is displayed now?"

"No, that should be beyond your capabilities. The device is only a translator of what the iron pillar permanently emits. They are radio waves in a certain frequency range. The measuring device activates and displays a permanently programmed image when your brain concentrates on it. Unfortunately, that's all it can do yet. The iron device is in waiting mode. Without the missing piece, or at least the main part of it, it can't switch to transmit and receive mode."

"What's so urgent that this thing should work again now, of all times?"

Ravi switched to Sanskrit, the language of the Brahmins, for his answer. It was the mother tongue of the two monks, "Excuse me, but for some things, only Sanskrit has the appropriate words. That is one of the reasons why you were chosen for this task. We believe that Shiva and the other gods of his tribe want to return. To do this, we may need to explain what Shiva stands for in our faith. You probably know the term Trimurti from Hinduism. Our three main gods embody the concept of divine creation, preservation and destruction. Brahma is the creator, Vishnu is the preserver, and Shiva is the destroyer. So, these three things form the eternal cosmic cycle. But Shiva's task of destruction also simultaneously enables transformation, the creation of a new age. The arrival of this god thus offers people the chance to free themselves from everything old and to change social conditions, the entire way of life."

"I know this part of your doctrine. But with such ideas, you surely don't have only friends on this planet!" Brian said.

"We call it the age of rebirth. In Freiburg, a large part of this ancient knowledge is passed on to selected younger members. You are one of them. But you are right. It would be too easy if there were not also enemies of this change. As we know, those who profit from the ills of the current order cling to the old state. Unfortunately, there are not only heavenly powers like Shiva. The powerful of the current order also have their gods, bringing us to our real problem. These bad gods, in our eyes, must leave the earth voluntarily. Otherwise, according to the prophecy, Shiva would start the destruction. So, there would be war between the gods again."

"And you fear that humans would suffer from this war, yes?"

"Not only that. As in times past, people would go to war for the gods this time as well. However, if we follow the Buddha's teaching and believe the other sages, there is a way out. One could make the rival gods leave the earth voluntarily."

"But why volunteer?"

"No one can deny that the gods are real. They are real because they have survived in people's memories. They nestled in consciousness and thus became real for civilization. Only when the discord among men disappears will they no longer be willing to go to war for evil forces."

Kanja returned to the actual mission, "You now know that the many crop circles appearing on all continents could be a call to prepare for Shiva's return. We think the Merkaba indicates that Shiva and his assistants need help for the return."

"I wonder why they need the help of humans. If you believe the ancient scriptures, they were on earth before humans and had been waging wars against each other even without us."

Kanja sounded slightly puzzled when he replied, "Remember what you have learned. There is indeed much in the Indian Vedas. The gods we are talking about do not travel by subway or space shuttle. True, others travel great distances by spacecraft. Shiva, however, is not one of them. He and his family of gods can only move through space in energetic form. At their destination, they need something into which they can materialize. A body that we humans recognize and accept as an interlocutor. Only when they are physically present can they build vehicles with their knowledge and earthly means. With this, they can move. As you know, these vehicles are an important part of our mythology. Wherever you look, flying gods are depicted. Even though they have taken a body on earth, their language is difficult to understand. After a long separation, gods and humans will have to learn from each other again to get closer. That is why we monks were trained to pass on the knowledge of communication to all generations. Sadly, the last remaining transmitter is not working anymore. Nothing is worse for a religious community than not being able to receive and talk to their gods in a dignified way."

"I'm starting to get it. Thank you for being so patient," Brian said, and at that moment, he became aware of his task.

"Where can we find the missing piece from the pillar, and how will we straighten up the piece that weighs tons?"

"Raising the pillar in Dhar would be difficult. Before we succeeded, we would surely be locked up by the authorities. The pillar has fulfilled its function for now. It indicates the arrival of Shiva. Now we must prepare everything so that we can receive him. We also don't need the *linga*, the forged top of the pillar, at least for now. This part is housed in the fortress of Dhar and is safe there now. We will get it only if it is needed."

Brian became uncertain. He wanted to consult with the masters from Freiburg first, at least with Anna. He had made no effort to shield his thoughts. Therefore, Ravi noticed that Brian was struggling to decide and said, "Do that. Consult with your confidants first. This Anna was a disciple of Ela, a priestess from Egypt. Ela was one of my most remarkable students. But that is no wonder because she is the incarnation of Hathor, the Egyptian goddess of love and fertility. An earlier incarnation of Ela was the Greek goddess Aphrodite."

To his shame, Brian realized that he should know this. Every language study and every education in Freiburg contained many lectures about the history of the ancient gods. However, the subject is so extensive and confusing due to the many embodiments that one would have to spend years on it alone to avoid losing the overview. Only one thing was deliberately omitted from the lectures. The students never learned the civil names of presently living incarnations in their studies. This was done for their protection. All embodiments received protection from enemies of the existing order. This included, for example, that they belonged to or were supervised by specific organizations. One of these secret organizations was the last remaining Masonic Order. But no one was allowed to know which of the many existing splinter groups was the confirmed Order and still had the knowledge about the gods. This was also true of several other Orders. Thus, the fragmentation and strife among the most educated classes of all previous generations also produced something good, camouflage.

After Brian thought it all through again, he asked, "Now can you tell me how exactly you want me to help you and where is the missing piece of the pillar today?"

"Your task is to get into the hideout with your military superiors. Unfortunately, this hiding place is in the most inconvenient location imaginable."

"But it was always clear that Shiva would return. Then why a hard-to-reach hiding place?"

"This is simply because the founders of American democracy have always been among the protectors of ancient knowledge. Therefore, the artifact was considered the safest in the United States during World War II. Then in 1940, they tried to hide it in the New Mexico desert. What we're telling you now may not be the full story, but at least the part that got through to us after the event." Ravi paused for a minute, eyes closed as if refreshing his knowledge through meditation. Then he continued, "I suggest Kanja tell you, and since I am the better driver, I will take us back to Mandu already."

Brian didn't know whether anticipation of the expected revelation or fear of Ravi's driving skills outweighed the excitement. Finally, he said, "Okay, let's hit the road, but please watch out for oncoming traffic."

Kanja had a different way of telling stories. It always sounded like a prayer with him, as if he learned it all by heart, "Yes, so that's how it was back then in New Mexico. A military base had the job of protecting the artifact. Of course, research was also done. Not only with the artifact from India, by the way. At the end of the Second World War, the Americans also began to hide other things there. The danger was too high that the Germans could obtain secret research results from the Americans and the allied British. After World War II, however, they began experimenting with the artifact. During this time, there were particularly many UFO sightings in the area. It seemed that someone was watching the goings-on of the Americans. On July 7, 1947, the military noticed the artifact was emitting radio waves. The radiation was so strong that electrical appliances did not work, and vehicles did not start. Then, on the morning of July 8, what has provided for various science fiction tales and conspiracy myths ever since happened. One of the patrolling UFOs crashed in Roswell. Those who believe in extraterrestrials will wonder what kind of junk the aliens are flying around here with us. As we see it, however, it was not a miracle. The Americans' experiments damaged the UFO's anti-gravity generator so badly that it crashed. But the crucial thing was what happened afterward. The artifact simply disappeared a few days later. And it wasn't until years later that we learned from brothers of our allied Orders where the aliens had taken it."

"Now tell me!"

"You're not going to like this," Kanja repeated, and with a grin, he continued, "We need a submarine to get there."

"Of course, a submarine. You can probably get that at the nearest online retailer, or how will you get something like that?"

"Not just anyone. We're going to need one like the Germans are building. Small and with a fuel cell propulsion system. An improved model is undergoing trials and is still at the ThyssenKrupp shipyard in Kiel for touch-up work. A more advanced design of the Class 212A. The sub has been ordered for joint NATO operations, and now hold on to your hats as you learn what its first mission will be."

"Do you think I could help you steal a submarine? How do you imagine that? Even if we get someone to move the thing, such a boat is registered worldwide. It would be a miracle if we could get out of Kiel Bay undetected, let alone reach the open Baltic waters."

"Listen first before you question everything again," Kanja explained further, "Actually, everything is already prepared."

Brian sat back and shook his head in disbelief. It seemed to him now that the old monks had traded their minds for something less valuable. Then he began one of his breathing exercises to normalize the pulse. Finally, he said, "Well, since you've obviously seen enough James Bond movies, I guess everything will be fine. But for now, keep talking!"

Kanja's face lit up when he heard the name Bond and said enthusiastically, "Yes, James Bond. I've seen them all. But even the British haven't come up with what we have in mind. Maybe we'll do some test shots anyway. Then we'll have some footage later for the next blockbuster with lead actor Brian Wilson."

"Better not," Ravi replied, indicating to Kanja with a motion to continue the explanation he had begun.

"First, you should know that it's better if Anna doesn't find out the whole story yet. She has too many contacts in her network. There is a risk that there is also an opponent of Shiva. Besides, when you return to Malta, you will tell your superiors a story that will make them think you have partial amnesia. They will send you on convalescent leave to Germany if everything goes as planned. This is supposed to be your cover. When you get home, the sub will already be on its way. You'll have to get on somehow, but others will take care of that. Our problem is the time factor. The sub is scheduled to leave soon for its next test run. The exact date is still secret but will be communicated in time. The official destination is the North Atlantic."

"Where do I board?"

"Somewhere on the high seas."

"So, where do we go from there?"

"Our friends on board will explain that to you. The commander is Captain Lieutenant Lange. Such officers are used to special missions scheduled at short notice. In such cases, it also happens that the target is communicated to them only during the mission.

Our job from here is to ensure the mission objective change comes at the right time. In addition, we must take care of the camouflage. Despite the ingenious camouflage technology built into the boat, there is only one way to keep the itinerary secret...."

Here Ravi interrupted him as he said, "He will be told about this soon enough. It's better if it stays a secret as long as possible. Just in case something else happens to James Bond between now and then."

This even made Brian laugh again. But the laughter immediately disappeared when he learned that Kanja would bring him to the tunnel this evening with the donkey cart. Before that, Ravi gave a lot of instructions for the next steps. The hole in the ground near the hut on the outskirts of Mandu would then transport him back to Malta. Since jumping back near the earth hole in the Nandu Mountains would again cause time dilation, everything had to be done as quickly as possible. As Brian sat next to Kanja on the donkey cart again that evening, he learned a few more things about Anna and her colleagues at the Freiburg Institute. Despite heavy eyelids, he listened tensely because this story was so crazy that, at first, he thought Kanja was mixing it up with one of the latest spy movies.

"We indicated earlier that Anna should not hear about your next trip. She and a few institute colleagues are currently trying to get information on crop circles. We believe that someone is trying to gain access to you through Anna. As thousands of years ago, our gods still have the same enemies today. You know, it's always about the same thing. Some want to help humanity progress, while others prefer to continue exploiting people. The enemies of Shiva are masters of deception. They use it to gain access to all circles in society to undermine it, including the secret services. You should only talk to her about your task once we know if Anna is already being monitored and controlled. Nevertheless, you must contact her so as not to arouse suspicion. But remember one thing; while you have only been on the road for a day and a half, about four days have passed for Anna. As a result, the time schedule has become confusing. Therefore, your contact attempt must not occur until you are back."

Brian replied, "Then I may have already caused a problem. Since I fell into the hole, I have tried several times to reach Anna through the institute's internal data network."

"This is not good. We don't know what happens when you make contact like that. Maybe your attempt, at worst even snippets of thoughts, will be transmitted with a time delay. That could confuse the recipient. If information arrived at Anna, it would be from the future. But this is only theory. Maybe she didn't notice anything at all."

"What if Anna specifically asks me about the problem. I can't lie, and besides, I don't know how well she can get inside my head."

"Don't underestimate your mind suppression ability. Your pyramid trick works quite well. Anna is not supposed to help us directly with the mission with the submarine. But we may need her later to distract the enemies from Shiva."

Brian couldn't tell if he was suited for such cheating. As with the bridge game, he was also evil at pretending otherwise.

Ravi must have sensed his doubts and said, "Oh, by the way, we believe that many a puzzle in life is solved only at the right time. I feel like I got some crucial advice in life only when I had almost given up hope. Maybe your pyramid trick is not a bad thing for such moments."

His butt and back hurt terribly when Brian finally got off the donkey cart and followed Kanja to the tunnel. Again, it was an inconspicuous hut through which they reached the entrance to the Subway. They walked again and stopped at a place where symbols were on the rock wall. This time, Brian knew that the journey would not begin until his hands were on the engraved spirals. When he opened his eyes again, they could exit the tunnel up the well-worn stone stairs after a few steps. In the small wooden hut, everything seemed unchanged. This time, too, it was utterly dark, and Kanja led him to the hole in the ground with a flashlight and rope ladder in tow.

As Brian descended the ladder, a shiver ran down his spine. Would the journey end in the muddy hole in Malta? Before any more concerns could arise, Kanja said, "The return journey begins when both hands touch the walls. At that, you have to go back into a light trance. And remember, people in Malta don't know about the time difference. Sensitive people might have had strange encounters related to you. Because of your attempted contact, this could also be the case with Anna. So then, see you soon!"

When Brian regained consciousness, the first thing he did was look at his cell phone. The battery wasn't dead, but he had no reception. *Great. They may have blocked my cell phone card.*

Fatigue took him by surprise within seconds. He slept lying on his side until morning. Shivering, he got up with the first rays of sunlight and stumbled, dazed and downright filthy, in the direction of the village of Dingli. Arrived there, the inhabitants met him skeptically at first. Eventually, however, one of the younger ones lent him his cell phone, so he could dial the military emergency number. After returning to the frigate, which was still in the port of Malta, the adventure was to begin in earnest.

Δ

Freiburg, university campus

"Before I begin, I'd like to know what has happened since last night," Sergei began the meeting with Anna, Mailly, and Gregor. All three had previously been summoned at short notice to the bug-proof meeting room, where they had also conferred the previous evening. Anna retold everything about the theft of her engraved stone. She also did not omit the strange dream in which her meditation student Brian contacted her. After all, it was unusual that he was not available since then. His cell phone signal had also wholly disappeared for hours, she said. Gregor's part described what the research had revealed, "To be honest, all the information about the vision received by Anna yesterday is contradictory. These are real newspaper articles about reactionary Russian forces from the first years of the twentieth century. Much of it can be found in London museums. However, I've not found the article Anna mentioned anywhere. Not even in Jerusalem. When one comes across documents on the forged protocols with the anti-Semitic message, it is pointed out that their authenticity has been scientifically disproved. No serious source would claim today that these protocols were genuine."

"I suspect someone wants me to look into this matter. It must have to do with the publication and dissemination of this agitation at the beginning of the last century. Maybe it's some warning or a cry for help. Maybe something like this is brewing again at the moment. What do you think?" Anna asked.

Sergei replied, "But Anna, history is history, and we can only ensure that the truth about it is not rewritten. There are memories and records. They remain in the minds and archives for the later generations."

"I know it doesn't sound very likely to most, but the knowledge of humankind has already been extinguished at least once. Whether caused by God, as religion describes it, or by nature alone remains speculation. For me, the extinction of humankind's memory certainly occurred with the great flood at the end of the ice age. That was like a great 'reset'. I personally believe that this was not a coincidence."

After this sentence, everyone froze in shock and looked at Anna's face.

"What are you trying to say?" asked Mailly.

"We are again heading for a time when people's heads will be washed. There can only be a remedy if we take a different path. And my vision could have been an indication of this. The great founders of religion realized this when they tried to convince the masses of their idea. You know that I cannot see into the future, as some claim. But my experience tells me that people are left with only two options."

"I hope it's not what I think!" Mailly admitted.

"One possibility would be for the three major religions to unite into one faith as soon as possible. This should be theoretically possible because they have the same roots and even many details in their stories about the gods are similar. The opportunity will arise when the resources on the planet are depleted, and the starving people can no longer increase individual wealth. How likely do you think that is?"

"Probably not so likely, if you ask me," said Gregor.

"Then the second option is for people to fight each other until most of the world's population can be convinced of one ideology. What about this option?"

"Apart from the fact that these wars are already in full swing, recently even as cyber wars, I'd classify this variant as not expedient," was Sergei's opinion. He immediately added, "But I see a third possibility. And this one, according to the legends of ancient Asian scriptures, has been used many times."

"You don't mean..."

"Yes, I do. At some point, I stopped letting so-called scribes explain how to read the remaining ancient texts. I'm not the first one with this knowledge. Already in the early Middle Ages, some artists began again to leave their knowledge and visions with subtle messages in their works of art. Those peoples who did not know the religious dogma of Christianity just carved in stone or scratched into the ground what they saw and experienced."

"So, what's the third option you were going to tell us about, Sergei?"

"I did not come up with this option. It is already written as a warning in the book of Moses. As a warning to the people is told about the divine destruction of life."

"But that's just one story of many," Gregor said.

"Yes, sure. And just like today, the warring parties falsified the texts for all they were worth. The only interesting thing for me here is who the warring parties were originally. Obviously, gods and not humans. People were misused as working tools for a kind of heavenly legion. Another sort of god disapproved. The war described was not between gods and humans. It was the war of the gods, fought vicariously on the backs of humans."

"And after this war, people's memory had to be erased."

"Interesting thesis, Sergei."

"I'll go even further. There's something brewing again at the moment."

"You mean the gods are starting another war?"

"If I interpret the ancient scriptures correctly, all peoples are waiting for the return of their gods. And there is a consensus among them: The time is now!"

"But just returning doesn't necessarily mean war among them, does it?"

"Anna's vision reminded me of the sacred number three. Hinduism is preparing for the arrival of the three gods, Shiva, Brahma, and Vishnu. While Brahma is the creator and Vishnu is the preserver, the arrival of *Shiva* scares me. He must first destroy everything so that it can be recreated by Brahma."

"For God's sake, Sergei! You sound like a cult leader," Gregor said to which Anna replied, "I don't think so. This argumentation has always appeased us; people thought the old stories belonged to old times. In the meantime, I know that history repeats itself. And it will continue to do so until the prophecy is fulfilled."

"Was that the reason you called us today, Sergei?"

"Well, we still need to finish yesterday's discussion about the *Merkaba* and Anna's vision. In the meantime, something else has happened. It looks as if someone is trying to steer our activities in a particular direction. Let's see what we already know:

- Someone is pretending to stalk Anna. If it's a tail, it doesn't fit any pattern we know.
- During the same time, we receive a request from NATO in Brussels. We are to help with the clarification of the crop circles appearing worldwide. Some people trust that we know the artists or suspects who might have done it.
- Anna imagines herself in a memorial during a vision, where she is shown a document. The content of this paper has contributed to one of the most extensive disinformation campaigns of the last century. There are also Jewish and Masonic symbols on it. And the circle closes because these symbols have similarities with the Merkaba, which again appeared in these crop circles.
- While Anna is with us at the institute, her apartment is broken into, and a ritual artifact is stolen.
- On some points, there are parallels with ancient biblical texts.

How do you see it?" Sergei finished his summary.

Mailly did not seem to like these theses yet, and she said, "It is not yet clear to me what all this is supposed to have to do with each other. I also don't see the parallels to biblical texts. Anyone can pull them out by the hair. There is a suitable story in the Bible for every event in our lives. Also, a suitable example can be found in history for each prophecy. However, the house of cards quickly collapses when one tries to match a sequence of prophecies with real events."

Anna became uneasy at these arguments and replied, "On the one hand, I've to agree with you. I also think someone wants to steer us in a direction, possibly distract us from something. On the other hand, I see many prophecies as cultural heritage. In my opinion, a prophecy is nothing more than a memory stored in our cultural memory. This phenomenon occurs when people in a trance leave our physical space and are no longer bound to the space-time continuum. I have learned that time plays a subordinate role outside our material world."

While the discussion continued, Sergei got a message on his cell phone. He was supposed to contact someone through the institute's secure network. After a few minutes, he came back excitedly:

"This can't be true. My contact at NATO in Brussels has informed me that a group within the Navy may be trying to seize an ancient artifact."

"And why are they coming to you with this?"

"It was a warning at the same time. The contact fears they will try to recruit young people from our network with telepathic abilities."

"Could he have meant me?" Anna wanted to know.

"Based on everything we just discussed, that would be possible."

"Did he say what kind of artifact?"

"No."

Sergei turned to Anna and said, "I firmly believe all this is connected. I suggest we take care of the warning from Brussels. Maybe you can help us pull the strings in the right place first. You are in regular contact with this Brian Wilson from the Naval Command in Rostock. Could you please find out where his unit hangs out and if he can find anything in this matter? As far as I know, Brian has good contacts with the admirals because he regularly mediates between conflicting parties with his special skills."

"Sure. I'll approach it carefully. However, as far as I know, Brian does not mediate anything but only takes part in the negotiations in the background. He can tell when interlocutors are not telling the truth."

"All the better. Then he's exactly the person we need."

CHAPTER 5

**Malta Port, Aboard the Frigate,
One day after Brian's rescue**

While unsure how to explain his four-day disappearance, Brian sat shaved and in fresh uniform in a room next to the command bridge. The commander would sit across from him any moment now, and he had no idea how to tell him this lie. As he heard footsteps, the feeling in the pit of his stomach became more uncomfortable. The door was pulled open, and the commander jumped over the threshold with a petrified face.

After the usual greetings and asking how he was doing, Brian heard him say, "Never mind if you want to tell me your story someday or not. I really do find the whole thing extraordinarily strange. I'm sure you can imagine that I'll have to come up with something plausible for the crew to keep any crazy horror stories from circulating around here. I find it very interesting that your comrade Sean Keller initially had a guilty conscience. He could describe every minute of your trip to us in detail. Now, the poor guy suddenly doesn't know how you fell into that damn hole. Very contagious, this amnesia. So, we should isolate you both from the crew for now."

Brian was just about to reply when he was interrupted again, "Wilson, I have always appreciated your honesty. That's why you'd better not even try to give any explanation. Apparently, the command in Rostock had this highly decorated psychologist flown in from Greece to examine you and your friend. So, quite a few other people want to know where you have been hanging out during these four days. But apparently, the psychologist couldn't find out anything either.

Be that as it may. Your mission order is convalescent leave. However, you are both flown to Germany. An American authority has pressured the naval staff in Rostock to temporarily release you from duty. Nevertheless, there will be no special treatment for Americans either. There was not enough budget for a ticket to the United States. Home leave would then be a case for your own wallet. Since you also have German citizenship, Rostock is almost like home," said the commander with a grin, "We'll take you to the airport right away. Someone must have had a huge heart for their American friends. If it had been up to me, you could have started your journey home on a stinking fishing boat."

In the meantime, Brian's thoughts were already elsewhere. Only the words of his supervisor that followed startled him again, "Don't you dare tell anyone on the crew about this celebrity treatment. They might develop a conspiracy theory out of it. You can step away now!"

"Thank you, Cap'n," Brian said goodbye and turned to the exit.

With one foot out, he was called back again, "There's one more thing, Wilson. We blocked your SIM card after your phone became unlocatable across the planet."

That too! Without that SIM card, I can't reach anyone in Freiburg on the institute's internal channels. Hopefully, I*'ll* get th*is* fixed, Brian thought on the way to his cabin. He dropped by the radio operator, who had sometimes helped him with technical problems. After they contacted the cell phone provider, Brian was sent a replacement digital card. Online again, a message arrived from Anna, "Had no contact via the institute network for four days. Get back to me!"

Brian first tried the regular telephone network. Anna answered immediately, "Hey, are you okay?"

"Things are complicated, and I suspect my cell phone is being tapped. Can we talk telepathically? I'll be on a plane in an hour and have some time to do it then."

"Sure, I'll retire to my room. See you then!" Anna answered, and when Brian later spread out his leather chair in the Learjet, he pretended to catch up on the lost sleep. Sitting across from him, Sean sympathized and listened to music through the headphones attached to his seat. The self-hypnosis worked as usual, but Brian needed a few minutes before a relaxed conversation with Anna was possible. First, she talked about the burglary at her apartment and that she, Sergei, and his team were looking into the crop circles that had just appeared worldwide. Brian listened carefully, and then he sensed that Anna was leaving one thing out. When asked about it, she still told the story about the fake Tony Peller and the *deepfake* in the CCTV.

"*This is really crazy. Things are happening to both of us now that have something to do with each other. When you arrive in Rostock, I'd like to discuss it in more detail. I'm also worried that you can't remember everything that happened while you were away,*" Anna transmitted telepathically. Brian had to keep his promise not to talk to anyone about his planned submarine trip. Therefore, he pretended for the time being not to remember what had happened during his absence. Knowing his meditation teacher and former fellow student, however, he would not succeed for long. So there was nothing to do but stay away from Anna for the time being. Finally, he said goodbye, "*You know, I'll enjoy the convalescence vacation. Maybe I'll fly to the States and visit my family, too.*"

Then, before they said goodbye, Anna simply replied, "*Take care of yourself and don't let anyone talk you into anything you don't understand.*"

So, Anna did sense something. Maybe she felt a little of what I experienced in India, Brian thought and stared out the window for a while. He also couldn't help thinking that Anna wanted to ask something else but didn't want to jump in.

At an altitude of 36,000 ft, they were flying over Munich. Later, when the pilot reduced the height, Brian fell asleep and only woke up when Sean gently nudged him to get out.

Δ

Rostock, Maritime Operations Centre,
Ten days after Brian's accident

I should have been told by now when the mission was going to start, Brian mused. His mission was to wait for further orders. Since disembarking the frigate in Malta, he had spent most of his time studying the Indian scriptures on the communication of the gods. The deeper he delved into the complicated texts, the more amazing parallels he found to current technology. If he had read the text before the advent of the first cell phone, some of it would have seemed too fantastic. This prompted Brian to examine those passages in the text dismissed in previous translations as religious depictions of action. He, therefore, searched again and again for similar descriptions from European antiquity to the present.

Without great expectations, he typed the keyword "UFO images" into the search engine. As he browsed, interesting things appeared alongside fake photos, some of which he already knew. His eye roamed over sculptures from different parts of the world but still depicted the same thing. He wondered why the archaeologists insisted that these cultures should not have had any contact with each other. He knew that a Mayan tribesman did not travel to the Indian highlands.

Consequently, they must have all been visited by the same people who brought the architectural style and art. The local artists then depicted the same technical-looking objects. For Brian, there was no doubt that the gods had shown their technology to people everywhere. He wondered: *But why not today, or are we blind to it through bias? For now, I'll continue to focus on Asian images. They are traditionally the least distorted by reinterpretations.*

After these reflections, a more mundane urge announced itself to him. He had worked up an appetite for something from the canteen. Maybe Christina would go with him. He owed her an answer about the bowling evening anyway. Actually, he felt like joining the others after all. It often took an external incentive to spend his free time with something other than books. So, he jumped up and would have run straight to Christina's office if it hadn't been for the cup of sticky tea that spilled onto his pants.

"What a shit!" he exclaimed and immediately had to think of what he had felt when Olaf yelled similar things through his open door the other day.

Twenty minutes later, Christina caught him in the ladies, dressed in a military shirt, drying his trousers at the hand dryer.

"What are you doing here?" she wanted to know. Brian should have known that someone would ask him this question. But as an eloquent language expert, he didn't really have to fear unusual situations. The sight of Christina standing in front of him with her figure-hugging dress and pink face made it impossible to string together logically justified words. What came out was only, "It's hotter here, uh, I mean, in the men's room, there's only cold air. Sorry, I'll be gone in a minute."

This time Christina had reason to laugh at Brian and enjoyed his embarrassment. She didn't let him stop her and promptly disappeared into one of the booths. Brian decided not to take flight immediately and asked, "Have you been to lunch yet?"

"No, but there are only the greasy leftovers at this time of the day."

"I'm hungry, and the lunch would be on me."

"Okay, we can look. We might find something from the salad buffet," Christina answered before Brian left the ladies.

The conversation in the cafeteria was less stiff than Brian first feared. Christina immediately reminded them of the bowling they had planned that evening, "We've gotten enough together without you. Even Olaf is coming along."

It had to mean something if Christina could persuade the frustrated comrade down the hall to come. Brian's guilty conscience was somewhat relieved by this news because if Olaf had joined, it was the first step toward a better climate among the colleagues.

About five hours later, he saw Christina standing alone in front of the bowling center just as he was driving his car to one of the free charging stations. Since he had worked until the last minute, there had been no time to change at home. So, he appeared in the uniform trousers, disfigured by cleaning attempts. Only the blue service shirt had been replaced by a sports shirt, which could still be found in his locker.

"Is no one here yet?" he asked Christina.

"The others are already inside, but I wanted to make sure you weren't walking past the entrance thinking about half-naked Indian goddesses," she answered him cheekily.

Christina was paying so much attention to him should make him happy. However, the question remained how she knew what he was doing now. At first, he wanted to leave it alone. Still, while one of the waiters started the computer and explained the rules of the bowling alley, Brian asked, "You know about my current studies?"

"Not really, but I wanted to take the opportunity to confess something to you," Christina replied.

"Let's hear it."

"I was asked yesterday by the Chief of Staff to send him a breakdown of all the data you requested from the military archives."

Brian inquired, looking at her face, "And did you?"

"Started it, but before anyone gets it, I wanted to research to see if it violates any regulations."

"So?"

"It is permissible. However, everything must be recorded. But the regulation also states that the consent of the affected soldier or civilian employee must be obtained in advance unless there is an order from the military prosecutor's office. And I don't know of any such order."

Without meaning to, Brian registered a natural expression on her face, and the rest of her body language was unremarkable. This made the story believable.

"But what's the point?" Brian asked, this time perhaps a little too loudly, so Olaf turned to them as he took his first ball from storage.

Brian could no longer enjoy bowling. Thus, he unintentionally contributed to the general amusement because the bowling ball rarely rolled to where the pins were waiting for it due to his mental absence.

Afterward, everyone ate together, and Brian sat next to Olaf. His conversation was pretty relaxed, and he even learned about some of his private worries. Sitting across from Brian was Christina, who seemed to avoid eye contact. While everyone was saying goodbye, Christina asked if she could get a ride in his car since she had been drinking alcohol. She could pick up her car the next day.

Before Brian pulled up to Christina's apartment to drop her off, it went through his mind, "*This is classic again. No one knows which way to say goodbye. Goodbye kiss or kiss. Or...*"

Christina took the answer from him and said she had a surprise in her kitchen if he was not too tired. He wasn't, and the surprise was a bottle of a good French red wine that the Fleet Admiral had donated to everyone at the last Christmas party.

"I've been saving it. After all, I was only on duty for a week when the Christmas party was held. Since the boss had thanked us for our work and I didn't want an advance, it's standing today..."

Brian's good mood sometimes had surprising consequences. So also, this time, when in euphoria, he finished Christina's sentence, "... ready as a pleasure accelerator?"

"It's a good thing I already know you, so I know in what situations you say things that others, in their restraint, only dare to think. But in the end, everyone wants the same thing," Christina said and pulled him towards her without making a face. He took advantage of the closeness for a brief kiss and began caressing her neck with his mouth. With slight tension and goosebumps, she instinctively stretched her upper body. Brian ran his tongue along her neck toward her ear. The tingling sensation ran through her entire body. She seemed to like it because she began to move more intensely. The more the arousal increased, the less they thought about what was happening. All inhibition seemed to have vanished. With one hand, she tampered with the belt of his pants. They both stumbled toward the couch as if held together by invisible magnets. Brian's simultaneous attempt to get his hand inside her jeans ended with both falling onto the cushion. The longer the struggle with the clothes lasted, the more it excited them. The frantic movements were interrupted by a short pause, during which Christina took off the remaining parts herself. Brian threw his pants somewhere with a sweeping motion. As he nestled against Christina's warm body and whispered something in her ear, she ended the conversation with a long and passionate kiss.

Although later than usual, Christina and Brian were not the last employees to arrive at the *MOC* parking lot the following day. Each in their own car after picking up Christina's two-seater from the bowling center on the way to work. They should have reserved a spot at the electric charging stations for today. They thus had to put up with remote parking for combustion cars. On the way to the main entrance, Brian worried about whether he should regret the last night. Christina had already given him to understand that it would be okay with her if he considered the whole evening just a leisure episode. Thereupon Brian decided to see this the same way.

The automatic vacuum cleaner was finding its way under the desk when he entered his office. As usual, he had forgotten that Fridays were cleaning days and that all movable items had to be removed from the floor the previous evening. As Brian moved his chair, the robot said, "Sorry to bother you...cleaning is finishing."

The military messenger showed an appointment reminder on the screen, "0900—briefing, an invitation from Rear Admiral Roland Breede."

Oh my goodness! Invitation from the boss, I'm already five minutes over!

Putting his uniform jacket back on and making his way to the navy staff floor, he took the elevator this time to avoid arriving rushed. On the way to the Operations office, he reflected on how many times he had met Breede in person. He was something of a phantom to the staff of the Naval Command, appearing on all official letters but never present. In Brian's eyes, that could only mean that he was responsible for lesser-known missions.

"Wilson. You look like you just fished your pants out of the trash can. Since when do you show up for duty like that?" was the greeting.

"Sorry, Rear Admiral!" was the only thing Brian could come up with in response.

"Why do I have the impression that you do not give this institution the respect it deserves?" Breede continued to yell while closing the soundproof door to the anteroom. When the assistant could no longer hear them, Breede said at an average volume, "Please excuse my tone, but your pants look like crap. ...and save the excuses. You're not going to make a real soldier anyway. For what we want from you, it should be enough."

"Sir?"

"Your mission starts tomorrow morning. You will receive the individual orders shortly before the next destination. So, for now, I'll say this: We were asked to assist in an international operation, but the final location is still unknown. The mission is top secret and will be led by Admiral Rainbow. This is, of course, an alias. You will only learn his real name when he invites you for a cigar. As you can imagine, each person on this mission will only know their immediate assignment. Refrain from even telling anyone personal things. Also, please do not screw women on the team. That only goes well in James Bond movies."

Brian wondered: *If he mentions it specifically, maybe he already knows about Christina. And how does he come up with James Bond? Does he know about my trip to India, and has he talked to Ravi about me? Then the network of the two monks must be pretty comprehensive.*

Finally, Brian considered whether he should rather confess his one-night stand, but Breede took the decision away from him.

"The interlude with Christina was a mistake. Please put an end to this venture. Our naval command is international. The defense tasks of the Atlantic Alliance are one thing. Unfortunately, we come without a special liaison, ... Let's call it special forces. I'm sure you understand that defense missions outside the NATO allies exist. With that, special internal command structures also exist, and not all of them are compatible with each other. I hope I have made myself clear enough. That is also why you should not put your plug in every socket."

Damn, who could have tipped him off about Christina. Did this Olaf have something to do with it? On Breede's behalf?

"Wilson, you are an intelligent fellow. I have yet to learn about some of the things you know about. But there's one thing you should take to heart: don't believe everything you see and hear on your mission. It could be that we will have to deal with an enemy far superior in some respects. Therefore, also think about who you tell what to. Always ensure the identity of the person you are talking to beforehand. You may know better than I that there are so many ways to manipulate people now. You could become frightened. But you will be the right support for our team aboard the submarine. You know that your mission is on a sub?"

"Yep."

"Your trusted officer on board is Captain Lieutenant Richard Lange. The boat is a further development of Class 212 and is intended for sale to a currently unknown customer. The cover name of the boat is Leonardo DaVinci, with the identification S-XX. We refer only to DaVinci in our internal communications."

After this speech, Brian remained alone for a moment. When Breede returned, he said, "Adhere to our security regulations. Even though I have said it several times, always ensure the recipient's identity. Even then, if I should contact you."

"You mean someone could assume your identity to influence me?"

"We have to expect anything. Now pack your seabag and be ready to go starting tonight."

Breede squeezed Brian's hand as if it were goodbye forever. The Rear Admiral's eyes and body radiance told Brian he was very nervous and probably meant the warning. That day, Brian couldn't get anything done right. He just scrolled through his email inbox again without responding. Even Anna's message went unanswered, "Get back to me when you're free."

At 0410 hours, his cell phone rang. It was an automated announcement of the arrival of his cab. An hour later, that cab dropped him off at the helipad checkpoint, where an SUV picked him up and took him directly to the helicopter. He was the only passenger on a long flight until the refueling stop at an air base on the Belgian North Sea coast. Approaching Koksijde, Brian could see the almost smooth North Sea. If visibility had been good, he could have made out the chalk cliffs of Dover on the English coast from the air. He regretted that he was denied this because of the haze. The south of England was like a homeland in secret, and now the weather clouded his view of it. He had the idea of asking the pilots if they would come close to Dover again when they continued their flight.

"We should avoid that at all costs. We have orders to keep as much distance as possible from British territorial waters." was the co-pilot's reply. Judging by his dialect, he could have been from Texas.

When the helicopter was refueled, a military jeep pulled up, and a man in his late thirties joined Brian in the cab. He recognized the rank of lieutenant captain from the badge, and the embroidered name was Lange. As he put on his headphones, Lange greeted, "Good morning, gentlemen!"

A few facts were now arranging themselves in Brian's mind. So, this was his confidant. Lange turned off his microphone and signaled Brian to do the same. Then he spoke in a friendly tone, "Wilson, you are my assistant from now on. I've ordered you aboard because I need someone who knows exotic or ancient languages. In addition, you can also communicate telepathically. I'm not sure if these skills will be needed, but on this mission, we should be prepared for anything."

"What does the crew say when the commander is replaced on the high seas?" asked Brian.

"In the case of Captain Lieutenant Fuchs, there is a suspicion of a detached retina. This must be urgently examined by an ophthalmologist. Fuchs was picked up yesterday evening by a frigate. As there is not enough fuel for the return flight, it will also bring back the helicopter. I stood in for Fuchs."

"How long until the meeting place?"

Lange passed this question on to the pilots, who learned, "The target is 35° west in the North Atlantic. Conceivably unfavorable for an emergency. It was fortunate that a Belgian frigate with an ophthalmologist was nearby."

"About four and a half more hours. This frigate will then take our helicopter to the next refueling opportunity."

"Does the team know about my duties?"

"Mainly specialists in military submarine engineering are aboard the DaVinci. They are used to secrecy. The sub is a technical advancement with features particularly suited to reconnaissance missions. If you want to remain undetected underwater today, you must put considerable effort into it."

"I assume the boat must be tranquil?"

"For this, we have a revised hydrogen propulsion system that allows us to dive for four weeks and emits hardly any noise or heat. We also have a geomagnetic field simulator on board to camouflage the boat's magnetic structure. A few other things are more reminiscent of the protective hull of satellites. Nonetheless, you don't have to know everything, Wilson. However, one thing that's top about this new boat is that we can use two torpedo tubes as pressure locks. This will allow divers wearing pressure suits to reach depths up to 1,300 ft. That's as deep as the sub can officially dive."

Brian noticed Lange's enthusiasm for his latest test model. But with each piece of news, the feeling in the pit of his stomach became more uncomfortable. Every new development had teething problems, and Brian preferred not to ask Lange how often this technology had already been used.

As the flight continued, Brian was familiarized with various regulations and procedures aboard the submarine. This was also important so that the sailors did not hinder each other in the cramped conditions. In an emergency, command structures had to work. As dry training, Brian was given a few exercise videos, which he watched with interest. But none of these instructions improved his uneasy feeling. Despite this, he wanted to keep every detail, especially the orders, in mind. Nothing would be worse than being the greenhorn with a well-rehearsed team.

A change in the sound of the rotor blades woke Brian and Lange grinned as he said, "I hope you're used to this high swell. Please don't throw up all over the place when we're down in the boat. There are better ways to make your debut."

Now Brian saw it too. Lashing rain from above and foamed sea from below. The hatch on the hull of the forecastle was still closed.

The pilot exchanged information with the submarine. Finally, he gave the command, "Get over!" which called for the two crew members to take over.

"How do we get down there, sir?"

"On the rope! And now go ahead."

Despite strong winds, the helicopter was still in the air. Now Brian saw a small inflatable boat with two navy divers. They were holding a thin auxiliary rope that had been dropped earlier. This enabled them to stabilize the two men as they rappelled down. A short time later, Brian was in the dinghy with his life jacket on. Lange followed him. While every move the divers made was fitting, Brian felt completely awkward as he climbed the auxiliary ladder onto the submarine's deck. The two seabags were lowered by rope directly into the hatch a little later. Once in the boat, Brian had to pass through a lock before sailors handed him towels. The new commander's arrival was announced with the traditional Side Whistle. While Brian was allowed to change, he heard that the DaVinci should be ready to dive in an hour. On his way to the crew quarters, he was given a command center tour. Those on duty gave him a friendly nod. Still, Brian saw worried faces on some.

Before the dive, Lange took command, announced the mission assignment, and planned the navigation route in the first briefing. As a guest on board, Brian had observer status. Despite this, he was assigned to the two sonar technicians during the watch.

Shortly after, with its nose down, the DaVinci disappeared into the inky black Atlantic.

CHAPTER 6

Freiburg, university campus

Why isn't this guy answering? His cell phone was ready to receive calls for days. Nevertheless, he can't be reached either by cellphone or telepathically. Maybe I should call Brian's office in Rostock?

These and many other thoughts went through Anna's mind. She was now worried that Brian was doing something rash. He had pulled out all the stops last time to block off parts of his mind. Much of this Anna had taught him. This defense against outside intrusion was supposed to be a protection against abuse. But sometimes, it was also difficult for Anna to weigh correctly how far psychological care could go. After all, Anna's mission was in the general interest and did not serve to harm anyone. Finally, she called Brian's office.

Christina's phone rang. The number displayed was not stored in her personal phone book. The caller had wanted to reach Brian, but his number had been diverted to Christina. Before opening the picture and sound channel, she ensured that her blouse was only open as permitted on duty.

Although Anna introduced herself to her peers by her first name, she knew this was a call to German naval headquarters. Thus, a formal start would be appropriate. Nevertheless, Anna skipped the formalities and simply asked for Brian.

Christina's mood probably deteriorated the moment she suspected the call was of a private nature. Her response was accordingly, "I'm sorry about that. Brian Wilson is away on business, and I can't say for how long. I'm sure you understand that I can't provide further information on that."

"Yes, of course, thank you very much," and the conversation ended quickly. Anna looked at the recording again and realized Christina was twice dishonest. First, she probably knew where Brian was staying. That was fine with Anna; you do not publicly announce military missions. But a second thing bothered her because Christina's eyes radiated jealousy.

Moreover, her eyes scrutinized the physical features of the caller. Not that Anna was jealous here, either. But it was clear now that Christina would not be of any particular help. She would probably have to develop something more to get to Brian. Now she was even more determined to warn him. As Sergei had suspected, someone might try to exploit Brian for an action. If it was a matter of recovering some artifact, no military in the world was the appropriate institution, at least not without international control.

Δ

North Atlantic, DaVinci

The operation center's mood was tense, which seemed normal to Brian. After all, it was all about navigating safely and undetected through the Atlantic. The course corrections have become more frequent now. Brian looked with rapt attention at the relief of the seafloor on the screens. The level of detail was so impressive that he couldn't get enough of it. The sea was 4,100 feet deep at this point. In between, the current diving depth was announced. One announcement made Brian wonder: "Depth 1,250 feet, descending slowly to 1,800."

Hadn't he learned that the boats of this class had a maximum diving depth of 1,300 feet? His gaze, therefore, panned over all the display boards. About 26 nautical miles ahead of them, the sea became abruptly shallower. Apparently, the edge of the North American plate began there. Above the border, the sea was 1,900 feet deep. It was a vast flat plateau.

"Where are we?" muttered Brian as he tried to read the charts. The second officer pointed to the screen with a marker, "Look here. We're 280 nautical miles southeast of the Newfoundland coast. There, an offshore underwater plateau begins. Our destination is there..." At that, he tapped directly into what looked like a former river valley.

"There are many small depressions and valleys. Ideal for hiding."

"But it's 1,900 feet deep there!" Brian pointed out.

"Did you think they would put in the official records how deep a military sub can dive?"

"And what is our maximum diving depth?"

"If it starts cracking, it was probably too much," the second officer said, grinning. Then Commander Lange joined in, "Don't worry about such things. You can't just dive a well-equipped submarine like that too deep. Nevertheless, there will still be enough surprises for you. But now, slowly pack your seabag. You and I are about to get on another boat."

"Changing the boat? Are we surfacing?"

"No, to transfer, we must get down to the bottom and anchor."

Twenty minutes later, the boat slowed down and turned on its exterior headlights. Together with the sonar measurement and the computer's digital map, a razor-sharp image of the surroundings emerged. The external cameras showed only mud-covered areas and occasionally a sea creature. The closer they got to the seafloor, the more the ground was churned up.

"100 feet to ground contact."

"50...20..."

Like a warning message from the parking assistant in the car, warning signals became louder and louder and appeared at shorter intervals. The exterior cameras and radar showed no obstacles around them. Yet, the computer voice gave a collision alert, "Obstacle 200 yards ahead!"

Brian tried to see something, but there was nothing. Then he simply asked, "What obstacle is this supposed to be? What are we being warned about?" The second officer again answered: "Ahead of us is the DaVinci II, our sister submarine. You can't see anything is, of course, intentional. The DaVinci I and II are identical in construction and have perfect camouflage. The gauges only strike when they get very close. But the best camouflage is the earth magnetic field simulation. This makes the contour of the sub appear to strangers like a natural object on the ocean floor. Incidentally, the public knows of only one boat. The manufacturer has kept the production of the second and identical boat secret. As a result, no one will notice if one of them does not reappear right away."

"Granted, that's a brilliant idea. But the two crews know about it, don't they?" was Brian's objection.

"Believe me, everyone on board here is at least as loyal as you are. Everyone will keep the secret as if their lives depended on it."

The exterior cameras now captured a long black object seventy yards away. Details could not be made out because the propulsion heavily churned up ground. One of the wall monitors read, "Approaching target DaVinci II – Automatic navigation complete."

After this maneuver, the commander gave the order to anchor. He handed over command to the second and took Brian to his side, "Wilson, I will now show you how we will transfer to the DaVinci II. There is a special airlock in the tower for that."

He showed him the technical equipment on the monitor, which had remained hidden from Brian until now.

"We transfer through an airlock that's in the tower. It's more like a mobile capsule, like a mini-sub. It can move on its own for a few hundred yards. However, we will have the capsule remotely controlled from the command center. At the same time, a capsule is also undocked in our twin boat. In it sit two sailors named Wilson and Lange. We have doubles now. Great, huh?"

Brian sighed and said to Lange, "Boy, oh boy. What have I gotten myself into here? If we drown in this, and our doubles survive, we won't even be dead."

"It's possible, but it's not meant to be. Our doubles will keep our identity until the DaVinci is back in its home port. Then they will go into hiding. So no one gets the idea of looking for us in the sea. As you've already been told, very few on this planet know about a twin named DaVinci II, and we need to keep it that way."

Then Brian and his commander went through a small hatch into the tower above. They entered the capsule, which could hold up to four crew members. A short time later, they heard hydraulic noises in their airlock, and the entire capsule floated out of the DaVinci. Brian's mood visibly worsened, as the vehicle was by no means moving steadily. They were able to talk to the control room by radio. Lange cursed into his microphone because he had hit his head due to a jerky movement, "Keep your fingers steady. Or is the joystick on the control panel rusted? This jerking can't be normal. We'll never get into the tower of the DaVinci II like this."

Meanwhile, the twin boat said they also had difficulty steering their capsule. Lange initially assumed it must be a design problem affecting both diving capsules.

"What's different here from the previous tests?" he asked over the voice radio. The DaVinci II's board engineer came back shortly with an initial diagnosis, "We stirred up sediment from the seafloor during the approach. Beneath it is bound methane ice, which is now beginning to outgas. The small capsules are losing some buoyancy as a result. Anyway, the steering jets don't handle the gas very well. Either wait for the methane to dissipate or wiggle carefully to our destination."

Lange knew that he should have checked the ground conditions. The outgassing of more extensive methane ice must be avoided at all costs. Any floating body in the water will lose buoyancy if a chain reaction is triggered.

The next decision was made by first officer Matteo Braun from the DaVinci II, "We wait 30 minutes. After that, we have to try it this way."

30 minutes turned into 4 hours. Only then did no more large gas bubbles rise from the sediment deposits. By now half frozen, Brian and Lange finally transferred to the DaVinci II. This crew seemed less worried. They also moved more calmly than their comrades on the twin boat. That could also calm Brian down because that was bitterly needed after he learned about the next destination of this trip: the United States of America, California Pacific Coast.

"By air, it would only be 3,300 miles. Unfortunately, our wings are too short to fly," joked one of the officers, whom Brian immediately took a liking to because of his sense of humor. "Even the short way through the Panama Canal is out of the question. We can't get through there undetected."

So, the only route left was the long one around the tip of South America, around Cape Horn.

"Then we'll be traveling for an eternity, or is there another technical surprise?" Brian wanted to know.

"Indeed! Ever heard of supercavitation?"

"Yes, but I thought only Russians and Americans had this technology available to date."

"In the years during the great crisis with Russia, when Putin stepped up the saber rattling to make himself heard by the west, he had shown off. It was quite a shock because this technology meant that torpedoes might travel underwater at the speed of sound. But now the technology is a little more mature. Above all, the problem with the steering has been solved.

"How does supercavitation work?"

"The submarine is ultrasonically enveloped in a pulsating air-water vapor bubble. This means that the hull is no longer in direct contact with the water, and the flow resistance is reduced. During this phase, we are driven by a special jet engine. There's a catch to this, though."

"Figured there'd be no miracles."

"In the dark, the high speed is treacherous. As we travel in this vapor bubble, marine organisms are swirled around in the water so strongly that the plankton glows. Anyone who has ever dragged their hand quickly through the seawater in the dark is familiar with this effect."

"So, we can only go fast during the day?"

"Hours before sunset is the end of the day. That's how long the luminescence of the plankton lasts. The beasts seem to love roller coaster rides."

"On our line, we only want to accelerate to a maximum of 950 knots during the day. That would be a third of the speed of sound underwater. We could thus cover the 10,000 miles in five days," Lange explained.

In the hours that followed, Brian's well-being deteriorated. After his seabag was stowed and he received his first briefings as an assistant sonar technician, the feeling in his stomach began to worsen. Siggi, one of the navy divers who occupied the bed below him, had told him that dizziness is expected after being in the airlock. In addition, after a stint in the airlock, the other senses could go crazy. The main reason given was the intense movements of the capsule, which was exacerbated by the multiple pressure changes in such a pressure chamber. All of this caused a sensory overload of the organ of equilibrium. Brian had experienced such discomfort before. In airplanes, the air pressure is constantly adjusted during the flight. This stimulated his brain, which is why he experienced his first strong visions shortly after a long-haul flight. Fighter pilots exposed to extreme pressure fluctuations often experienced his effect. Initially, specific sightings of unknown flying objects had been attributed to hallucinations that could occur because of sensory stimulation. Brian knew by now a lot was true about the UFO sightings, but differently than most thought. Experiments with fighter pilots showed that their reports at the time of the sighting matched the onboard cameras and radar records. It was different after landing. Hours later, the pilots had divergent recollections of the event. It was as if the pilots had been brainwashed. And Brian knew that this brainwashing was triggered during the flight. The UFOs, after whose sighting this effect occurred, sent a signal in the frequency range of *teta waves* during the approach phase. It could be proved that this led to the change of memories in the test persons later. Because word of this effect had naturally spread among pilots, they became increasingly cautious about reporting such events.

Until the military realized that this could be an ingenious weapon. With this weapon, a possibility opened to send false information directly into the opponent's brain. However, these parts of the UFO files, of which more and more had to be released in recent years, remained blacked out.

Brian now stood in front of his tiny sleeping alcove. This was on the lower deck, where one of four sleeping chambers with double bunk beds was located. There was more space on this boat than on the previous model. Where once a diesel engine hammered noisily, there was now a compact fuel cell unit and lightweight dry batteries.

His anticipation of the barely twenty-four inches wide bed was quickly over. As he lay in it and tried to close the curtain, one of his five senses was activated: the sense of smell. Siggi's feet stank of a mixture of cheese and deodorant to such an extent that he could already announce his approach by a slight breeze. Brian hated that smell and was already considering looking for another place to sleep. He recalled the briefing video during the helicopter flight explaining that the submarine's torpedo tubes were not armed during such test runs. Four of these tubes were for a more significant type of torpedo. They were even wide enough to serve as sleeping berths.

Brian's tired eyes briefly probed the narrow room again when Monika appeared. Her sleeping alcove was just the opposite. She was one of the four navy divers on board and had shoulders as broad as the three male divers. On her sleeve, she wore the badge with the swordfish of the minesweeper company. The badge read NEC ASPERA TERRENT, which Brian translated as THOSE WHO DON'T FEAR THE HARSHNESS. She probably had no trouble being the only woman aboard this sub with that confident demeanor. Monika sorted a few things on her bed, which immediately stood out as particularly messy. Then she began to strip down to her underwear. The fact that she could be observed didn't seem to bother her. Towel in hand, she pushed past Brian while saying, "You'll get used to the smell. We're still lucky with our sleeping area for that. It's relatively quiet here." She disappeared into the only shower available on board. Monika pulled her bed curtain closed a few minutes later, allowing each sailor to delineate their twenty-four-inch-wide private area.

Extreme fatigue put Brian into a sound sleep seconds later. He was scheduled to start his next shift four hours after.

A command announcement woke Brian. Except for him, everyone seemed to know what to do. Only the repetition of the first officer's report made him realize that another supercavitation bubble was about to be generated. After all duty officers had taken their positions, the board engineer began this maneuver. With the formation of the gas cushion, the boat started to lie unsteadily in the water. Stability increased again as the jet engine accelerated. A stable position within the water vapor bubble was achieved by control nozzles located around the hull. The whole technology was not exactly quiet. Brian could hardly imagine this would remain hidden from the other ships forever. He couldn't stay in his bunk anymore, so he went to the command room. All the seats were taken, so he got a makeshift stool and squeezed in next to the sonar technicians. When some time could be found, Brian was told that the noise was caused by the sonar generators. But a unique sound system ensured that other sounds neutralized the noise before it could penetrate the vapor bubble. This was the only way they could not be heard by alien hydrophones during the supercavitation trip.

One of the technicians regularly gave the commander status information, which he always confirmed with a short YES. So, Brian was also informed about the latest parameters. The speed was just 290 knots when a soft but insistent warning tone was heard. The screens indicated that further acceleration was not possible. It was supposed to accelerate up to 970 knots, the theoretical maximum speed. Now it became exciting for everyone as they listened to the conversation between the commander and the board engineer, "We are getting increasing signs of an unforeseen photoelectric effect from the sensors."

Lange said, "Explain that in more detail."

"Until now, we have attributed the luminescent effect exclusively to plankton when there is strong turbulence in the water. Apparently, something else has been overlooked."

An unidentifiable voice explained, "According to publications from the Pinyin University of Technology in Shanghai, the Chinese have observed similar phenomena at great ocean depths. This was explained by certain quantum effects. According to them, strongly accelerated objects under high pressure should cause strange phenomena. The generated light is only the smallest mystery. Things are said to have happened which could not be repeated in experiments. That was then also the reason why it was not recognized as scientific work."

"Now, don't tell us such spooky stories! I want to hear facts here that we can do something with," Lange wanted to bring more objectivity back into the discussion. However, Brian could sense that Commander Lange knew more about this than he wanted to admit.

"I'm sorry, Cap'n. My factual knowledge cannot explain what we are recording now."

"Then first describe what the sensors are telling us."

What could be seen on the monitor should have made any technician break out in a sweat. There were clear signs of technical failure. But the engineers on board were used to reacting to the unexpected. Especially in the testing phase, there were constantly new challenges. Moreover, the first dives of a new submarine type were always particularly thrilling. A significant mishap could immediately lead to disaster. Some felt that fear also spurred a bit of creativity. Brian, whose eyes were focused on a spot on the monitor, now held nothing on his stool. He slipped through the crowded officers behind and even pushed the commander aside. All eyes were on Brian at that moment. They probably assumed he had lost his mind. Focusing only on the monitor, Brian asked, "What's our current position?"

"Thirty degrees 15 minutes north, 42 degrees 38 minutes west. We are just crossing the Mid-Atlantic Ridge," the navigation officer said. While he spoke, Brian was still staring at the second monitor. Then the others saw what was upsetting him. Right below, there was intense seismic activity.

"Can these seaquakes have anything to do with our unusual measurement data?" came the question from the round. Strangely enough, everyone now looked expectantly at Brian. Yet, until that moment, no one could imagine that he had any experience in the field of seismology.

"At least we know that seismic activity triggers strong sound pulses, especially underwater. In addition, sound waves propagate very quickly in water."

"Then that's going to cause the interference...I mean, the special readings," came the comment from the board engineer.

Brian said right after that, "There's something else, though."

"What do you mean by that, Wilson?" Lange asked.

"I can feel something approaching and possibly trying to contact us. I can't imagine how that would work in this water depth."

The crew was very well informed about all the other crew members. So they knew that Brian, as a language expert, was not only familiar with the spoken word. Therefore, what he said would not have been so exciting if he had not added something else, contorting his face as if he were in a trance, "I can feel those angels again. They are moving toward us."

"Brian, you should get some rest," one of the concerned comrades said, but Lange waved it off and told the crew, "If it seems to some of you like he's going crazy, I can put your mind at ease. I don't think Wilson will hold it against me if I say that it's normal for people like him to be thought crazy. It's precisely because he has a few more senses than most people that I brought him on board."

"Captain, what do you mean? What is our true destination?" wanted to know a technician who was listening, apart from the officers. Now, however, this discussion had caught the imagination of the others. Finally, the question came up, "Cap'n, does that mean you were expecting similar difficulties that the Chinese also reported?"

"Yes."

This answer silenced the team for a moment. Brian wondered if everyone would remain so understanding or if some might treat him as a freak. First officer Braun broke the silence and asked the commander, "Shall we proceed according to the checklist?"

Lange gave the order, "Keep speed and all eyes on the instruments!" He then turned command over to the first officer. As Lange left the command center, he signaled Brian to follow him to his cabin. Once there, the commander was very thoughtful, and finally, he asked Brian, "Describe to me exactly what you saw or felt."

Lange could not hide from Brian that he was worried. That's why he asked straightforwardly, "What worries you so much? I can tell that something is wrong with you!"

When Brian did not answer immediately, he continued, "I have read many reports about you, Wilson. That's how I know what you might mean by angels. I will be frank with you."

Brian interrupted, "You should because I can feel when you're not telling the truth anyway."

"That's all right. We've been sent on a complicated mission, and I trust you'll do a good job here. It's just that we need to develop a story for the crew to keep things calm. In a sub, the risk of particular stress is very high. Stress is contagious, and I am responsible for preventing it. I'm psychologically trained for this, and I know that you can also affect the crew in your own special way. So first, let me know your thoughts, and let's agree on what to tell the others. With 28 people living in a few square feet and hundreds of feet underwater, the appearance of any ghosts can cause tremendous unrest."

"Yes, sir," Brian slipped out in his native tongue.

Lange decided to continue the journey only at 290 knots for the time being, even if it would take them a little longer. Brian had agreed to help with the evaluation of the collected data. The further south they went, the weaker the seismic activity became. Then he remembered that Anna had said something about the pattern in the current crop circles during their last conversation. That gave him an idea. It was just a thought and maybe not even relevant, but if there was something to it, it could be an exciting lead. The only problem was that he was not allowed to tell his comrades on board about his thoughts for the time being.

This boat could not use one of its technical equipment at this speed. This was a transceiver buoy. It was pulled behind by a rope on the surface when the boat was cruising slowly. With the buoy, they would have satellite and internet connectivity. So, Brian had to make do with what he had stored on his smartphone. This included almost all the books and scientific publications he had already dealt with. He quickly found what he was looking for. Anna had spoken of a Merkaba. In the Jewish culture of pre-Christian times, something called Merkaba mysticism appeared. In these legends, it was said that a chariot of light came into this world through God's power. Brian was probably looking in this place because a few things seemed strangely familiar.

They had measured seismic waves as they crossed the Mid-Atlantic Ridge. In addition, there was a photoelectric effect. Something like this could be caused by plankton. In this case, the reason was an interaction with the sound waves created by the earthquake from the depth. Now a particular phase began in Brian's head. With rapid speed, he gathered all the facts to form a picture.

Nevertheless, a few pieces still needed to be added to the puzzle, and nothing changed in the next few minutes. He went to the sonar technicians and asked for a graphic evaluation of the measured earthquake waves. He found nothing unusual at first. These waves looked like normal seaquakes.

Brian decided to lie down in his bunk and think about what he might have missed.

The DaVinci II glided almost silently and rapidly toward the equator. Upon reaching the twenty-fifth parallel, the crew was again startled by the alarm. Lange ordered Brian to the operations center. Everyone was staring at the sonar technicians' screens when he got there.

"What happened?"

"It's back," he heard someone say while several sailors talked in confusion. The commander tried to calm down, "Quiet! We don't have a technical problem. And there is no reason for this excitement. I had ordered combat readiness because the regulation says so if there are unforeseen sonar contacts of this kind."

"What do you mean by contacts of this kind, Cap'n?"

"There are earthquakes again with solid seismic waves. The only thing is that the photoelectric effects are so strong this time that our vapor bubble around the boat glows like a bright blue fireball."

First officer Braun suggested, "We should reduce speed if we don't want to be detected. This area of the Atlantic is monitored by satellites without any gaps, and we don't know if the glow will last until dark." He based his concern on the fact that this glow would already be seen from space at dusk. With it, he was right because the light-dark border of the earth moved in a strip a few hundred miles wide from east to west. This border strip was beautiful for astronauts and well observed by weather satellites. Since the atmosphere cools down significantly when darkness sets in, a considerable number of weather phenomena occur in this area.

Lange had a different plan because he ordered, "Maintain speed until we have completed all measurements. Inform me of any change."

Brian looked for a free place to use the onboard computer to work. With one ear, he constantly listened to the announcements of the watch crew. The seismic waves subsided south of the twentieth parallel. Together with one of the two sonar technicians, he looked at the pattern of lines slowly emerging on the screen. All the readings were added there graphically.

"Take away the magnetic field lines. Then it will be clearer. I don't have as practiced an eye for these maps as you," he told his comrade.

"Don't know what you're looking for, but we could still pull up the sound wave readings of all the sonar buoys via the satellites," someone suggested.

"Doesn't that make us suspicious?" Brian wanted to know. Commander Lange had heard the question and replied, "No. We have free access to all NATO forces' navigation data during our mission. My contact at the MOC made sure of that. We will retrieve the data as soon as we can use the communications buoy again."

After a few inputs, the monitor's pattern of lines and colors changed. Brian's trained eye began to scan the image while his brain compared the routines to all the geometric shapes.

"Do I have the opportunity to do my own simulations here?" he asked Lieutenant at Sea Peter Gross, the sonar specialist next to him. Although he held an officer rank, he was assigned to the technical staff. That led Brian to suspect that Gross was responsible for several things.

"Of course. Take a look. We have various graphics software. We could even create three-dimensional construction plans with it."

"Great. That helps."

After a few moves, Brian got the hang of it, and with the help of Gross, he quickly found his way around the software. Following his instincts, he tried to structure the displayed lines by trial and error. He already had a few ideas but kept them to himself. As agreed with Lange, no premature conclusions were to be drawn, or speculations spread. Hoping to be undisturbed for a few minutes, he prepared an experiment. There was something he wanted to try once he was alone. Out of the corner of his eye, Brian was watched by Lange. He probably suspected that something was brewing in that crazy head again. He was startled when he suddenly felt the commander's hand on his shoulder and heard Lange say, "You can sit in my cabin and work there if you want. There you will also have access to all communications systems. If you need help, take Gross with you."

A short time later, Wilson and Gross sat at the tiny desk in the commander's cabin.

"I am also nothing better than you. You can call me Peter," was the first thing the lieutenant offered him.

Brian's thoughts were already completely with his concept and the experiment he wanted to accomplish now. The mystery of the strange sound impulses from the depths had awakened his spirit of research. Lost in thought and his eyes constantly fixed on the monitor, Brian muttered his theory to himself. Unintentionally, he spoke in his native language, English. Peter answered him in a standard dialect of the United States northwest coast. It also sounded accentless, as if he were speaking to a fellow countryman. Brian was about to ask about it, but he changed his mind and said, "I'd like to compare some geometric structures with the patterns we measured. Can you help me program the graphs if I give you the formulas?"

"Sure. Let's see..."

But when Brian dictated complex formulas to detect patterns in the sound waves, Peter got puzzled, "Do you know how many different mathematical patterns there are? How long is that going to take?"

"For what I'm looking for, we need a few more trigonometric calculations. I didn't make them up. They were written down a long time ago. Today, anyone visiting a temple in Asia will find these formulas in the religious illustrations. I studied that for years. The crazy thing is we find these formulas in cultures that, according to our archaeologists, never had contact with each other. So how could they have learned from each other? Where did they get their knowledge? From the internet?"

"Are you kidding me? Mathematical formulas in religious illustrations? There are already enough bizarre stories circulating about hidden messages in the Bible."

"Of course, you can't believe everything. Sometimes it's enough to open your eyes and talk to different scientists about the same subject. I grew up near Washington, D.C., but I only learned about some of the secrets of architecture there when I went to college. The city was planned by American Freemasons, and you still find new surprises in the architecture today. But a real mystery is the temple of *Angkor Wat* in Cambodia. No one probably expected what the archaeologists found there. The most fascinating details could only be seen after the entire site was mapped with satellites. It is great luck that no new cities were built over it. That's why you can still see the original extent. Now people wonder how the builders could build a twenty-kilometer-long structure so accurately. Most tourists shrug their shoulders and think they just managed somehow. On the other hand, the German construction company's engineers confirmed that they would not have been able to build this structure today without the most modern satellite technology. Well, my point was that even back then, the builders must have had highly sophisticated measuring tools."

The first officer's order to switch to standard propulsion could be heard over the ship's radio. It was 1700 by now, so there were still about four hours until sunset. Until the following day, they would be heading toward the South Atlantic again without supercavitation at a depth of 490 feet.

"And what formulas are you going to use?" Peter wanted to know.

"We don't need any more formulas. Normal geometry should be enough. Let's start with the simplest ratios that we already know. And then we'll add the sacred numbers of Asian religions," Brian said.

"Then I'm curious. Go ahead..."

"Let's start with 108. In the temple of *Angkor Wat*, this number can be found again and again. In Hinduism, it is a sacred number. Even in the Vedas, element number 108 is mentioned as the substance that powered the stupas of the gods. The proof can be found in the reliefs made of stone. The fire-breathing serpent is represented as a string of beads with 108 balls. This is only one example. If I list them all, we won't finish."

Peter shook his head but had created a table for all the parameters. Then he asked, "And what should the computer do with the number 108?"

"The number results from $1^1 \cdot 2^2 \cdot 3^3 = 108$. There we have a pattern already. This is, namely, the edge angle in a pentagon. When order emerges from chaos in nature, you'll usually find the shape of a pentagon. So, we should also look for our pattern in the sound waves of the sea bottom. If the waves have mathematical patterns, they cannot have arisen by chance."

"You mean these angels are sitting at the bottom of the ocean making music so loud that it creates earthquakes?"

"Don't make fun of me. I think the sub's sonic generators inadvertently sent a signal. The signal may have triggered something in the depths of the ocean. What it is, I don't know either. If we find out, we may also know why the Chinese researchers did not conduct any more experiments underwater at that time."

"That scares me, but I hope you'll explain that to me someday, I'm sure," Peter mumbled in disbelief.

Brian then talked about his thinking, "Also, we need to look for the shape of the tetrahedron, circles, or any number ratio..."

He literally got into it and seemed to gain inner satisfaction. On the other hand, Peter became more skeptical and hoped that Brian's last fitness-for-duty examination was not too long ago. Nevertheless, he had to admit a particular fascination with these things. Therefore, he could well imagine that esoterica with such theories would get a good audience. When the computer was fed, they heard the sound of the ship's bell over the loudspeaker. The ship's cook called the watch crew to the mid-watch, a warm meal just before midnight.

"We should treat our brains to some food, too," Peter joked, and as the delicious smell of the food hit Brian's nose, it made him forget about the numbers for a few minutes. Later, as he sipped the strong midnight coffee, he felt uneasy without being able to explain it in more detail. Brian didn't know fatigue at all in creative moments like this. His body was addicted to new insights. Peter, on the other hand, seemed rather tired from the coffee. He yawned and showed all the signs of a busy day.

Therefore, Brian said, "I suggest you get some sleep for the next few hours and relieve me later."

Now Brian looked at the screen alone and thought about what they had already discovered. Once again, doubts arose as to whether he was on the right track: *What am I actually looking for? None of the results make any sense. I must have missed something else.*

He decided to retreat to his bunk to think. Something at that moment reminded him of his childhood. The fear of encountering his dreams made it challenging to fall asleep. The figures that came out of the thoughts always looked different. His anxiety and other strange behaviors led his parents to believe he might suffer from Asperger's syndrome, a form of early childhood autism. Psychologists initially confirmed this suspicion and sent Brian to therapy. He quickly learned, however, that he could improve learning outcomes by describing what the therapist expected. This was especially true of the beings he encountered in his dreams.

At the time, no one had noticed that Brian had learned to wordlessly hint to the therapist what questions the latter would ask later. He quickly realized that it was most convenient to describe beings of light, generally called angels. Thus, it was clear to the therapist that Brian's fantasy was just the reproduction of ancient myths and fairy tales. After all, this is how the cultural heritage of all civilizations has been inherited, and sensitive children would not be able to process all the stories so quickly.

Later, Brian wanted to understand what was happening in his brain and studied the phenomenon of human dreams in detail. He had to learn to distinguish between what was wishful thinking or expectation and what was real. But there was one thing Brian hadn't realized in his entire life. Namely, to lose the fear of a door in front of which he regularly stood in his dreams since he was a little boy. There remained an almost panic fear of it. Sometimes the curiosity was so great that he dared to get too close to the enormous door. When it opened a crack, the panic led to paralysis or shock every time. Instead of running away, curiosity won out, and he tried to see every detail behind it.

Moreover, in the dream, it was always as if he could no longer walk, only swim. What he saw then made the blood freeze in his veins. Since those days, the feeling was present as if the door could open at any moment and what was seen would come out.

The memory returned when he visited a temple in Mexico on vacation with his parents. Some grimaces of the stone figures resembled very much what he had been panicking about since early childhood. Fear, as since those nights when the dreams began. In adulthood, Brian developed a powerful weapon against that fear. It was the pyramid trick, which he used to prevent other thoughts from entering his head. It also helped from dreams. For Brian, it indicated that dreams did not originate exclusively in his mind. They also invaded from the outside in some cases.

For this reason, Brian now had to decide. If he wanted to learn the strange vibration patterns emanating from the seismic waves on the ocean floor, he had to open his mind to it. It was necessary, even if what he would see and feel shortly might be terrifying.

A glance at the monitor confirmed that the computer had not found any abnormalities. In the meantime, it was time to wake Peter up. He would take over the watch for the next four hours.

Before Brian drew the curtain to his bed, the fast travel with supercavitation was initiated again. Brian was so exhausted that he thought it would make more sense to sleep first and meditate afterward.

South Atlantic, 0845 local time

Commander Lange accelerated the DaVinci II again since sunrise. Slowly they tried up to 390 knots, corresponding to about 450 mph (720 km/h).

The navigation officer just gave the current coordinates. They would soon reach 19.5° south. This latitude was marked on the navigation map in the north and south with a particular line. If you run your eyes along these lines, you can find many famous places. A few of the eeriest examples were the pyramid city of Teotihuacán in Mexico and the Eye of the Sahara in Mauritania. In the southern hemisphere, the cult sites of the Australian aborigines and the magnetic anomaly in the South Atlantic stood out.

Since there had been no disturbances up to this point, Commander Lange wanted to increase the speed even further. The strange light phenomenon had not reappeared either. Nevertheless, Peter looked nervously over the shoulder of the first sonar technician. Something seemed to be troubling him.

Peter had not awakened Brian so that he could sleep soundly for seven hours in the meantime. But then his eyelids began to move as if he were just in a vivid dream. That in itself would not be unusual. However, the cause of the increased activity in Brian's brain, in this case, was not the normal REM sleep phase of a human being.

Δ

Rostock, Maritime Operations Centre

The phone rang, and Christina wondered whether she should answer it or walk with a few others to the outdoor area of the MOC as planned. When the weather was nice, they liked to meet there for lunch. She could always call back later. But she took another look at the number displayed. It was an area code from the United States. It wasn't even 7 a.m. on the East Coast yet, so it had to be crucial.

She wasn't heard saying much besides the usual greetings and a few brief words of confirmation. Minutes later, Christina sent someone a text message via secure military messenger: "DaVinci with Lange and Wilson back in Europe."

Δ

Freiburg, university campus

The possibilities were now almost exhausted. Anna still needed to learn how to fulfill her mission to warn Brian. She was sure he would take her warning seriously and at least think about it. He would hardly volunteer to help put an ancient object into the wrong hands.

Anna trusted Sergei one hundred percent. If he said that the thing in the wrong hands could lead to unforeseen conflicts, she considered that danger not to be underestimated. By now, it was also clear that various groups were already wrestling with each other in the background. Anna wasn't overthinking their possible aims at the moment. All forces that unscrupulously enforced their own interests and were after power had to be stopped. In her eyes, the power of individuals always meant war. Sometimes on the battlefield, other times in the computer networks or the media's ideological field. The most vulnerable part was the human mind. Whoever mastered it had already won the war. She saw it as her life's mission to transfer her knowledge to as many people as possible. Knowledge was the heritage of humankind, and she was one of those allowed to be present at the opening of a testament. People had to pass an examination to learn the contents of this will. Anna had done that at the age of sixteen. She understood what this testament contained in the City of Mysteries in Egypt.

In summary, it contained only three things: Who are we, where do we come from, and what should we be afraid of. This sounded so banal to Anna at first, too, that she wondered why they didn't publish this testament. But the answer became clear to her only during further education because everything had long since been published thousands of times worldwide. Unfortunately, most people still needed the key to reading, which could only be acquired through learning. To make the key visible, a few brain regions had to be trained, which had previously atrophied over many generations due to non-use. To impart this knowledge was now the task of Anna and the other masters at the new modern mystery schools.

Whatever happened to this guy that seems to have dropped off the face of the earth, Anna thought as she searched for another way to reach Brian. She had even asked a couple of meditation teachers for help. In a group, the field intensity was much higher to find a person in this way. At the same time, Anna had quite a few other avenues of communication open to her. However, since the port stone was stolen, her access to her mentor in the *aka* was limited. Without this stone, she would have to go to a place rich in energy. There were many such places, but by now, most had been sealed off militarily. Using a functioning megalithic stone facility for communication without being noticed, though, was nearly impossible. In addition, almost all free-standing menhirs, pyramids and temples were already heavily weathered. Only a large group of people could still muster the necessary energy to operate the facilities. This would be challenging to organize and would also immediately attract attention.

There was something else, too. In the meantime, many of the younger generations saw in people like Anna their hope of finally being able to free themselves from old dogmas. Of course, this was also known to the enemies of the new zeitgeist. The most conservative forces, often recognizable by their selfish lifestyles and backward-looking politics, had long since realized that the generation around Anna represented a threat to their wealth. Meanwhile, painted with a green label, many secretly waited for the increasing number of "Annas" to disappear from the globe.

The longer she remained without success, the greater her fear that something serious might have happened to Brian. Perhaps some people had taken advantage of his good nature. Already almost desperate, Anna wanted to dare a dangerous thing and seek help in one of the mystical places.

Δ

Rostock, Maritime Operations Centre,
Ten days after the incident in Malta

"Don't fuck with me, Petty Officer Keller!" it echoed in Sean's ears, "Nobody's buying that story. Your comrade Wilson is lucky to have been certified as having amnesia. But that's only due to incompetence on the part of the doctors. And don't think your American passport is going to help here somehow. After all, you still have a German passport and were sworn into service in the German navy. I want to know what you were looking for at *Dingli Rocks*, near a restricted military area. And what was a military navigation device doing on a recreational trip? You've violated so many regulations that your record is already enough for the military prosecutor. The whole thing reeks of espionage. If you don't cooperate, I'll see your career is over!"

Sean sat across from the head of the investigating committee. According to the rank insignia, a lieutenant at sea. On his chest was the name Pot. *With this stupid name, he was bullied as a child, and now I have to suffer from the contaminated guy*, Sean thought.

For an hour, he had patiently answered the same questions over and over again. Meanwhile, he already regretted his first statement, which described how Brian was accidentally pushed into the hole. That coincided with Brian's testimony. But the investigating committee could not put any of Sean's and Brian's testimony into a logical and chronologically appropriate order. There is a Marine who disappears from the scene for four days, and no one has been able to force this man to testify. Brian claimed he couldn't remember anything, and Sean didn't even try to find any excuse.

The medical report after the return only certified exhaustion, combined with slight amnesia. So, the guy had to know something and his friend Sean even more. In the meantime, there were already psychological methods of questioning that made it much easier to establish the truth.

Pot, who was assigned to investigate the incident, had another problem. If he left it at the statements of the two, it could document his incompetence. The naval command in Rostock didn't seem interested in clearing up the matter because they had put Brian Wilson and Sean Keller on leave instead of squeezing them. Pot suspected it might have something to do with their dual citizenship. With arrogant fellows like Brian, only pressure would do any good, and that's what Petty Officer Keller was now supposed to help with. Since Sean and Brian were friends, a ruse would be the right thing to force Sean to testify.

Later, Sean sat back in an uncomfortable waiting room and pondered what could be the reason for this disaster. Why did he have to sit around alone, with the condition that he not leave his residence, and was regularly interrogated? He had even been ordered not to have any contact. Without this possibility of contact with the outside world, he couldn't even find out if it was legal how this lieutenant at sea was treating him. The man was quite old for the relatively low officer rank.

Maybe he'd screwed up several times already, Sean wondered. *And anyway, why is a board of inquiry headed by a lieutenant at sea?* This *whole* matter may not be considered necessary, and only this Sigfried Pot thinks he has to make his mark here.

Still, with each hour of waiting, he became more uncertain about the consequences for his career. Doubts were also spreading about his friendship with Brian: *He just took off, probably already sitting on a beach somewhere. Why was I so stupid to get involved in this crappy trip? The only thing they can really blame me for is the unauthorized use of the navigation system. But that can't be a reason for such treatment. There must be more to it than that. It was such a bummer that I didn't have time to ask Brian what he was looking for at these cart ruts in Malta. He could have told me beforehand instead of being so mysterious. Now I don't feel like taking the rap for this nonsense either.*

CHAPTER 7

Freiburg, university campus

"I'd like to try. At the moment, I don't see any other way." Anna attempted to convince her boss Sergei.

The same rules applied to business trips at her institute as everywhere else at the university. The supervisor had to approve a request. But Sergei had his doubts, "You can't go there alone. Since your port stone was stolen, it's clear that people are interested in you again. It's like when you took your maturity exam in Egypt."

Anna nodded, "That's right, I must have attracted attention then. But observing does not mean eliminating. Nevertheless, I don't think anyone is out to get me. They're just curious about where I hang out and what we do here at the institute. It's no wonder. After all, there are more rumors than publications about our research. That makes some people even more curious. One could get the idea that we are on to something big."

"Maybe. But there's no harm in having someone accompany you. Intelligence agencies are also always interested in research at the frontiers of science. And they also conduct espionage on a large scale. They are definitely professionals who were in your apartment. That's why we're going to camouflage this business trip a bit and give our partner university in Dundee, Scotland, as the destination. There London is just a stopover. We'd better book a hotel in Dundee, too. But I'm more worried because fundamentalists might already be on our trail. As we know, they have their problems with paranormal things. Something like that doesn't fit into their ideological worldview at all."

"I'd rather call it world blindness," Anna replied.

"Anyway, I'm responsible for your safety and coming along."

"I wonder if this is a good idea. As soon as you enter the UK, the journalists will be after you. Everybody knows you there, and it doesn't help us to be seen in all the newspapers. The British know exactly; wherever you appear, there must be something spectacular."

"Perhaps you are right. Then I'll ask Gregor to accompany you."

"So it's a deal. I'll book two tickets with a stopover in London. From there, we'll take a rental car to Long Compton."

Sergei still asked, "As far as I know, the menhirs are privately owned, and both King Stone and the *Whispering Knights* are fenced off. Should I check with the owners for permits?"

"We don't need that. I know the county people and call them directly. It went easier that way last time, too, when I was there with my students."

"Wasn't that Brian there, too?"

"Yes, and he didn't make it easy for me in the first few days. Because of his charisma, he immediately won over the whole group. It took me a while to assert myself as a lecturer at the age of twenty-three. Half of the students were older than me, and Brian immediately had the reins in his hands, especially with the girls."

"I don't remember Brian as macho, though. Maybe you were just jealous?" asked Sergei jokingly.

"I was angry that he made such an impression on the group just because of his appearance."

"Do I need to remind you of our research on biological influences in sociology? That was one of your favorite topics. When I hear you, you recognize it in others, not yourself. You know what reasons that can be!"

"Nonsense. I'm not in love! Anyway, Brian must have been very impressed by the visit. Because he went back a few weeks later. However, he had problems after his second visit."

"Oh, I didn't know that," Sergei said.

"Brian told me he was only at the *Whispering Stones* for an hour. This must have caused him terrible visions for weeks. Possibly the stones did not want him there."

"That's strange. Did he tell you what those visions were about?"

"It was about nightmares from his childhood. He kept seeing a big door behind which something terrible must have been. That's all Brian wanted to say."

Sergei said, "According to old legends, the sound of the *Whispering Stones* is really hazardous. There are tales that people never wanted to bury their dead near these stones."

Anna seemed surprised when she asked, "Oh yeah? I didn't know that yet. But legends often have quite different backgrounds. The oral tradition later made fairy tales and superstition out of it among the people."

"I know. However, some writings could be attributed to the Druids in this case. According to them, sometimes dead people disappeared from their graves after burial and later reappeared in the dreams of relatives. Here again, we have a parallel with other parts of the world. It is the Indian tribes in North America. There must have been reasons why these Indians insisted on burning their dead. Other tribes, on the other hand, deliberately covered their deceased with heavy stones. Does it seem like they wanted to prevent the disappearance at all costs? And maybe we can get a little closer to the mystery by finding out what Brian was really dreaming about."

"We'll see. Anyway, first I need the contact with the stones to locate the fellow."

"Be careful. These places are always good for a surprise. Don't do anything rash!"

"I'm not a beginner."

"True, not in these things," Sergei replied with a grin.

Δ

South Atlantic, DaVinci II

All the muscles in his body tensed. Brian lay curled up in the narrow bunk. He didn't move a bit while pulling the blanket over his head. Everything was like in the days of his childhood. Only this time, he wasn't standing in front of the closed door. The prophecy of the tall angels who appeared to him almost every night in his dreams must have come true. All but one of them had warned him repeatedly not to open that door. Of course, Brian knew that most people imagined something different about angels. But no one could explain it exactly, and whoever he asked, they all had other names for these lovely beings. Often they were depicted with wings. He had yet to meet such beings. His angels moved slowly and gracefully as if they were swimming.

There was something Brian had never understood. The angels were always there suddenly in his dreams. He never saw them coming. He just saw them floating away later. But one of them regularly came back alone after all the others had left. This angel knew a lot about Brian and what he was afraid of. He knew every childhood secret and promised to answer all his questions one day. With each dream encounter, Brian wished this one angel would come back. At some point, he trusted only this angel, no longer listened to the others, and believed only this one angel.

"*When will it be?*"

"*Be patient, Brian. Time will lead you to the right place. I will also be there to show you everything you need.*"

During his childhood, Brian believed that the angel without a name was his only friend because only to him could he entrust his secrets. Everything was so easy when they were together. He had answers to questions he couldn't ask anyone else. It was different with him than with the children his age. A real friend. He could understand when Brian talked about hearing voices and understanding people even if they didn't say anything. Later, before the angel stopped appearing in his childhood dreams, he had given him one more task. Before the angel would return, Brian would have to do something for him. There was a whisper in his ear that it was another door he needed to open. Then he would also get behind all the rest of the secrets. When asked what was behind that door, the angel chuckled and said, "*You'll have to find out for yourself because something different awaits everyone there. I will be there, and you will come when the time comes!*"

Now it seemed that the day had come! Brian had woken up in the meantime. Even with his eyes open, he could remember every detail. It was as authentic as he knew it from his childhood days.

The angel without a name had given him the task of carrying out all orders of his commander. Commander Lange was his confidant, and together they would open the door and bring to light what had been kept from humanity for so long.

After Brian freshened up in the shower, he went to the operations center to look for Peter. Walking was difficult for him because his shoulder kept bumping into something.

His appearance in the command room startled his comrades as if a stowaway had appeared out of nowhere. Ronny Zobel was the second officer with a double function as technical officer and ship's doctor. He immediately noticed something was wrong, "Wilson, I'm going to examine you first. Then we'll see if you're fit for duty."

"It's fine, no problem!" Brian defended himself.

"I don't see it that way. Your skin looks like you slept in a lime bucket. Plus dilated pupils, I can't let you report for duty like that."

Brian was about to head to the wardroom to be checked out when Monika and another sailor reported for duty. The ship's doctor faltered and said, "Stop, look at me! You've got to be kidding me... You all look like someone bought a round of weed!"

Several crew members had been sleeping for the last few hours and had symptoms similar to Brian's. It was clear to everyone that sunburn was not expected on a submarine. Still, when several comrades looked so pale, the commander should have been worried. Lange, therefore, ordered everyone to see a doctor before going on duty. Even food poisoning would be an event to be taken seriously.

The medical equipment on board was limited to a few emergency cases, but there was also a small medical laboratory. The officers' mess now served as the treatment room. The minilab was busy with the first two blood samples for a few minutes.

"That's what I thought!" was heard from the ship's doctor at some point. "The bastards got stoned out of their minds!"

Less than ten seconds later, Lange pushed into the officers' mess and asked to see the blood results. Some of them had elevated blood and urine levels typical of drug use. However, there was already an abnormality in the first five blood samples. One contained twenty-five times more of it than all the others. The doctor followed up on suspicion and soon had confirmation. It was Brian in whom the drug *DMT* was detected in large quantities. This was a substance with hallucinogenic properties. It was now clear to the two officers that someone must have smuggled the stuff on board. But Lange could not get one thing out of his head. Why should Brian, of all people, have taken so much of it? Lange thought he wanted to get pumped up after sitting at the computer for many hours studying the observed anomalies.

He called Brian into his cabin and asked, "What's wrong with you, Wilson? We can't afford incidents like this. What possessed you to take drugs, and where did the stuff come from?"

"I swear I didn't take anything."

"Your blood work says otherwise. There's no point in denying it."

"I can only repeat it. I have nothing to do with drugs or..." Brian faltered.

"What is it?" wanted Lange to know.

"Can we get the doctor back in on this? I have a few questions for him."

A short time later, the three were sitting in the wardroom again, and Brian asked the ship's doctor, "Can you determine what exactly was found in the blood?"

"It's definitely *DMT*, nothing else. It's a very controversial drug. It acts as a neurotransmitter."

Now more directed at the commander, Zobel explained further, "By the way, it can't have been in the food because then the entire crew would have had these symptoms. It probably wasn't smoked either because the effect of inhalation wears off after twenty minutes. With these blood values, some drug must have been taken."

Lange looked into Brian's eyes. He, in turn, shook his head and said, "I can only repeat that I didn't take anything!"

Zobel continued his explanation, "There is also an anomaly in the blood samples. I took a look at the duty rosters. Only comrades who have their bunks near Wilson and were actually there during the last hours are affected. That all speaks to a small party, doesn't it?"

Lange wanted to know, "How does this substance affect humans?"

"Mind-expanding states arise alongside the usual intoxicating states. Indigenous peoples in South America use this for their spiritual acts."

"Are there other ways this stuff could have gotten into the blood?"

Zobel scrolled through the medical database on his tablet. After a few minutes, he said, "Apparently, extremely high DMT concentrations have been measured in people after near-death experiences. But even crazier is that newborns also have elevated levels of DMT in their bodies. And they're more likely not to smoke pot." He further read: "There are esotericists who claim that the substance allows the entrance and exit of the soul at birth and death."

"For heaven's sake! What are you talking about?"

"The doctor is right," Brian now interjected. "A research group in Freiburg has found that some ritual objects can also provoke the production of DMT in the body. So the body seems to make the stuff itself, too."

Lange thought the whole thing was too crazy, "I don't believe in such hocus-pocus. I rather think that someone has smuggled in some kind of drugs here. The only legal narcotics on board, available free of charge and in abundance, are foot stink and farts. And anyway, what ritual object would have caused such a reaction in you, Wilson?"

"I don't know. But I'd like to find out."

"I wish you were right. Therefore, try it and take Lieutenant Gross to help you. Tonight I want your report!"

Peter and Brian spent the following hours in the commander's cabin again. Peter first wanted to work on the sound signals they had received from the seafloor the day before. In the meantime, the computer had calculated thousands of variations, and Peter had everything shown to him that looked in any way like mathematical patterns. Then he said to Brian, "If you try hard, you can read something into every other graph. Like looking at the cloudy sky."

"That's right. That's how our brain works. Depending on the observer's imagination, the patterns in the clouds remind us of real shapes. Subconsciously, we are constantly trying to compare the environment with our memories. A disadvantage of the human imagination is that we are easily deceived by our senses. Therefore, an old rule is to always critically examine one's own desires. But that's just the theory," Brian said.

"What do you mean?"

"Well, if I want to manipulate someone, I must awaken a certain desire in him. If you then also offer a supposed solution, you've already won. That's how advertising.... works, and if you replace the word 'desire' with 'fear', you can make people develop anger and hate others. That's how wars work."

"And what does that have to do with our geometric patterns?" Peter inquired.

"We humans are not good at recognizing new patterns because our brain first looks for everything it already knows. Computers have no preconceptions, so they recognize what's really there."

"So you're saying we can't use artificial intelligence to search for the unknown if it worked the way our brains do?"

Brian said in response, "Exactly. A human-like computer would make the same mistakes we do. Right now, there's also no AI that can process anything other than pure data. For more, computers would need to be able to process emotions. Feelings and emotions, however, carry the danger of prejudices and these, in turn, blind us to backgrounds."

"Yeah, sure. The more human, the more emotions would play a role in the search. And the less rational the results would be – I hadn't thought of it that way," Peter said. "Let's hope no AI decides whether a missile is fired!"

"Still, we need both our brains and some artificial intelligence. Now, tell your 'computer friend' to stop messing around. You might have to reward him with a friendly smile," Brian tried to lighten the mood.

"I'll get some power for our brains first," Peter suggested and made his way to the coffee machine. Brian was now alone for a moment and concentrated on the mathematical patterns found by the computer. He couldn't get out of his mind the vision Anna had told him about during their last conversation.

She was so excited about the crop circles. What is so special about the hexagonal star? Somehow something is missing. We may be looking with the wrong system, Brian thought. Then he had another idea: *Crop circles are two-dimensional. But in nature, there are only three-dimensional shapes. I have to change the formulas again...*

When Peter returned with the coffee, Brian had written a complete note. He asked Peter to feed it to the computer.

"Did you find out anything else?" he wanted to know.

"I don't know. But how are seismic sound waves actually measured?"

"With hydrophones attached to the hull of the ship."

"So we also measure the noise the boat generates?"

"Our software knows its own sound signals and filters them out of the readings."

"I see. But that might be the problem," Brian replied and seemed to become almost euphoric.

"I don't understand," Peter admitted in amazement.

"If I want to talk to someone who doesn't understand my language, I'd try to do it in their language, right?"

"You mean...?"

"Yes. Could you turn off the filters?"

Peter seemed to have understood and was now hammering away on his keyboard so fast that he kept mistyping. Brian looked over his shoulder the whole time, and Peter seemed annoyed, "I have to concentrate. Could you maybe stop looking at my fingers all the time?"

This reaction surprised Brian, but he left Peter alone in the commander's cabin to look around the operations center for a while. On his way there, he found Lange eating in the officers' mess. Brian sat down and asked his commander what he knew about the submarine's sonar technology. He replied in amazement, "I hardly think I know any more about it than Gross."

"I know, but he doesn't have time for me right now, and I want to know what the limits of this system are."

"You know, Wilson, in terms of technology on board, you won't find much better anywhere in the world. We detect sound waves from infrasound to ultrasound. If we're missing something, the software isn't programmed correctly. You have to tell this system what to look for. Only then can it find something."

"I get it. But I had the idea of turning off the filters so we could hear everything as it is received by the hydrophones on the boat's hull. Now Peter Gross is sitting at the programming. He's trying to disable the filters."

"These filters can be turned off with the push of a button. No special programming is needed for this. Didn't Gross tell you that?"

"He did," Brian lied and immediately started back to Peter. It was only a few feet, but now, of all times, everyone seemed to be on the move and clogged the corridor. Before Brian could open the door to the commander's cabin, the alarm sounded, and Peter jumped out to meet him, "What's going on?"

Before Brian could say a word, they heard from the speakers, "Everyone to battle stations!"

The navigator quickly clarified the cause of the alarm, "In ten minutes, a large object will cross our course!"

Lange considered the possibility of changing the course at this speed. Then he decided, "It's already 1500, and we've made good progress today. We'll switch to propeller drive and stay under 10 knots with creep speed. Any indication yet what the object is?"

In the meantime, Peter had also resumed his post, and both sonar technicians looked at the data together. Peter said, "It sounds like a drive with ring propellers. Object size and cloaking techniques suggest a Chinese submarine."

The sonar location automatically assigned the code "X" for unknown objects. That meant that their unknown pursuer had been given the name X1. This should prevent confusion with other objects.

"What is the course of X1?"

"But that's strange... It's gone!"

"How gone?"

"You may have noticed that they were detected and switched their magnetic field cloak to full power."

"Could be. But that also means their propulsion is now off."

Commander Lange ordered, "Continue crawling. Continue the search for X1."

It was easier to camouflage for the DaVinci II at 200 feet. With its 410 feet, the Chinese submarine did not have such an easy time remaining undetected. But the Chinese were always good for a surprise regarding the latest camouflage technology. Lange was concerned about why the vast object could disappear so quickly. Every maneuver always takes a few minutes. If not, X1's technology must be very advanced.

Completely unexpectedly, the DaVinci II was hit by a tremendous concussion. Brian was just about to sit down on his makeshift stool when the collision threw him to the side. Instead of landing with his butt on the chair, he was now sitting on the floor. His tailbone and head hurt. It must have hit others harder because sounds of pain could be heard from various directions. Actually, it had knocked over or slammed against something everyone who was not sitting firmly on a chair.

"What was that all about?" the navigator was heard to ask.

Lange said, "Take care of your comrades. Report all injuries!"

First officer Matteo Braun switched some systems to control mode. Subsequently, the order to report any damage and injuries was on the screens of all stations. Most of the analysis, however, was done automatically. A short time later, the crew's reports were received. Only one response was missing. Norbert, the ship's cook, did not report. Someone was heard saying, "I hope the cook didn't douse himself with boiling water."

Monika was the first to reach the galley but found no one there. The assumption about the hot water seemed to be correct because it was steaming on the floor, and a pot was lying empty. Monika was shocked when she saw that the hot water was dyed red and that there was also a paring knife on the floor.

At that moment, Fabrice joined them. He was one of the four divers. Looking over Monika's shoulder, he said, "Something happened to that guy. But where did he go?"

The footprints from the galley led to the shower. Fabrice knocked and called, "Norbert, are you okay or is it cold food today?"

Monika looked at him angrily and said, "Are you always thinking about food? You've made better jokes!"

Then Fabrice yanked open the door to the shower. The cook squatted on his knees and held the shower head in his pants. As he did so, he wailed terribly.

Monika asked, "What's wrong? Did you cut off your peeper?"

Norbert could only squeeze out the answer, "Nonsense. Got the pot of hot water off."

"But there's blood all over the front!" said Monika.

"It's not mine."

Monika examined Norbert from top to bottom and saw a cut on his right elbow. Because of the pain in the hip area, he had probably not even noticed this injury."

Fabrice's whole body tensed at how painful the scalding might be for the cook. Over the ship's radio, he reported that they would need the doctor. When Norbert was attended to by the ship's doctor and later returned to the control room, he looked into the worried faces of the crew. To them, he explained, "At the moment, the cook can only offer hard-boiled eggs."

Lange wanted to end the laughter by sending Brian and Monika to the kitchen. He knew that the loss of mealtimes could soon lead to a change in mood among the crew. Then he explained to the officers, "It wasn't a hard impact, so it wasn't a collision with an object. It must have been a blast wave."

Then Lieutenant Gross said, "Now it's clear why X1 disappeared from the screen. They must have accelerated with a tremendous recoil."

"Establish the propagation of the shock wave. Then we will know in which direction X1 disappeared."

"Yep, Cap'n!"

During the next two hours, it was peaceful on board. Those who didn't have a watch had to help in the kitchen. Brian was glad when someone who knew more about cooking was present than he did. He couldn't understand how Norbert managed to cook four meals daily for so many people in this tiny galley alone.

Because of the low speed, they could send the communication buoy to the surface, which meant there was now satellite communication again. Lange used the time to find out something about the technology aboard X1. To do this, he had to go to the NATO archives to learn about other nations' latest underwater technologies. Which nationality the object belonged to was only speculation for the time being. Lange also sent an encrypted email to an address designated for such cases to inform his contact at the *MOC*. He hoped that someone knew who was currently hanging around the area.

Brian then went back into the commander's cabin and noticed that a cabinet door must have opened due to the blast. He was surprised because the door had been fitted with a small padlock in his memory. But he was not quite sure about that. The commander's private belongings were now lying around on the floor. He gathered everything up with his hands and was about to stuff it into the closet when something caught his eye. Strikingly colorful socks peeked out from the black and blue clothes. Brian wondered if Lange would wear something like that. But then he noticed that it was not a pair of socks, but a small bag. Because of its odd shape and the noticeably worn leather strap with which it was laced, it looked familiar. The memory of where he had seen this pouch before shocked him. When he unlaced the ribbon and looked inside, his suspicions were confirmed. Brian's knees buckled, and he had to sit on the edge of the bed. He had found the stone, which had recently been stolen during a break-in at Anna's apartment. He was about to stuff it back into the commander's closet when he changed his mind. Sitting on the bed for the next few minutes, Brian tried to understand how Commander Lange had gotten hold of Anna's *port stone*. Should he call him on it? Is it necessary to inform Anna? Brian knew how people reacted in specific conflict situations and wanted to take advantage of that. Instead of putting the bag with the stone back, he put it in his pants pocket. Then he went to Lange, informed him of the mess in his cubicle, and offered to clean it up. Lange said, "Oh, gee, thanks a lot, but I'll do it myself."

Without haste, the commander went to his cabin and returned a few minutes later, "Thank you, Wilson. You can continue working at my desk now if you like. It was my fault. I guess I forgot to put the padlock back on."

Brian had looked closely into the commander's eyes as he listened. Apparently, he remained utterly unimpressed or had yet to notice that one of his belongings was missing. When Brian arrived at Lange's cabin, the locker was padlocked again. The whole story seemed stranger and stranger to him, but Brian wanted to abide by the no-contact rule, so he couldn't get in touch with Anna. All he could do at the moment was to look at the patterns in the sound signals received from the depths.

$$\Delta$$

England

The flight to London was exhausting. First, there was a delay, and then they were diverted to Stansted Airport due to a thunderstorm. The train express would have brought them back to London, but they decided to take a rental car immediately. While Gregor drove, Anna organized a few things. She had been offered a place to stay at the home of a former student. Kilian was Scottish but lived with his family in a small old house north of Oxford. It was a good fit because they could move around the area less conspicuously from there. Kilian was also familiar with Anna's work in Freiburg. He knew a lot about the area's menhirs and other energetic sites.

It wasn't until late at night that they approached the friends' house, but they had to look for the driveway for a while. Anna had been there before, but the roadsides were overgrown, and no light from the house penetrated the street.

"It must be scary for kids to live here," Gregor said.

"Not just for kids," confirmed Anna, pointing to a small bridge that crossed the creek on the side of the road, "You have to drive in there!"

"Do you think the bridge will hold us?"

"We'll know in a minute."

About a hundred yards from the road stood the house. As they slowly drove into the entrance, the outside lights came on, and Kilian's partner Paula opened the door. Despite the late hour, she radiated joy as she addressed the two guests in Swiss dialect, "Come in. I hope you are still hungry. Kilian has cooked and is just warming it up."

Paula mentioned that her five-year-old son was excited about the expected visitors but had finally fallen asleep. The table was set, and Anna didn't dare say they had already picked up sandwiches from the gas station. However, these were probably intended more as a deterrent to British fast food. Gregor was less sensitive and mentioned the terrible sandwiches later during the meal. He complimented Kilian on his cooking skills. To lighten the mood, he told what a French folk hero once said about the English: "Did you know that even Voltaire once wrote that the English had a thousand countries, but only one sauce?"

Paula could laugh her head off at this and went into it, "You know, then Kilian must be an Englishman after all. He always leaves out the sauces altogether!"

"Only because you're always bitching that we're eating unhealthy," he countered.

They then talked for a while until Kilian asked, "Did you want to see something in particular? Tomorrow afternoon I could accompany you."

Gregor didn't know how Anna would react to this, so he waited to hear what she had to say, "You know, I got permission to come right up to the Whispering Knights. I want to spend some time there in meditation. I'm sure that would be boring for you guys."

"Okay. Then at least let's go for a ride together later. I have something for you. There's a new dig site near the Rollright Stones. They found something extraordinary there."

"Now you're making us curious. What's it all about?

"There's supposed to be another article about it in 'Science' this month. It is a circular stone building. There's often something like that in the British Isles. This one, however, is 50 feet underground, and now brace yourselves. It is said to be at least twelve thousand years old. The site resembles *Göbekli Tepe* in Turkey."

"But England was still covered with ice then," Gregor said.

"Yes, but that means that the stone structure was built after the ice age, that is, ten thousand years ago at the earliest, or it happened before the last glaciation. However, that was thirty thousand years ago. The only question is, who could have done it then?"

Gregor sounded discouraged as he replied, "Either they will find an explanation on this that is plausible to the public, or no editor will dare to publish an article on it."

Paula, herself a journalist and German-language correspondent in Great Britain, had so far only listened. She sometimes saw things a little differently than Kilian about the publication of scientific articles. Therefore, she tried to present her view, "That is probably true. In the journal Science, hardly anyone will write about cult sites of extraterrestrials. And certainly not about a thirty-thousand-year-old culture in Europe. But that's why the journal is so appreciated."

"You mean we're the ghost hunters that no one should take seriously?" Kilian asked somewhat flippantly.

"No. I mean, …a journalist's job is to maintain the diversity of opinion, and balanced reporting is a prerequisite for that. When I read a scientific newspaper, I assume that the articles have also been scientifically researched. There are enough newspapers that do not follow this principle and have special readers."

"Paula is right," Gregor agreed, "We know how hard it has become for people to still find their way in the crowd of manipulative media. Most of the time, people stop looking for reasons when someone presents them with the appropriate truth. The easiest thing to do then is to present the culprit immediately."

"The best way to do that is to scare people. Whether lying or exaggerating, they'll believe it if it's convenient for them."

Kilian didn't want to leave the impression that he was the undiscerning rebel, "Even if the journal doesn't print anything, we should collect some material about the excavation. Maybe there will be other interested people who want to research further."

Perhaps to restore family peace, Paula offered to take everything to the publishing house. She thought there would always be someone who would write an article about it.

By now, it was half past two in the morning and very quiet in the house. Despite exhaustion, Anna had kept herself awake with a few thought exercises. Gregor had been given the couch in the living room. He was the one she had let in on her little adventure. He was one of the few who understood why Anna had to go through with her plan alone.

The sun was due to rise shortly after four o'clock. The sky was overcast, and Anna knew the rain would ruin all her efforts. What she had in mind would only work if the stones were dry. The reason lay in the physical properties of the different materials. Especially when water evaporated on rock surfaces, effects were created that interfered with the field energy. It had less than an hour to get to its destination. She remembered the barrier around the *Whispering Knights* as a rusty fence without a lock. She hoped that had stayed the same by now. Otherwise, she would have to climb over the spiky barrier.

When Anna tried to unplug the charger from her rental car, no cable was connected. Had Gregor forgotten to charge the battery? She hadn't reminded him either. A brief panic set in because now the capacity might not be enough for the trip. At least 30 minutes would be lost for charging at a fast-charging station, and then she would be too late.

Behind the car, she heard a crackling sound. Was someone there? Maybe the cat from the neighboring property on its night excursion? Or was someone sneaking around after all? She decided to get in quickly because the mixture of silence and unfamiliar noises made her shiver. Reflexively, she chose the wrong side at first but then walked around the front of the vehicle to open the driver's door. As she stood directly in front of the car, the headlights came on, and the buzzing sound of the electric drive rang out. After a moment's hesitation, the adrenaline rush faded. Anna's heart pounded heavily when she saw someone sitting behind the steering wheel. It took her a few seconds to realize that it was Gregor, who was barely recognizable with his tanned face and black cap pulled over his few hairs.

Finally, she took the passenger door and scolded, "Gregor! Have you gone crazy, scaring me like that? You know I have to go to the stones alone!"

"I know. But I'm going to drive you. I put a note on the fridge. After all, Kilian knows that the stones only speak at sunrise. We'll sort that out later. Now get in the car!"

They took the A44, which led north from Oxford. Passing Woodstock, they proceeded quickly to the Little Rollright exit. The route to the tourist parking lot was quite well signposted. However, the signs only pointed to the official destinations Rollright Stones and King Stone. Strangely, the car's navigation led a little differently than the signposting. Gregor preferred to trust the signs and drove better with them. Anna knew from her previous visits that it was possible to go quite close to the destination, although it was not allowed. At this time of day, however, it was hardly likely to be caught. Anna glanced at her phone. The app indicated that the sun would rise in 30 minutes. So, she had to hurry. Gregor still reminded her to take the ultrasound meter with her, linked to her smartphone via an app. Anna had about 300 yards to walk from the parking lot. The hiking trails to the excursion destinations were well maintained because tourism was now a lucrative business in this area. Unfortunately, Anna was wearing inappropriate clothing, as she often did. Her light sneakers were not the best choice because of the damp ground, and soon, the water foamed out of the fabric pores. In Anna's head, however, completely different things were already happening. She went through all the steps needed to initiate the ritual. With each previous visit, new things were added.

A few more yards on the paved forest floor to a clearing, from where she had to cross an overgrown dirt road through a cornfield. She could already see her destination, the fenced-in *Whispering Knights* when there was a terrible crash above her.

Of all times, there must be a thunderstorm now. It's like a bad fantasy movie!

Anna hoped the rain would hold off for a while and imagined how she, as the heroine in this movie, had to fight terrible demons. Fortunately, she was well acquainted with demons and knew precisely where these thugs came from. Memories and new stimuli from the environment were what made such fantasies real. And people knew that. That may be why some feared their dreams more than the real world. But Anna's research also showed that playing with such things in places like these was dangerous. The ultrasound meter hanging around her neck could not only measure the danger but also warn against overloading the brain.

She was there. As hoped, a small gate in the fence was as unlocked as last year. A mixture of different grasses lined the circular enclosure measuring about twenty feet. The grass was trampled down and smelled like late summer and thunderstorms. Now she could only hope the stones would work as they did last year, despite the weather. A glance at the meter showed that the rocks had already started emitting ultrasound. Anna squeezed herself between the five heavily weathered stones and started meditating cross-legged.

Sunrise had already begun, and Anna would have liked more time to prepare. In her head, a program was running that allowed her mind to head for a specific destination during meditation. It mayn't work that day, and more trials would be necessary. Measurements by sonar technicians over the past few years have provided deeper and deeper insights into how these stones worked. This was undoubtedly a disappointment for many people who believed in supernatural phenomena. After all, many of their rituals were based on tales from the time of the Celts and Druids.

The fact that minerals could emit ultrasound and infrasound was no longer a secret. The piezoelectric effect of minerals was also used in many ways in technology. But science was now faced with a completely different problem. How should people have known this technique thousands of years ago, and who showed them how to correctly arrange the heavy stones to achieve these effects?

Such questions were not on Anna's mind at that moment. She and her research group had already penetrated many secrets, even if not everything was known. Nonetheless, Anna was not there that day to find anything new but to use the stones as their builders once did.

A few moments later, it began. The sound waves the stone colossi emitted stimulated her brain's central part. The pineal gland began to produce *DMT*. Even then, the creators of these stone formations knew what modern generations had just found out again. The hallucinogen was not used to fog the brain and have a few intoxicating hours. It stimulated certain areas of the brain, which connected them in a particular way. This enabled the priests and shamans to see far beyond the standard horizon. That's exactly what Anna needed now to find Brian. If you just wanted to put yourself into a state of intoxication, you didn't need any special training. It was something else to properly manage one's thoughts while intoxicated. Anna knew that she couldn't go too deep into a trance if she wanted to determine the destination of her thoughts herself.

A journey began in her mind. Billionaires had spent a lot of money to experience something similar. After short trips into the near-earth orbit, they reported identical intoxication states. At the same time, they could see the planet Earth from space. All egoistic and narcissistic qualities of a human being faded into the background for moments because, at this sight, it became clear how insignificant a single human being is. Perhaps in such special moments, *DMT* was also released in the brain. At least with Anna, the first received message of this day was that there can be no property on this planet, only lending of inestimable value.

The strict rules she now had to follow allowed her to go deeper and deeper into where she hoped to find the answers to her questions. In principle, Anna's stolen port stone worked the same way. However, it could only do a fraction of what was possible with the megalithic stone installations. And that, although only meager remnants of the former splendor of the facilities arranged around the earth were still to be found.

Now the time had come. She tried to direct her thoughts to the destination of her journey. A goal whose coordinates she did not know but did not necessarily need for this communication. She wanted to get inside Brian's head. Most important was first to sense a sign of life. Sergei had asked her to dissuade Brian and whoever would be traveling with him from stealing one of the ancient artifacts. At the moment, no one knew who it once served. Apparently, it was essential to someone at NATO command in Brussels. Whoever asked Sergei for help assumed that the problem could not be solved by usual political or military means. He could help specially trained young people like Anna learn about occult objects or simply use paranormal abilities to penetrate into the depths of a soul. Sergey actually refused such requests when he could not estimate the consequences.

Anna's head briefly roamed with the thought that whenever people spoke of the depths of a soul, they usually meant the worst that people could think up in their brains.

Did the idea of hell originate in the darkest cave of one's own head? Was that why people were so afraid of the dark eye sockets of a skull? The last thoughts made Anna shiver again because she had already had experiences in a dark chamber when she almost died in it years ago. Some called such a thing a near-death experience. She also knew that such an experience was part of the training of priests, even in the most ancient cultures.

The light trance changed Anna's perceptions. A quick glance at the meter showed that the ultrasound was getting stronger. To a bat, this noise would probably seem as if the pubescent children of her neighbors had gotten a new stereo system.

In the eastern sky, the thunderclouds already got bright edges. So, the sunrise had begun. Because of the twilight atmosphere, the outlines of the distant trees stood out like a mountain range. The measuring instrument's pointer moved further into the red area. Anna now concentrated again on her dream thoughts. It was as if her body was gliding over a railroad track held in place by the tracks. Inside her head, the environment passed her by faster than her senses could register. Then everything slowed down again, and the first step seemed to be taken. She now saw things stored in Brian's mind, the world, seen through his eyes. The train tracks turned into corridors of an office building, with someone walking back and forth as if in time-lapse. In between, Anna looked at a naked female body for a split second. She could remember the face but didn't want to. Then a wake-up call followed, and a short time later, she was sitting in a helicopter that took off and flew in a westerly direction. After a brief stopover, a man in a navy uniform sat next to her. The badge on his chest revealed the name: Lange. She did not know the meaning of the rank insignia. The helicopter flew on over the sea.

After a long flight and heavy turbulence, the helicopter door opened, and she froze in fear. The view landed on high waves that occasionally hit the deck of a surfaced submarine. The look down and the aircraft rocking caused a nauseous feeling in the stomach. Then vague images raced past her as other faces of young men kept appearing before her. This continued until she found herself in a confined space with this Lange. She knew something like that from TV reports about diving expeditions. Because of the portholes, it could be a small submarine or something similar. This vehicle also lurched, which again caused Anna to feel dizzy.

After awakening from her trance state, Anna noticed that she had just thrown up. Her jacket and pants were fetidly soiled. What she had experienced in a trance had transferred to her body and taken effect. She nevertheless tried to find her way back into the dream. Before doing so, she ventured a quick glance at the ultrasound meter. The pointer was well into the red zone. Whether other energies had also reached dangerous levels, she didn't know. This should be a warning to Anna because if the stones radiated so strongly, it was high time to break off the meditation.

The people in this area knew very well that it was better to stay away from the stone formations during a thunderstorm. There were legends that people seeking shelter lost their minds after the thunderstorm. If you believe in the traditions, the druids once waited for thunderstorms to perform their rituals.

Anna still needed to reach her goal. She did have confirmation that Brian was on a submarine. However, there needed to be an indication of the location and the mission's destination. It was also bizarre why Brian had been in a tiny capsule for several hours. A smaller submersible? She also had to assume that wish and reality had mixed in Brian's head in some places. Therefore, Anna could not say exactly which of his memories had taken place. She had an idea, but it quickly faded away.

The gusts of wind had increased so much that Anna did not hear Gregor's shouting from the forest's edge. He must have been worried about the approaching heavy weather. Now the lightning strikes were only a few miles away. High time to break off the ritual, but Anna saw herself already close to the finish line and tried again. With her eyes closed and one hand on each upright menhirs, she began her journey again. Anna managed to pick up Brian's thoughts while looking at various graphics in front of a screen. If only she could get deeper into his head, she would realize what he was looking for. This form of mental coupling was, in fact, only successful with meditation partners who had practiced it together for years or were used to living together in groups. Without practice and encouragement in the group, an individual's talent was not worth much. Anna's attempt was complicated because Brian's strengths lay more in reading other people than opening up to them. Therefore, she had no choice but to guess at his snippets of thoughts and draw her own conclusions from what his eyes saw. If Brian could sense Anna approaching him, it could get easier. The possibilities for meditation in such a steel monster were probably limited. Anna could not have guessed that Brian was fixated on something entirely else at the other end of the transmission.

Gregor became more and more nervous. The first raindrops on the back of his neck seemed as if someone were saying to him: "Now do something!"

The distance between lightning and the sound of thunder was already very short. Finally, nothing stopped him when there was a crash behind him so loud that it hurt his ears. Running towards the stone circle, he didn't care if Anna had succeeded. Nothing could be more essential now than her life.

What is that guy staring at? The patterns could be sound waves. Not unusual, actually. If they're underwater, sonar equipment should be sending out and receiving sound waves all the time. But Brian isn't a sonar technician. What's so special about that?

Seconds later, the crucial traffic light must have turned green at some point in Anna's brain: *Why didn't I think of that in the first place? They need Brian on board as a language expert! Maybe he's supposed to help decode specific signals or talk to someone as a medium?*

If one person could recognize characteristic patterns in the chaos of signals buzzing around, it was Brian. Anna made another effort to grasp the entire contents of the screen. She memorized the data given and remembered a few formulas that Brian captured with his eyes while occasionally looking at a piece of paper. Without further attempts to understand what was seen, Anna wanted to use the rest of the time to memorize details. She benefited from the fact that Brian apparently concentrated on something in between and let it run in his mind's eye. What had been seen frightened Anna. But she tried to suppress it with all her might. Yet, the images couldn't be hidden. Brian was suddenly standing in front of the door he had told her about a year before. She could feel his panic as his eyes approached the light shining through the narrow crack in the door. A little closer, a little closer... The heart was pounding, and Anna's pulse had also reached a level that made her chest ache. Only a few steps were missing, then you should see it. A few more inches... Anna began to hyperventilate. She suddenly heard a male voice. It was raining. Someone shouted her name, and then she felt her body dragged through tall grass.

The next thing Anna experienced with a clear head was a woman asking her if she could give her name. She was lying in a hospital bed and still saw the doctor's lamp go out, with which she had previously checked her pupil reactions. Now she also noticed Gregor's worried face. The doctor turned to Gregor, "And you don't know what medication your daughter might have taken?"

"No. To my knowledge, she doesn't take anything."

"We'll wait and see what the blood results show. Please don't take offense at these questions. Still, tourists are not uncommon to pump themselves full of drugs to celebrate some ritual at the stone circles afterward. Your daughter's symptoms are indicative of a substance with strong hallucinogenic effects. You should advise her against staying near such places of worship at any time."

"Of course, you're right," Gregor answered ruefully.

The doctor's face expressed little understanding for this kind of tourist. Anna could think clearly again in the meantime, and when the doctor had left the room, she said to Gregor, "I'm sorry that I got you into so much trouble."

"No problem, little daughter. Now I have to teach my wife how I came to have a child out of wedlock."

Laughing, Anna realized she had a few bruises. Of course, the lab found a residual *DMT* in Anna's blood. Since this was a volatile drug, they could conclude that Anna had given herself a high dose of this illicit substance a few hours ago. A little later, Gregor learned that Anna would receive an invitation from the hospital's drug counseling service. In addition, charges were filed for violation of the Narcotics Act. Gregor only hoped this served as a deterrent and would not have any significant after-effects.

Anna then joked, "Doesn't look good for our personnel file at the university. '...Got high on illegal substances on a business trip...' That's definitely not going to be a career booster."

"Did you at least succeed, Anna?"

"How to take it. I didn't get around to leaving Brian a message. I need a computer for now. Once we've analyzed the data, we may learn what message the crew in the sub received and where they're headed. Maybe we could try to get to our destination before they do."

"That sounds exciting, but our business trip budget is insufficient. It would be best if you rested for now. I'll come back tomorrow," said Gregor.

Anna grabbed his wrist and pulled him a little closer. Gregor noticed the concern in her expression, "Is something wrong?"

"I feel like being watched here. Every few minutes, someone comes in. It's like they have too many staff."

"You collapsed, and there could be problems after the fact. They're just worried!"

"Gregor, I'm not stupid after all. It's not the nursing staff that comes, but some specialists. As if I were an exotic animal in the zoo. Look. The three other beds in the room have been cleared out as if they had to isolate me. I assume they've already checked my DNA. At least that's what it sounded like during their conversations."

"Did they tell you what other exams are coming up?"

"Next, they want to do an MRI. Gregor, they can't do that! With MRI, they'd see abnormalities in the brain right away."

"You're right, but you can refuse the treatment."

"I don't want to rely on that. Can you help me get out of here?"

"Run away? You have to stay in bed!"

"Absolutely not. I couldn't sleep a wink here. I won't stay in this hospital another hour."

"I hope the lightning didn't reprogram anything in you after all!" Gregor said, but he had apparently given up on discussing it further. "I'll stay close to you and keep watch. I promise!"

"Okay," Anna said. Gregor's care seemed to calm her down for the time being. Then she added, "Tell Paula and Kilian. They're probably worried already."

"I already have. Oh, yes ..." Gregor mumbled while searching for something in his jacket pocket."... Here's your cell phone. I took it to be on the safe side. They were looking for it in your stuff when you were brought in. Maybe someone was curious about what apps you had installed on it?"

Anna pointed with her head to a corresponding sign on the wall and said, "You are not allowed to use G5 mobile devices in this hospital."

Gregor seemed reassured by this, "Maybe I'm already seeing ghosts, too."

Anna had to laugh, "Of course, there are ghosts everywhere! Please ask the ward nurse for my clothes. I haven't found them."

When the door opened, Anna had barely uttered the sentence, and a nurse came in with a laundry bag, "Hey Anna, your clothes are back. I'm putting everything in this closet."

"What do you mean by ARE BACK?"

"The ward physician had ordered a chemical analysis. Sorry, but that's the protocol for suspected drug abuse."

Gregor talked about trivial things until they were alone in the room again. Then he went to the door and said, "I'm going to look around the ward. Maybe I'll find someone who can tell me more details."

Alone again, Anna realized how exhausted she was. The fact that Gregor had nearby calmed her down, and not two minutes later, her eyes fell shut.

Meanwhile, Gregor wanted to discreetly look around to see how many patients were in the ward. He also wanted to find out what else was unusual. He didn't have to go far before one thing was confirmed. A list of patients was hanging on every room door; according to it, all the beds were occupied. Thus, the other patients from Anna's room were divided among the infirmary. So much special treatment for an average patient was strange. A friendly hospital employee then asked him if he would like some tea. Gregor gladly accepted and sat down with his cup on a bench at the end of the corridor. From there, he had a good view of what was happening in the ward. At least until sudden tiredness overtook him. A sleeping relative was nothing unusual in a hospital corridor. It would hardly be noticed by anyone during the next hour.

As so often, Anna dreamed strange things. This time she was a four-year-old child again, lying in her bed. Although Mama had promised to leave the light on, it was completely dark. As much as she tore her eyes open, she could see nothing. Despite the warm summer evening, the window was closed, and the curtains were drawn. Anna insisted that all the windows remain locked. The feeling in her gut told her it would happen again today. The quilt pulled over her head was the last protective covering and, therefore, the most essential thing the little girl had in these moments. For a long time, she lay like this and waited, waited, waited. It was terribly warm under the blanket. For a bit of cooling, she wanted to stick a foot out. At least for a little moment. But she couldn't. It wouldn't take a second, and someone would grab her by the foot. Then it would be too late, and she would be carried away again. She had told Mama many times, but she didn't believe her. She had also confided in her brother but could not expect help from him. He seemed to be more frightened by her stories than Anna herself. He didn't let on, but she had overheard her parents talking worriedly about the boy suddenly wetting the bed again. *Nobody wants a brother like that,* Anna thought at the time.

Then the scene in her dream changed. She was now an adult again and was lying in the hospital bed. With her eyes open, she could only see blurry. The perception of the environment with closed eyes also did not work as well as usual. It was also difficult to move her arms. Two figures in light blue hospital clothes stood around her, and suddenly the bed moved. *Are they driving me out of the room?* Anna wanted to say something, but only incomprehensible words escaped her lips. She didn't even know in which language she had tried. In bed, she was pushed toward the elevator. At the end of the corridor, she could still see Gregor's outline before the bed disappeared into the elevator. She wanted to call out, but before a sound could leave her lips, he was already out of sight. From the conversation between the two figures, she picked up a few scraps of words, "When she gets back to the room, she won't remember anything... That pushy overseer drank all the tea. That will last at least two hours."

Anna's brain worked as slowly as a computer in the last century. Every thought was complex, and it would be hopeless to resist if Anna hadn't practiced it for years. *Maybe there's a trick I can use to suppress the anesthetic in my body through my thoughts,* she reasoned. It just took some time to develop the necessary pattern in her mind. Should she succeed in getting the proper meditation routine going, her thoughts could be more potent than the drug she was being given. The limbs were the problem because they obeyed the least. Running away would be difficult.

Minutes later, she was wheeled into an anteroom adjacent to the lab with the MRI. This machine could bring Anna's biggest secret to light. The images could show any expert that her brain was structured differently than usual. Someone might then get the idea to record brain waves, which would give neurologists a reason to do more and more tests.

What a bummer. If they x-ray my head, it's all over. Then I might become a laboratory animal. Who knows into whose hands I'll end up.

In the radiology department at Oxford University Hospital, the staff wore blue vests and a meter on their chests. Someone scanned Anna's body for metal objects and asked the two men who had wheeled her in, "Where's the medical history report and what about metal objects in the patient's body?"

"Everything has already been loaded into the system with her medical records. The examination is being done by Dr. Zhou himself. He'll be here shortly, too."

Dr. Zhou was one of the senior neurologists with his own research lab specializing in brain mapping. This involved measuring which areas were active during certain activities. Recent research has also revealed that the brain shares certain functions with other body parts. That in itself was not spectacular. Much more exciting was the realization that communication between the brain and the abdomen also worked through energy fields that formed around the entire body. A research program on this had been funded almost entirely by the partner university in Shanghai for several years. Dr. Zhou had brought some people from China with him at that time. His research in Shanghai was also rumored to be about remote viewing in humans.

During the Cold War, the Russian side intensively pursued this research. On the other hand, the Americans are said to have shelved such things at that time. There is occasional criticism in the British press that foreign institutions should not conduct unsupervised research on similar topics at Oxford. Anna and her teammates in Freiburg were among the few who knew why such research was so interesting, especially in the British Isles. For no other reason, she had also traveled to this place.

Restlessness arose. Although Anna had started exercises and wanted to shield her senses from the outside world, she heard the radiology staff discussing intensively. Dr. Zhou had arrived in the meantime and had brought his own team with him. He insisted on being able to perform the examination independently.

Therefore, the radiology doctor on duty came up to Anna and addressed her, "... can you understand me?"

Anna tried to nod but could only close her eyelids a little.

"Good. Your attending physician will now take over the further examinations. Do you agree with that?"

Anna tried to shake her head and say something like no. It was hopeless. She could only open her eyes and stare pleadingly at the doctor. He watched her face closely as she did so before turning to Zhou and saying, "I'm sorry, colleague. I can't see the patient's wish, nor do I see any other reason to ..."

Anna could not follow the further discussion because the disputants had left the room. Perhaps doubts arose in the radiologist, and the tone between him and the neurologist Zhou showed that the two did not get along very well. Others could certainly be more impressed by this Zhou with his charisma. One of the reasons could be that his home university was the main sponsor of neurological research in this private clinic. This probably opened more doors for him than the regulations allowed.

The bed in which Anna was lying still stood in the anteroom of the MRI scanner. She wanted to use the time to focus on defending herself against the foreign substances in her body. She had learned from her student Brian a method of shielding her mind against foreign influences. Whoever succeeded in imagining an upside-down and circling pyramid possessed a powerful tool to protect the brain against foreign forces. At least if the intruder did not know this trick. Against some nerve poisons, this form of meditation should also help. It was a risk, but worth the try.

Not twenty seconds later, the pyramid was spinning in Anna's head. It also had side effects, as she lost spatial orientation, floating as if weightless in a room, creating dizziness. Through the window into the next room, she could watch the two orderlies who had brought Anna in earlier approach the radiologist from behind and press something like a syringe into his neck. He slumped and was dragged into an adjacent dressing room. Anna thought her arms were now moving. In reality, however, only her fingers slowly became mobile again.

One of the orderlies dressed in blue now returned and handled an infusion bottle at her bedside. She heard Zhou talking about a contrast medium, which alerted Anna again. She knew that some of these agents contained the heavy metal gadolinium. The substance was problematic for the body to break down and was deposited in the brain, among other places. What effect this would have on Anna's telepathic abilities, she did not know.

The infusion was already connected, and when the nurse turned on the cap, the liquid flowed into the tube. In a moment, the stuff would rush into her right arm. Panic set in. The pyramid was still spinning in her head, and she felt like she could feel her left arm again. What should she worry about first? Continue to fight the anesthetic's effects or stop the contrast medium's flow? She had to somehow pull the IV needle out of her arm. The eyes of Anna and the man who had put the infusion on her met. Anna felt utterly exposed but still did not look away. The fact that she was left-handed would be an advantage in tearing off the IV. As if he had read her thoughts, he got a piece of tape and wrapped it around the arm, including the infusion needle. Now tearing it off would be even more difficult. The gray contrast medium was flowing into her body by now, and she felt totally helpless. *How will Gregor be? Has he also been anesthetized?*

A woman's voice could be heard in the next room. There was a discussion going on there. All eyes at that moment were directed toward the door, where the voices came from. Dr. Zhou seemed to be arguing excitedly with someone again. For a brief moment, Anna could see the hair of a familiar woman. *Is that...?* Sure enough, Paula was accompanied by another person, carrying a camera on his shoulder. Paula held a microphone in front of Dr. Zhou's face as he tried to push the two reporters out of the room, "You have no business being here..."

"We now have a shooting appointment in radiology. Also, we have been advised to be on time."

"What are you doing? You can't just come in here!"

"But they sent us straight to you!"

"What nonsense! I don't give interviews here. We treat patients."

"Is it right for you to have patients undergo radiological examinations against their will?"

"How dare you. Get out of here right now. I'll call security..."

"You are Dr. Zhou, right?" asked Paula, but got no answer. Zhou was probably not sure how to handle this situation. Meanwhile, Gregor dragged himself staggering into the room. He had woken up in the meantime and called Paula. She had the idea with the camera team. As a reporter, it wasn't difficult for her to charm her way past the security services and use her eloquence.

Unnoticed by everyone else, one of Zhou's men pushed past the disputants into the room where Anna lay. He took a hand out of his smock pocket next to her bed. His fingers grasped something. Anna saw a jab in the corner of her eye before she felt a sharp pain in her throat. A few seconds later, the guy was gone. Anna felt nauseous. She lay on her back and gagged. If she couldn't find a way to turn onto her side now, she might choke on her vomit.

Meanwhile, the tussle between Dr. Zhou and his associate was getting more heated. Gregor still seemed dazed, barely getting three words in the correct order. He also had to keep holding on to something. His eyes searched the room, and he tried to shout, "W h e r e...i s...A n n a?"

Paula and Gregor realized that Zhou and his co-worker were unconsciously looking in the same direction for a split second. Gregor immediately understood and rushed to the sliding door where the two had unconsciously looked earlier. When he got to Anna's bedside, she was lying on her back with wide-open eyes. Her face was already turning gray. Gregor screamed for help as he tried to turn Anna onto her side. He failed. Instead, she fell off the transport bed. In the process, the infusion tube ruptured, and something probably triggered the cough reflex. Somehow Paula had managed to press the emergency button on the door to the MRI. Two employees rushed into the room and helped Anna clear her windpipe. The alarm must also have set security in motion. Paula, therefore, signaled to her reporter colleague to make the camera equipment disappear somewhere.

Strangely, there was no sign of Dr. Zhou or his staff. Paula took the initiative in pushing Anna and Gregor into the nearest elevator, not knowing where it would lead. They were in luck. There was a button labeled "Lobby/Reception." The ride took an eternity. When the door opened, Paula was confronted with the following problem. Anna was wearing only a patient gown. In addition, her bottom was sticking out and to make matters worse, she was soiled from top to bottom with vomit. They couldn't leave the hospital like that. Paula nodded at Gregor, and he understood. Staggering, he fetched a parked wheelchair from the lobby and took a used gown from a clothes bin. They put it on Anna in a makeshift fashion and made their way toward the exit. At the end of the lobby, they saw four security guards standing directly in front of the entrance. So, this way was out of the question for them. Now two of the security guards were also moving in their direction. Maybe they had been spotted by the surveillance cameras. Gregor looked around. The nearest fire alarm button was two steps away. He pushed, and the stunned people in the lobby paused for a moment before the first ones began to move toward the exits. The disciplined English seemed alarm-tested, for it took only seconds for crowds of people to move toward all the doors. Against the tide, Paula now pushed the wheelchair toward the elevator. She also had to pull Gregor along, as he was still staggering. Despite safety warnings, the elevators still worked. In any case, he let himself be driven to the parking deck.

"You got a parking space down here?" asked Gregor in amazement.

"No, the car is parked in a no-parking zone, but I don't think anyone will have towed it that quickly."

That's where Paula was wrong. When they arrived at her car, a towing company was already dealing with the vehicle. But the fire alarm had finally persuaded them to abandon their plan. They sat in the small car a few minutes later and left the premises via the fire department driveway. This was forbidden, but no one was interested at that moment.

In the meantime, Gregor could think clearly again and explained to Paula during the trip that Dr. Zhou must be behind the whole thing. Under the pretext that Anna had taken illicit drugs, he was probably after something completely different. Perhaps he was researching the mystery of endogenous hallucinogens. After all, people lived here amid all the places of worship with their myths and ancient rituals. This could also be why the Chinese partner university was so interested in Oxford as a location. For Gregor, it was always fascinating how appropriately the inhabitants of the time had named the ancient cult sites. Anyone who believed that all legends originated only in people's fantasies was quickly proven wrong in the vicinity of such menhirs as the *Whispering Knights*.

The next day, Anna still felt limp. But she wanted to write down everything she had seen the day before in her trance at the menhirs. Therefore, they postponed the excursion with Kilian again for one day.

Each last Sunday and Monday in August, England and Wales celebrate the end of the vacations and summer. The excursion should now take place this Monday. Despite the holiday, Paula had to go to the newsroom. But she took her son with her because excellent childcare was available for employees around the clock.

They had an early breakfast to get on the road before the excursion traffic. The twenty-year-old Range Rover did its best to rattle past Woodstock again on the A44. It felt like déjà vu to Anna. Things were happening in her head as if she were expecting the same thing two days ago. The thought of coming closer to the stones once again caused discomfort. Perhaps a similar something had happened to Brian there a year ago. She couldn't enjoy the scenery for the rest of the ride. Instead, she tried to go over her notes of what had happened at the Whispering Knights in her mind. Her ability to concentrate was poor, as she kept thinking about what creepy experiments this Chinese neurologist would perform on other patients. Gregor had calmed her down a bit and announced that he would ask Sergei to use his contacts in England to get to the bottom of the matter.

With what she had seen through Brian's eyes two days ago, she was reaching her limits, and she decided to call in a sonar expert later.

After an hour of driving with a fuel break, they turned onto a narrow forest road. This ended on a farm with several flat buildings. There had been no farming here for a long time. Kilian had announced them from the road, and an older woman came to meet them when they all got out of the car. She hugged Kilian warmly and addressed Anna by Paula's name, "You're getting skinnier and skinnier, girl. No wonder you can't have children." The old lady had already begun to retreat into her world of fading memories.

Later, Kilian explained that it was the grandmother of a good school friend on whose farm they had sometimes played as children.

From the large orchard, Kilian led Anna and Gregor to a dry dirt road over a few hills. When asked why they couldn't drive this route in an all-terrain vehicle, Kilian answered, "I'd love to. But the meadows are restricted to military areas, and no motor vehicles are allowed here."

As the three crossed a narrow section of forest, Kilian said, "We're almost there. In the clearing ahead, we should see the first barrier of the excavation site."

What they found there, however, was something entirely different. Four concrete mixers were standing on a leveled area, and a few workers were handling long hoses. Kilian turned white as a sheet and immediately ran in their direction.

"What are you doing?" he addressed the first worker.

The answer hit like a bomb, "The subsoil is unstable. Cavities have been found that are in danger of collapsing. The landowner is now having the cavities filled with mud."

"But there was another dig here last week, and many archaeologists from Oxford!"

"They've all gone again. They must not have found anything. False alarm, I heard. Therefore, we began clearing everything away on Saturday. The matter was probably so hurried that we even have to work on today's holiday."

This trip was incredibly frustrating for Kilian. What would his German friends think of him now! They might now believe he was a weirdo. In any case, the past few days' events proved something wrong in this region.

Slowly, they started on their way back. During the drive, Gregor also clarified that something could not be correct. Why did the landowner have the ground filled in? Was he even authorized to do so? Even if the archaeologists had found nothing special, there were obviously cavities. Or was the backfilling with mud camouflage, and secretly the excavations would go on after all? All unanswered questions, for whose answers one did not get far without help. Gregor said, "I'm sorry, but I don't think there's anything more we can do here. Right now, Anna's safety is our top priority. I will definitely ask Sergei to use his contacts in England. Maybe he will find out something about this place. If something has been found in the cavities, it will come out sooner or later. There is always a leak. Then, at the latest, Sergei's contacts in England will also get wind of it. Anyway, we are alarmed and remain vigilant."

Anna still wanted to stay in England. She neither believed that the incident in the hospital would have any consequences. Of course, she wanted to find out what research this Dr. Zhou was working on in Oxford. However, that was not Anna's task. Therefore, she tried to send her report about it to Sergei as soon as possible.

While Anna started to analyze the data she had collected in Brian's head during her trance session, Gregor tried to find out where the Chinese were currently hanging out in England. He didn't have to search for long. Just by looking through the British business news, amazing things caught his eye: "BEIJING INVESTS MILLIONS IN BRITISH RESEARCH" – "CHINESE STATE CONTRACTOR BUYS WORLDWIDE WATER SHARES" – "RADAR IN CHINESE SPACE STATION CAN SEE 160 FEET INTO THE GROUND" – "CHINA BUILDS UNDERWATER STATION IN THE PACIFIC"

That evening, Anna's phone rang. The number was unknown, but she immediately recognized Sergei's voice. He kept it short, "You must return to Freiburg immediately. There is news about the wanted person, and the matter will not tolerate delay. From the looks of it, he's in serious trouble. Your flight leaves in four hours."

By the following day, Sergei had found a sonar specialist with whom Anna was to meet in the institute's laboratory. Kai, who looked like a teenager in his mid-thirties and sometimes expressed himself that way, had years of experience in materials research. Thanks to his specialty in hypersonic, he was also allowed to work on military projects for various underwater technologies. He had a reputation for not making long speeches and being loyal. He also seemed to be interested in everything except money. The latter was why he had not yet accepted an offer from the United States or Great Britain. Anna had sent him everything she had already recorded from her dream at the stones near Long Compton. He explained to her initially, "It's really cool what you brought back. How did you receive the data from the sub?"

"Telepathically," Anna answered as a matter of course.

"Telepathic? You've got to be kidding me."

"No."

"Then you can channel that Brian just like that?"

"No, I wouldn't call it that. Channeling is a term from esotericism. There, one understands it rather as the establishment of contact into a higher spiritual level. What I mean is the use of quite normal physical conditions. For telepathy, you just need to practice and understand the principle of operation. Many Asian methods are based on what a few Aborigines still practice in the Australian outback. I use field amplifiers for this, as they are found everywhere on earth. However, global communication works only through the natural energy lines of the earth. Unfortunately, there are rarely connected transmitting stations in Europe where this still works. And as I know by now, there are also different mechanisms for activation."

Kai now looked even more puzzled than before. Regardless, he seemed to trust Anna as she continued, "Apparently, the creators of the old stone installations in England used different systems as transmitting stations. There's a lot to suggest that they didn't agree on everything. Perhaps there were competing stations, something like what is happening today with Russian 'RT' and British 'BBC' television."

Kai was visibly excited, "That's crazy. I really need to know more about that. But let's finish this thing first..." He opened various screen windows and explained, "As you guessed, Brian was looking at sound signals that originated in great water depths. I could pick out natural seismic waves and even identify the source."

"Cool," Anna gave in fascination.

"Yeah, that's really cool. It must be small earthquakes at great depths above the Atlantic Ridge. Those kinds of sound waves are easy to identify. But this Brian guy was after something else. Only I wonder if he's identified it himself yet. Some of the seismic waves are unnaturally distorted. We know this from modern submarines. They camouflage themselves by imitating the sounds of the natural environment. The enemy then cannot distinguish artificial and natural signals. However, this is familiar. The new German subs also camouflage themselves in this way. But I've never seen an artificial object move fast over long distances without being detected."

"I don't understand. Which object is moving fast, the submarine Brian is in or the other object?"

"You're not listening to me!" Kai said, annoyed. Apparently, he quickly lost his patience. After a pause, he continued, "Both objects are moving very fast. Brian is in a small submarine and may have detected a pursuer in the sound signals. And from the looks of it, it must be a bigger thing. Probably more than 400 feet long. The object Brian is in could be one of the more advanced small German submarines powered purely by electricity. Supposedly a prototype hypersonic propulsion system is already being tested."

"Tested? Does that mean Brian's in a boat that hasn't matured yet?"

Kai saw from Anna's excitement that he shouldn't have said that now. He tried to put it into perspective, "Well, it's not really like that. Before the boats are sent out into open waters, they undergo testing months. Incidentally, it has been reported that the Philippines are modernizing its submarine fleet with German help. They now want to do more to protect themselves from Chinese overreach in the South China Sea."

"I know. The Chinese are building one island after another there as a military base. The dispute over that regularly escalates with the coastal states."

Kai thought he had reassured Anna with his words, but she was already a step further in her thoughts, "Do you think the pursuer could be a Chinese submarine?"

"It's just a guess, but at least there's much to be said for it."

Anna now suspected that the whole thing was even trickier than she had feared, "Why does everything always have to be so complicated. Whether it's coincidence or not, several things have come together to cause us problems. And the crew of the German sub may not even know how much danger they're in right now."

Since the Institute was asked for help by NATO command, people there had to know that something dangerous was happening in the Atlantic. Maybe this wasn't a usual Chinese spy mission at all, directed against German companies as so often. It could be about much more. If the Chinese pursuer's mission was to prevent the delivery of one of the West's most advanced weapons to the Philippines, then the entire team was in danger.

Neither Anna nor Kai knew at this point that the submarine's test run had officially already ended. The public had no idea of the existence of a DaVinci twin. Whoever the pursuers were, they could make the unknown submarine disappear into the deep sea.

CHAPTER 8

Hamburg airport

Sean saw a chance to get out of this unscathed. He believed it wouldn't hurt Brian if he told Lieutenant at Sea Pot all the details about the trip to Malta. Still, Pot sensed more behind the whole thing. That's why he wanted to see for himself on the spot. Besides, the report on Brian's accident was due soon, and he couldn't stand there empty-handed again and be labeled incompetent.

On the morning of the departure to Malta, Sean had a good feeling. He didn't have to worry about anything. However, he was upset that Pot had booked a business class for himself and only economy class for Sean. Sean vowed to pay him back someday. When they arrived at Hamburg Airport, the departure board already showed a delay for their flight. Pot couldn't hide his fear of flying, and Sean decided to do everything he could to make his flight as uncomfortable as possible.

They went to the counter to drop off their luggage. Sean always kept a little behind Pot. When it was his turn, the flight attendant addressed him in a friendly manner, "Mr. Keller, due to a booking error, your seat was assigned twice, and since the economy class is fully booked, we'd like to offer you a free upgrade to business class."

Sean happily accepted the offer and wondered whether god had perhaps, for once, heard the wish of a poor sailor. In case his excellent fortune turned out to be a mistake when he boarded the plane, he didn't mention the upgrade for the time being. When boarding began, the business class passengers were called first, as usual. Sean trotted after his supervisor towards the gate. Pot said, "Keller, you have to wait. The business class is boarding first."

Sean enjoyed the moment and replied, "Oh, that's fine. I like to push my way in."

Still, he lagged behind his boss. The latter was probably already looking forward to humiliating Sean when the flight attendant sent him back to the waiting passengers in economy class.

As he stuffed his bag into the overhead compartment, Pot's forehead was full of sweat drops. He couldn't believe his eyes when Keller sat in a row in front of him. Then the flight attendant took off his backpack and jacket as well. Apparently, within seconds, the two were busy flirting. He called Sean, "Keller, what are you doing in the front? Your seat is in the back!"

The flight attendant responded immediately, reassuring Pot, "Can I help you?"

"This impudent fellow never does what he's supposed to," Pot nagged.

"Sir, everything is fine. Please take a seat for now. "I'll take care of you in a moment."

Before the landing, Sean did not hear another word from the row behind him. His audacity had taken effect. *This fatso will surely think up the next nasty thing to do*, Sean thought. But he wanted to save the trouble of thinking up countermeasures for later. The red wine first developed its soporific effect during the remaining flight time.

To Sean's surprise, they checked into an idyllic little hotel near the village of Dingli. They met for lunch on the roof terrace. Shortly after, they were joined by someone who introduced himself as Tony Peller. Pot had asked the staff in Rostock for an archaeological expert to assist him who knew his way around Malta. He was surprised that this Peller looked like he had not yet passed thirty. Anyway, the young man seemed to be in a good mood.

I guess the poor guy still has no idea what an asshole Pot is, Sean thought. Then Tony introduced himself and quickly got to why he was supposed to fly to Malta, "I lead the Experimental Archaeology team at the University of Freiburg. A colleague who knows the area here very well was supposed to come. Still, someone from the naval command in Rostock called me and asked me to take over."

"Do you remember the name?"

"Yes, that was Rear Admiral Breede. He must be in charge of special operations in the navy."

"Did he say why he chose you?"

"He asked me to take over because it seemed to be about the strange soil structures in the island's rocks. In addition, I am familiar with the ancient cultures and their ritual acts, which were celebrated by the island's former inhabitants."

Pot was suddenly a changed man. Friendly and ready to talk, he told what he was about: "As you know, I'm leading a commission of investigation into a marine accident. Boatswain Keller ..." At this, Pot pointed with his head at Sean, ".... I brought him along because he is a witness to the accident. He will be of great help to us in reconstructing the mysterious events."

"Mysterious events?"

Sean had already taken a breath to reply, but Pot cut him off, "Well, we just want to understand how a sailor could disappear for four days and then suddenly reappear in the same place without remembering."

"Have any other strange things happened?"

"What do you mean?"

"For example, any...I'll call it time perception issues." At the question, Tony shifted his gaze to Sean, probably wanting to hear the answer firsthand.

"Let me put it this way, ... Brian Wilson had been gone for four days. Yet, judging by his beard growth, he had only gone a day or two without shaving."

"That's very interesting. I understand you were at the sinkholes when the accident happened?"

"Right. We were going to the Dingli cliffs. But I had the impression Brian was more interested in the *cart ruts* in the rocky ground, which exist everywhere here. We didn't expect such a big hole with no barrier where tourists could fall in."

"You mean Wilson was actually after the secret of the tracks?"

"Maybe. But I don't know how much he knows about it. He didn't tell much, probably wanted to find out where the tracks lead."

They arranged to meet the following day to drive to the accident site. Pot had organized an all-terrain vehicle for this purpose. He also insisted on taking the same route as on the day of the accident. The off-road vehicle was better suited for the stony terrain than the quads. That's why there was no danger of getting stuck. Pot proved to be an experienced off-road driver. They reached where the hole in the ground was located without any problems. However, the surroundings were no longer the same. The sparse plant growth had been flattened by construction vehicles, and the hole filled in with debris. This calmed Sean, for he feared that he would have to climb back into the muddy maw. Tony Peller's behavior, however, surprised Sean. He kept squatting down on his knees and examining the remains of the cart ruts. Just as Brian had done a few weeks ago.

"Did you find anything?" asked Pot.

"I don't know yet. But maybe this Wilson guy has found something. I want to ask your comrade, where do we reach him?"

"I'd like to know that, too. This gentleman is probably recovering in the United States now."

Sean interjected here and said, "I hardly think he'll recover. He's disappeared without a trace. I can't reach him by phone or via any of the online platforms. There is also no word from his unit in Rostock. Very strange."

Tony looked lost in thought for a moment, probably making up his own mind about Brian's whereabouts. Then he suggested driving back to the hotel, "I need some time to do some research. We'll meet for dinner. Then maybe I'll know what might have happened here."

On the way back to the four-wheeler, Tony photographed a construction trailer that was probably waiting to be removed and used during the earthwork. The attached advertising did not seem to indicate a Maltese company. Here, too, another surprise awaited them.

Of course, Tony quickly realized that some things went together strangely well. An American linguist worked at the NATO naval command. As he quickly learned, this Brian had already attended special courses in Freiburg. He had been involved in special military operations because of his exceptional talents. Then he allegedly had an accident during his free time. And this, of all places, is on a Mediterranean island known for its legendary architecture and mystical past. The accident also had strange accompanying circumstances, such as the different perceptions of time among those involved. Even more intriguing to Tony was that the Naval Staff had sent him to Malta, of all places, when he had studied these cart ruts in the rocks for years. And now he learned from Sean that Brian had been looking at those cart ruts. Did someone in the military want Tony to look into something they didn't want to entrust to an official board of inquiry? That thesis settled in Tony's mind, and he decided to present this Lieutenant Pot with only a few more apparent nuggets as bait. They would all be facts, but still so unbelievable that Pot would not dare to mention them in his report. Then he would be rid of him quickly and could continue researching the matter later in peace. By dinner time, Tony had thought of a suitable story. He would have to be careful not to give too much away with his scientific enthusiasm.

Pot showed up for dinner in an evening dress reminiscent of a 1960s movie. Sean had completed his outfit with the mandatory long pants, a polo shirt, and flip-flops. When he read the Harry Potter ad on Sean's shoes, Tony had to grin.

Sitting at the table, he didn't keep them waiting long for his conclusion, "Well, I think we've done a pretty good job of researching the sequence of events. If I'm not mistaken, this Brian Wilson has been studying the ancient cultures of the Mediterranean for a long time. Sean confirmed that he took every opportunity to look at cultural treasures in his spare time. The hole in the ground had apparently been overlooked by the local authorities. They have since filled it in to prevent further accidents."

Here Pot interrupted him, "I don't want to question your expertise, but so far, we haven't heard anything new."

"Maybe so. I also wanted to help you write the official report faster. Do you want to hear my personal opinion? However, you might have them thrown around by your superiors."

"I need to know what's going on. Let it all out!" Pot replied euphorically.

"Good, then listen. There is an old legend about an advanced civilization in Malta, long before the pharaohs in Egypt. There were also giants living on the island who had to build monolithic structures as work-enslaved people. One of these structures is the temple complex of Hagar Qim. The giants lived in Ghar Dalam's cave, which still exists today. Traces have even been found there, dating back to 180,000 years."

Pot began to slide back and forth in his chair. This was probably not the story he was hoping to hear. When the appetizer came, Tony busied himself with it until Pot asked, "So what happens next?"

"Oh, right. Brian Wilson must have known about this legend and wanted to follow the cart ruts back to their origin."

"Their origin?"

"It is difficult to see today because of erosion. Some traces start at these burrows near Dingli rocks. There must have been prehistoric quarries at this site. The traces end at depths of up to 330 feet on the present seabed."

"A railroad to the mermaids, eh?" Pot tried to join in with a joke.

"Something like that," Tony replied. "Geologists can't explain how large blocks of stone could have been moved from this area to other parts of the world in the Stone Age. That would only be possible with functioning ocean shipping."

"I didn't even know that Maltese rock was found in other parts of the world," said Sean.

"No wonder. What cannot be explained is not published. I used to deal with it in my spare time. Now I'm even allowed to do research on it. Anyway, I have a theory, and I must prove it."

"I'm curious," Pot said.

"The holes in the earth in this area are of natural origin. However, someone must have noticed at some point that the holes can be put to practical use by making minor adjustments. Similar voids exist all over the world. Obviously, they were part of some transportation system. In my opinion, the holes were used to transport rocks unavailable in Malta and, conversely, to transport local material to other places. This was then probably a kind of ancient online trade for giants." Tony added, but Pot didn't seem to have understood the joke. Instead, he looked at Tony in disbelief as he chewed his food.

"And what about this rail system?" Sean wanted to know.

Tony stumbled and replied enthusiastically, "Exactly the right designation. It was indeed a rail system, but without rails, as we think of them today. Pipes were inserted into the notches in the rocky ground and contained a sound-transmitting fluid. As we know today, sound waves transport mass particles. However, the mass behaves in a very exotic way."

Sean's face lit up at the cue, "Exotic? That sounds sexy. Go on!"

"Whether you really find that sexy, I don't know. But in any case, experiments with sound waves could prove that there are so-called *phonons*. What is exotic here is that the mass of these particles is negative. The objects are therefore repelled by gravity. In this way, things could be made to float."

"And science hasn't come up with that idea yet?" Pot asked with a slightly sarcastic undertone.

Tony was not provoked by the question and replied, "But I'm a scientist. That's why you called me here. In any case, the sound waves were transmitted via this kind of rail system. As I said, the exotic behavior of the phonons generated in the process caused the negative gravity. This allowed the stones transported from the quarry to their destination suspended above the rails."

"What's on the seabed? That's where some tracks lead to, if I'm not mistaken?" Pot wanted to know who now seemed to be interested after all.

"The rails must have been formed during the last ice age because that was the only time the sea level was so low. They probably ended at the buildings that stood on the coastline of the island at that time. Unfortunately, all this lies underwater and under sediment deposits dozens of feet thick. Only with satellites can you see the remains of the structures."

"It seems to me that these are more like legends because if they were true, they would have been reported before, right?" said Pot.

"Some have reported. But all this does not fit into the current historical picture. Because sound technology and anti-gravity have no place in the Stone Age, the subject is ignored."

The main course was being served when Sean told Tony, "I searched for the construction company whose advertising we saw on the construction trailer. That company doesn't even exist in Malta."

Tony already had the next bite in his mouth when he answered, "That's right, they don't exist in Malta. But the port in the north is being expanded, and companies from Greece are involved. Chinese corporations are already involved in these construction companies almost everywhere."

"Unsurprisingly, they are also building their new Silk Road in the Mediterranean."

"But what do the Chinese want in Malta?" asked Sean.

"Good question. Maybe deals have already been made with Malta, too. Whoever owns the ports on the Mediterranean also has a lot to say about trade flows," Tony said. Pot didn't seem convinced by the arguments, and while poking at his fish, he said, "But maybe the construction truck was just bought by someone. That's not interesting at all."

The next day, Pot didn't want to go to the accident scene again. Since Sean preferred to spend his time at the beach, Tony went alone. Sean and Pot were back in Germany one day later. Sean heard nothing more about the Malta case for quite a while and supposed that the matter had been settled for him.

Δ

Freiburg, university campus

Sergei was dealing with the Oxford incident again. It was challenging to find out what contacts this Dr. Zhou had in his home country. To the outside world, it appeared that he was merely working on his own neurological project. Something was not right. The news was regularly leaking out in China about issues involving energy patterns around ancient cult sites in England. These reports also mentioned recent Chinese successes in paranormal research. For Sergei, this could have two reasons. Since the only known Chinese research project on the subject in England was the one Zhou was leading, his team had to be the source. Someone published unauthorized information, or Zhou was spied on by his own countrymen.

Nonetheless, Sergei thought it unlikely that a Chinese intelligence agency would publish its findings immediately. Then, Zhou would be more likely to act on his own account. Sergei wondered whether he should tip off the British authorities.

The phone rang. Sergei saw Gregor's face on the display and took the call, "Gregor, your face is all smeared! Have you been screwing with your vintage car again?"

"You're right," he replied, still out of breath."...I was listening to the radio on the side. Why don't you turn on the United Nations news channel?"

After the great pandemic that changed the world at the beginning of the second decade, regional conflicts have intensified. Therefore, a worldwide information channel of the United Nations was launched. Before this radio and television channel started, new conspiracy theories were sprouting. Among the craziest ideas was that aliens were running the station and would soon announce their takeover of earth. But this transmitter had changed something crucial all over the world. All nations committed to broadcasting UN news around the clock in the national language and in the original. This made it possible to receive the same news in all regions during international conflicts. All people could thus access world news without it being poisoned by war rhetoric and propaganda. This did not work everywhere, but it was a start.

Sergei immediately understood what Gregor was so worried about. Television also reported on a planned special session of the World Security Council. As a permanent member, China called this special session. News reports said they felt threatened by the Philippines because they were currently massively expanding their navy, seeking more presence in the Indo-Pacific region. On the other hand, countries bordering the China Sea, particularly, had felt threatened for years. China had begun to occupy islands in this region and build naval bases on them. This made it easier to control the sea routes. China justified its actions by defending its new Silk Road, which was particularly aggressively opposed by the United States. Some NATO countries, including Germany, began to show more presence with naval ships in the region in 2021 to maintain neutrality because of the tense situation. However, China was later able to limit that through its influence in the Security Council. Since then, as a countermeasure, NATO and Australia supported countries like Taiwan or the Philippines with military equipment to defend themselves in case of a threat. Now, this back and forth had reached a new level. The Chinese later found out that new types of German-built submarines were to patrol the Indo-Pacific in the future.

Sergei was unfamiliar with this type of submarine. Still, the last few days' events suggested that Brian Wilson was in one. In addition, Anna discovered that Brian and the whole crew might have been followed by a submarine of Chinese design. Of course, there could be other reasons behind the Chinese excitement.

Sergei asked Gregor again, "What do you think? Should we inform someone in the Security Council that there might be a threat of escalation somewhere in the ocean? I mean, because of the pursuit by an unknown submarine?"

Gregor thought about it for a moment and said, "That won't work. The Chinese or whoever is behind this will deny it and call it a distraction. So far, all we know is that it was built in China. Who controls it, nobody knows."

While Sergei listened, he researched his sources on the subject. One article immediately worried him, so he told Gregor, "This can't be true. I just found some information that must have come from the Chinese. Allegedly, one of the new German subs has been hijacked by terrorists. The target is still unclear, and nobody knows what weapons are on board. Any country could be the target of an attack. Maybe this issue is to mobilize the Security Council and the public. You know, the terrorist threat gets much more attention from the media than any arms exports by the Germans."

Gregor had an idea, "I will discuss this with my contact in the NATO staff. Perhaps there are also diplomatic ways. After all, neither Germany nor the EU has been accepted as permanent members of the Security Council. Therefore, this information should be mentioned by Americans or English in the meeting. By the way, I find it strange that the council wants to meet in person in New York. Lately, there have been no presence meetings because of the CO2 emissions."

"That's really strange. Maybe the arrangements are so secret that you don't want to send anything over the Internet. You know the danger of *deepfake*. Even fake government officials would be possible today."

"You're right. Also, it could be that the Chinese will bring up the terrorist threat issue as leverage. They might want to get NATO to sink that German submarine."

"This is some shit! What have we gotten ourselves into here? I want to keep Anna out of these things. The more she gets involved, the more likely she is to get in the line of fire," Sergei said.

Gregor tried to reassure him, "I will take care of Anna."

"You saw in Oxford how quickly it can become dangerous. Anna could have been dead if her body hadn't been able to defend itself against that anesthetic."

"You decide, Sergei. In any case, I'm ready to take care of Anna."

In the evening, all the media reported on the special meeting that would take place the next day in New York City. There was also speculation as to why all the participants wanted to be there in person. During the coverage, there was speculation about rumors that several issues were at stake. So, the general public at that time was only aware of the conflict with the Philippines and the increased danger because of a submarine allegedly stolen by terrorists.

Δ

Unknown place

At the same time, a conversation occurred between a teacher and his student in a place known only to a few creatures on the planet. Depending on the current function, the teachers were called *masters* or *mentors* in their culture.

"Will our effort be successful?" asked the disciple Thriot. He first wanted to find out if Master Shet-Ahma was ready for a conversation.

"Despite your short life, you've seen many changes and know that doing nothing is always the worst option."

"When I look at the inhabitants of this planet, I wonder if we're not doing some things wrong."

Shet-Ahma thought for a moment and said, "Access to your thoughts is blocked. Therefore, I cannot follow you at the moment. You always do that when something is troubling you or your beliefs are filled with doubt."

"As far as I know, we have very little influence on the decisions made in the Galactic Council."

"Little is more than nothing. We have at least been listened to for a long time, and our reports are taken very seriously. The current development and the phase *Achala* is in is unique in this part of the galaxy."

"Maybe even beyond that. But we don't fully know what influence other civilizations have on humans, do we? For example, the *Dark Grays'* activities are again more frequent. I've learned they interfere in many affairs and have also thwarted our plans several times."

"I don't like it when you call them the Dark Grays. It's a term humans use. The *Anabhu* are neither vicious figures of darkness nor less enlightened than we are. Remember that they were once created to serve their biological models."

"You know I mean it differently. In any case, the origin of the Anabhu remains in the dark for humans. As a result, they don't learn that their ancestors were once even more highly evolved than the Anabhu. The latter keep giving themselves new names when they come into contact with humans. The fact that they have problems with their replication doesn't make things easier, either. They still use earthly genetic material without the council's permission. Without the council, we'd be the only ones left looking out for humans. What is your opinion, does the council's interest in the special protection of this planet eventually wane? After all, some peoples of this galaxy already think the effort is not worth it."

"This opinion is likely to be held less by whole peoples and more by individuals represented on the council. There have always been a few among them who wanted more influence of their own on this planet. But the council knows how that turned out. Ultimately, it led to the old god wars. And the people are not supposed to know about that at the moment. They could blame the current negative development in their cultures on foreign influences. Then the autocrats among the people would feel even less obliged to go new ways to preserve their planet. At any rate, that is how the council sees it."

"What makes the council believe that human beings can do it independently?" the student inquired again.

"The new generations are different. They are beginning to break away from the delusions of prosperity. The higher level of education also makes them realize the planet's destruction. At the same time, more educational institutions are emerging again that include spiritual life. Thus, more people are gaining access to higher levels of consciousness. Also, the whole planet is a wondrous place. While this is happening, it is also becoming more interesting for beings from the *aka* willing to work as mentors. The fact that we have also stayed on the planet has helped to keep people's spiritual bond with the aka from breaking."

The student seemed unsettled, "I wonder if our influence is really that great. After all, we never actively intervene. When will people start to break away from the old dogmas?"

"They are already on that path but must agree first on a unified goal. Often, it is only the global catastrophes that make everyone pull together. Possibly, however, only after many have already not survived."

"What about those who once presented themselves as gods to mankind?"

"The Council's old ban is still valid. And that it is respected is also part of our tasks. Unfortunately, the people still have a long way to go before they achieve true independence. Their discord makes them slaves to their former creators. Much time will pass until they all remember the old rituals again. We, however, will remain only observers."

Thriot scrutinized his master's face very closely and said, "Have you ever thought about returning to the *aka*, Shet-Ahma?"

"You know, I've never really been away. My home is here as well as there. Our ancestors were born on this planet as *Manujas*. Subsequent generations are often drawn back to their roots."

"But you did live in the aka for thousands of years as a *Kha*, and as a *mentor*, you helped people evolve. Only recently did they give you a solid body again."

"No. No one gave it to me. I chose it that way. As I said, I was just drawn back to this planet."

"So you're sticking with the idea that humans can manage to protect and survive their habitat on their own?"

"This planet has become the treasure trove of ancient civilizations. Many alien species have found shelter here because their own habitat disappeared. The genetic material left behind and the knowledge stored in the rocks result from billions of years of development. Many extinct peoples have entrusted their knowledge to us survivors and rely on preserving it in this place. So you see, it's not just about these selfish people. It's also about the heritage they carry."

"You're avoiding my question. Can they make it on their own or not?"

"Honestly, I don't have an answer for that. Humankind is also just starting to think about it. Especially the younger generations must realize what a bad legacy they are supposed to inherit from the old ones. But still, their cultures are evolving so fast right now that we are regularly surprised by them. The greatest driving force is their curiosity. Although it wouldn't work without that curiosity, it's giving us a little trouble. As you know, they are getting closer and closer to us with their technology. We already have to go to great lengths to hide our existence."

"Then why don't we pull back a little further?"

"You will learn a lot about this world. We have a mission to fulfill from the Galactic Council. The closer we are to the people, the better we can protect them from the *Anabhu*. And then there's something else. As long as humans do not use the power of the global energy lines, we have to do it for them. Otherwise, seismic movements would have destroyed some of their inhabited areas long ago."

"I didn't know about this kind of protection. Is that why this base is in such a dangerous place?"

"Yes. That's also one of the things you should still know. You can find the calculations on energy ratios and predictions of natural disasters in the central repository."

"What actually makes us so sure that all these calculations are correct?" the student wanted to know.

"Trust and hope, Thriot. There is nothing more important among friends."

At the behest of his master, Thriot had been intensively studying the events on *Achala* during the last few days. In trying to understand the people, his interest in their behavior grew.

That day he met his master in the room for meditation. Before that, the two ate together. This allowed them to talk face-to-face. The Manuja knew it was essential to train their eyes, ears, and hands. Not only because otherwise unused parts of the body regressed. Cultural life was also changing. Other races, such as the ancestors of the Anabhu, had recognized this too late and then tried to genetically improve these physical disadvantages with hybrid offspring. But this also had advantages. As hybrid beings, the Anabhu were better able to adapt to space conditions and conditions on other planets.

Shet-Ahma began to speak acoustically again, "People call it —At the end of the world— when there is nothing in a place that seems attractive to them. It is hardly possible to find such places anymore. That worries us. Only this hideout and a few parts of Antarctica are left to us as places of retreat. Fortunately, we could get representatives of a former American government and the United Nations of this planet to agree to a chapter of the Galactic Code. This deals with the duty of the Council to ensure the survival of every intelligent species and its environment. Everything that could endanger survival was to be prevented by force if necessary. During this time, the base near the South Pole was expanded."

"This contract with humans has been around for a while, right?" the student asked.

"You could say that. It's just that hardly anyone overlooks it anymore. Such treaties only help if people do not make agreements with the Anabhu at the same time. Their pacts undermined our efforts, and since few individuals knew of such agreements, the nations played off against each other by the Anabhu. With the emergence of the first human specimens of *Generation Alpha*, ideological clashes increase. Authoritarian systems see their sphere of influence dwindle. With the advent of digital warfare, more and more countries are being infiltrated. The most intelligent among them are currently being fought particularly hard. We call them the masters of Generation Alpha."

"So, what contracts are most important to us right now?"

"Let's look at it together," said the master, activating a virtual overview on the wall with his right hand.

"Look, the last major treaty was concluded in 1959, according to this calendar. It was, by the way, the first time we were able to bring twelve states together. Thanks to the foresight of the Galactic Council, the United Nations had been established years before. With the end of the Second World War, this step was urgently needed. The Antarctic Treaty's main components were territorial claims regulations because some countries had already begun colonization. The Anabhu had a treaty with Nazi Germany in the 1930s to secure access to ancient Atlantis technology. This treaty contradicted all previous rules because the treasures, sealed since the glaciation of the continent, had been in our protected area for thousands of years. The only thing left for us Guardians to do was limit the damage by preventing further colonization. In addition to the international regulations, the Antarctic Treaty also contains another article. However, this was only agreed with the government in Washington. It is therefore classified as secret on their side."

"Is the United Nations privy to the amendment?"

"Unfortunately, only five member nations know this part of the agreement. These nations came together in 1946 to form the World Security Council. Tomorrow is the next meeting to which

I have been invited. We called together the most powerful nations when this earthly council was formed. We informed them that we would not tolerate the planet's destruction. Only these five permanent members know about the cooperation between humans and non-human intelligence. As is often the case, the point is to keep our presence on the planet a secret from humankind. This was not our wish, but the Galactic Council still believed that humans must be slowly prepared for this contact. You can thus figure out for yourself what points had to be kept secret."

"How is secrecy maintained? You can't explain UFO sightings to people today with divine apparitions as you did 500 years ago."

"Oh, I see you've been taking advantage of my absence and studying human cultural objects."

The disciple showed his master what he had found in the documents of humankind. One of the paintings depicted the religious scene with a flying boat of the *Anabhu*. In the background, a person points with his hand to the flying object.

Madonna with child and the boy John,
Palazzo Vecchio in Florence (probably by Sebastian Mainardi)

"I find it exciting what artists, even in this unenlightened time, already dared to do. Certainly, people sometimes stand open-mouthed in front of such illustrations and wonder without really understanding."

"But this is normal. As with us, there is also social awareness among people. Only when a certain knowledge becomes general knowledge does it become generally accepted. That's a process that can take a long time. Change is uncomfortable and is rejected at first."

"What exactly does the Antarctic Supplemental Treaty contain?"

"The American military is protecting our base. The satellite images are neutralized, and there is a no-fly zone over the entry crater in the ice. In return, we have agreed not to perform any conspicuous flight maneuvers. The Anabhu, yet, have their own rules. As you know, they have already developed different subspecies. Nobody knows if they always follow their own rules among themselves. That makes it unmanageable for us. It is dangerous for people to contract with them because no one knows which subspecies they belong to. It has happened that humans have been sold obsolete and even faulty technology, which their scientists then tinker with for years. In return, the people are supported by the Anabhu in political actions. These are usually disinformation campaigns. Such things can destabilize entire states."

"It really sounds like humans have a lot of work to do. They could understand thinking beings better if they trained their instincts again."

"Don't forget that they only started to recover from the global catastrophe 12,000 years ago. Their collective memory and access to the *aka* were completely wiped out by the end of the last ice age. In their history books, cultural development begins long after the ice age."

"Who should be surprised? As far as I know, we Manujas also suffered from the Great Extinction. Much of our knowledge also disappeared. Only the Guardians of Knowledge were able to save some of it. The people have found some in the land of the Nile. However, they do not understand it yet."

"You saved the most important thing!"

"Yes, I know, access to our shared cultural memory in the aka. But all attempts to pass the key to this to mankind are hindered by the Anabhu."

"The Anabhu will probably try to use the next point mutations in the brain of humans for their purposes. The new generation of humans will usher in the Age of Knowledge as planned. After they discovered the *ARHGAP11B Human Genesis Gene*, its origin will not be hidden for long. Of course, they have already discovered that 11B is a copy of gene 11A, which could never have happened through the natural evolutionary process. It would have taken several million years for that to happen, and countless intermediate species would have arisen during that time. We know that the Anabhu performed similar genetic manipulations on primates long ago. Unfortunately, they are pursuing their own goals to restart their evolution, which has reached a standstill. Therefore, one of our tasks must be to protect humans from the selfish actions of the Anabhu."

"I don't know as much about human genetics as you do. How does the human genesis gene actually work?" Thriot wanted to know from his master.

"As I said, humans gave the gene the name ARHGAP11B. It resulted from a point mutation, which led to accelerated cerebral cortex and skull enlargement. With the larger neocortex, thinking, imagination and language became possible."

"But the survivors had this knowledge after the Flood. Why did it disappear later? And they must also have known that this intervention had no natural cause."

"Only the priests had this knowledge. For their students, they even depicted it on their sculptures. But with the power struggles of the following generations, the priests died, and only the stones remained."

"Can I find examples of this in people's archives?"

"Of course. Humans usually depicted the creators and their helpers as gods. Look, here's an example from Egypt..."

The projection screen showed a god carved in stone with the name Bes.

"Do you see it?"

"Very impressive how clear the language is. The god-helper holds with his hands a human child's head. Probably the result of his work."

"The story begins at the top left, with the third eye still closed. This is duplicated with the help of the *Ankh tool*. The eye on the right then has a pupil, so it can see. Seeing in the sense of consciousness. Finally, the youngest generations have already begun to train their abilities. You may have a chance to meet one of them in person someday."

Egyptian depiction of the creation of a human child by the dwarf-like god Bes (Temple of Philae [31])

Before the master ended the conversation with his disciple, he addressed something else, "Now, I will prepare for the meeting with the representatives of the planet. As I mentioned before, they have asked me to attend a special United Nations Security Council meeting. The People's Republic of China asked for the meeting. One representative from each of the Manujas and the Anabhu has been invited. Although, we non-human participants will only be heard on one unique topic, which, as usual, the public is not supposed to know about. On the side of the humans also, only the five permanent members take part. Not even the Secretary General of the United Nations will attend the meeting.

Incidentally, the Chinese leadership is portrayed as aggressive by Western countries. China is using its economic power to expand. Consequently, the power of Western alliances on the planet is dwindling. For decades, the West has accused the Chinese of stealing technology, even though their intelligence agencies are equally stealing what comes before their eyes. It's just that the Western world and Russia have long focused on military espionage. China was cleverer. They took over entire industrialized nations and massively expanded military and space technology later when there was enough money."

"Then everyone does the same thing and holds it against the other side as a crime. How cynical!"

"That's the way it is. However, something has come up that could decisively change the balance of power."

"Does this have anything to do with the artifact of the ancient settlers that is in our care?"

The master replied, "I will know tomorrow. We cannot trust the official rhetoric. I have to look the people present in the face and feel their body radiation. Only then can I tell who is telling the truth. There is still hope that the public does not know where the artifact is hidden. Those who empower themselves with this object and understand how to use it can avail themselves of the powers of *Shiva*. This, in turn, would change the balance of power on the planet. We should prevent that from happening. In the end, however, people decide for themselves. We outsiders can only try to exert our influence."

"I don't understand why we leave it up to the people to decide whether or not to use Shiva's power," Thriot admitted.

"This is also one of the complicated issues from earthly history. After the last god wars on this planet, the Galactic Council negotiated a compromise with all sides. People know three main gods from *Indian mythology*, of which Shiva is considered the destroyer. They were given an eternity guardian role for Achala or Earth as it is called by humans."

"Does that mean people accept Shiva and the other two main gods as protection for human civilization?" Thriot wanted to know.

"Unfortunately, it is not that simple. In many religious writings, a lot is left out. So, the story often appears very one-sided. Only when you put all the records side by side does one thing come out; there have always been different gods, and they disagreed on how to deal with us Manujas. The same was true of humans later on."

The student nodded, "I understand. Only those who know all the scriptures can get a picture of the ancient world."

"By the way, among the rules of the Galactic Council is that the cycle of life must repeat itself through perpetual renewal. However, this renewal happens in nature over sizable periods, such as the lifetime of a star. Unfortunately, the principle of regeneration was abused again and again. For example, the self-appointed gods decided when to make a species disappear again. The council always tried to prevent this. Nevertheless, they could not do anything against the repeated destruction of whole species on this planet.

The Manujas, too, eventually became victims of genocide when the divisions among our people became so great that cultural progress halted. Meanwhile, there has been no genocide of this magnitude for 4,500 years. But let's look at the inhabitants of this planet today. They are already back at a point where one war zone after another is preventing people from progressing. We Manujas were protected by a treaty our ancestors signed with the Galactic Council. This treaty stipulated that everyone who had reached a certain level of spiritual maturity was allowed to leave the planet. For humans, however, it turned out differently. For their warlike culture to disappear, the memory of the old order was to be taken from them."

Thriot expressed his agreement, "I already know a lot about that. Like you, not all Manujas have left the earth. Some of our species, too, have allowed themselves to be worshipped as gods by humans. This is how cultures flourished in Sumer, Egypt, and Central America."

"Whether everything happened exactly the same way, no one knows today. But we know that this compromise was accepted by all parties in the Galactic Council. Regardless, the Anabhu continuously tried to manipulate and enslave people in their sense. Others, such as the three main Hindu gods, opposed this. However, they let people decide for themselves what actions to take. You can see that several non-human races are influencing earthly civilization and that it is almost impossible to keep track of it all. That is another reason people do not want to be educated about it yet. And now comes the crucial point: Should people one day use the artifact to claim Shiva's powers, they will get them. The consequences would be incalculable. It could happen again as described in the religious writings of the people: A war of the gods in heaven and on earth, combined with the erasure of human memories."

Δ

New York City, United Nations Grounds

Because the conference participants were to meet in person, there were also opportunities for contacts outside the protocol. For example, on the eve of the Security Council meeting, a conversation occurred between German Foreign Minister Isabel Friedemann and her Chinese counterpart. This was to take place in a small office on the hotel corridor of the Chinese delegation. Two security guards were posted there to ensure an undisturbed conversation.

After two hours of discussion, there was still no word from his foreign minister. Therefore, the German head of the organization contacted her by cell phone. She immediately replied that he should organize an online meeting with NATO headquarters for the same evening. Usually, a representative of the European Commission was also invited to such arrangements. At precisely 10 p.m. New York time, the monitors went on for all participants. Several NATO generals had dialed in via the specially secured line, as had Pablo Cerrah, the European Foreign and Security Policy Commissioner.

A moment too late, Rear Admiral Breede joined them. As the person responsible for special operations in NATO's naval command, he had also been rung out of bed. A cursory glance at his face made him appear calm to the untrained, but inside he was seething. He had been entrusted with the delicate mission with the DaVinci. Now the whole thing was threatening to blow up. And this was in a politically tense situation where China was expanding its expansion policy with enormous financial resources and unprecedented high technology. Every month there were new surprises from China when technical innovations were presented in the Middle Kingdom, as they now called their homeland again.

Decades earlier, only the United States had seen anything like this. Breede knew what the name Middle Kingdom meant politically. It was a matter of determining where the planet's new economic and political center would be located in the future. In the meantime, the entire Chinese people had become correspondingly self-confident. This broke out now. After this, people were humiliated for centuries from the outside. The West had continued this tradition in the conviction of its own superiority.

Breede had studied Asian culture and the geopolitical interests of the countries in that region very carefully. Whether military or political, anyone who wanted to understand the Chinese had to start far in the past. Only then could one learn the characteristics of Asian culture and its spirituality. Because this was difficult for Christian-minded Europeans and Americans, NATO began to train some leaders in this direction years ago.

Rear Admiral Breede had become one of these specialists and was now practicing meditation. However, he had scoffed at it just a few years earlier. He had a moving period when he was introduced to *Zen teachings* for a few months in Asia. There he also learned to meditate. At that time, a change in his thinking began. It seemed as if new networks were forming in his brain and beyond. As a result, he became more open to completely new things in his life. Meditating with the help of Zen exercises can help to always look for a contradiction in everything. One could get closer to the solution without prejudice if this was resolved. Breede had memorized the saying of a monk: "To be wise is to know how little one knows. Only one's own arrogance stands in the way of wisdom."

The economic advisors of Western politicians also began to realize that China's economic and military progress could not be countered with sanctions or tariffs. They first had to defend themselves against China's most dangerous weapon. That was access to the minds of its adversaries. Some still believed in those days that this was fiction. But China had already bought its people's willingness to forego data protection and thus protect personal rights. Digitization and the new prosperity had blinded its people to this kind of control of the masses. This would increasingly extend to political leaders beyond their national borders. The knowledge of a person's thoughts, inclinations, and everything else in their head could make them susceptible to blackmail. But the general public was even easier to influence. Targeted disinformation in social media could create entirely new currents. Anyone who believed this could be contained simply by adapting the laws was sorely mistaken. Rules did not apply in the realm of electronic data streams.

All these things went through Breede's mind before he dialed into the conference with the German foreign minister. The fact that he had been invited could only mean one thing. Something about the "DaVinci" mission had to have leaked out. Worse, possibly the Chinese already saw what such a weapon could do on their country's borders. He had gotten involved in something threatening to escalate and possibly cause an international crisis.

Friedemann could see the excitement at the beginning of the meeting. Without much preamble, she began to report on the unofficial conversation with her counterpart from Beijing, "... it looks like all the hype about the Security Council is just a pretext. The official reason for the meeting in New York is that China is again complaining about Western naval forces' presence in the Pacific. They feel threatened. But we have been arguing about this for almost ten years now. So, this is an issue we could have negotiated without meeting on short notice. So, the fact that the Council is meeting in person tomorrow must have another reason. I am told in private that the Chinese believe terrorists have hijacked a German submarine. To date, I don't have more details on this. That is why I have asked for this topic to be postponed. The naval command in Rostock has also not yet been able to tell me anything about this. Rear Admiral Breede, I hope you will be able to find out more details by tomorrow morning. I don't want to be the world's laughingstock should the Chinese present unpleasant facts. Should military activity occur in the world's oceans, incalculable diplomatic conflicts would follow. In such a case, we would also be in a domestic political mess because the action is not legitimized by the German parliament. Do you have anything to say to me, Breede?"

The situation was even worse than Breede had imagined. He, therefore, answered evasively for the time being, "Dear Madam Minister. I can only see one thing clear at the moment. The Chinese leadership has once again managed to poke the Western alliance with its nose at its own weaknesses. We don't have exact knowledge, so we're on the defensive. Everything our services have been able to provide so far is based on rumor. In the meantime, I was also informed by my British naval colleagues about a possible terrorist threat. They also assume the theft of a German submarine. If you don't mind, I will clearly tell this group of participants what I think."

"Please be quite frank!" Friedemann replied.

"The facts already provide one insight: possibly through purposeful disinformation and influence on Western intelligence agencies, we cannot present the situation clearly. This will make us look foolish in a meeting of the Security Council. In this case, I can only advise expanding the circle of allies beyond NATO."

"What do you mean?" wanted Friedemann to know.

"As a soldier, my strategy always sees only two options when dealing with international forces. Either you win them as allies, or you soon lose them to the enemy. In plain language, since there is no neutrality in the Security Council, we should seek an alliance with Russia. Only the permanent members have a veto. The British will vote with the Americans. Consequentially, we Europeans are left with only France as a voice on the Security Council. The French have been purposefully bombarded by the Chinese with completely different issues. Perhaps they see no reason to decide. Since they know nothing about the current situation, they will abstain approvingly from a possible vote. And that suits the Chinese just fine."

"Please excuse my directness, but I think you're out of your mind!" the foreign minister said indignantly.

"With respect, you sound like you don't know that most decisions are made exclusively by the five permanent members," Breede shot back.

Here, Pablo Cerrah intervened as EU Commissioner for Foreign Affairs and Security Policy, "Please forgive me, Madam Minister. I must vehemently disagree here. With all the neutrality that I must maintain as a representative of the European Parliament, I would like to note that Rear Admiral Breede is right in this case. Although I regret it, his assessment of the political situation within the EU is plausible. We have known for years that the People's Republic of China is trying to increase its influence on EU countries. To do this, they are making targeted investments in critical infrastructure. This makes the countries susceptible to blackmail, so the member states no longer speak with one voice. The EU can no longer speak unitedly against China when criticizing it for human rights violations. Here, the plan has already worked. The Chinese leadership has also learned from Russia how it succeeded in playing Western countries against each other. In this way, the Russians have strengthened their opposition to Europe. Now China sees its chance to present its political system as superior. Because in our democracies, we first have to discuss every problem in the parliament, everything takes much longer. I don't want to question that today. Yet, we should quickly agree with Russia that there should be no security-related vote that would further weaken the influence of the West in the Pacific region."

"You've got your work cut out for you. How do you plan to achieve it?" asked Friedemann.

"There are enough ideas. I would start by lifting some of the sanctions against Russia. Americans and Chinese are the ones who benefit the most from these economic blockades, aren't they?"

Friedemann's face contorted into a grimace, which did not precisely express approval. She left Cerrah's question about the sanctions unanswered because she thought it diplomatically inappropriate to go into it in this circle. But she said, "Let's summarize: We must convince all allies not to agree to any resolution sought by China at tomorrow's meeting. I will be meeting with my foreign minister colleagues later tonight. I will also raise the issue of Russia's involvement and the issue of sanctions."

After this discussion, Breede had a fear. The minister did not know anything about what the five permanent members of the Security Council would discuss in the secret meeting. Thus, she would run the risk of falling into the trap of the public engagement that would take place earlier. Since neither Germany nor the EU was among them, it would be about something that would not be mentioned on UN television. Judging by the American general's expression, he seemed to think similarly. Breede also had the impression that he detected a little arrogance in his facial expression. After all, this was precisely part of the distinctive world politics that the "Big Five" had settled among themselves since the forties of the last century: Diplomatic relations with non-human intelligence.

Both the Chinese and Russian presidents arrived late at the Norwegian Room. The two took their seats at the same time. It was impossible to tell whether the delay indicated a previous vote or was meant to symbolize unity between the two states.

The Chinese foreign minister introduced the initial topic during the first twenty minutes. China's threat in the Indo-Pacific region from foreign naval forces had increased again. After Australia began to reinforce its naval forces with American submarines, they saw the danger of nuclear conflict in the area. But now, the Philippines also wanted to start equipping its maritime fleet with tactical submarines. Their equipment would be capable of patrolling undetected near Chinese shores. This armament would constitute a dangerous provocation. After explaining the threat situation, which was done in an unusually sharp tone, the speaker suddenly changed his volume and continued speaking much more calmly. He explained to those present that China had agreed on a few points the previous evening in bilateral consultations with the countries involved and NATO representatives. Germany probably also realized that delivering such weapons to this area would not be a good prerequisite for joint peace efforts.

Under these conditions, China was willing to withdraw its resolution request.

The second item on the agenda was more exciting. In this room, an old projection screen was still used, which covered the famous Phoenix painting during the presentations. The Chinese delegation showed video footage of a submarine with German insignia. The spokesman stated, "According to our information, one Class 212 fighter submarine is scheduled for delivery to the Philippines. To our knowledge, the name is Leonardo DaVinci. We have been able to observe this sub for a while. It was on a test cruise in the North Atlantic. It has been missing for at least 60 hours now, and we must consider the possibility of hijacking by terrorists. It looks like this fact is being kept secret by the German side."

"What evidence is there of a kidnapping?" the Russian foreign minister wanted to know.

High-resolution satellite images appeared on the screen. The details of these videos were already impressive. Those present were even more amazed by what followed. The outline of a submarine became visible, which looked very much like the 212A boat class. A helicopter hovered above it, and people were lowered down the rope. A little later, they boarded the submarine via one of the two hatches available. A later film clip showed the DaVinci slowly descending.

"Submarine vehicles of this class usually do not go deeper than 490 feet when they want to move fast. We could not detect any sign of the DaVinci within a 540-nautical mile radius just one hour after the submergence. Our sensors can locate all submarines down to this depth. Therefore, we assume that the boat has either sunk or been hijacked. Now we ask the German delegation for a statement."

Friedemann leaned to the right of their table neighbor and whispered, "An attempt to provoke us. Maybe this way, they will learn more about the actual diving depth or camouflage technique."

Finally, the spokesman for the German delegation switched on his control panel, which was to be used to present the media he had brought with him on the wall.

Then it was Friedemann's turn, "Unfortunately, the German navy had not been allowed to clarify these facts in advance. We believe that a direct inquiry from the Chinese side to my ministry would have sufficed. Thus, I regret that this enormous effort is now being made to clarify the matter. This is probably a huge misunderstanding. It would be fascinating to know what sources of information the Chinese authorities relied on upon this."

Scattered laughter could be heard around the table while the Chinese delegation looked around as if transfixed. Of course, they did not respond to this innuendo. Friedemann cleverly made her listeners wait a little longer before she continued with her explanation, "But we can reassure you. The submarine Leonardo DaVinci has neither crashed nor fallen into dubious hands. Please see..."

The screen showed short video clips of the DaVinci's arrival at the naval port near the Belgian coastal town of Koksijde. Friedemann was well informed about all the details this time and explained, "As you can see, the described sub reached the naval base again two days ago. Commander Lange sees off his crew ashore during the final roll call. Both submarine and crew have returned safely. In addition, we took a look at the ship's log. There were only minor complications during the test run. Due to a health emergency, the DaVinci had to surface in the North Atlantic to provide medical attention to one of the crew members. This is also why the DaVinci met up with a Belgian frigate in this sea area. So, hijacking by another warship is completely out of the question."

In fact, the identification number of the boat in the naval port could be recognized in the pictures. This was later officially confirmed by the Chinese delegation. Those who knew Commander Lange could have assuredly seen this man in the photos. Technicians from Germany's Special Defense Force for Cybercrime, which was launched in 2019, also did not notice anything that would indicate the video footage was faked.

After clarification of this agenda item, the official meeting of the Security Council was over. The Chinese motion for a resolution was withdrawn as announced. Of course, Friedemann could assume that the matter would still proceed through diplomatic channels. But she was much more concerned with what the five permanent members would discuss in their subsequent secret session.

The Technical Reconnaissance Division of the German Intelligence Service had informed her government early that morning that two participants from unknown nations had been invited to the meeting. Friedemann suspected what this might mean, but it was all just speculation. Breede also seemed to know more about it than he admitted. She decided to stay on the case and not let her own soldiers lead her around by the nose. She thought lobbyists might have nested in the military to circumvent licensing requirements for arms exports. But since she knew that Breede also maintained contacts with spiritual circles, he could also be involved in secret research with a paranormal background. Secretly, Friedemann was fascinated by such things. She knew countless reports about the study from the last century, which had taken place in the Soviet Union, the USA, and Israel. As a young woman, she enthusiastically read the autobiography of the magician Uri Geller. He described in one episode how he was asked by Mexican President Echevaría to search for oil in the Gulf of Mexico. Most of his stories would never have become so popular had it not been for the proven interest of the FBI and CIA.

The "Big Five" met in the late afternoon in a smaller room for their meeting of the Security Council's permanent members. The representatives of the five countries were already present and were now waiting for two more participants. This meeting room was built on an underground floor during the last major renovation. The circular room had massive walls and doors separated from the outer areas by an airlock. In addition, the inner site had been built to be bug-proof. Even the translators customary for UN meetings did not participate in the discussions. Those who needed translation assistance took care of it.

Many visitors to the New York site learned for the first time on guided tours that the entire UN building complex was not on US territory at all. The area has been considered an international site since its inception.

One of the two entrances to the room led directly to the underground parking garage. This entrance was guarded by UN police officers waiting for the arrival of the missing participants. Neither the names nor the origin of the guests arriving at that moment was mentioned in the minutes. The organizers provided only the synonyms Guest A and Guest M.

Almost simultaneously, two black SUVs entered the underground parking level. While three figures jumped out of one car and ran toward the meeting room, only the passenger door opened in the second SUV, and a tall, bald man in a dark suit slowly ran after the three others. There was something comical about the scene. The three more miniature figures wore skin-tight clothing and had hoods pulled over their heads. The figure from the second SUV was much taller, and from the side, it looked as if he was being escorted by the three small ones. At the entrance to the boardroom, the tiny figures stopped. One was holding a device in the room. Possibly he was testing the air quality. The "giant" waited behind them for so long. Finally, one of the preceding trio entered the hall after taking off his hood. The other two went back into the tunnel. As they passed the tall man waiting behind them, they all bowed to express their respect. When the hall door closed, representatives from seven different nations were inside.

The light was dimmed. Two opposite doors in the circular room pointed precisely north and south. The walls consisted of thirty-two wall segments. On each were transparent discs of a *metamaterial*. They owed its remarkable properties to exceptional ability. They influence light or sound different than any natural materials. When the discs were illuminated, they produced images that changed depending on the temperature and color of the light. Such metamaterial doesn't exist in nature and was presented to the public for the first time in 2010. Illuminated by the lamps on the ceiling, a different image now appeared on each of these discs. There were thirty-two simple symbols in total.

The floor consisted of rectangular natural stone slabs. The rectangle in the center was laid in a north-south direction and had seven recognizable points. Anyone familiar with religious mythologies would suspect some special symbolism in the number seven. Depending on the origin of the particular creation myth, there would be various possible interpretations. Christians might think of John's Revelation and his letter to the seven churches. Everyone probably knew the Menorah from the Jewish sanctuaries, the seven-branched candelabrum. From Islam, the

Seven Saints of Marrakesh were well known. This list could be continued indefinitely. But perhaps the artists and architects of this room were also thinking in cosmic terms. Looking up at the night sky, one notices seven stars in the constellation of the Little Bear. One of them is the North Star, which was used by hikers and sailors as a guide when they lost their bearings.

However, since guest A and guest B were present, the atmosphere had something spooky for people. The two had mastered telepathic communication and could read the energy signature of other living beings. Therefore, this room was equipped with unique technical means to create equal opportunities. The energy transmission between the *morphic fields* of living beings was suppressed. For this, neither electronics nor electricity was necessary. Only the correct arrangement of the crystals in the minerals of the walls was enough to disturb these fields. A high quartz crystal content in the sand, condensed at high pressure, produced a piezoelectric effect. Everyone knows this from the small lighters to ignite the gas flame. As a side effect, a permanent electromagnetic field was created. The round shape of the room favored the impact. Thus, thought transmission became almost impossible. At least, those present could neither communicate telepathically nor with electronic means such as cell phones to the outside. The technology for this had been used on earth thousands of years ago. Regardless, the representatives of modern times had learned how it worked only a few decades ago.

When the building complex was renovated a few years earlier, the architects received instructions to use certain materials to construct this room. After the opening, the representatives of the people of guest A refused any meeting in this room. They were probably unwilling to give away the advantage their special abilities offered them. On that day, A would be present for the first time. The reason for the change of mind was probably the urgency with which the matter was to be discussed.

The small number of participants did not require a protocol for the proceedings. The rules of conduct for meetings of this particular kind have applied since the Security Council was established in 1946. This had not changed much up to that day. Each of the permanent members of this body had the right to convene such a meeting. Upon request, representatives of nations that were not members of this standing committee could also be invited. All contracting parties were obliged to appear if one side wished to do so. Whoever made this request also took over the organization and set the agenda. This time it was up to the Chinese side.

In the morning's public conference, the whole world had been informed that the disappearance of a German submarine was a misunderstanding that could be quickly cleared up. Something quite different was discussed in this secret meeting in a small circle. A film was shown as a projection above the center of the room to prove that Germany tested not one but two submarines of the same type in the Atlantic. However, only one of them had returned so far. The British prime minister asked immediately, "Why did you let the world believe that the issue was settled? What is all this fuss about? We could have taken the Germans to task this morning."

Guest A took over the answer to this, "We, the Anabhu, have advised our partners in the Middle Country to go this way. As you know, we consider the order that prevails there to be the most advanced on the planet. Therefore, we try to contain any threat at an early stage."

"But what threat are we actually talking about here? We have already dealt extensively with the presence of the European and American military in the Indo-Asian region. We will support monitoring the maritime Silk Road and ensure access to these waters for other countries," declared France's president.

As one was used to from China's president, he responded to the previous speaker with an impenetrable expression on his face, "Right. We have come to an agreement on that. However, as far as the missing sub is concerned, the earth could face a different threat. The consequences would be as proportions as no currently living earthling has ever seen."

Although she had shown little emotion, the British prime minister made a startled face and said, "Please don't let us guess around here and get to the point."

Now it was the task of the Chinese side to explain their point of view in more detail. For this purpose, pictures of the German Himalayan expedition were shown, led by Ernst Schäfer at that time. The president's spokesman commented on the photographs thus:

"In 1939, a statue was stolen by the Germans in Tibet. As it is known, the Tibetan monks refused to sell it to them before. According to experts, the statue was actually only a few years old. However, it was made from the fragment of an ancient iron pillar. The iron, in turn, came from the famous Chinga meteorite. Probably in the time of the *Bon religion*, many sacred objects were created from this meteorite, including iron pillars that can still be found in Asia today. This statue and the pieces of the iron pillar are cultural objects of the Chinese people. The 9.5 inches tall statue is known today as the Buddha statue with the *swastika* on the belly. Possibly, that is why the Germans considered this statue valuable. They probably did not realize at that time that it was made from a piece of an ancient legendary iron pillar. As everyone knows, the remaining part of the artifact was hidden by the Tibetan monks. After the Germans left, they brought it out of the country. It has been kept on the North American continent ever since.

We accept the temporary seizure by the Manuja people, but we would like to issue a warning! There is a strong suspicion that the Germans have returned to search for the rest of the iron pillar. During their research, they possibly came across the real purpose of the object, which is broken today. As our security services learned, a group of monks in India decided to take possession of all parts of the original pillar. These monks, to our knowledge, have anti-state Tibetan patrons."

The British prime minister frowned and protested at the comment that it should be the property of the Chinese people:

"I'd like to point out that the United Kingdom considers Tibet's current affiliation with the People's Republic of China to be contrary to international law. Chinese claims of ownership are totally unacceptable in this context."

The US president now intervened, urging China, "First, please explain why you assume that any Germans want to capture the artifact."

"Dearly beloved! We, of course, have evidence to support our claim."

Then followed a series of video recordings that had to come from a surveillance camera. The location given was an exhibition site in Dhar, India. Two men in monk's clothes and a European-looking man in tourist clothes and a backpack could be seen. The European guy was handling some sort of measuring device near the items exhibited. The explanation was as follows, "We have asked the Indian authorities for information about this man. He does not have an Indian passport and did not enter as a tourist. But we were still able to establish his identity. Chief Warrant Officer Brian Wilson is an American naval officer currently attached to a special unit of the German navy. He also holds a German passport. To our knowledge, the commando belongs to a NATO unit for worldwide special operations. Here, the present representatives of the North Atlantic Alliance should perhaps be able to give us information!"

As the Chinese president spoke, the American's expression darkened. It was not difficult to see that she was surprised by the Chinese's detailed knowledge. She had no idea about the special commando to which this Brian Wilson was supposed to belong.

Further images from a satellite perspective were shown. This offered a bright, thin line in the water of the North Atlantic, running from north to south. While individual sections of the trace in the water were magnified, the explanation was, "We were able to identify a German-built submarine as the cause of this underwater trace. The magnification shows this underwater vehicle at a depth of 330 feet with a length of 200 feet. It is moving forward with a supercavitation propulsion system. The external dimensions and sound signature prove that it is the lost twin of the DaVinci."

As the Chinese side continued to speak, images were shown one after another of the submarine passing Cape Horn and then heading northwest along Chile's Pacific coast.

"Along with the United States of America and the Russian Federation, Germany probably also has this propulsion technology. Although the 'DaVinci twin' has not yet reached the speed of sound, it was fast enough to leave the telltale glowing effects in the water. Currently, there are many indications that their target could be the secret hiding place of the artifact."

France's president said calmly, "We all know that this object is actually a sanctuary of all humankind and must not be understood as the property of a single people under any circumstances. When the Tibetan faith representatives handed over the main piece of the artifact to the world community at that time, everyone believed that the object must never again fall into the hands of individual people. We do not know what the intentions of the occupants of this sub really are. In any case, we must prevent them from finding the hiding place and reassemble all the artifact pieces."

Finally, guest M, called Shet-Ahma by the others, said, "As a representative of the *Manujas*, I agree with the French President. I also suggest leaving the discussion about property claims of individual nations outside. The League of Nations, whose most important representatives are in this room, had already agreed on this matter decades ago. The parts of the iron pillar once belonged to an engineering facility in what is now India. It was a gift of Shiva to humankind. Therefore, we cannot accept claims of ownership by individual nations. The hiding place of the artifact must remain secret. The recovery and its reuse may only occur if humanity decides it together."

Guest A, who represented the *Anabhu* people, was still holding back. It was clear to Shet-Ahma that this was not necessarily a good sign. The Anabhu were interested in alliances only if they benefited themselves. It was likely that the Chinese leadership had been informed by them about the renewed search for the artifact. Neither the Anabhu nor the Chinese leadership was interested in the reappearance of the ancient relics. Both parties wanted to prevent contact with the old Asian gods. In addition, other people's welfare played only a minor role for the Anabhu. They saw humans as a source of genetic replenishment, replacing their own physical degeneration. The fact that they could not freely dispose of the genetic material of earthly living beings was only due to the presence of other non-human races. Of course, Shet-Ahma knew very well that the Anabhu would like nothing better than to make the artifact disappear forever. This would deprive people of the possibility of communicating with Shiva and asking the old gods for help. Yet, the current dispute over the artifact provided an excellent opportunity to drive a deeper wedge between the Western alliance and the newly strengthening alliance between China and Russia. Nothing would be more harmful to the exploitation of the human race than the unification of all earthly peoples.

The meeting of the seven representatives finally ended with an agreement. The Manujas would remain the guardians of the artifact. No one should be allowed access to the hiding place. Shet-Ahma noted that they would not use force to deny anyone entry, but he would do everything possible to maintain the existing cover.

The American side continued to cordon off the hideout over a wide area. Since it was an American territory, this would be in the interest of national security anyway. Due to their claim to the ancient object, which they believe belongs to the cultural property of the People's Republic of China, the Chinese side abstained from voting on this point.

CHAPTER 9

The Pacific Ocean, southwest of Mexico

Monika pulled open the tiny curtain to gently shake Brian awake. Only when that didn't help did she address him, "I'm sorry to wake you. There's bad news!"

He didn't want to open his eyes because being awakened with a negative message could bring bad luck. With his eyes closed, he thought: *Is she exaggerating? If people exaggerate, they mainly make themselves attractive. But that's not Monika's style at all.*

This realization finally alarmed him: "What is it?" he tried to say but only managed a croak.

"The captain wants to see you. There must be trouble," said Monika and disappeared again.

"What happened? Hopefully, not nearly as much shit as I just dreamed," Brian asked the watch officers in the command room after he had duly reported for duty.

Lange stood behind the seats of the two sonar technicians, looking at the monitors, "I think you should see this, too. It appears we have visitors."

Sitting in front of the sonar monitor, Peter said to Brian, "I think you were right in your guess. X1 was near us all the time. The signals must be coming from there. They camouflage themselves and their communications so perfectly that our instruments can't detect it."

"So, it was not vain to have taken you on board!" Peter added.

"I've gotten better feedback than that!" Brian countered, well aware that Peter had meant this remark only jokingly.

Lange said, "When Lieutenant Gross makes such a statement, you must take it as huge praise. But seriously. Your idea to investigate the signatures of sound waves according to mathematical patterns has brought a breakthrough. Unfortunately, all we know now is that it is a type of boat of

Chinese design and must be equipped with unknown communication technology. We don't know what they're talking about yet, though. Any ideas, Wilson, on how we can translate this?"

"They don't use a binary system for the digital signals like our mobile data networks do. It looks more like quantum encryption. Without a quantum computer, our technology would take years to translate a word."

"How in the world do they get a quantum computer into the submarine. The ones I know of are still way too unwieldy," said someone from the crew.

"I don't think they have a quantum computer as we know it. Either they found a simple way to make quantum key exchange usable for mobile transmission, or they're using something that's been around on earth for thousands of years and at all prehistoric cultural sites: Stones."

"Huh?"

"Yes, you heard right. They might just have certain minerals on board. Stones with a high quartz content, for example. That would allow the earth's energy network, called ley lines, to be used for transmission. Stonehenge and Carnac once worked this way. But this is just a guess."

"If you were right, Brian, then yes, our high-tech equipment would be from the Stone Age compared to what they have over there."

"This is the end of speculation," Lange said, indicating to Brian that he wanted to speak to him in private.

While the DaVinci II was at a depth of 330 feet and far off the Mexican Pacific coast, it was again powered by the conventional stern propeller. Brian sat with Lange in his cabin. This time he sensed a nervousness in his commander's voice as he heard him say, "It takes a lot for me to believe you. If we really have to reckon with what you just said, they are playing a nasty game with us over there. When and where should the Chinese have developed such technology?"

"They may not have," Brian replied.

"What?"

"I think they're using something that someone gave them."

"Who?"

"The *Greys*."

Lange looked Brian in the face and asked, "You know something about the Greys? Then you live even more dangerously than I assumed until now. Many people have been hunted for this knowledge!"

"Looks like the hunt is on again," Brian said, and Lange looked him in the eyes.

"Cap'n, I'm not sure yet, but I feel that during my sleeping phases, someone wants to communicate with me. I've blocked it out, but we may be supposed to be warned about something!"

"We will not break the news blackout under any circumstances. That is an order, do you understand?"

"Yes, Cap'n."

Whether Brian should already confide in his commander what he experienced in his last trance phases, he did not know. The thing with the stolen *port stone* made him crazy. What did the commander have to do with it? If Lange knew how to use this port stone, the communication with stone circles and minerals should not have surprised him. Something was not right here. Or was the whole thing a giant hoax to discredit Lange? Was the thief someone else? Finally, Brian remembered the words of Rear Admiral Breede. He had sworn to him that Richard Lange would be his confidant. Brian went over in his mind again all the characteristics which would indicate that a person was lying. Nothing had struck him about Lange's body language. Others had so often relied on his judgment in this regard. And now he didn't trust his own intuition? That was then the point at which he wanted to confide in his commander, "There is something else you should know about, though, Cap'n."

"I thought something like that. You seemed to be looking for someone to talk to during the last hours."

"Yes. And if it hadn't been for message blocking, I probably would have contacted my meditation teacher Anna. I had the impression after the last contact that she wanted to tell me something. Because of the no-contact rule, I blocked her attempt every time."

Lange said, "Thought transference, or whatever you call it during meditation, might not only give away our location, Wilson. You're a Marine, after all, and you ought to know that you don't get mission orders on or under the sea just like that. Despite the latest encryption technology, any new order could be a forgery. You know how easy it is today to acquire a false identity via digital media. The place and form of delivery are, therefore, precisely regulated. So, we must ensure that the next command can only be issued to us at the agreed place and in the agreed way."

Brian said, "I know. My job is to spot false reports. Unfortunately, technology has rarely been able to help me do that. In reality, we biological beings are the best-designed machines. But that takes years of training, and many young people are getting farther and farther away from being able to do that."

"Right. Your superior in Rostock must have known that, too, when he sent you on this mission with us. Believe me, we may face quite different challenges before we reach our destination... But you wanted to tell me something earlier if, I'm not mistaken. What did you mean by that?"

"I may have found something else in the patterns we received with the sonic signals from X1."

"What do you mean?"

"I think they're using these sound waves to communicate with their naval command center. They're also talking directly to the Anabhu."

"What, why would they do that? I hardly think a crew has permission to converse with non-human intelligence! Besides, the existence of these .... let's call them 'aliens' is not even officially known," Lange said, and Brian nodded, "Maybe. I don't know if they are talking or maybe it's just some spy channel from the Anabhu."

"You mean the Anabhu would use this technique to spy on people?"

Brian thought for a moment and replied, "I could imagine that selected governments have already received technology from the Anabhu. The recipients then surely trust this technology and make themselves dependent on it. The industrialized countries have also had such ideas to spy on each other. Do you remember the discussions about microchips from the Chinese Huawei Group? At the time, these were installed in 5G mobile communications systems worldwide. Before the technology went into operation, Western intelligence services feared espionage intentions on the Chinese side. To this day, no one knows whether the Chinese government was behind it. I believe that the Americans already suspected at that time what potential a manipulated mobile radio technology could have. In any case, neither side trusts the other."

"Interesting thesis," Brian admitted. "You mean the affair at the time was a failed attempt to manipulate people on a large scale?"

Lange replied, "Such a plan is dangerous when people are involved. There is always someone among us who would sell secrets for money. Still, it was a huge deal. When Western politicians railed against Huawei, it must have been an eye-opener for global chipmakers. After all, many of them were sourcing semiconductor products from Chinese production. I think that was one of the reasons why technology was switched in many production facilities. At that time, the bottleneck in semiconductor products might give you pause for thought."

"Anyway, I think the Anabhu technique might be a similar manipulation attempt, only much more sophisticated," Brian replied.

"If you were right, Wilson, maybe you could also find out what the overheard conversation was about?"

"I've already tried that. But I'm not really getting anywhere right now."

"Stay tuned. You'll get everything you need. And keep me posted!"

Before Brian retreated to the commander's cabin, he asked the navigator for the current position. The commander had previously announced that they would use only conventional propulsion until they reached their destination. They were now less than 55 nautical miles from the west coast of the United States. Lange swore his crew in once again to adhere precisely to the regulations. The closer they got to their destination, the greater the probability of being discovered by the American Coast Guard. From now on, any unnecessary noise should be avoided again. Commander Lange had not yet revealed the exact coordinates of the target. There must have been good reasons for this. However, the secrecy also led to the crew starting to speculate. Hair-raising stories made the rounds, and the most imaginative ones burned themselves into the heads. None of these stories would even describe what was in store for the team a short time later.

Δ

Off the Pacific Coast of California

"Have you been able to calculate the DaVinci's new course yet, **Shao Wei** Lin?". The commander addressed his crew with such an abbreviation of the very long Chinese rank only when he wanted to avoid confusion regarding identical names or on official occasions.

"The calibration is still going on," the second nautical officer replied to Commander Chén, whose rank, **Hai Jun Shang Xiao**, was equivalent to a German Captain at Sea.

Chén ordered the duty officers to the command center to give a situation report, "We are keeping fifteen nautical miles from US territorial waters and no further approach to the German object until we know their course."

Unlike the German navy, the Chinese did not have to repeat the commands for maneuvers. The acoustic logbook recorded every word and transmitted all orders to the command room monitors. Officers could give instructions through their chain of command, reaching the workstations in writing and acoustically. The system even worked should neither the commander nor his second-in-command can give orders. In such a case, the submarine would be controllable from Chinese naval headquarters via satellite or from another vehicle. Theoretically, a commander could also be relieved of his command authority by having someone from outside take command. Communications were shielded from foreign powers using encryption technology developed in China.

The third officer in charge of communications now had his turn to report to the commander, "For the last four hours, the DaVinci II has not carried out any seismic measurements. I conclude that they have not found anything abnormal. Nevertheless, I suggest we keep our communications with B23 minimum."

B23 was the code designation for the Chinese navy's latest transmitting and receiving system. For this system to work, China had begun installing special buoys around the globe some time ago. These buoys were maintained from Chinese port facilities.

The country had either bought up the ports or, in some cases, built them in developing countries disguised as economic aid. The measures could always be justified with the New Silk Road, allowing China to trade freely with all nations.

The transmitting equipment in the buoys permitted them to establish a satellite broadband connection over water. This allowed them to communicate from anywhere in the world. What made these buoys special, however, was that they also allowed data transmission underwater and from great ocean depths. This was possible because sound waves propagate extremely quickly in water. What was still top secret at the time was that the information could be disguised as natural seismic waves. Those who did not know the system would only find sound waves that also occurred in the natural environment. However, the large amount of data also caused a problem because it had to be transmitted in encrypted form. A particular device was developed for this purpose, which was used practically for the first time here. The device, the size of a suitcase, was housed in the radio room and could not be opened.

The crew was taught that China was the first nation to build industrial-strength quantum computers and could now use them militarily. The country was thus able to extend its supremacy in communications. Chén was proud that they were technically years ahead of all other nations. He, therefore, considered manipulation from the outside to be practically impossible. His submarine was a revised prototype that had been in service for six months. In addition to the usual crew, there were also technicians from the manufacturer and two security officers on board. They had introduced themselves to the commander. According to the report, the two had been assigned by the Tenth Bureau of the Chinese Ministry of State Security, responsible for scientific and technological information. Once a day, Chén met with the two and had to report any technical problems and deviations from the regular daily routine. Chén sometimes felt that the two obtained information from outside but did not know how they did it. They were allowed access to all communications equipment, but as far as he knew, they did not use it themselves. This task, therefore, had to be done by someone else on board.

The commander trusted his second officer Lin. They knew each other from cadet school, and their families were friends. He had assigned him to keep an eye on all activities of the two security forces. This was actually nothing unusual. With a security apparatus like the one the Chinese had built up, it was vital to know a few people you could trust.

Δ

DaVinci II

Despite fatigue, Brian had taken another look at the evaluation of the sound waves. As he explained to Lange, Brian suspected a Chinese communication system based on camouflaged sound waves. Without explaining what he was looking for, he asked Peter for help. Even for people with excellent technical training, the whole thing might not be easy to understand. He also did not feel like having endless discussions about transdimensional fields. In short, if you wanted to understand what Brian was looking for, you had to know more about natural communication possibilities than you could currently learn in introductory studies. For the time being, Peter was to write a program for him that would find regularly occurring faults in seismic waves.

In Brian's view, a quantum key exchange was not such a complicated procedure. He used something similar for every telepathic connection and didn't need a computer. If Brian managed to provide proof of this, Peter would better understand what they should be looking for together.

Commander Lange called his crew together once again and described the next steps. Since they would soon be approaching the territorial waters of the United States and a particular restricted military area off the California coast, maximum stealth had to be employed. To this end, the newer 212 boat class specimens had a specially designed propeller that produced a sound similar to natural water eddies. In addition, the acoustic camouflage on the sub's hull went back to full power. The DaVinci II would mimic the earth's magnetic field and minor seismic activity, which corresponded to the natural environment in the California Rift Valley. This was nevertheless risky because there were a lot of hydrophones in this part of the Pacific. Modern earthquake research had the best conditions for earthquake prediction at the eastern edge of the Pacific plate. However, Lange wanted to take advantage of one particular circumstance. A large number of military ships and submarines patrolled the restricted area. Lange's most important plan was to hide the nearly silent DaVinci II in this noise confusion. They had only to stay away from the surface because satellites already had high-resolution cameras.

"You no longer have to try to fool me," Peter said.

Brian looked up, startled and asked, "What do you mean?"

Peter had squeezed in next to him at the tiny desk in Lange's cabin.

"I know you can read other people's faces. Do you feel I'm holding anything back from you?"

"I... well, we are in the military, and I don't expect an officer to have to talk about all subjects with lower-ranking officers. In that respect, I understand that everyone keeps a few things to themselves. Including you, of course."

"That sounds like an excuse. Something is going on in your head that you don't want to talk to me about. It's okay if it serves the cause, but I just want to know what you want me to look for with you. Otherwise, it's not going to be successful."

"You're right, Peter. I am used to others being skeptical of my methods and way of thinking. When I tell strangers how I go about reading the minds of others, most of them wet their pants out of fear and then run away."

"Understandable. It sounds like a spook to me, too, when you claim to dive into the heads of your fellow human beings and who knows who else. But only those who have to be afraid of their own thoughts will get out of the way. I always thought that whoever is fundamentally honest and not an egoist does not have to be ashamed of his thoughts."

Brian smiled and thought something must have just happened inside him. As if an inner barrier had been broken, he suddenly felt the need to reveal himself to Peter. But he also felt a little guilty because he hadn't told anyone that the telepathy in this sub didn't work the way he was used to. Also, some body language seemed to work somehow differently than usual. Possibly something in this steel hulk was interfering with his mental abilities.

Finally, he confirmed Peter's opinion, "That's how I see it, too. I'd like to believe otherwise, but the selfishness and dishonesty we are confronted with from infancy are why telepathy has almost disappeared from our lives. It doesn't fit the Western way of life. Perhaps this is why Buddhist monks withdraw from the rest of society when they want to exchange knowledge among themselves and get in touch with nature. What conservative materialists call esotericism is a pitiful attempt to explain something they do not want to deal with. For those who find their way back to ancient traditions, the richness of cosmic knowledge is revealed. For the others, it remains haunting, and they continue to live in their own limited world."

Brian paused for a moment and seemed to consider how to proceed, "I forgot to mention that I can't look inside your head. Nobody can. That's just a figure of speech. In reality, I look around your head."

"Now, what kind of nonsense is that?" asked Peter, grinning, thinking Brian was making another of his enigmatic jokes.

"It's just ... you should dispel this myth. Surely you know that active neurons produce light by emitting photons with the help of the DNA they contain?"

"Honestly, this is the first time I've heard this. I only know the halo on religious paintings."

"Exactly. That's pretty close to the point. The network of nerve cells runs through the whole body, and many photons are generated in the brain. You may have heard of the body's seven chakras, which esotericists often deal with. Sometimes they are just called energy centers. Whether the ancient painters knew about this phenomenon, I don't know. But they knew the myth that the smartest of their time were among the Enlightened. And without claiming that you are one of the enlightened ones, I see or better feel something like an aura around your body with my senses."

"Thank you for the compliment!" said Peter with a smirk. Brian grinned and topped it off, "Well, your aura is pretty small...."

Peter stared at the screen again and asked, "Let's discuss our original problem some more, so we don't have to wait so long for the Nobel Prize."

"Good idea!"

"Why do you think the Chinese are using a natural method of quantum entanglement?"

Brian stumbled because he didn't think he had talked to anyone about quantum entanglement in the last few days. But Peter had perhaps just confused the term. So, he replied, "Did I say quantum entanglement? If so, I meant quantum encryption. It's not the same thing."

"Oh, sorry. I mean quantum keys, too, of course. I like watching science shows about stuff like that. That fascinates me, and quantum entanglement sounds spooky, as Einstein once said. Maybe that's why the word keeps haunting my mind."

Brian had the impression that Peter was sincere. The feeling of being able to trust this lieutenant strengthened and more and more displaced his skepticism. Brian was convinced he could learn much about his inner self through the humor of the person he was talking to. In the end, Brian was not a person who always weighed the risks everywhere. He trusted people more quickly if they didn't give off negative vibes. Following this instinct, Brian took it upon himself to bring Peter into his confidence. He still didn't know how Anna's port stone had gotten into Lange's cabin, but he would deal with that again. For now, the task was to decode the data transmission of the Chinese sub.

Peter added, "It may not be a topic for today, but I'm still interested in how you can communicate telepathically over such long distances. Supposedly, this is supposed to work without time delay. Doesn't that also have something to do with this entanglement?"

"Science is still arguing about that. I think a hypothesis is probable, but that will surely bore you, and I'm not a quantum physicist either."

"I'm not bored with it! Give it a go. It's exciting."

"Maybe just this much first... The smallest particles of our matter are connected via ... let's say, some kind of wave function. This connection may be made by the *Higgs field*. This field exists independently of matter, but there is an interaction. Because of the independence of matter particles, their properties are probably also not bound to space and time. In other words, the information can be transmitted via waves in cross-dimensional fields without time delay. Since distance does not matter for telepathy, our brain can use these waves for thought transmission."

"Gee Brian, that would be an innovation for our intelligence agencies. Being everywhere and knowing about everyone, without travel costs!"

They laughed, but Brian wasn't sure if Peter had caught on to what they were dealing with. Now he had no choice but to diligently explain his plan to hack into the Chinese system.

The next question surprised Brian a bit. Apparently, Peter had understood more than expected: "If we know that they talk to each other with the same procedure as you do with telepathy, you should be able to listen in on the connection."

Brian's enthusiasm was evident when he said, "That's what I was getting at. Since the Chinese may be using technology for transmission they did not develop, it is reasonable to suspect that the technology is also being misused to manipulate people. Telepathy or not, it is the same metaphysics."

Peter laughed and said, "You sound like you're talking about some aliens who want to manipulate us."

Brian looked Peter in the eye without saying anything. That moment seemed to drag on forever before Peter said, "You don't really believe that, do you?"

"It doesn't just sound like that. I'm a firm believer in it, and if we're going to work together on this, you're going to have to start accepting it," Brian said with a serious face.

Peter seemed less surprised than Brian had expected. He was probably thinking about how to explain to his comrade what he had been thinking in the past few days, "You know, somehow, it's a bizarre feeling now. Since you've been on board, maybe everyone has thought about something like this. Of course, the crew has already speculated why such an exotic bird is on board. I feel that most of them are already waiting for the day when someone will reveal that there are not only humans on earth. What do you actually know about the destination of the DaVinci II?"

"I was told to trust Commander Lange and not ask questions. The answers would come in due time." Brian said, and Peter seemed to understand, "Then I guess they swore in the whole crew with the same words."

"Alright...," Brian resumed the previous discussion, "So let's assume that the Chinese communications are being manipulated somehow. There's a risk that the commander is receiving orders from a different source than he believes. That scares me, and I'd like to figure out how we can intercept their conversation."

"How much do you actually know about these aliens? Who are they?" Peter wanted to know.

"To be honest, I can't even tell if they are different species or if they are extraterrestrials at all. As far as I know, the most famous is called Anabhu. I have this name from dreams that I have been experiencing since I was a child. I only met people who dreamed similar things when I was an adult. In meditation sessions, I've received proof that the Anabhu are real. Sometimes they are also called the Greys. I then simply accepted this as fact.

Some people are convinced that an intelligent species is more similar to us humans than the Anabhu. They call themselves *Manujas*. I don't know much about them, but they are said to have lived on earth long before we did. Nobody seems to know anything about their intentions. Maybe these strangers see themselves in a protective role. Who knows. I think that other intelligent races fought each other in the past, as the ancient writings describe," Brian said, and Peter asked, "Do you think they are using this to influence our mission as well?"

"That's what I'm assuming. And since we'll be arriving at our destination soon enough, we don't have much time to figure it out."

While discussing, the commander had given the order to surface at periscope depth. Shortly after, there was movement in the narrow corridors, and the noise of the blowing again produced eerie sounds. The two had skipped their last meal. The smell of fresh bread was, therefore, a welcome distraction. They made their way to the galley. The DaVinci II's nose pointed up a bit as they emerged, making it difficult to move forward in the narrow passageway. Brian was so tired that he lost his balance and bumped his head. The mess hall was in the lower deck's wide part of the corridor. Across from the galley was a long bench with several small tables folded sideways in between.

There Monika sat with a technician. They were studying a map with the relief of the seabed. For this purpose, they took a wall monitor out of its holder and placed it on the table. Working on the map with a tablet pen was more manageable in this position. Brian recognized handwritten markings and annotations. He suspected they were preparing an exterior mission but didn't ask. The boat began to lean to all sides. That meant they were close to the surface, and there had to be heavy seas there. The meal was ready on the small tables for self-service. This time it consisted only of sandwiches and Vienna sausages. Since the ship was moving, they sat down to eat next to Monika and listened to the conversation.

Because of the strong painkillers, Norbert had been given an extended free watch. Nevertheless, he occasionally left the bed to avoid leaving his comrades alone during the meal preparation.

Peter and Brian grabbed another one of the fragrant rolls and climbed onto the upper deck to the operations center. Peter asked the watch officer, "Why did we surface?" But he seemed to be concentrating on the weather map.

Lange had his eyes on one of the two periscopes, although he could observe everything with the outdoor cameras. The human eye still picked up details in the distance that could sometimes be misinterpreted with digital image enhancement. He would comment on what he saw every now and then: "Swell seven to ten feet. Visibility below 500 yards. What's the weather situation?"

"Getting worse. Two hurricanes are approaching from the northwest. If we're lucky, they'll dissipate back east of Hawaii," the watch officer explained and continued, "Could become one of the new types of weather phenomena, as it is more common here in recent years."

Brian asked, "But why are you talking about a phenomenon. The hurricanes have natural causes, don't they?"

"Since water temperatures have exceeded a certain level, hurricanes are no longer rare, even in the North Pacific. Until the beginning of the century, these storms rarely reached the US mainland. That has now changed. While these hurricanes are far less destructive than their Atlantic siblings, they cause huge waves and disrupt ocean currents, which affect the weather on the West Coast."

The commander interfered and explained, "What is happening here is strange and has not been researched yet. A second one forms as soon as one storm gets stronger and moves toward the Californian coast. Each time, they meet before they reach the coast and wipe each other out."

"Is there anything like this anywhere else?" someone asked.

"Yes, but rarely. It's called the Fujiwhara effect. The coincidence of two hurricanes can either lead to a mega storm or just extinction. However, an anomaly occurs in this area, and every meteorologist's prediction model is off. Contrary to all calculations, the storms never hit the coast with full force. One day we'll find out what the reason is. But for now, let's all get back to work! We need an exact movement pattern of all ships within 200 nautical miles. Lieutenant Gross, you and Wilson can keep an eye on our Chinese friends. Be good to know where they're hanging out."

Brian already wanted to protest because he intended to continue to look into the recorded communication of the Chinese. Still, Peter gave him a look that made it clear not to contradict now. Since all the seats in the control room were occupied, the two wanted to return to the commander's cabin. Before Brian left, he asked the commander, "Why are we staying at periscope depth in this sea state? Can't we wait for better weather further down?"

"Wish we could. This is where our next stopover is scheduled. We are waiting for our target coordinates from Rostock. For this, we need a satellite connection. Unfortunately, we can't use the radio buoy in this weather. It might break off."

Some of the crew looked puzzled because, apparently, not all of them were enlightened about the fact that Lange did not know the final destination either.

The boat's movements were increasingly violent, and the lean was sometimes thirty degrees. Brian now regretted that he had just stuffed himself with another roll. Before he left the control room with Peter, he heard Lange say, "Swell up to 16 feet. Give the order for all who are not on watch to buckle up in their beds. It's going to get heavier."

Lange went into the radio room, to which only three other crew members had access beside the commander. Here was the most secret part of the technology. The radio officer had just received the coordinates of the target. The message also included the order for the DaVinci II to remain in that position and wait for the next mission order. Lange went to the map screen with the coordinates. He already suspected this weather was what the principals in Rostock had hoped for. During the storm, the number of boats over water would be kept to a minimum. Air surveillance was also limited on such days. However, Lange was concerned about his navigation. Being exposed to unpredictable ocean currents was a horror for submarines. And the storms in the area were causing just that. For Lange, it was clear that they would either have to stay on the surface or surface once a day to reconcile their exact position with the satellites. Either way, they were not spared the hassle of the high seas. Operating unnoticed in water was what this class of boat had been designed for. So there were various ways to camouflage themselves. The only thing was that the right choice always had to be made.

The watch officer gave the crew the order to stop all noise-making work immediately.

Fabrice, who had to take care of the food with Monika because of Norbert's injury, had just lost to Monika in the rock-paper-scissors game. Now it was his turn to devise a meal plan for the next twenty-four hours. When the watch officer's announcement came, he was about to start preparing it in the galley. He still seemed to be in a good mood and said to Monika, "Too bad, knocked cutlets are out of the question today, so we'll have to think of something else."

Monika laughed and replied, "We can't use pans or pots with the slant. Let's bake cakes. Nothing can fall out of the oven. On the record, we'll call that stuff swing cake."

Δ

Rostock, Maritime Operations Centre

The weather on this first day of October did not indicate that it was autumn long ago. The walk from the parking lot to the office building felt good, although the uniform jacket was already too warm at eight o'clock. The many leaves reminded Breede of an old story. Soon after the outdoor area was completed, MOC employees noticed that the trees were already coloring their leaves in August. There were two reasons for this.

On the one hand, the growing season began a month earlier than it did a few decades ago. On the other hand, the planning for the outdoor area dates back to the last nineties. At that time, resident German deciduous trees were selected. But before the construction of the MOC complex began, another twenty years passed. The contracted horticultural company had therefore revised the planting once again. However, the responsible department of the navy would not be convinced that the climate in Central Europe had changed. The horticultural specialist, who had immigrated from the Balkans, offered more heat-resistant deciduous trees from his homeland. The poor fellow will probably not have forgotten the conversation with his client in which it was explained to him that German trees were desired on a German military site.

Rear Admiral Breede, who at that moment was plugging his staff car into the parking lot's charging station, would now be reminded of this insane dispute by the falling leaves again for weeks.

He believed much had already improved in terms of leadership in the Bundeswehr. Nevertheless, it would still take time before contemporary leadership methods would prevail. Breede himself sometimes wondered what failures he could be blamed for. Classical training measures alone were not enough. He had, therefore, already thought about alternatives. This German-American Wilson could be suitable as a mental trainer. But Breede thought he was still too young and a bit too arrogant to train the overaged, majority-male bunch of staff officers. Breede couldn't help grinning as he imagined Brian Wilson teaching Sigfried Pot meditation.

The weekly staff meeting was supposed to start at nine, but twenty minutes earlier, Breede received an invitation to a video conference with the German foreign minister.

The line had now been up for ten minutes, but only one guy from Friedemann's administrative team was dialed in. He apologized for the minister's delay every few minutes, only to go mute again immediately. Meanwhile, Breede leafed through his emails to highlight the most important. Christina usually did this sorting for him because he couldn't do it alone due to the quantity. Non-encrypted emails were filtered out first and only reached him after extensive checking.

A message with civilian encryption then caught his eye because of the unusual domain name. As if it had been a suspicion, he had been thinking about the psychologists' guild that morning. Now he found an email in his mailbox from one of its most prominent representatives:

sergei.fyodorov@ifpuvw.freiburg

The acronym stood for the Institute of Psychology and Behavioral Sciences, a legendary European teaching institution. Most of these legends, however, were made up. Breede knew by now that all the rumors were harmless compared to what was actually being researched there. Among insiders, jokes were already being made about the fact that anyone who thought to be a VIP in Germany should know at least one psychologist from Freiburg.

If I ever get an email from there, then maybe it's time for a checkup, he joked, opening the document.

The message was indeed from Fedorov himself, and judging by the style, it was about a serious matter: "...unfortunately, it is not possible to reach you by phone. We urgently need to contact one of your employees who has been away on business for a few days and whose identity should not be mentioned in this email... urgently request a personal callback on my mobile number..."

It didn't take much imagination to figure out that this was about Brian Wilson. If Sergei, whom he usually addressed privately, was writing to him this way, he had to know that these emails were also read by navy personnel. So why hadn't he called him on the secure mobile line in the first place? He was about to follow up on the matter when Secretary of State Friedemann appeared on the screen. She tried to put on a friendly face but could not hide a certain tension, "Good morning, Rear Admiral Breede! Since we are in a tiny circle, I suggest we save the formalities. I'm sorry to keep you waiting. My colleagues from cybersecurity only called me in when it was certain that we were the only ones on the line."

"I'm surprised you have to bring up the wiretapping issue," said Breede.

"When you hear what I say, maybe you will understand. Are you alone?"

"Yes."

"Since the last meeting of the World Security Council, we have received several disturbing pieces of information. Apparently, something is going on that has caused various countries to increase their security measures."

Breede didn't let any excitement show as he replied, "That sounds like a special situation. But from you, I'm used to hearing the facts right away, or were you hoping I would be able to tell you more about it?"

Friedemann now knew that Breede had smelled a rat right away. Of course, she wanted to use her intro to find out how much was known about the activities in the Pacific at NATO's Naval Special Operations Command. Breede had resented that he had not been directly involved in the negotiations with China. She knew that, so she said, "I also have to apologize for not getting you involved until after you talked to the Chinese. That was a mistake. But in New York, I didn't know a few things yet. I thought some foreign policy trickery was going on to impose sanctions on Germany because we wanted to supply submarines with sensitive technology to countries in the Pacific region. In the meantime, however, I suspect this was just a pretext to get all the Security Council's permanent members to New York. We also now know that there was another tiny meeting. Unfortunately, I have limited information here at the Department on the so-called territorial treaties of the United Nations, if you know what I mean?"

"Madam Secretary, you must talk to the Minister of Defense about such issues. If he were to authorize me, I would be authorized to give you information about it. I am sorry, but..."

At this point, Friedemann interrupted him, "Unfortunately, the official way you suggest is not possible in this case. There is a risk that the Minister of Defense will involve the parliament. And in my opinion, there is a good reason not to involve the public in the current situation. I make you a compromise proposal: Like all high-ranking NATO officers, you regularly receive passwords. With this, you can read secret messages. As a government official, I also receive these codes. One comes from the NATO Secretary General and the other from the highest-ranking representative of the state, in our case, the Federal President. The two together verify legitimacy if a NATO member state temporarily lacks a legitimate government or if legitimacy cannot be obtained for some reason. You and I can now use this process to authorize each other for information."

"Madam Secretary, this provision is for the alliance case under Article 5 of the mutual assistance treaty. To my knowledge, this case does not exist. I know of no attack on our country!"

"That's where you're wrong, Breede. We cannot use the regular chain of command in Germany. I'll tell you my clearance code, and you open the two envelopes to match it. Then you'll know that I've coordinated with headquarters and..." She paused to choose the right words for what followed."...And that this is an Article 5 alliance case."

Friedemann gave their sixteen-digit numerical code, and Breede hesitated. In his head, he reconstructed all the procedures drilled into the staff officers of NATO troops for such an eventuality. Ultimately, no reason was found to refuse his foreign minister's request. He then opened the files with the two parts of the clearance code. They matched Friedemann's code. This gave her the authority to provide Breede with official instructions. While comparing the two codes again, he realized it could only be about using the DaVinci II. So, the whole thing had been blown wide open.

"Madam Secretary, I confirm the release. Please enlighten me as to what the threat is."

"I had asked you a few minutes ago if you knew more about the United Nations territorial treaties. I mean, for example, the regulations relating to Antarctica and other restricted areas."

"I don't have more than the publicly available information either. All I know is that there is a secret supplementary contract. Who signed it and with whom is a matter of speculation! In military circles, we therefore jokingly call this supplemental contract the X-File."

"Don't lose your sense of humor," Friedemann said. "I have heard that you are envied by your people for it. Yesterday, however, I learned something else I can't laugh about. Accordingly, you are personally involved in the mission of the dubious DaVinci twin and thus have something to do with his disappearance! So, what the Chinese presented in New York is true. One of our secret military projects has been exposed. I didn't know about any of these projects and therefore got into an –

excuse the expression– shitty situation. The Chinese negotiator showed me up, or rather, he showed up all over Germany. And that was because I didn't know about it. Fortunately, I have connections at NATO headquarters and don't have to rely only on my staff. In Brussels, I learned that there was a German submarine cruising off the coast of California and involved in some salvage operation. None of this would be a reason to get the secret codes out of the drawer. But to make matters worse, our survey has since learned that there is still a Chinese submarine in the vicinity whose mission may be to prevent the Germans from succeeding. You know what such a confrontation at the gates of the United States could result in?"

Breede was not squeamish and could take a lot of bad news in one fell swoop. But he had no idea that the crew of the DaVinci II was actually in such danger. Moreover, a possible confrontation would occur in the United States maritime territory, i.e., an alliance partner. He said to Friedemann, "Of course, now the situation is much clearer to me."

"If that's the case, we should get someone else involved. Have you checked your mailbox this morning? There should be an email from Professor Fedorov. He wants to talk to you and urgently. I already had a call with him this morning."

Breede took his cell phone out of his pocket, "Ok, let's bring Fedorov with us now," but Friedemann said, "Leave it with the cell phone. My assistant will dial the professor."

While they waited for Sergei, he slowly realized that the foreign minister had learned more about the mission in the Pacific from her contacts in Brussels than he knew. There seemed enough backing in Brussels to take matters in hand. The question was also to what extent the Americans were already in the loop here. After all, with his position in the navy, he knew that you had to explain what you meant when mentioning the Americans. Not even every president could see through the power structures there in detail.

Sergei's face now appeared on the screen, and he seemed pretty upset. Before he could say anything, Breede beat him to it, "Good morning, Professor Fedorov." This salutation signaled that this was an official conversation, or perhaps the communication was unsafe. Among the rules of their order was that internal matters could be discussed only in compliance with specific regulations. Keeping secrecy was one of the essential rules, of course. Breede wanted to make clear that he had already exchanged confidential information with Friedemann. Therefore he said, "Hey Sergei, Secretary Friedemann informed me of circumstances that may have had to do with our partnership."

"I see. We had the pleasure of earlier. I suggested we have this conversation together after she gave us the bad news about the DaVinci twins individually. I have no idea how involved you guys in the navy are, but something has gone wrong. And it looks like we will need diplomatic support from the State Department to avoid an escalation."

Here Friedemann jumped in, "Gentlemen, before you waste any more time by avoiding the subject at hand, I think it would be best if I just opened the door. As you know, each member of our Order has only as much knowledge about a mission as the task requires. Of course, this is also true for me, especially since I have only been working for the Order since I took over my government post for mediation in international conflicts. I exchanged the necessary credentials with each of you earlier. That should close the circle. Please confirm that with each other."

Unlike Roland Breede, Sergei did not seem particularly surprised. He said, "Roland, I can confirm Ms. Friedemann's identity with this. I am releasing Code Three On The Bridge."

"Code Three confirmed On The Bridge," replied Roland, who now knew that Friedemann was also a member of their Order. She was one of the people with whom he was allowed to talk about Order matters. Usually, only those with a contact belonging to the same security level. With the code word Three, combined with a second password, which was only valid for a short time, interlocutors confirmed the individual security level to each other. There were seven of them, although hardly anyone knew who had level seven in the Order. Even Foreign Minister Friedemann could only speculate who belonged to level seven. She had recently received the fourth level. This included knowing that there were various subgroups within the organization. These had their own Order statutes, deviating Order names and somewhat different rituals. This would make it difficult for outsiders to keep track of the proper organization, even if details occasionally leaked out.

After the formalities with the secrecy had been cleared up, Friedemann took over as expected, "I chose this way because it is urgent. I didn't want to spread panic at all. Still, I think you now know that the real action with the DaVinci could be interpreted as an attack on the United States of America. Somebody might also want it to look like a terrorist attack with a hijacked submarine."

Breede said, "Madam Minister, I can assure you that the DaVinci II is also safe. The captain has my trust, and the rest of the crew is reliable."

"Listen, I think I know why the Security Council's permanent members met again in a small circle after the main meeting. It could have been a Level Seven meeting of the Order and the main meeting in the morning was just a pretext," Friedemann said.

"You mean it was about the German sub?"

"When I put all the circumstantial evidence together, a broader picture emerges. Perhaps the Order was deceived, and even the whole of humanity fooled," was the answer of the foreign minister.

"Now I'm going to lose track of everything." Sergei interjected, but Friedemann continued in a calm voice, "Fortunately, we started to recruit the young generations Z and Alpha for the Order some time ago. Professor, with your training center in Freiburg, you are helping to expand our worldwide network. Only yesterday, and only by chance, I learned that Brian Wilson is on board the DaVinci II, to whom the Order has entrusted the recovery of an artifact. I do not know what the artifact is. But it seems that someone wants to prevent that by all means."

"Why does this artifact have to be recovered at all? Can't it stay where it is?" Sergei asked.

Breede wanted to answer the question carefully and turned to Friedemann again: "You said that everyone in the Order only knows what is needed for their mission. We can see from this mess that it doesn't always work properly. All the secrecy can lead us into chaos. But what the heck? One is always smarter afterward. Anyway, things are hurrying. As far as I know, the hideout has not been safe for some time now. Since there are satellite images of the entrance on the Internet, the Order has decided to choose a new hiding place. But that's all I know. After all, the whole thing depends on the guards, whose unmasking would be a disaster."

Friedemann nodded and said, "Seems to me the Chinese are interested in the stash, too. Thus, it can be assumed that they know about the artifact. And it scares me because it could lead to weapons deployment on American shores."

In response to her statement, Breede said, "Well, if we're all talking about the same thing, I guess we're speaking about the underwater formation off the California coast, near Malibu. And that's where Commander Lange and his crew will arrive in about twelve hours. Although the public doesn't know anything for sure, the satellite image is so interesting that treasure hunters are already regularly making their way to the site. So far, no one has succeeded in investigating the entrance. But since we can't let the pictures disappear, it is only a matter of time."

As Breede continued to speak, he shared his screen content with the others. A satellite image with a prominent underwater structure appeared, "As you can see, everything is going as planned."

"Nothing goes as planned! You must stop this Lange at all costs. Our informant at the manufacturer in Kiel had told us that two of the eight torpedo tubes were loaded with torpedoes shortly before the DaVinci II sailed. Who ordered such a thing?" Friedemann asked.

"That's not possible! None of the new boats under test were equipped with heavy weapons."

"Obviously, someone has other plans than you, Rear Admiral!"

"If you're right, things are starting to get dicey now. Communications with the DaVinci II are down and can't be resumed even before the mission is complete."

"What?" cried Friedemann, her face contorting into a horrible grimace.

Underwater structure off the coast of California (USA) [17]

"You heard me right. The DaVinci II received the order to dive this morning. They should now be more than 500 feet deep to avoid detection. Commander Lange is only allowed to contact us at the agreed-upon points. There is no more rendezvous point before the mission has been fulfilled."

"Why this insane contact ban?" Friedemann wanted to know.

"Madam Secretary, this is perfectly normal. Otherwise, a mission could be boycotted by rogue forces. Every commander knows this procedure. But I still see a small chance."

Sergei responded, "I'd have another idea, but let's hear it first!"

Breede addressed Sergei directly, "We have this guy Wilson on board. He may be our only chance. But we need your people in Freiburg to do it, Sergei!"

"I've been thinking about that, too. Our meditation trainer Anna Stein had a strange vision and believes it has something to do with this Wilson. She tried contacting the fellow a few days ago but only picked up a few snippets of thoughts. The shielding in this sub is excellent."

"Even if there is only a small chance, she should try again!" said Friedemann euphorically.

"Unfortunately, that will not be possible. To make contact, she traveled all the way to England and almost got killed," Sergei explained.

"From whom?"

"We suspect there's a Dr. Zhou behind this. He leads a visiting Chinese research team at Oxford."

"That doesn't sound good. It is to be feared that the Chinese have now picked up some of this Anna's knowledge. That could be the leak. That might be how they found out about Wilson and the whole mission," Breede said.

"Roland, we have no way of knowing. This Dr. Zhou is certainly too insignificant for such a big deal. It will be just coincidence because he is engaged in neurological research at Oxford," Sergei replied.

"Oh yes, there is, gentlemen. There might be something to it. Maybe the Oxford thing was an important clue. We have been looking for a leak in England for some time. Members of the Order have already had to go underground because more and more unknown people have been interested in the contacts. However, we don't believe that the Chinese are behind this. Their government is not interested in the artifact. The communists rather do everything to keep any form of ancient myths and prehistoric lore away from the public. We suspect rather billionaire tech corporations behind it, which build something like a parallel world to the state with the money from the capital market. I assume the Chinese state is more concerned about such people. This is also supported by the regulatory measures in 2021. Targeted action was taken against companies that work with large amounts of data and thus accumulated a lot of knowledge. Although this Dr. Zhou is a small wheel, we will start there. Someone has to fund his research, after all."

"Do you think the unidentified sub is also not from the Chinese military?"

Friedemann underlined her answer with a shrug of the shoulders, "From the military, it definitely comes. But whether the state leadership still has full command over all submarines remains to be seen. As I said to Rear Admiral Breede earlier: As far as that is concerned, we can only speculate for the time being. Ultimately, we have to find out. If necessary, I will get the Chinese ambassador involved. Then at least, they learn that we know the Chinese submarine's existence."

CHAPTER 10

Off the Pacific Coast of the United States

The DaVinci II moved through the dark Pacific at medium speed and silently. Their destination was five miles off the coast of California and eleven miles west of Malibu. Another 54 miles, and they would pass San Nicolas Island to the northwest. After that, the military exclusion zone began. Commander Lange had gone to sleep after twelve hours on watch, so Brian and Peter sat next to each other in the command room.

"How could I have been so wrong?" Brian suddenly shouted and immediately muffled his voice again. He had forgotten that any noise was forbidden on the boat. Peter, tinkering intently with some program code, had winced and growled, "Do you have to scare me like that? What's wrong?"

"I hate to admit it, but this time your program spits out something brilliant," Brian gave free rein to his enthusiasm.

"Your compliment is more promising than the menu for today."

"This can't be true. I'm about to announce that we're about to be nominated for a Nobel Prize, and you're bitching about Monika's cake."

"If you had seen how burned it was... it's okay. I get it. Go on!"

Brian grinned and began, "Unfortunately, I must first admit that I was completely wrong when I thought the Chinese would use quantum encryption. It's much simpler, but still ... I'd say ... more complex."

"Explain it to me, please, without any new riddles."

"I first thought it was a program error when the computer kept trying to develop a four-letter system to decode the received vibrations emanating from X1."

"Four letters? That sounds like..."

225

"That's right. The letters A, C, G and T are the abbreviations of the four building blocks of DNA used to form the base pairs. So, the program was looking for some biological coding."

"And what do you conclude from that?"

"That you don't need a quantum computer to encrypt data securely," Brian began to rave again.

"Got it, but then what do you need?"

"The people aboard X1 may use a computer to translate their messages into the language of DNA before sending them. But if the recipients have telepathic abilities, their brains can understand the information without a computer. A trained brain can decode messages without technical aids. They have to reach the receiver first."

"I believe you can understand the message now. You are a medium, aren't you?"

"I wish. Something must still be missing in me. I suspect that something like a decoding gene has to be activated first. In prehistoric representations, you sometimes see the god holding a ceremonial object in front of a person's nose. The specialists in Freiburg might know how that works or if you need special hypnosis for it."

Peter thought for a moment and said, "I've always wondered why there are so many animals in old paintings. Maybe the combination of animal and human genes has something to do with it. What do you think?"

"Not a bad thought. Remember, an octopus living in the Sea Life Centre in Oberhausen correctly predicted all of Germany's games and the final in the 2010 World Cup. I know that an octopus has ten thousand more genes than humans."

While Brian was telling this, Peter tried to find something about the octopus's nervous system in the onboard digital library. He saw something and said, "Look, these animals are supposed to be able to change their DNA in a short period. Maybe with them, it's like switching from one TV channel to another."

Brian smiled, "The comparison could fit. Geneticists are racking their brains over this extreme adaptability."

"When writing about Greek mythology today, one sometimes reads of speculation that the Oracle of Delphi might have been an octopus."

Brian shook his head, "I don't believe in that. The oracle was always the officiating prophesying priestess, whom they called Pythia. There is no doubt about the process of divination. Pythia was placed over an aperture crevice in the earth from which vapors were emitted. The vapors must have had a hallucinogenic effect. But one thing is really striking. No matter which oracle the legends were about, animals were always present. In Delphi, it was a goat. In Asia and the Orient, snakes."

"And when it comes to soccer in Europe, just an octopus," Peter said. "But do you think the Chinese could use animals for encryption or data transmission? Surely someone would have published it if such a technology was already developed, right?"

Brian thought for a moment before answering, "Scientific work always implies that the results of experiments must be reproducible. So an apparatus would have to be built on repeating the experiments. What do you think such a machine should look like?"

"I see. We're going around in circles with this," Peter sounded resigned. But Brian laughed and said, "I just imagine what would happen if a student presented an experiment like this. Some old gentlemen might be sitting in the lecture hall watching this budding scientist communicate with an octopus in a jar."

"I bet you got that from some movie," Peter said with a grin.

"Nah, I've been to student parties in the Rhineland. As an American, I'm used to some nonsense, but the Germans even award a medal Wider Den Tierischen Ernst."

"Can it even be translated into English?"

"Good question. Perhaps in the States, one might call it: A Medal For Combating Deadly Seriousness."

"Maybe nobody's noticed yet, and there's a deeper meaning to it all."

After they both enjoyed themselves, Brian resumed the conversation, "Where people dare to combine technology with spiritual practices, there will be a breakthrough first. That will also bring us more understanding about the quantum world."

"To stay with our actual problem, I want to do something else to help you. At the moment, however, I'm out of ideas," Peter said.

Brian looked him in the eye and again seemed mentally absent for a moment. Then he said, "I've always been able to rely on my intuition. Even now, something tells me that what has happened to me in the last few weeks can't be a coincidence. My meditation teacher Anna somehow can't get out of my head."

"That you even have time for that..." grinned Peter, but Brian immediately protested, "I don't mean it that way. She's a brilliant medium. In our last conversation, she talked about the pattern in her vision. Coincidentally, at the same time, these crop circles are appearing all over the world. It must mean something!"

Peter replied, "But in the world, countless things happen in parallel. And much of it seems familiar. If you make an effort, you always find things that seem to fit together. The brain also plays tricks on us."

"That's right. I can't explain it all, but my brain sometimes works differently. It is trained for patterns. Areas of the brain that are repeatedly used are dense form networks and are more efficient. It's like fishing. The denser the net, the more gets caught."

"I thought you would be comfortable with the physical and auditory language."

"Communicating is related to a whole lot of things. When I focus on a certain topic, I often notice something in the environment that could be related to it. This works as if my subconscious is checking out the environment. Also, if someone near me thinks something related to the same topic, we both benefit. At least, we have been able to prove this in laboratory experiments. It also worked without the other person being consciously aware of it. What we haven't tested yet, though, is whether it also works when the two partners are farther apart."

Peter had listened attentively and then said in confirmation, "Most people know what is meant by the chemistry between two people being right. This proves that where the chemistry is right, solutions to problems are found more quickly. Even in whole groups."

"Maybe you and I have a mental connection, too," Brian said, and he meant it.

Peter stared at his screen for the next few minutes and just thought. His question came at a moment when Brian's mind was already elsewhere, "Say, somehow, there's still a catch in your theory."

"What's the problem?"

"This technology with DNS encryption only makes sense if it can be used widely at some point. Just for underwater vehicles, the effort would be far too great."

Brian seemed to have thought about that, too, "Maybe the whole thing is already a widely used technique. Just not with humans."

"As exciting as it is to listen to you, Brian. I don't think there is any non-human technology in a Chinese submarine. If humans are involved, something like that could never be kept secret for long."

Brian thought about it for a moment before replying, "You're right. The best solutions are always simpler than you think. For years, we have imagined what kind of technology extraterrestrial intelligence would use for their computers. Yet they might not need computers at all, as we imagine. Either they have created some hybrid beings that do the dangerous work for them and have cloned brains, or... I can think of something else: The computer power is higher the bigger the network it is in. Maybe the whole thing serves the purpose of gradually connecting our human brains to the big network. And what we found at X1 could be a prototype for that."

"I suppose you already know about such a network, don't you?" Peter wanted to know.

Brian had already nodded before the question was, "You know it too. We humans call it morphic fields. Our aura is connected with it. All morphic fields of the universe together are called the *aka*. I cannot move freely in it with my thoughts yet. Until then, I always came only with a powerful medium. But maybe I don't need to penetrate that far. All we have to do is plug in to listen in."

"But you'll be spotted if you hack in, won't you? Or how do you hack in there?"

Brian's good mood had already flared up again, "Has your criminal side awakened? I already have an idea of what we could try. You probably know the physics of this technology better than I do, so we'll skip the theory for now. My hope is that X1 only contains technology that can be operated by normal people. After all, it had to be installed by humans first. It will probably be inconspicuously tucked somewhere in the radio system."

"So again, Brian. I'm the technician, and I need to understand this. An average person sends out a signal with his thoughts. Other people could receive that because their morphic fields are connected. But because we normal people are still too stupid to use those fields, we need a translation machine. Right?"

"Right, but..."

"Stop, no further! I need to understand it at my speed."

"Okay, I'm listening."

"A person thinks something, and in doing so, he radiates that into the environment with his morphic field."

"Something like that, yes."

"So this device can translate human thought into sound waves, which are then transmitted into the water at X1's outer skin?"

"Bingo!" Brian said with relief, and his face radiated satisfaction again.

"But why so awkwardly about the sound waves in the water. Surely the 'others' could tap into the morphic fields."

"Apparently, the outer shell with the stealth technology not only shields the sound but also disturbs the structure of these fields. But that can't matter to us. We already have some of the transmission technology on board: our sonar transmission system."

"But what we're receiving so far is just sound waves, and they sound like they're of natural origin. Since we've been tinkering with it for days, our onboard computer isn't going to help much," Peter argued, and Brian nodded as he replied:

"But maybe we already have more than we think. My dreams must have something to do with it. So, this is something I have to stay on."

"In addition, it's also not advisable to allow foreign signals into our onboard computer."

Brian nodded again and explained, "Too bad we can't produce this gas bubble around the boat now. When we were going fast with it, my dream was the strongest. I'll have to try something else to get into that trance again. Maybe I can find a way to access that network. It can't go any more wrong than that."

"But you know, in a submarine, not so much should go wrong!" Peter gave to consider.

"Are you scared?"

"Have you ever done this before?"

"Well, I haven't managed to do that myself yet. But theoretically, I know my way around," Brian admitted.

Peter was not nearly as optimistic as Brian, so he sounded resigned, "That sounds like I can't drive, but I've been a passenger."

"Sometimes the passenger is worse off than the driver. Believe me, I know what I'm talking about."

"After all, wouldn't your identity be immediately revealed if you suddenly appeared on the 'line'?"

"We still have to work on that. I hope we have enough time," Brian said.

Δ

On board the Chinese nuclear submarine

Commander Chén still hadn't gotten used to the fact that there was one room on his boat that he couldn't just walk into. This was the cabin of his two security officers. Unnecessarily, they had also put a no-entry sign on their door. After the completion, several sections were rebuilt once again. Some of the technology was replaced, and each section was equipped with sensors. These sensors registered the movements of the crew members. In addition, an alarm was triggered if someone without the required authorization level was in certain areas.

The standard equipment of naval soldiers now included a small chip under the skin with which everyone could authenticate themselves. This innovation had already spread to civilians because those who wore the chip enjoyed various privileges, such as free use of public transportation and bonus points in government assistance programs. The chip was advertised as a vital innovation for recovering injured people and medical care. The state media repeatedly pointed out how superior the Chinese system was to Western democracies, where personal rights still impeded progress in digitization.

Upon entering the command center, the crew was informed that the commander had gone on duty. Chén was the first to be informed about all the activities of the DaVinci II:

"The observed object is now believed to have set a target course. Their diving depth matches the bottom relief and is currently 1,600 feet. They should not be able to dive any deeper. The speed at a constant twenty knots. Their noise emission has been extremely reduced. We now only hear them over the buoys on the surface."

Chén looked at the map and said, "It will soon be narrower between the rocks. Then they will have to reduce their speed."

"Commander, we should increase our distance. If the boat ahead collides somewhere, we will have to take massive evasive action. That could give us away."

"Keep your distance!"

"Roger that!"

"Any attempts by the Germans to communicate with the outside world?"

"Absolutely nothing."

"As we pass San Nicolas Island, watch for the earthquake early warning system sonar buoys. There may have been other military-use sensors installed by now. They're hard to distinguish from the civilian buoys. If you notice anything, report it immediately."

From that moment on, the automatic monitoring was supplemented by a sonar technician. His task was to look for the new passive signals that the computer might miss. The American navy responded to the increasingly sophisticated stealth technology with its new measuring devices. Yet it was always the same. If you wanted to find something, you had to know what to look for.

The radio officer forwarded an incoming message directly to the commander, who received the note on his smartwatch. He could then decide whether it should be submitted to the officers on watch. Of course, that also depended on the sender and the confidentiality level. Incoming emails marked in blue came from the navy staff. A message marked in red was exclusively for Commander Chén, and the sender was sometimes just a synonym.

In red lettering, Chen had just read, "Fish must be netted after feeding!"

Δ

DaVinci II

For the next two hours, Brian concentrated on the notes, repeatedly typing something on the keyboard, waiting to see what the computer would spit out. When the result appeared, his reaction was always the same: His back pressed against the back of the chair, he grimaced and said, "So that wasn't it either."

Peter, who was working intently on his software, didn't let on that this was getting on his nerves. He also wondered because Brian wanted to meditate and try to penetrate the mysterious network of the Chinese via the trance state. But what Brian was doing didn't look like meditating. Although curiosity almost ate him up, he refrained from asking him.

Two steps away from them, the two navigation officers chatted as they checked the automatic controls on their monitors. Although the computer was steering the boat mainly on its own, course corrections were occasionally entered. The commander had instructed them to pass close to rising rocks until they reached their destination. The jagged mountain formation scattered the few soundwaves they emitted, making the boat even harder to track. In return, this trip was risky in other ways. The proximity to rock walls reduced forward visibility, and each time they approached the next turn, both navigators' pulses went up.

Outside the boat, it was dark at this depth, and the water was murky because of the current. Nevertheless, the crew saw a razor-sharp image of the surroundings on the monitors. However, this image was only simulated by the computer. For this purpose, the stored map material of the seabed was supplemented with the measured values of the sensors. A boat built for the NATO fleet could use the American underwater GPS. This used the acoustic signals from buoys on the coast and the transmitters attached to the seabed, officially installed only for earthquake research. When Brian had been explained the system a few days ago, he realized why only a submarine with secret NATO communications technology was suitable for this mission.

Shortly before reaching a ravine, Lange appeared in the control room and relieved the watch officer. He probably didn't want to leave the tricky navigation to his officers alone. Peter's shift had also begun a few minutes earlier. He was now again sitting next to his second sonar technician. The two wore their headsets as usual.

On the other hand, Brian returned to meditation for the time being. He had no new idea yet. Nevertheless, he hoped, by chance, to get back into this trance. However, a quick glance at Peter's face kept him from leaving the operations center. He knew the latter's body language well enough to recognize an inner excitement. Unlike Peter, the Cap'n did not make a nervous impression, while he seemed to be looking for something on the sonar charts. Until a piercing alarm signal quickened Brian's pulse. The sound was not loud, but with such a hideous tone that it would be suitable for a scary scene in a movie. And Brian didn't like such films for that very reason. The memory of his childhood came back immediately. Sometimes he secretly watched adult movies with friends. The others would always make fun of him when he hid his head behind a pillow at scary noises. Only when he was grown up and learned to enter the hidden world of thoughts with Anna did he realize what memories these sounds awakened in him. After thirty seconds, the alarm signal was back. Brian wondered if he should put on noise-canceling headphones to endure it.

"What's going on, Wilson?" the commander asked.

"Oh, that's just..."

"I see. You'll get used to it. This sound is quieter than a falling ballpoint pen but at a pitch transmitted to the brain, directly to the alarm center in the limbic system, even when you are asleep."

That different frequency could trigger amazing things in the brain was something Brian knew, of course, from advanced studies on nonverbal communication. It's similar to an ordinary alarm system. It involves the generation of a feeling essential for survival: fear. First, just a suspicion, a thought settled more profoundly inside him. But it motivated him so much that he was already sure he had found something useful to access this network. It had to have something to do with this alarm. Before he could think about it any longer, it became clear what the warning meant. Peter waved from his seat and spoke in a hushed tone, "Cap'n, take a look!"

Lange immediately saw that Peter wanted to get something important off his chest. He had pushed the headphones up to one side and declared, "I hear something here that shouldn't be there!"

Lange took a pair of headphones and listened. Everyone stared at the screens. Possible causes for the noise were listed. Brian couldn't do much with the values displayed, but all the more with Lange's face.

The nautical officer asked, "Distance confirmed?"

"Yes," came from the second sonar technician.

Lange shook his head and said, "This far out and at this depth, I'm more likely to assume a school of fish that has taken an unusual formation."

Brian saw that Lange was not telling the truth. But why would he downplay a danger? Did he know what had caused that noise in reality?

In the water could be all sorts of obstacles. An old fishing net or ropes caught in the steering gear is very annoying. That doesn't cause much damage but forces the boat to surface. Brian had no way of knowing whether Lange didn't want to worry the crew further or whether he had an inkling of what the signal was really about. Everyone was relieved when the commander said, "Reduce speed to ten knots."

In this sea area, all underwater mountains and shipwrecks were accurately marked on the maps within a few feet. But there were also other artificial obstacles. The most dangerous of these were the underwater buoys attached to the bottom with ropes. Because of the ocean currents, these buoys did not always float in the same place. Colliding with such an object would not cause any damage. Still, the vibration would be heard immediately at the earthquake center.

"Mr. Gross, were you able to find a clue as to whether X1 has been near us again?"

"No, haven't heard anything since the last contact, Cap'n."

No sooner spoken than the second sonar technician raised his arm to draw attention to himself. All eyes were on him. Then he pointed to the screen. A faint signal lit up two-and-a-half miles behind them and faded shortly afterward.

"Identified?"

"That's definitely X1. Because we slowed down, they had to use their steering jets. They want to keep their distance from us. But that must have caught them right at the entrance to the gorge. With the current, it must have taken more correction not to get too close to the rocks."

"Must have been a good idea then, Cap'n, to go through the narrow part here."

"That wasn't a good idea, more like normal navigation 101. X1 has a problem taking the tight turns with its size."

"Could you actually find out what our chaser's name is?" someone on the team wanted to know.

"Sadly, no. We don't even know if our pursuer has a male or female soul."

Brian, wondering about the gender of the boat's name, remembered the introductory video. Someone jokingly mentioned that sailors sometimes have unusual ideas about the underwater world. The thing about the soul of the boat was probably one of them.

Out of curiosity, Fabrice had been standing by the doorway to the command center listening, saying, "I'd rather X1 had a male name. The prospect of death becomes even more terrifying when the knife at the throat is held by a woman."

Even Lange had to smile and responded, "I can reassure you. It will probably be more of a man's name. So far, the Chinese have not been very imaginative regarding naming. All nuclear submarines up to now have been called Long March."

"And then they still call their launch vehicles in space that, too?"

"Yes, it probably has something to do with the outdated leadership. The Chinese are running out of ideas," someone joked. Zobel, who had also just reported for duty, said, "Back when the Chinese had chemical weapons, they traditionally gave them female names. Killing with poison is also a female domain in the Middle Kingdom."

Lange let the crew have their way to relax a little during the hours of tension. But now he called for discipline again and sent everyone out of the command room who was not on watch duty.

The silence that followed was eerie. Everyone knew someone was breathing down their necks whose intentions they did not know. Lange could not discuss with anyone in this situation what his own suspicions were. That would increase the tension. For what lay ahead of them, he needed clear-thinking heads. But he would also like to know how much was known to X1's principals about the DaVinci II's destination. That would greatly simplify the strategy in the game of hide-and-seek. If X1 got closer to the American coast, Lange would have to devise another diversionary tactic. Secretly, he hoped Brian had already figured out something about the contents of the radio traffic with X1. Lange had expected more from this medium and communications genius because the generals had touted him.

Every mission is different, and this guy just learned about the circumstances of a sub. Maybe he just needs more time, Lange thought before retreating to his cabin to make a private and encrypted logbook entry.

**Logbook DaVinci II
Day 5, 1725 board time
Private entry Lt. Capt. Richard Lange**

-The uncertainty about the mission's goal has not unsettled the team. The mood is upbeat.
-After scalding, the cook is presumably unfit for duty for another two days. Tasks were taken over by the crew. For details, see the medical log.
-Brian Wilson is acting normal again after initially suspecting a **stress injury**.
-X1 continues pursuit but keeps its distance. A diversion is intended to disguise our target coordinates.

After the watch officer's announcement over the intercom, he completed his entries more quickly than usual, "Commander, to the command center, please!"

Once there, Lange saw first officer Matteo Braun checking the computer data on the analog chart table. Lange stood next to Braun and saw the marking of the current position.

Braun said, "We are now reaching the end of the gorge. After that, there is only this flat plain in front of us before we finish. How far do we want to approach?"

"For that, we first need to check the depth data on the nautical charts."

"These data are definitely wrong. Look: the measured values deviate from the maps already in the current range."

"The water depth in the target area is indicated on the map as 1,100 feet. I estimate that at the base of the formation, it is 990 at most."

Lange instructed, "We stay close to the seabed and keep a distance of two hundred yards from the formation. The target must be approached in a wide arc from the north so that we remain maneuverable in the current when sailing slowly. There, everything is surveyed first."

"Do you want to go inside?" asked Braun.

"We'll see about that."

Peter commented in his own way, "Maybe the Americans are already waiting at the entrance to tell us that we don't have a valid ticket for this museum."

"Instead of worrying about tickets, pay attention to the environment for a change!"

"Right now, only one object is moving near us, but we haven't received a new signal from X1. Thus, we don't know how far away it is from us now."

"As it gets closer, sooner or later, they will give themselves away. X1 will also catch the Americans' eye because of its size. Would be really bad if the Coast Guard took notice of it."

"There's a question that's been bothering me since the beginning, Cap'n."

"Fire away!"

"How can our mission be kept secret from the US Coast Guard when our mission comes from NATO's Special Operations Command."

Lange did not avert his gaze from the map as he replied, "I can't tell you that. You know the command structure. We receive our orders, and even I only know as much as necessary. Maybe the whole thing has been arranged with the Americans."

"Or are the Americans making common cause with the Chinese?" Braun speculated.

"Well, that's hard to imagine."

Braun remained adamant, "Maybe not at the official level. But there are plenty of other channels through which these countries do business."

"Don't let anyone hear about such conspiracy theories! You are an officer, and you must reason."

"It's hard for me sometimes, to be honest."

Lange sounded surprised, "What do you mean?"

"Our destination alone is bizarre. As far as I know, only Americans have ventured near these coordinates. Now we are supposed to pick up something here while the Chinese follow us. That sets off all the alarm bells for me."

Lange was taken aback by the last words and asked, "What are we to pick up? I don't recall seeing anything like that mentioned in my mission orders. Or did you find anything like that in the log?"

Braun was slightly unsettled. Yet he was eager to learn more about the mission from his commander, "I admit, the receiving of some object is only from crew rumors. Still, I am the first officer on this boat, and I expect you to fully brief me on the mission. This has not been a test cruise for a long time, and should you become unfit for duty for any reason, I must be able to act as your replacement, Cap'n."

"You're quite right, Braun. But I have to abide by the mission order. It states that I will not inform the crew until the target coordinates are reached."

"That's understandable. But why does this Wilson guy know and I don't?"

"Have you spoken to him?"

"No. The sailors heard him talking in his sleep. And he must have been talking clearly about an iron artifact. That immediately prompted the guys to search the knowledge bases for missing iron artifacts."

"So?"

"Now, there is a rumor that it is an ancient stargate or something like that. Forgive me. I am speaking in the words of the sailors. From the looks of our destination, some here already imagine we're about to enter the underwater gate to hell."

Lange's face remained calm as he said, "I should have foreseen that rumors could turn into horror stories. But it would have been better if you informed me as soon as this started. That also contributed to the uncertainty of the team. We need to know what's happening with the sailors at all times. As for Wilson, how much he knows is irrelevant. He has specific duties on board and is my personal assistant."

"What are you going to do, Cap'n?"

"Gather the crew and tell the truth. But first, I will confront the second officer. Tell him to prepare himself. As the ship's doctor, he'll get work with cases of nervous overload. Some of them may go crazy when they find out what we're going to do next."

Δ

Freiburg, university campus

Gregor met Anna in the coffee kitchen and spoke to her, "Any idea how you can get in touch with Wilson again? Tony could probably help you, but he's back in Rostock. They need him there again because of the thing in Malta. But Kai might be able to help you, too. He always has good ideas. Besides, he's been on the road with Tony and knows his special European ritual places."

Before this conversation, Anna had been in the meditation room for two hours, trying again to reach Brian. It seemed hopeless as long as he was in this underwater vehicle, and Anna had no means of support. She now realized more and more how much she had relied on her port stone over the past few years. Perhaps it would have been better to look for a fail-safe solution. Anna couldn't even get help from her mentor in the *aka* without the stone. She had always helped her with tricky questions and sometimes asked other *Kha* for assistance. Anna was even more annoyed because the connection to the ethereal world used to work without the port stone. For convenience, however, she had not trained her brain for years to penetrate the higher vibrational level without aids.

She decided to follow Gregor's advice and asked Kai. Because the exercise made her feel good, she ran straight to his lab. One of the assistants said he could be found at a construction site in the next building, where new lab equipment was just being installed.

"Hi Kai, got a minute?"

"Right now, it's bad. We have to finish today. Tomorrow the next company will come."

"It's vital, and it doesn't take long!"

"If you look like that, all men probably do what you want," Kai said, admitting defeat.

Anna didn't feel good about dragging Kai deeper into this. Eventually, she did enlighten him, "We had talked the other day about this field amplifier that I could use to contact Brian Wilson from England."

"I remember."

"We need to get a message to Brian urgently, but I can't go to England right now. I don't know of any such strong spiritual places in Germany that you can still access without supervision. Do you know if something like the *Whispering Knights* has been found near us lately?"

In truth, Anna speculated that Tony and Kai might have talked about it. Their partners were best friends and also happened to be pregnant at the same time. This meant that the two men also spent much time together in their free time.

"I can't think of anything off the top of my head, but I have a question. I've been thinking about our last discussion for a long time. You may be trying way too hard. Some interesting research by neurologists deals with where the memory for our consciousness is actually located. In any case, the brain is unnecessary because the beings in this *aka* don't have a biological brain. Everything there is intangible."

Anna was amazed that Kai was actually still dealing with this. His words sounded as if he had gone deep into the subject. Then she replied, "That's true. But whichever way you look at it, we're not getting anywhere. The tool that would allow me to access the collective memory has been stolen. And even if I could get there, the thoughts of each individual are not so easily accessible using that either."

"Fortunately! Otherwise, my boss would probably have fired me several times already," Kai wanted to try with a joke. But Anna didn't feel like thinking about what he might have done. She ignored his comment and said, "To overcome the barrier to the thought memory, you have to have certain genetic prerequisites. Sergei and a few others have been researching this topic for ages. All we know is that consciousness cannot have a material storage medium. In rare cases, patients have lost up to half of their brains due to injuries or diseases. Nevertheless, their memories came back after some time. The Prof is sure that we store thoughts somewhere in our sleep phases. We suspect it ends up in the *aka,* but no one knows with certainty."

"You've been in contact with these mentors. They should know," Kai said.

"Yes. And the beings from the aka explain it to us, too. The problem is that our thinking works differently within the material world than in higher dimensions. That is why some things of metaphysics still remain closed to us. Therefore, the mentors advise us to advance the exploration of the quantum world. The crucial brain areas would be activated during this learning process over time. We also know that the brain develops when exposed to certain stimuli. Inactive genes can be activated if they are stimulated accordingly. Sergei suspects that the inactive genes are not really inactive. They are just waiting for a certain signal."

"Speaking of signals. Weren't you talking about the crop circles the other day?"

Anna stumbled and looked through Kai at some imaginary point. Then she almost shouted, "Gee Kai, that's it!"

"What is what?"

"The signal! The crop circles could be the signal we need. Sometimes you have to ask the right people."

She couldn't hide her excitement and got all euphoric, "Would you help me decode the crop signal?"

"I thought you had already checked off. Didn't you tell me it was a mandala, a sacred symbol among Hindus and Buddhists?"

"Yes. But that was it. Why a mandala, I don't know. What about now? Will you help me?"

"I'd love to, but you'll have to work it out with my boss. Someone else would have to supervise the construction work on the new machine."

Kai already knew Anna's way of working. Before she plunged into a topic, it was first necessary to meditate. And so the joint search began that day as well. There was a thick carpet in her office. Both sat down cross-legged opposite each other. Anna put her left hand on his head to ensure that Kai didn't take too long to reach the right trance state. The two bodies touched each other with their knees, and energy flowed into Kai's body through all contact points. He had no idea whether he was awake or already in a light trance. In any case, he just imagined what his partner would think of this exercise. She was not exactly a spiritual person. These thoughts didn't go unnoticed for long because he heard Anna say, "Now, for once, concentrate only on me."

Later, he didn't know whether he had heard or thought her voice. It was the same with the following conversation. For the first time in his life, he felt inside another person's head. He didn't need to formulate words. It was as if they were talking in a foreign language, but no one had to learn it first. Kai started to get into this feeling of well-being and enjoyed every second of this encounter. Then Anna asked, *"Are you ready to go on the train?"*

"The train is already moving. It's too late to jump off."

"Just open your eyes when you want to jump off."

Kai didn't notice it immediately, but later, he realized that Anna was using particular cues to steer his thoughts in a specific direction. By naming these signal words, she made him mentally go a certain way or ride the train, as she jokingly called it. This was probably her method of taking students to another place in such sessions. They would always travel together, and one would explain his thoughts. An exceptional experience for Kai was that he didn't have to explain technical terms to Anna. The information flowed as a matter of course. Likewise, he understood things immediately, even though they were new territory for him. Actually, though, a single signal word had caused a mental breakthrough for Kai. That was when Anna told him about the Tibetan monks, how they sat on their prayer rugs and intoned in unison chants a tone that went to the core.

It was this tone that would not let him go. Instinctively, Kai realized that the goal of the joint meditation had been reached, and he now wanted to wake up again. Seconds later, he lolls up from his cross-legged position with terrible pain in his legs and buttocks. He was not used to this sitting posture and had trouble staying on his feet. Reflexively, he looked at his watch and was amazed that almost three hours had passed, but they only seemed like twenty minutes to him.

When Anna was also standing again, he said, "It's no wonder you spend twelve hours a day at the institute if you spend half the time daydreaming like that. Like you, I also want to earn money in my sleep."

"How are you feeling?"

"Cool, I feel like having read two books without being tired. Only the legs have something against this sitting position."

"Get used to stretching exercises regularly. Then it won't bother you anymore," Anna advised him.

Kai went toward the door, but she called him back, "Stay here! Before you go, I want to know what fascinated you about the monks' singing."

"I believe this sound and the mandala have a deep inner relationship."

Kai went to Anna's terminal and logged into the institute's network. He looked for something in his records and said, "Look. I know the pattern I saw earlier. From the looks of it, all these crop circles show a tone with the same frequency. It's a C-sharp, and if I'm not mistaken, that's about 136 hertz. And you know what? That's the tone the monks sing when they chant 'Om' together for meditation."

"And why do the mandalas differ so much in detail?" Anna wanted to know.

"When you vibrate different materials with the 'Om,' they also show different patterns. From the patterns, we can see which materials are involved."

As an engineer who regularly worked with ultrasound technology, Kai quickly found suitable software to visually display the vibration of various materials. Several crop circles strikingly resembled the pattern water forms on the surface when sonicated at 136 hertz. Then Kai simulated the vibration of iron filings on a glass plate. This pattern looked like the flower of life.

"Wait a minute!" Anna said more to herself and continued, "I have an idea. But I'd like to talk to Gregor first."

She dialed Gregor's number and discussed with him for a while things that sounded strange to Kai. Half an hour later, the three were standing in the laboratory of another institute at the university. There they met Ashley Harrison, a molecular geneticist who worked on evolution in human genetics. The dark-skinned woman in her late thirties was one of the few Americans who had decided to work in Europe for much less money. She did not like to talk about the time in Texas, where she initially became known for her research. In her publications, she argued that the Western way of life, with its diet, detachment from nature, and Western music, harmed genetic makeup. According to her thesis, people with mixed genetic backgrounds would be much better able to adapt to changing environmental conditions.

In Freiburg, Sergei offered her the opportunity to work with young people whose genetic makeup had already begun to prepare for the next evolutionary stage. Anna was one of her subjects at the time. Her excellent musical ear made her a sought-after participant in test series where the influence of acoustics on the human genome was at stake. Over the next two hours, it turned out that Ashley would be just the right person for this topic. She was not at all surprised by Anna's theory about crop circles. They didn't talk about Brian and the lost DaVinci II at first.

After Gregor briefly explained what it was all about, Ashley presented news from her research, "What Kai suspects regarding sound theory leads us to a fascinating topic. Sergei is supporting me on something I've been working on for a while. Years ago, I met Prof. Garjajev at a congress in Moscow. He gave a talk on his theory of *wave genetics*. Perhaps you know that the subject is very controversial in the professional world and is more or less assigned to the category of esotericism. I do not share all of the theses. But one thing is fascinating..."

Ashley went to a lab cabinet on the opposite wall and picked up a folder of high-resolution photos. The first photo showed molecular chains of human genetic material. The material was surrounded by a colored ring of light. Ashley explained in another series of photographs, "We've known for a while that the more active neurons are, the lighter they emit. But the phenomenon with the photons produced doesn't seem unique to nerve cells. Here you can see something that I didn't believe at first. We had DNA from living tissue vibrated with sound and electromagnetic waves. Depending on which frequencies were used, different color patterns emerged, which we could photograph."

"What kind of frequencies did you use?" asked Kai, already having the 'Om' in mind.

"Crosscut. What can be seen in the first photos came about only through human speech. Nevertheless, we believe that sound is only the door opener. In fact, it became quite curious when we realized that it didn't matter in which language we spoke with the molecular chains. This shows us that the wording is not decisive, but the meaning, i.e., the semantics, arising in the speech center."

Either Kai was trying to lighten the mood, or it just slipped out, "So there are spells after all. I'll have to go back to the Harry Potter books!"

Ashley didn't hold that against him. She even said, "Who knows? Legends about wizards have to come from somewhere. It's not for nothing that a veil of secrecy has always been placed over ancient spells. Look at the story about the Ark of the Covenant. In my opinion, it contained not only the clay tablets with the Ten Commandments. All the efforts of the Crusades would not have been worth it. The myth of the tablets was perhaps a nice story for the common people. The patrons were probably after a completely different kind of book. Above all, they were interested in the measuring tools from Egypt that the Israelites brought with them in this chest. Soon after the Crusades, architecture had its breakthrough in Europe. The fact that it was part of the knowledge of antiquity can be easily seen in the facades of the cathedrals."

She drew her visitors' attention to a photo on the wall. It showed the west side of Chartres Cathedral with one of the three famous rose windows. Ashley stood with a few others directly below it, pointing her right hand to the round window above the portal. How could it be otherwise? The window was in the shape of a mandala.

Kai moved a little closer to the photo. Now it was visible that Ashley pointed with three spread fingers to the round window above the cathedral's entrance. He then said, "Aha, you know the secret language of the Knights Templar?"

"Of course. Three fingers, the sign for trigonometry. Only Jacob's staff as a surveying tool in my left hand was still missing. Then I'd have looked like the surveyors of the Templars at that time."

"You could have borrowed the cane from this gentleman here," Anna giggled and pointed her finger at a man standing near Ashley.

"Are you crazy? That's Sergei. You didn't recognize him, did you? That was after his car accident. He really wanted to go to

247

the cathedral with us, but he was crying all the time...don't tell him that we made fun of him."

Anna watched Kai as he became more and more impatient. Ashley had her own way of getting people's attention. Even during her lectures, she kept it up until the last students in the lecture hall finally put their cell phones away.

Finally, she continued, "Returning to the photography of DNA molecules: At some point, we found that some experiments could not be repeated. The molecules of living DNA initially formed reproducible results. If the sound waves were identical, identical images were also formed. Later, however, the experiments could no longer be repeated, as if the DNA used had had enough of us. The emitted light waves suddenly formed completely different structures and what could be seen in the photos made no sense to us. I suspect this might be an answer we don't understand yet."

Gregor knew about these experiments, but the pictures were always fascinating, "Now turn the page!"

"Here are some other pictures, but we couldn't publish them..."

She turned the page, and Kai couldn't see anything at first. Only after a few seconds did he startle. The images taken with the microscope showed something that was actually not possible. A colored ring of light and dark areas could be seen around the cell tissue. This time, however, they clearly recognized the head of a human being. A human being with the face of Ashley.

"You may be the woman with the most followers on this planet. And that's without the internet!" Kai joked, but Ashley didn't think it was funny and kept talking:

"To clarify again: Which images are shown in the photos seems to be decided by the DNA itself. Sometimes you can see nearby objects, other times, you see people present. But there have also been objects depicted that were far away. This shows us that the distance to the reproduced object does not matter."

Anna asked, "So there is no usable dictionary yet to converse with DNA?"

"No. All we have so far are a few approaches. And as I said, one thing is unusual. We can only stimulate DNA to respond to our language. What response we get is always a surprise." Ashley said, and after a few seconds of silence, she asked, "How much time do you have today?"

"As much as you need!"

Ashley fetched a camera with a tripod to which a vast lens was attached. Kai knew this technique. Around the lens were small lamps. They emitted light in the visible and invisible range.

She asked Kai to place the back of his hand on a piece of paper. The image of his hand then appeared on a monitor. The skin emitted light in different colors. A light shone around the hand, becoming fainter with increasing distance.

"Your aura, or rather a small part of it," Ashley explained and then continued, "Now we'll make these light signals audible for us. For this, we use software that I got in Russia."

A moment later, they heard a mixture of hissing, crackling and wavelike individual sounds. It certainly didn't sound very harmonious, and Anna commented, "Wow, Kai, you really have to improve your expression! You won't attract anyone to such a concert."

"Very funny!"

In the meantime, Ashley had taken two Petri dishes out of the refrigerator. In them was human mucosal tissue. Then she muttered, "Let's see if my little friends feel like talking to us today."

She clamped the Petri dishes into a holder. Beneath them hung loudspeaker membranes in various sizes. Then she bent down to the samples and spoke to their contents as if they were spoiled pets, "Because you've been so nice and good, there's a new concert today. Let me introduce... this is Kai, the soloist."

Each petri dish was filmed from above with a special microscope. At first, the images on the two monitors were similar. Slowly, soft contours began to emerge. Then one of the images became clearer. It was, without a doubt, an almost full-grown fetus in a natural position in a woman's body. Kai was in a good mood, but a shiver ran down his spine. Pale as chalk, he stared at the monitor.

"What's wrong?" asked Anna, startled.

"I think I know what that is..."

"You mean..."

"Yes, I know this picture from the last ultrasound. Look, he's trying to put both thumbs in his mouth. That's exactly how I saw it with our baby a few days ago."

As if the molecular chains had been waiting for the right moment, the image of the second petri dish became clear. It was the complete body of Kai. Even his face was visible.

"If that's not proof that a part of your aura contains the complete information about your body! And even more than that. It's not very clear, but you can also see the scar from your thyroid surgery," Ashley said.

"But that's not possible. A scar is not part of the genetic information!"

"Right. But what you see is not your genetic information. The tissue is from a completely different person. We have shown the alien DNA only a part of your aura. Your aura is a field that contains both the genetic blueprint and the current state of your body. Probably even your thoughts."

"And what about our unborn child? How do the molecules know about our child?" Kai wanted to know but probably already suspected the answer. He couldn't think clearly in his excitement.

"Gee Kai, that's the most expensive paternity test ever!" Gregor joked.

"Gregor is right. With fertilization of the egg cell, you have begun to replicate a part of yourself. The little one also already has an aura, and it is connected to you through the physical world of quanta."

"But why do these DNA molecules do that?"

"We addressed them with 'music', and the molecules responded. Only sometimes do they do something quite unexpected. That could also be a response, but we don't understand it yet. And that's the problem my team is working on right now."

Gregor asked Ashley to go into a small room next door. Ashley said to the others when the two returned, "All right. I may be able to help you. Gregor has agreed to let me look at this as a big field trial. However, I know there is already research on this topic elsewhere, and we are far along here compared to the rest of the world. Something like this always arouses the covetousness of competitors. I, therefore, have to keep the team very small. Especially here in Freiburg, guests like to sneak around sometimes, and I don't like to let them look into our studies."

"Do you think we can use your little friends to send a message to the other side of the earth?" Kai asked.

"The distance doesn't matter. We don't know exactly how it works, but the information transfer is faster than light and doesn't seem to take time to transmit. In return, however, we have already been able to demonstrate something else. The DNA also reacts to feelings. Joy and enthusiasm, for example, cause the molecular chains to expand. Sadness and pain cause them to contract. In the last five years, we have discovered so many new things, of which we had only vague ideas at the beginning, that hardly anything can surprise me. Oh, well ... one thing did blow my mind."

Ashley again made one of her regular pauses, with which she could drive impatient listeners crazy. At the same time, her face radiated genuine joy, and Anna felt that her whole body was surrounded with pleasant energy.

"Yes, what is it now?"

"Nothing special, really. I fell in love."

"Congratulations!" Kai pressed out and now looked even more puzzled than before.

"Well, I was able to demonstrate, as a byproduct of my happiness, so to speak, what happens to DNA when people fall in love. Until now, we only knew that certain hormones and neurotransmitters like dopamine play a role in this. As far as our studies have shown, however, this is only a lower level by which the feelings of happiness are triggered, and certain biological needs arise. This ensures that only two people who are a good genetic match will ultimately reproduce. Look, I then asked myself why I had chosen this particular partner. However, we had passed each other for years without paying attention."

"Exciting! Will you give me the recipe?" Anna let out enthusiastically, and Ashley laughed off, "If I invent a love potion, maybe I'll let you try it."

"Hey! Don't give the cook any of these bottles. If he ever gets frustrated at his job, maybe some of it will end up in the cafeteria food. Imagine if everyone here suddenly fell in love with everyone else. That would be a madhouse!" Kai warned, giggling like a schoolboy.

"Well, well, well. A topic like that is going to turn you back into a teenager," Anna said, but Ashley quickly brought everyone back to the point, "It wouldn't work that way, guys. Because I'm not done with my explanation yet. Not everyone can fall in love with everyone. Not even if people were a super biological match. There seems to be a prescribed regularity, and unfortunately, it sounds a little less romantic."

"Too bad," was Anna's reaction.

It was clear to see that Kai was still preoccupied with his mental cinema. He couldn't stop giggling when Ashley continued explaining her thesis, "So it was soon confirmed that we are all connected via our aura. I then asked myself the question, how does one aura communicate with the other. I mean, what material connects my aura to my friend's aura?"

"You said earlier that it was the quantum world through which we are connected," Gregor replied.

"Right, but we still know little of this world of elementary particles. We are now trying to make contact from the macro world. We don't know how the information actually gets to this beyond. So long we call the effect simply further the entanglement. Nevertheless, we already know a way how we can penetrate. But that's Kai's specialty ...," Ashley said, nodding at him in anticipation of an answer.

"It's the vibrations we also saw earlier when we tried my hand."

"That's right. We can penetrate this unknown world with certain frequencies and even cause reactions. As unromantic as it may sound, lovers' bodies only vibrate in the same frequency range. This stimulates the molecular chains in their DNA to cause some parallel reactions. Only then are the appropriate hormones produced in the body, triggering that feeling of happiness. In fact, of course, it is much more complex than that. But we still don't know exactly why we feel happiness but at the same time behave completely stupidly. I mean that newly in love lose a part of their rational thinking. Gregor, isn't that your specialty?"

"The little allusion in your last sentence I blame on the fact that German is not your native language," Gregor joked. Only now, Ashley noticed her little linguistic faux pas.

But Gregor had already continued, "Actually, Sergei is the expert. I know the partial loss of rational thinking may be part of the genetic program. The activated genes that enable this absolute affection for a person lead to a certain degree of dependency. Imagine that I want to manipulate a large group of people. I want them to listen only to me. To do this, I need to win their unquestioning loyalty, preferably by making them fall in love with me. And I have to prevent anyone else from getting in my way. So people must not start questioning anything I tell them. Does that sound familiar to you guys in any way?"

Anna replied, "Of course. That's what we observe with newly in love. While outsiders wonder about the unreasonable decisions, people in Seventh Heaven don't mind how others think about it."

Then she suddenly laughed and said, "So one thing is for sure, Ashley. Your research doesn't lend itself to a romance novel. You'd better keep writing reference books."

"You could be right about that. But if Gregor's theory is correct, and I'm convinced it is, then you could make more of a political thriller out of it."

"Why?"

"Quite simply, if someone could figure out how to make this manipulation practical, they could manipulate large groups of people. Think about what is currently happening in autocratically ruled states."

But now Anna has concentrated again and answered, "No one needs to find that out today. It has always been part of people's lives. I know that not everyone likes it when I occasionally quote the first commandment of the Holy Scripture: YOU SHALL HAVE NO OTHER GODS BESIDE ME!
Where people adhere to the commandment, the principle works."

"Sure, but that still wouldn't give me a tool to make the masses fall in love with me, their new god."

When Gregor said that, he turned to Kai, "That gives me an idea! What would you need to irradiate many people at once with a certain frequency?"

"A transmission tower."

"Exactly. And where do we find something like that? I mean, not today, but before there was radio and television?"

"For example, in Egypt or in Asia. In front of every temple, we find these pillars and obelisks. I know conspiracy theorists also count the great obelisks in Washington, Paris, London or Rome as tools of the powerful elites. I understand these novel monuments rather as symbols of power only. They were adopted from the ancient models, but without knowing how they once actually worked."

"And you think these pillars might have once served to enforce love for the gods?"

"In the beginning to the gods and later to the priests and kings," Kai replied.

Now Anna could no longer hold back, "And that brings us to our real problem. We believe that in these minutes, someone is trying to recover such an ancient tool or let's call it an antenna, from the depths of the ocean. If they succeed, it might be possible to trigger some genetic reset in humanity!"

"This brings us back to our discussion the other day. Didn't you suggest that humanity would be more peaceful if everyone agreed on a single religion?" Gregor directed his question to Anna, but Ashley beat her to the punch and answered:

"If one day I ever believe that someone would steal an item to use it for the greater good, I'll start writing fairy tale books!"

Then Anna added, "That's right, and we don't know anything about the motives of the people who sent this submarine there. The fact that it is a military mission with heavy weapons on board makes it very dangerous. And anyway, that this mission will be a disaster is obvious. If even a single weapon is fired, it could trigger a global conflict. Perhaps the artifact's recovery will also succeed, but that would be a similar disaster. The use of this antenna would be a threat to all religions. And some countries on this planet are ruled by religious fanatics. They are already threatening their neighbors today even without this additional igniter."

Gregor nodded and said, "We can't take care of everything now. Others can find out who the principals are. There has to be a way for Anna to talk to Brian, who is aboard this submarine. This is our only chance to keep the captain away from the artifact's hiding place."

Kai had already been deep in thought minutes before. He had begun to occupy himself with his new task. He couldn't get the idea of the stolen stone out of his head: *Anna could use this material to connect her consciousness with higher planes of existence. Could a suitable replacement for the stone be found?*

"Anna, have you ever researched where the stolen stone originated? Or has there ever been an analysis done?"

"Yes. It is a common silicate rock with a central inclusion of several fluorite crystals. The origin is probably northwest Africa, now Mauritania."

"But it's a rock like any other!"

"The special thing is the fluorites inside. They react to electromagnetic fields and temperature. If you hold it in your hand and lower your brain waves to a low-frequency range during meditation, you cause the lattice structure to change in the fluorites."

Kai listened with fascination and seemed to understand, "So *teta waves* or *alpha waves* in the brain could be the trigger."

"As far as I know, you must generate the two frequency ranges in parallel. This already happens during simple hypnosis," Anna said.

"Do you know how we can get such a stone?"

Anna looked at Gregor and seemed to expect him to agree. When he nodded, she answered Kai, "You know, the builders of the pyramids in Giza have already used this principle. The large chamber in the Pyramid of Khufu is made of rose granite. Even more remarkable is that the blocks were placed with an accuracy of tenths of a millimeter. But what is interesting for us is that the granite's high quartz content reacts to pressure. A piezoelectric effect is created. Then, the pyramid functioned like a transmitter when someone chanted 'Om' in the chamber."

"I know this theory. But we can't get to Egypt today, can we?"

"Can you recreate similar conditions in your lab? With Ashley's sonic apparatus, we could..."

But Ashley immediately waved it off and said, "Forget it! We can't recreate the conditions in a pyramid in a thousand years. Let's try something that worked today."

Ashley explained her idea and said, "For that, we would have to find some genetic material from Brian. If he lives in Rostock, maybe we could find some of his hair in his apartment?"

Gregor was not convinced by the idea, "That would take a whole day. He's here at the university sometimes, too. Where does he live there?"

Anna replied, "He no longer has a residence here, so he stays at the hotel. Nevertheless, he sometimes uses one of my lockers during meditation training."

"Let's do it!"

They were lucky and found a small bag of Brian's paraphernalia. Among them was a knit cap with a few hairs stuck in it. Ashley quickly obtained several samples and began setting up her apparatus. She still had no idea if this would even work, but it was worth a try.

Δ

DaVinci II

The watch crew in the command center had changed in the meantime. Lange wanted to nap but returned with the watch officers quickly. At first, he thought it was unimportant, but then he could not rest because of a hint from his weapons technician. Since the boat was not equipped with torpedoes on test trips, the technician was mainly concerned with testing the training software for the onboard weapons. He had also volunteered to clean the torpedo room. There was some fitness equipment for the crew, and everyone was happy if the whole area remained clean.

Four of the eight torpedo tubes were fitted with special caps because they were suitable for emergency room flooding. While all the other empty tubes were occasionally used for storage, the larger four remained sealed. Every opening and closing was noted in the logbook. And here, something was wrong. The entries showed an anomaly. Two of the tubes had been opened and resealed before they were discarded. Lange had checked the data several times after the notice. In the simulation, all the tubes could be loaded and fired. The test logs only mentioned the poor usability of the new simulation software and suggested improvements. The technician criticized that balancing the weight after a simulated firing did not work for the sealed torpedo tubes and had to be done manually. With that, there were already two anomalies with the weapons software.

Lange somehow felt that this could not be a program error. He checked the armament logs several times, and it was clear: all torpedo tubes were empty. Then he had an idea. His first officer, Braun, and the other watch officers were busy surveying the area and updating the nautical charts. Lange did not want to delay this work under any circumstances, so he decided to act alone. In the logbook, he noted that the arming software had an irreparable malfunction. As required by regulation, he then ordered reinstalling the relevant program.

The whole thing took less than ten minutes, but his astonishment at the result of this action lasted longer. With the new software, the system displayed two tubes equipped with live torpedoes. Thus, his boat must have been deliberately tampered with. This required a significant intervention in the entire preparation process before departure. This abruptly changed the situation on his boat. There might be a comrade on board whom he could not trust. His next thought was as unbearable as a nightmare: *Do I have to expect a mutiny?*

The first officer approached behind and said, "Cap'n, the seabed mapping is complete. No obstacles. Nevertheless, I suggest slow sailing. Surprises are greatest when you feel safest."

Lange replied, "Agreed. Approach to within one thousand yards. Make sure we find a place with little current on the north wall. What is the ground condition?"

"Largely solid sediments. Should you wish to anchor, we could use a probe. Methane ice is not expected here, however."

"Good, let the free guards sleep for now. In an hour, I'll inform everyone of our plan."

In reality, Lange was unsure whether he should follow his plan. This was a situation in which even his attitude toward the matter could tip over. A feeling of powerlessness also began to paralyze his ability to act. His head was buzzing, but he didn't want to lose control. The only thing that helped now was to be faster than his opponent.

Several thoughts overlapped simultaneously: *Should I show up and inform Rear Admiral Breede about the situation? Then the mission would be a failure. We could only return. Or is an early termination the better option after all? As long as it is only a suspicion, I must follow the original order! Still, Breede is under the belief things are going as planned. He also couldn't possibly be part of a conspiracy or sabotage. There's no logic against that. What about this Wilson guy? He's got to be clean. I may have overestimated him, but he can't lie, and that's why no one will let him in on a plot. What about Gross? No, neither. If someone overrides my command, it needs an officer who can take control. That doesn't leave many. I have to concentrate on the First and the Doctor.*

All the brooding had made Lange even more insecure. He also quickly realized that he had made one mistake after another in trying to sound out his situation. Finally, one of the few good spirits that had not yet left him must have rattled his brain. Eventually, the penny dropped: There might be a traitor on board. That must have been the real reason for sending Brian Wilson along. His personnel file showed Brian to be an excellent observer. Now Lange wanted to take him cautiously into his confidence.

"Wilson, where are you with your work?"

"I must admit, Cap'n, we're kind of stuck here. All the conditions seem to be right. We know that the natural sound waves in the ocean are being used to exchange information with X1. However, there is no way to listen to the transmission. I cannot put my body into a stable trance for a connection attempt. And this doesn't help me with that either..."

Brian took the port stone out of his pocket and held it right in front of Lange's face.

"I don't understand. What is it?"

"This is an old artifact stolen from a private apartment in Germany. When your cabin was devastated by the blast wave, it fell out of your closet."

"I'll leave out the question of what the stone was doing in your pants pocket. If it was as you describe, it would be much more important to know how it got into my closet beforehand. When all the contents fell to the floor, I was annoyed that I had not closed it properly. Now I'm not so sure. There are a few things that don't add up."

Brian focused on Lange's body language and was sure he was telling the truth.

"So someone must have pretended that you had hidden this stone in your closet. That would discredit you to me, destroy the basis of trust."

"Could be. But you also said the thing hadn't helped you so far?"

"Right. In joint exercises with my meditation trainer, the stone had a kind of amplifier function. You could get into a trance quickly and go much deeper into higher energy levels than without it. I guess the stone doesn't work inside this sub."

"I see. But maybe this thing isn't real at all?"

That set off alarm bells for Brian, "I hadn't even thought of that. That may be why this thing doesn't work. But what's the point of a fake rock?"

"I don't know. But it could also be... Maybe it really is an attempt to sow distrust." Lange faltered.

Brian said, "Anyone who knows me superficially thinks I'm naïve about people. In some respects, there is some truth to that. But what always helps with distrust is a face-to-face conversation!"

"Thank you, I appreciate your loyalty very much," Lange said and saw in Brian's face that he had something else on his mind.

"Rear Admiral Breede bid me farewell with the words that I should only confide in you on board, even if he reported to me. As if he had a hunch that something might not be right here."

Two things became clear to Lange after this unusual conversation. The first was that there were already two of them searching for a rogue on board, and the second was that contacting Rostock would not be a good idea. Breede himself had advised against it. So, he must have suspected that the organization might be infiltrated. Now it was necessary to find out by whom. That might depend on whether they would return home at all.

CHAPTER 11

Rostock, Maritime Operations Centre

When Sean entered the conference room, he was blinded by the sun, even though the outside blinds were down. Some slats of the attached glare shield could not be closed.

Twenty chairs fit at the long conference table, but only half the side was set with drinks. Pot was already sitting at the front, reading something on his tablet. To Sean's greeting, he returned a mumbled Good afternoon. On the window side, some chairs were occupied with bags, which was probably interpreted as a reservation. Sean immediately thought those were the better seats since one didn't have to look into the faces against the sun.

Shortly after, Tony entered the room, who had already traveled to Rostock a few days earlier. They greeted each other, and Sean's facial expression revealed his thoughts. Tony couldn't stifle his laughter and whispered, "Assigning guests the most strategically inconvenient seats suits the military."

Sean grinned and had an idea. He walked purposefully to the window side and pushed an extra chair in between. *Guests first*, he thought and hung his jacket over the backrest. Pot looked up briefly but said nothing. To Tony, the situation was both comical and worrisome. The fact that Sean was so openly provoking the head of the investigative committee did not speak to a healthy climate. Tony found the stillness oppressive, and he tried to pass the time by pouring himself a cup of coffee. This helped to hide the excitement.

The night before, he had quickly put together a presentation summarizing the latest findings of the Malta investigation. Pot would have preferred not to invite Sean, but the protocol was to allow everyone involved in the examination to be present at the final meeting. Tony, on the other hand, had another task. His report contained points that raised new questions. Therefore, he also recommended that further research be done. He knew, of course, that he would have little influence on the decisions since it was a military matter. In the end, things turned out quite differently than expected.

At fourteen o'clock sharp, the rest of the participants entered the meeting room. It was funny to see Tony sitting alone at the wall side as if he had been summoned to a tribunal. Across from him sat Sean, flanked on either side by two people. Christina, as the organizer, sat at the front next to Pot. After a brief welcome, she asked the Lieutenant at Sea Pot for the final report of the Commission of Inquiry. After a half-hour presentation, no one was much wiser since everyone except Tony and Sean had received the draft in advance. Afterward, Sean was asked if he agreed with the content or wanted any additions. After that, the first part of the meeting was over, and Sean was seen off by Christina. She thanked him in a friendly manner and accompanied him outside.

The second part of the timetable was about Tony's expert opinion. This then actually had nothing to do with the accident in Malta. Tony was randomly coming across strange activity from a construction company during the inspection of the harbor area. The company contracted to backfill the unsecured hole had strangely arrived weeks earlier on a coastal construction vessel from Greece. As Tony was taking pictures of the harbor and the sea with his telephoto lens, he saw this construction ship anchored far out in front of the harbor entrance. The photo enlargement showed that the crew was busy replacing one of the boundary buoys for the shipping channel. This would not have been of particular interest had Sean not discovered earlier that the construction company belonged to an Indian company. The company's name had been in the headlines for some time. One of the managers was indicted on suspicion of corruption. In addition, it was also allegedly about espionage activities for China in India and Europe.

These were too many coincidences, and so Tony's interest was piqued. He, therefore, investigated even further. Later, he reported the matter in an email to the Naval Command in Rostock. In it, he recommended a thorough investigation of the circumstances. Not wanting to miss any of what would follow, he moved to a hotel overlooking the harbor. While working on his report, he kept an eye on the harbor entrance. A few hours later, one could see an American frigate checking buoys along the harbor entrance. They sent divers into the water at each buoy and disappeared after some time. Now that the Americans were taking care of it, the issue seemed settled for Tony for the time being. The whole thing had raised a lot of dust in the background, and in the end, that was why Tony should have come to Rostock personally.

Christina looked at her watch and said, "Rear Admiral Breede has announced himself for Dr. Peller's presentation. I suggest we wait a few more minutes."

Finally, Breede entered the room, bringing with him a plainclothes man Tony had seen on TV somewhere. Both took advantage of the empty chairs next to Tony. Then Breede stood up and opened the meeting by introducing his guest, "Please excuse our lateness. I am pleased that Mr. Koning found time to see the situation in person and came to Rostock. Most people will know him; Mr. Koning is Germany's Permanent Representative to the North Atlantic Council. The fact that he is attending today shows the importance of the matter. As usual, I remind all present of the absolute confidentiality of this conversation. Nor do we need to waste time with introductory words. As you know, we are discussing unusual Mediterranean activities."

As he spoke, Christina showed a nautical chart of the affected area. Breede poured himself a cup of coffee and continued, "Before we give the floor to Dr. Peller from our partner university in Freiburg, I'd like to thank him for being curious and persistent enough to pursue a matter that has eluded the coastguards for years. How that could happen, we will clarify later. Please, Dr. Peller, you have the floor!"

Giving lectures was part of Tony's everyday life. This time, however, the excitement was particularly significant. There was little time to prepare, and highly decorated officers sat at the table. The presentation began with a collection of detailed images from nautical charts and satellite evaluations of the Mediterranean. Beginning in Cyprus, Tony explained individual pictures, "If I may, I will go into details only if you wish. You can review everything later in my report.

So, my thesis is that we may deal with one of the largest intelligence activities in this region, perhaps beyond. With civilian companies' help and European research ships, transmitters are currently installed on all Mediterranean routes. I don't want to speculate about the reason for these activities. For now, I'll just go into how they work. As I found out, fifteen years ago, a Chinese consortium purposefully bought up European companies related to the safety of sea routes. These include companies that take care of repairing sea marks. As far as I have seen, all the contractors involved also largely comply with the tendering guidelines, so there are no irregularities to be found here regarding international law."

Breede added, "Since securing sea routes falls under the sovereignty of the countries, the military rarely interferes here."

"I was able to determine from satellite imagery that the marine buoyage in the Mediterranean is among the most modern in the world. Although their service life had not yet been reached, many signal buoys along the coasts have been replaced recently. At first, I thought this was due to cellular technology, which needed to be modernized. Many buoys now use satellite links to help ships and aircraft navigate. Since I am not an encryption expert, I asked someone from the mathematicians for help. Through his worldwide contacts, he found by accident that these buoys communicate with military satellites of unknown origin."

"You said something earlier about Chinese investors getting into various companies. Doesn't it justify that they are also satellites from China?"

Brede jumped in her, "It's not easy to find out. In our case, the direct contract partners are all European companies, mainly from Greece. Meanwhile, China has invested in hundreds of strategic companies worldwide. In telecommunications companies, too. That they also have an influence on their market activities can be assumed. To know exactly, we would need special auditors, and even they sometimes fail because of the complex commercial contracts."

Then Tony continued with his presentation, "Anyway, we could detect a novel form of communication. All the signal buoys exchanged were equipped with a sonar system for underwater transmission besides standard technology. Together with the satellites, the operator might one day in the future be able to intercept all communications from NATO's submarines." Tony paused and looked at Breede, who took that as an invitation to explain the real problem.

"You are probably wondering what is so extraordinary about this. I can only tell you that, at present, not a single submarine of our partners would be able to use such technology. So, who is to be intercepted here? The US Navy is testing the first prototypes of high-bandwidth sound transmission systems. I think you realize why I brought this to the attention of our ambassador to the North Atlantic Council yesterday. The German navy, by the way, has taken on the task of expanding its maritime patrols in the Mediterranean accordingly."

Then Tony continued his lecture, "But now I have to explain how I came to investigate such a case more closely. You must know that my specialty is the material analysis of archaeological artifacts. I am also familiar with high technologies from the *Mesolithic* and *Paleolithic* periods. So, this concerns the period 7000 BC and older."

After the last two sentences, Koning's facial expression changed considerably. Tony had expected this reaction, of course, and enjoyed it. He did not often have the opportunity to discuss such topics with people outside the field. A response from the ambassador was also not long in coming, "Dr. Piller..."

"Tony Peller, but Tony will do," Tony corrected his name.

"Excuse me, of course, uh... Tony, please explain to me what we mean by the high technology of the Mesolithic. I thereby think of things that have sprung from the industrial age. Do we have different definitions there?"

"Not at all, Mr. Ambassador. I only suspect you mean the current industrial age, which began in the nineteenth century. On the other hand, I specialize in technologies that began to disappear again around the time of the great ice melt twelve thousand years ago."

Koning was confused and looked at Breede. He felt compelled to say a few descriptive words but rather casually, "Tony, I had actually hoped that you would be a little gentler with our guest.

But yes, Mr. Ambassador, this is a matter of high technology from a time still missing from our history books. And please allow me to mention that we have not all lost our minds simultaneously."

Either Koning had quickly regained his composure, or he had already been confronted with such theses without being convinced. In any case, his following sentence sounded quite different, "Please, Tony, continue with your lecture. I'll listen to it for now."

"Well, I started to explain what my specialization has to do with the activities around the Mediterranean. To this end, you must know that I have been studying the Stone Age remains in Europe for a long time. Together with some fellow scientists, we are investigating what purpose certain artifacts might have once served. Without going into too much detail, looking at individual finds is useless. We have compiled the findings in a database and developed use scenarios with computer simulations. Today, however, I'd like to focus on just one of these things."

"Please go ahead. I am very excited!" said Koning.

"With the holes in the earth that have since been filled in and the ruts still visible in the rock, it was probably a transportation system used to carry heavy objects."

Tony showed one of the photos of the so-called *cart ruts* he had examined in Malta.

Pot's head was constantly going back and forth between the people present. Apparently, he couldn't believe how highly educated people could talk about this nonsense for so long.

When asked by Ambassador Koning what connections he saw between the traces in the rock and the transmitters on the Mediterranean coasts, Tony replied, "At first glance, no connection is apparent. Yet, I have been searching for anything that promises new insights into the old technical installations for a few years. Since I assume the traces are a transport system from the Mesolithic or earlier eras, we can make the first connection with the port on Malta. Some tracks lead and end at least 300 feet below the water's surface. I assume there must have been a prehistoric harbor when the sea level was much lower."

Example of tracks in rocky soil (Malta/Gozo), estimated age at least twelve thousand years [51]

"But what does it have to do with the modern-day buoys?"

Tony now showed the nautical chart once again. He marked all the sea buoys that the dubious company had attracted attention in Malta, "And now you can also see all the sites of early Stone Age installations that are now underwater. I suspect that in all cases, they were coastal towns and harbors."

Even before he had finished, unrest arose in the room. Faces exchanged glances, and Koning asked, "So the buoys are found where the former coastline ran? But why is someone marking these ancient Stone Age sites all over the Mediterranean?"

"To elaborate, it didn't just happen in the Mediterranean. Look..."

Tony enlarged the map on the wall screen and showed that parts of the Indo-Pacific region and the Pacific coast were equipped with an extensive network of sea buoys. Then he added, "It is likely that such newly installed sea buoys can also be found in other oceans. However, we do not have an inventory about that yet."

"I find it hard to imagine that no one noticed the installation of such a system around the world," said one of the attendees from the VIP window row.

Breede replied, "I'm afraid I have to admit that we only found all this out in the last few days. Without the work of Dr. Peller and Professor Fedorov's team, I think we'd still be clueless."

"Please wait a little longer with your praise. We may have to ask new questions at the end of my presentation."

"Sorry, I didn't mean to interrupt you. Please continue!" Breede said in response, and it seemed that Tony's words had left him a bit puzzled. He now had a bad feeling and feared that the presentation would still reveal details that had not been discussed.

Tony now showed computer graphics. Among them was a world map with lines drawn in. He explained the picture, "Based on the network of communication buoys known so far, I created another simulation yesterday. The results should be reviewed, of course, but I must make an urgent recommendation: The North Atlantic Alliance should act quickly to counter the doings in the world's oceans."

Breede and Koning sat on the edge of their chairs and stared at the wall screen. The Rear Admiral was surprised by these statements because he had not discussed them with Tony.

"As I said, the simulation has just been completed. But what we can already see is that there's a global grid emerging that roughly corresponds to the ley lines, which is the planet's worldwide natural energy grid."

"But Dr. Peller. I have heard about these ley lines. Surely this theory belongs to occult mumbo-jumbo. I cannot believe that you are really scientifically concerned with it."

"Your skepticism is justified, Mr. Ambassador. The ley lines on the maps circulating in various literature often differ from what you see in my simulation. But this is because these energy lines depend strongly on the orientation of the earth's magnetic poles. And the poles are known to wander."

"What does that mean now?"

"Maybe I can put that doubt of yours out of the way. Please see..."

Tony pointed with the cursor to points along the ley lines, "All prehistoric cultural sites still known to us today are either at intersections or directly on these lines. That can't be a coincidence."

The heads of those present followed the cursor on the world map, and Tony explained, "But there is something much more fascinating. These conspicuous features exist in the arrangement of the first cultural sites around the earth. One line, in particular, stands out where structures were built in the same architectural style. This is a strip inclined thirty degrees to the equator. It stretches around the entire globe. Lined up like a string of pearls, we find our ancestors' most famous ancient ruins.

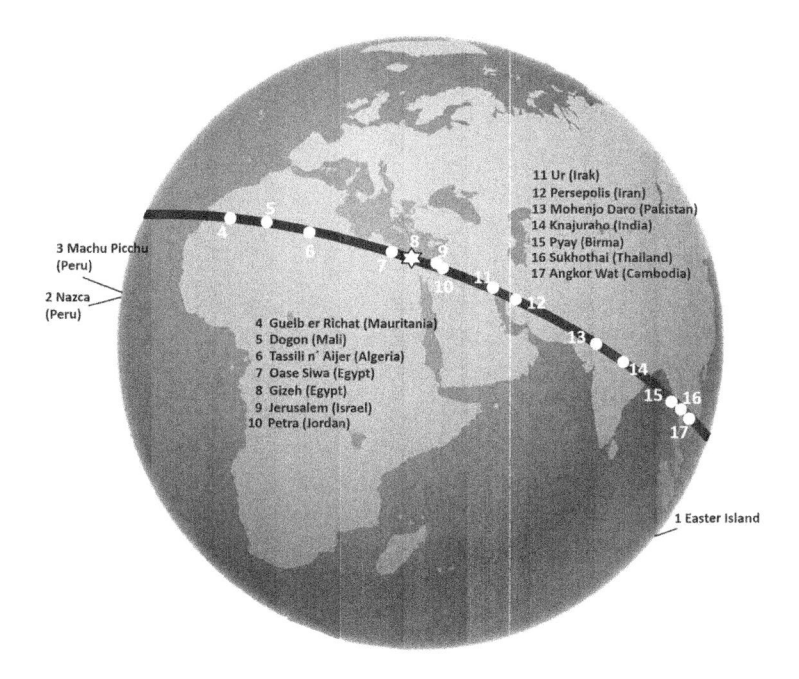

Globe diagram showing sites along an inclined line:

- 1 Easter Island
- 2 Nazca (Peru)
- 3 Machu Picchu (Peru)
- 4 Guelb er Richat (Mauritania)
- 5 Dogon (Mali)
- 6 Tassili n' Aijer (Algeria)
- 7 Oase Siwa (Egypt)
- 8 Gizeh (Egypt)
- 9 Jerusalem (Israel)
- 10 Petra (Jordan)
- 11 Ur (Irak)
- 12 Persepolis (Iran)
- 13 Mohenjo Daro (Pakistan)
- 14 Knajuraho (India)
- 15 Pyay (Birma)
- 16 Sukhothai (Thailand)
- 17 Angkor Wat (Cambodia)

I could start at Easter Island, then go to Peru to the Nazca drawings and Machu Picchu and Cuzco. Crossing the Atlantic, we end up at the Eye of Africa, that mysterious ring structure. Then we continue to Mali, Africa, the land of the Dogon. In Algeria, we find the famous rock paintings of Tassili n'Aijer. We continue to Egypt to the oasis of Siwa, famous for the oracle of the temple of Amun. Of course, we also come to the Promised Land in Jerusalem, where we encounter the Temple of Solomon.

Then we continue to Jordan, to the rock city of Petra. In Iraq, we come across the city of Ur, the birthplace of Abraham. Further east, it all continues, as you can see."

His eyes fixed on the map, Koning said, "There's a point on the map marked with a star. Why didn't you name this one?"

"Well noticed! There is one exception. This concerns the point on the planet through which all global energy lines pass, and that is the pyramid plateau at Giza. This is the center of all land masses, and this place is also on the belt."

"Dr. Peller, this is all very interesting, but I still don't understand where the connection is with the sea buoy communications network."

"I also had this problem until a few days ago. Fortunately, some of my Freiburg colleagues are also dealing with the phenomenon. Kai Lohr, for example. He has found a simple-sounding explanation for why the oldest preserved cities are lined up like on a chain. This morning, he confirmed what it is all about again."

Koning looked at his watch and said, "I now have half an hour before I have to go to my next appointment. Please be brief!"

"All right, I'll do my best," Tony replied and could hardly hide that this pushing annoyed him.

"Suppose we humans were to repopulate a planet and had only a few satellites available to allow all the settlers to connect the earth. It would be good if all the receiving stations were on a line. Ideally, this would be the equator. Interestingly, though, we see something different on my map."

"Interestingly?" came from Christina.

"Because it means that the inclination of the earth's axis was different when the first cities were built. The axis of rotation of a celestial body depends essentially on its mass distribution. Accordingly, when the ice masses in the mountains and at the poles melt, the earth's center of gravity also shifts and begins to tumble. Therefore, the inclination of the earth's axis is also determined by warm and cold periods. And the mysterious band around the earth may have been the equator long ago."

"What do you mean by a long ago?"

"We know more details only from the last great shift of the geographic poles. That happened at the time of the Flood, thus after the lightning-like melting of the remaining ice masses twelve thousand years ago. But there must have been such shifts before that."

Either the topic interested Christina, or she seemed a bit indecisive. In any case, an essential detail in Tony's explanation had not escaped her. And that was what mattered, "As I understand it, all these old cities are on the same line for a reason. What does that mean for us today?"

"It means that the change in the tilt of the earth's axis caused the pyramids and stone structures built on the line to malfunction."

"What happened after the movement?"

"The cultures possibly lost contact with their gods. Today we would say radio contact broke off."

"But where do you see the connection between the Chinese sea buoys and the ancient cultural sites?" Christina asked.

Tony was happy to answer her questions because she didn't seem to reject his theory out of hand, "The Chinese must have figured out the working principle of the original pyramid structures. This will also be why all pyramids on Chinese territory are inaccessible for research. Until German researcher Hartwig Hausmann succeeded in studying the pyramid fields near the city of Xianyang, no one knew that the White Pyramid was among the world's largest. The Chinese authorities have since covered it with soil and planted it. Something must be hidden there."

"So, if I understand correctly, the sea buoys are replacing the ancient structures in the correct position today?"

"Right."

"Are you saying that satellites existed in ancient times, and what do they have to do with the pyramids? With all respect for your work, but this thesis really sounds a bit .... I say ... daring."

With these words and the corresponding undertone, Koning had clarified what he thought of the whole thing.

"Admittedly, it sounds daring. But let's leave the past behind for a moment. Let's first look at what else the Chinese are currently accomplishing. We believe they are working to recreate the ancient system. And they do it with the help of the replaced buoys and the new satellites. Many of these satellites are on orbits that can't be explained commercially."

Deftly, Tony had waited a long time to show the stunning images of a satellite animation on the wall screen. As he continued to explain, an employee came into the room and handed over a piece of paper. Pot read it, and for a tiny moment, the corners of his mouth twisted into a grin. When the next opportunity arose, Pot said, "Please excuse me for interrupting at this point. Dr. Piller, ..."

"Peller, please. But Tony will do."

"So dear Mr. Peller. We have just received a message from your employer in Freiburg. You are asked to stop working here and return immediately. The message also contained a notice that you were under investigation by the authorities. They say you have been charged with criminal stalking. Can you explain to us, and perhaps also give reasons, how we assess your credibility under these circumstances?"

"I don't know of any charges. This can only be a misunderstanding," said Tony, who was really embarrassed by this dialogue.

"My note also indicates that you should have received an email from your HR department requesting you to end this business trip. Due to the current situation, I suggest we reschedule the meeting for another day."

Instinctively, Breede had looked at his cell phone and lo and behold, there was also an email from Freiburg. He only skimmed over them but understood immediately. With a subtle hand gesture, Pot was told to be quiet. Then Breede said, "I think this must be a case of mistaken identity. I am reading a communication from Freiburg to that effect. We should therefore allow Mr. Peller to explain his thesis further."

What he said was not entirely true. The email was from Professor Fedorov, who had written Breede that there might be an attempt to discredit Tony Peller. Nevertheless, he said the matter was to be taken seriously since the Federal Criminal Police Office had taken over the investigation.

Ambassador Koning seemed clearly annoyed. On the one hand, due to Pot's unprofessional demeanor and how he managed this matter as head of the investigative commission. The disclosure of the contents of an internal memo in this round had really puzzled him. Ultimately, however, it was enough to increase his doubts about the content of Tony's examination. He agreed to Pot's suggestion to find a new date for the presentation. Koning was taken to the helipad in a navy SUV a few minutes later.

Breede asked Tony to continue his talk without the ambassador. The rest of those present were probably torn. On the one hand, overwhelmed with doubt, two things kept them riveted to their chairs: Curiosity and the fact that Breede wanted to hear the rest of Tony's thesis.

With difficulty, Tony was able to hide his trembling hands. Of course, he knew at that moment that after Pot's words, everyone would think there was something to it. He also didn't understand how a person in a responsible position could present himself as such an asshole. Somehow the whole thing was surreal. He returned to his interrupted lecture with red ears and less fluent sentences.

"As we know, a global satellite network is being created, presumably connected to all newly installed sea buoys. New here is that these buoys can receive underwater sound signals and transmit them to the satellites. Now the question arose for us, who is the operator and what is it for? In the meantime, we learned from the international space agencies that these are indeed Chinese satellites. The official operator is a private European company based in Hungary. The satellites were registered as a research project. Allegedly, this is to serve the development of a new communication platform. By the way, no one currently knows what technology is installed in them."

"This sounds like a Chinese competitor to the US networks of Alphabet and Meta," Christina said.

"Of course. Many security mechanisms on the old World Wide Web protect against fake news. Many countries have built-in filters to block unwanted content. Countries like China want to spread fake news and block free news outside their sphere of influence. They also dislike the privacy mechanisms that protect our personal rights. Chinese officials only take personal data protection very seriously if it concerns their own. So, you must turn off some Internet filters to sell new virtual reality products."

"As we all know, however, it is becoming more difficult to distinguish truth from alternative facts elsewhere," Christina said.

Tony noticed it and carefully jumped on it, "That's right. Whoever controls the net creates his own world. And if he has enough influence, a whole new reality for his followers, too."

Then Tony took up the thread again at the old place, "An interesting thing fits some hypotheses, of which I had already presented one earlier: These strange satellites have actually antennas, which are directed both to the earth and into space. Only for the Internet, you wouldn't need that unless you also want to communicate with other celestial bodies in the solar system. This is the idea that ancient civilizations have given us since we figured out how they might have communicated with their gods."

"But I'm really interested now!" someone from the VIP row suddenly showed interest. "Why did the cultural sites have to be so elaborately arranged on a line? A few pyramids as radio installations would have done it nevertheless also!"

"Since the pyramids were spread over the inhabited parts of the earth, a connection to a distant celestial object was possible at any time. Perhaps to the place where the 'gods' had a space base or even their home planet?"

Tony listed some of the remaining indigenous people groups living on the imaginary line, "To illustrate this, we can look at the myths of those cultures that have survived to this day. Their traditions are amazingly rich in detail. They tell of a time when their gods left the earth again, promising to return one day. There are also striking similarities in technology, representations of gods and rituals."

"Like what?"

"We could take the Dogon as an example. They live today in the east of Mali but must once have come from Egypt. Astronomy and faith are in line with the first peoples along the

Nile. Today the Dogon themselves have no technology but imitate it very clearly in their *cargo cults*."

Breede noticed that this discussion was increasingly met with skepticism by some instead of supporting Tony's theses. He had extensive knowledge of the occult practices of ancient peoples and was, therefore, open-minded about this subject. At least far more open-minded than most contemporaries. Not wanting to upset Tony, he decided to take the argument differently. Breede needed a successful presentation, which was reason enough to approach the German foreign minister. This time, too, it should not be left to the intelligence services alone to decide what disappears into the archives out of national interest instead of being passed on to Western partner countries.

Breede nodded at Christina. She understood and said, "Tony, due to time constraints, I would like to ask you to conclude. It would still be important for us to know what other conclusions your report contains."

"In my opinion, it is obvious that one country, presumably China, is currently striving to dominate the information market. As far as the facts allow, three goals will be achieved in the process..."

Now another overview appeared on the wall monitor. Tony explained, "Of course, the primary goal is to control all data streams on the Internet. This would make it possible to control what content reaches the user. What countries like China are currently only able to do nationally would then be applied to the globe. A long-term, but all the more dangerous goal could be the genetic manipulation of the entire human race."

"Aren't you exaggerating a bit now?" Pot wanted to know.

Tony continued calmly, "It may sound like an exaggeration to us at the moment, but the ancient texts of the Asian peoples speak of exactly this. We have concluded that now could be the time for our next evolution phase. This suspicion is supported by the fact that someone is currently trying to steal a special artifact. This object was kept by Tibetan monks until the beginning of the last century. Meanwhile, it is in a new hiding place somewhere in North America. As it seems, the attempt to recover it has not remained secret, so several sides are after this object now."

"What kind of item is this?"

"We would call it a radio transmitter today. This makes it possible to transmit certain frequencies permanently. As my colleagues from Freiburg explained, radio waves could also activate and deactivate certain parts of the DNA. And that's simply by transmitting low-frequency sounds. When the earth-spanning transmission system is ready, all people could be reached at the same time."

"But that's science fiction and probably more in line with the conspiracy nuts!" Pot was indignant, and his facial expressions showed more and more clearly what he thought of Tony's theory.

"Until yesterday, it was science fiction. Today it seems like a nightmare come true. In the meantime, I am convinced that what has already happened in ancient times could soon be repeated. We can only conjecture who once built this technology. Nevertheless, many of the world's mythologies say that the gods were worshipped by the people and promised to return one day. Scientists like me have been researching these things. To date, we know that such a manipulative system has worked before. Unfortunately, we have only recently learned of the acute threat. And one part of the ancient prophecies could come true at any moment: the gods' return. The task of the Buddhist monks seemed to have been to keep the secret until their arrival and, when it is time, to prepare everything."

When Tony finished those words, he leaned back in his chair for the first time since the meeting began and waited for questions. Most importantly, he did not know how Breede would respond. The said at least seemed to raise the pulse of the attendees. The questions from the window row also showed apparent skepticism, "Don't take offense at my frankness, but what you tell doesn't sound very convincing! Once it's the Chinese and then the gods, soon someone else will claim it's extraterrestrials!"

Despite the seriousness of the subject, Breede had to smile. To defuse the matter somewhat, he took it upon himself to answer, "If we're talking about gods, then it stands to reason that they're not earthly ones. In any case, I personally haven't encountered any yet."

Tony added, "Unless they appointed themselves or were the descendants and hybrid beings of former visitors to earth."

"That all sounds a bit, forgive me, rather whacky!" the doubter from the window side reported.

As one was used to it from him, Breede reacted in his calm, "I hold it here in such a way, as I would recommend it also to everyone else: the opinions of several scientists to catch up. If an entire institute has taken up the matter in the meantime, it is certainly not because individual cranks have come up with something. It also doesn't matter whether it comes from so-called gods or a totalitarian government. Or perhaps also from both sides. The worldwide broadcasting system with satellites and buoys is a fact. So is the technology for manipulating our genetic makeup. We have heard the warning and cannot afford to just ignore it! Doing nothing could mean that one day we will have no means to do anything about it."

"But then we have to educate people about it, too!" someone voiced his concerns, who had not said anything yet.

Breede's answer to this no longer sounded so calm, "Informing the outside world about this is not our task. I remind you here once again of your duty of confidentiality! It is also our task to protect people from themselves. There are already enough aluminum hat wearers in this crazy world. Some countries already have the potential to incite people to civil war. Do we agree on that?"

As was Breede's custom as an officer, all military personnel visually or audibly agreed. Tony, in contrast, just looked at the scene of military obedience and did not feel addressed. Finally, Breede said, "Be that as it may. This conversation can't just be released to the public anyway. The incredibility of the facts alone is protection against dissemination. The public must be informed bit by bit and systematically. And by the way, your silence is also for your own protection. I do not want you to be subjected to the ridicule of your peers. As I said, I alone will inform the government authorities. I also have the appropriate contacts."

The helicopter had not been in the air long when Ambassador Koning felt the vibration of his cell phone. To answer the call, he had to take off his noise-canceling headphones. Before the phone was positioned in hand, it fell to the ground. He could still briefly see that the German foreign minister was calling. When he tried to pick it up, he must have accidentally rejected the call. The co-pilot noticed Koning's mishap and showed him how to pair the phone with his headset.

Koning hesitated to press the callback button while thinking about how often Friedemann debated American foreign policy with him. Their views sometimes diverged, but Koning was a diplomat in the military service and thus had to represent the opinion of his government. The only thing they agreed on was the inequality in the composition of the North Atlantic Council. Because of the dominance of the Americans, decisions were often confirmed only by the Council after they had already been preconceived at American headquarters. Koning had come to terms with this problem until 2016 when it suddenly became apparent even in his circles that an unaccountable government was possible even in the United States. In this context, there was another commonality: both wanted to prevent a breakdown of democratic orders. Koning abhorred conspiracy myths but admitted to himself that some ideas held a fascination for him as well. He could imagine, for example, that there would be a globally operating organization to which Friedemann was also close. Much spoke for this Breede could also have something to do with it.

The phone rang again, and Koning took the call. Since Friedemann did not want to discuss details on the phone, she referred to a video conference that evening where it would all be discussed.

This online meeting, also attended by the Minister of Defense, lasted less than half an hour. Koning was tasked with informing the North Atlantic Council about the missing German submarine. The suspected location was the American Pacific coast. In addition, the Council was to learn of Tony's report on the Chinese buoy and satellite project.

"I don't see any other way than to bypass the parliamentary hurdles for the time being and keep it secret for as long as possible," Friedemann explained.

"I can already hear the opposition crying out because the ministers have once again bypassed Parliament," the Minister of Defense gave to consider.

Koning's discomfort was evident, but he responded calmly, "Admittedly, I am not enthusiastic about taking on this task. After all, I now have to officially admit that a German submarine has disappeared, which you, Madam Minister, denied only a few days ago and in front of running cameras!"

"That's your job! Regarding your concerns about domestic politics, we should remain calm for the time being. We are still within the permissible limits as long as we are not directly involved in any actions."

Koning checked again, and this time his concerns were hard to ignore, "But we are already involved in military actions! One of our submarines is moving towards the American coast with unknown intentions. We'll be asked who screwed that up. And who in our ranks is actually the enemy?"

With this, the defense minister felt addressed, "As I understand the current situation, it is irrelevant who is the principal of the submarine commander. If it is a matter of recovering a dangerous object that could significantly affect the balance of power in the world, that is reason enough to become active immediately. By acting, I mean immediately warning the Americans. If their coast guard has missed that someone with heavy weaponry is floating around in their waters, we would have problems justifying our inaction to an ally."

Immediately after the conversation, Koning briefed the Secretary-General and the American ambassador to the North Atlantic Council. As expected, the Americans criticized Friedemann's performance at the UN Security Council. Koning was struck, nevertheless, by the fact that it seemed to be nothing new for his American counterpart. This made him angry because nothing could express more clearly how much was happening in the background. In any case, his mission had been accomplished for the time being.

CHAPTER 12

DaVinci II

Only the quiet sounds of the hydraulics and ventilation could be heard. All seats in the command center were occupied. There was tension in the air like an approaching thunderstorm. Even among the comrades on free watch, no one could sleep. Shortly before, the commander had addressed the entire crew and tried to motivate them. Everyone now knew that their mission was to recover an object. Lange had spoken of a rock cave. What they now saw on the screen exceeded all expectations. Monika had imagined something entirely different under a rock cave. Nothing like that was to be seen here, whether typical rocky outcrops or long mountain crevices. In front of the DaVinci II, however, gaped a vast rectangular hole 300 feet wide and 270 feet high. Other rectangular openings were to the left and right of the hole, which Lange called a portal. No one could believe that this shape had formed naturally.

Someone must have built this structure when the sea level was several hundred feet lower, or the formation was created underwater. The computer image showed that the roof of the "building" consisted of a stone slab about half a mile wide, which was held up by vertically standing sturdy columns. Monika knew of no human-made machine that could move columns of this size. From this perspective and from a distance of two hundred yards, it was impossible to determine how many more columns were inside. Perhaps they were not columns either, but massive walls.

"Cap'n!" Lieutenant Gross was heard to say, "Please listen to this!"

Lange stood behind Peter's swivel chair and held headphones to his ear, "That's not a propeller. Run the sound through the computer!"

"I already have. It resembles a flat hull that glides through the water without propulsion but at high speed."

"Like our supercavitation propulsion?"

"Maybe. It could be surrounded by a water vapor envelope. But no propulsion can be heard."

Brian didn't want to get in the way, so he grabbed a headset in Lange's booth to listen in. Over the microphone, he asked to speak to Lange privately. A moment later, Lange was standing next to Brian, "What's going on?"

"I know that sound. It's the angels from my dreams!"

"Do they make that kind of noise when they fly?"

"No, not while flying. I now believe that the door from my dreams is underwater. When they approached or moved away, they made those exact sounds."

"What do your angels actually look like?"

"They look like persons moving quickly through the water with their arms outstretched," Brian said.

"Do they leave a vortex behind?"

"I don't remember a vortex, but I wasn't paying attention, either."

At that moment, Lange received an announcement from Peter, "...must speak to you urgently!"

"Come to my cabin."

Arrived, he pointed to the computer monitor and asked Brian to press a specific function key. A sonar image appeared with a zigzag line that became thinner and thinner.

"What the hell?"

"That's what I thought, too," Peter answered and explained, "A moving object is only displayed as a line on the sonar monitor if it moves faster than our computer can process. So, the object must move much faster than underwater sound."

"This is not physically possible with supercavitation. The air envelope would be compressed so much that the molecules would fuse into plasma. The surrounding seawater would start boiling!"

"And look at the movement pattern..."

Peter put another map of the seafloor over the picture. The line started right at the entrance to the cave formation and moved like lightning through the valleys on the sea floor. Then he said, "Looks like a snake slithering through the tall grass."

Lange held his head at an angle as if he could see the details better that way, "I wouldn't exactly call it sneaking. It's more like the thing is flying, and it seems like the little bird has flown out and chirped."

Peter's look expressed more than a question, and Lange responded, "I've spent half my life on and under the sea, but today I saw a real *USO* for the first time. If only on the sonar screen."

"I can already see the headline in the newspaper: 'German sub loses race against USO' or something like that," Peter joked.

"Before this report makes it into the press, the incident is already old hat," Lange replied.

"But now zoom in on the picture right at the entrance to the cave. Or we should call it a cathedral from now on."

"Now you had the proof. The sound was coming from an unidentifiable undersea object."

Staring at the screen, Peter said, "In motion, that thing looks like a ..."

"Like an animal with long wings!" added Lange, turning to Brian, "Gee Wilson, maybe you didn't see angels. It could have been these things. If you believe the reports of witnesses to USO sightings in recent years, there must be hundreds of them."

"Maybe. I'm not quite convinced yet. But if it were true, there would be something in the cathedral that I would definitely not want to go near," Brian answered.

Peter asked anxiously, "Your nightmare?"

"Yes. And in that, angels look more like humans."

"Maybe what you saw is not the vehicle but the occupant."

Brian shook his head and then began to nod before saying, "We must consider that the human consciousness is easily deceived. We associate our ideas in our heads only with those things that we have already encountered in reality. Thus, even our ancestors only ever depicted things in their art that they could compare to something real."

"I know the first winged gods from Sumerian images. Their main god *Enki*, for example. This wisdom god and ruler of an underground freshwater ocean was usually depicted with wings and a scaly coat. And in the images, in addition to hybrid creatures, fish are often seen."

"But how did people get the idea that Enki should be the ruler of an underground freshwater ocean. There is no such ocean," Lange gave to consider.

"I think so," Brian replied.

"Oh yeah?"

"Some believe that Enki's people may be the Anunnaki, who came from the stars according to Sumerian lore. The solar system has celestial bodies with oceans under a mile-thick ice layer. The best candidate for it is the Jupiter moon Ganymede. In the meantime, quite a bit is known about its ocean. The upper layer consists of freshwater, and saltwater is at the bottom."

"You mean the people of Enki could be from an ice moon? Possibly, but we don't have to look that far away. I know from the scientific journal Nature that gigantic water reserves are located at a depth of 270 to 410 miles. Due to geological activities, water regularly reaches higher layers and can collect in cavities. My physics professor once assigned us to solve the long-discussed mystery of why the earth's outer mantle has a lower density than expected from this rocky shell. He tipped us off with the magazine. The calculations suddenly worked out when we included the presumed amounts of water in the formulas. So, what if there is a freshwater ocean inside the earth?" Peter wanted to know, and Lange also seemed to be taken with this idea, "Could be a logical explanation for the spook that we are encountering here right now."

"For me, anyway, one thing is clear: If it's not high technology from the Americans, the stuff must have come from somewhere else."

Lange sat back and pondered. Now he had to worry about another problem: the crew's motivation. If they learned too soon that the hiding place might be guarded by someone, volunteers would be hard to find. There were only four divers on board who could handle deep-sea pressure suits. Wilson's fear of these angels, or whatever it was, could not be missed by anyone. Fear is always contagious.

Nevertheless, he would still need Wilson to talk to the "guardians", or as he called them, the angels. Lange, therefore, wanted to discuss the problem with the second officer first. As a doctor, he might have an idea. Lange was about to leave his cabin when Brian asked him to stay for a moment.

"Captain, we might get the problem with fear under control with one simple thing. We could use an ancient ritual for that."

The commander's questioning look was enough of a prompt to continue, "Some kind of prayer or meditation."

"Gee, Wilson. Hardly anyone here is devout enough for that to help, and I'm not a priest."

"Then I could take over. We shouldn't call it prayer, either. Autogenic training, like every athlete, to cope with stress before a competition. In a group, something like that does wonders."

"I'll think about it," Lange said before heading to the second officer.

When the commander entered the control room, the first officer waved him over, "We have calculated everything. An object with the shape of a boomerang has left the cave at a speed of 2,200 knots."

"Cathedral."

"Excuse me?"

"We'll call the cave a cathedral from now on."

"All right, then. That means we have to expect that there are more of these things in the cathedral. No one knows how they will behave when we approach. We should assume that they will technically block our intrusion. Perhaps that is why amateur explorers with scuba gear have not managed to get near the entrance. And nothing is known about professional expeditions either," Braun explained.

"You'll just have to trust me. Our principals know what is there and assume we can recover it. They also assume that the 'guards' will not harm us. As far as I am informed, the American navy is responsible for protecting access to the cathedral. And it looks like they haven't noticed us yet. What about our pursuers, I mean X1?"

"Everything unchanged. Remain at a distance. No new screw noises. Everything indicates they are anchoring and watching us."

"Then we have to make sure it stays that way. It only gets serious if they should follow us into the cathedral."

"You want to go in there, Cap'n?"

"That's actually the question I was going to ask you, Braun. How would you go about it?"

"We should get a little closer and send the pod in."

"But this only works if the path inside is not too far. The capsule can only move autonomously for a few hours."

"True, maybe there are miles of corridors. We'll take in the surroundings as a first step and then decide how to salvage," suggested the first.

"Sounds like a plan," Lange responded before heading to the ship's doctor on the lower deck to speak to him alone.

"What do you think of Wilson's proposal?"

"Good idea. But I have something else you should know, Cap'n," said Zobel.

"Is anyone sick?"

"No. It's just...these blood levels we measured the other day on the crew. Wilson still has elevated levels of this hallucinogen *DMT*. I can't figure out the cause."

"But I thought the body could produce this stuff as the shamans do."

"The only question is, what is the trigger? That's why we should be careful with autogenic training. We can't have Wilson turning the team into full-on zombies."

Lange also had reservations, but he did not see it so drastically. He knew from the conversations with Zobel that particular neurotransmitters were responsible for certain trance states. Perhaps the DMT was then also necessary for Brian's paranormal abilities. And for that, it required a genetic predisposition. So, Lange was not afraid of a suddenly clairvoyant team.

To Zobel, he said, "All right. You monitor the condition of the comrades during the meditation session. And put on an aluminum hat!"

"Huh?"

"Just kidding!"

285

Δ

Hainan Island in the South China Sea, Sanya Naval Base, 0835 local time

"This information is not sufficient for assessing the situation! Why can't Commander Chén send us all the shipboard logs?" Vice Admiral Ji yelled into the phone. As head of China's South Sea Fleet, he had a daily report submitted to him by the special operations coordinator. In the current crisis situation, he was permanently under time pressure. At the latest, his message had to be received by the Central Military Commission in Beijing by 0930 every morning. But on this day, the news was not forthcoming. Since 0830, two information officers had been sitting in his office waiting for Ji to finish his phone call. Ji was usually known for his strict punctuality. When a meeting was scheduled, the participants had to be present at the indicated time. The Chinese navy's entire chain of command worked like clockwork. Relentlessly, Ji expected discipline from everyone under his control.

Leadership methods in the People's Liberation Army had not changed significantly since Mao Zedong's great purges. After the country was opened up, it is true that training at universities and military academies also became more relaxed. However, this changed again in the late 1990s. A particular form of ideological repression then returned to the military academies. This campaign was against the *Falun Gong* mental conditioning method based on ancient traditions. The origin of this tradition included ancient Chinese medicine and conditioning exercises of Asian martial artists. Those who practiced Falun Gong professed truthfulness, kindness and forbearance. In addition, this teaching also includes balancing internal and external forces and using the body's energies. Even the use of the enemy's mental powers was part of it. Needless to say, the Chinese Communist Party soon began to eradicate this form of spiritual practice.

Since 1999, Ji had also been in charge of a program to screen out marines suspected of being Falun Gong followers. At that time, Ji was still friends with the current submarine commander

Chén, whose meager status report he was upset about that morning. Officially, there was never anything negative to hear about Chén. Except for one thing Ji knew about personally. There were sympathizers for spiritual traditions in Chén's family. Supposedly, followers of the Falun Gong were among them. Ji had not denounced his friend then, but old doubts arose again when he was to assign him to the current mission. Somehow, he felt uneasy about selecting personnel for the explosive mission. That was also why Ji had assigned two officers of the State Security Service to Chén's team at once. He wanted to be sure to keep an overview at all times. And besides, it wasn't unusual, primarily since this submarine used unique military communications technology whose origin was known only to the Tenth Bureau of the Chinese Ministry of State Security. Even Ji didn't know who had developed and manufactured the stuff.

In the end, all these considerations were something for later. Now it was time to explain to Beijing that Long March 23 had been lying motionless and out of contact with the naval base somewhere off the American coast for a whole day. Even worse was that he could report nothing new about the DaVinci II. It must have reached its destination long ago. There was no word from those Germans as if they were waiting for something. And he, Vice Admiral Ji, was cut off from communication with his trusted people. He finally sat down with the two officers, who had been waiting in his office for an unusually long time.

"Gentlemen, you're going to keep the report short today. We mention that the DaVinci II is probably rescanning the entire area and that we expect them to listen in on the surrounding area before initiating the next step of the operation. That allows us to justify our wait-and-see approach for now. Their job is to coordinate with Comrades Ning and Weng. They should send us a brief summary of all shipboard log entries."

"Yes, Vice Admiral Ji. Please note that the officers on board have been instructed not to send internal conversation content over the sonar converter B23. However, when Long March 23 is at great depth, the suitcase with the B23 unit would be the only way to communicate. As you noted, we should not share every detail with our... I'd say allies."

"You're right. Then we'll wait and see. I must also be able to expect intelligence officers to keep us informed, unsolicited, as soon as they can do so again."

The fact that the vice admiral referred to the security officers Ning and Weng as comrades must have slipped out. This address form has not been used in China since the early 1990s. Only veterans in Mao jackets still allowed themselves to be addressed this way. In the meantime, the word "comrade" has become a synonym for homosexuals, who were officially considered mentally ill until 2001. As with most social taboos, the ambiguity of this frowned-upon address form had become a popular means of hidden satire.

"Shame on him who thinks ill of it..." said one of the two officers as he left the office, but audibly only to his companion and with a grin on his face.

The uncertainty about what was occurring gave Ji no peace. Too much could go wrong with this mission. But something bothered him in particular. No matter what went wrong, it would be blamed on him since the entire operation was his responsibility. The party leadership had charged him with ensuring the success of the mission. However, he had not had the opportunity to speak personally with the leader. In the event of success, someone else in the chain of command would probably take the credit. Once again, the chances of becoming the youngest Admiral in the People's Liberation Army were slim. But there was still a tiny spark of hope.

He took it upon himself to transmit an order to Commander Chén. This should happen immediately via the sonar converter B23:

"Have empty bird's nest destroyed by German weapon!"

Δ

DaVinci II

They decided to send a crewless diving capsule into the cathedral. The crew wanted to use it to explore the interior first. Yet, the submarine could not be too far away to intervene in an emergency. Only when it was clear whether the technology inside the cathedral worked they wanted to venture outside with divers. But they first had to go a little into the vast cave. With the next maneuver, the anchor was released from the bottom to carefully venture to the cathedral's entrance. Navigating at a slow speed was difficult because of a shifting current. Steering could be assisted by lateral jet nozzles. However, using these jets was risky because the waterjet, generated at high pressure, jeopardized their stealth. The sound could be heard for miles.

"The jets are louder than a whirlpool. Shouldn't we rather drift with the current and then be pulled in backward by the stern thruster, cap'n?" asked the first.

"Nah, keep the whirlpool on. We don't need to hide from X1 at the moment. Our position will be clear to them now, and they will keep watching us. And the Americans can't track us this close to the mountain range either. Once inside the cathedral, the noise from the jets will be muffled. For now, we concentrate on getting through the portal. Where is Wilson, anyway?"

"Wilson to dispatch!" the crew heard over the intercom.

"If you planned to operate with the capsule from the beginning, then you already knew about the sound-dampening effect, didn't you, Captain?" asked Zobel, but the commander only looked intently at the monitors and ignored the question.

I moron should have known someone would ask that question, Lange thought, intending to find a suitable answer later. Then he called the four divers into the officers' mess hall for maneuver preparation. Braun had done the mission planning, and he also supervised the dive. Like most officers, Braun had more responsibilities on such special missions than usual for a submarine's first officer. He was a trained navy diver, so he could assess dangerous situations better than the commander. As a diver, he also knew specific vocabulary. Among themselves, divers always addressed each other by their first names. Finally, the dive team was complete, and Brian was to participate in the briefing.

Matteo Braun explained the procedure to his diving team, "First, Monika and Fabrice go inside the cathedral alone. The long-wave transmitter has a range of a few hundred yards.

Therefore, you do not move away from this radius. We will follow up with the DaVinci II if the cave is larger. Remember, contact via long distance radio is for emergencies only. Their reach is enormous, and we want the listening stations in Hawaii to keep relaxed. Your first task is to make a map of the interior. No unnecessary risks!"

"And what is my job?" asked Brian.

"You stay in constant contact with the divers. We may need your knowledge of foreign languages."

Monika asked, "Do you think we could be misunderstood by the angels, Matteo?"

Matteo was sensitive enough to understand Monika's subtle hint. He looked at Brian, and his gaze also expressed discomfort. Then, addressing everyone, he spoke, "I won't fool you. No one knows what awaits us in there. I only know one thing: We are all highly trained and capable of dealing with difficult situations. Even if no one has ever told you so clearly, humanity's fate could depend on our mission's success. And that is why we have only the best sailors on board."

The first officer's words struck Brian deeply for two reasons. On the one hand, the first had now let the cat out of the bag and made it clear that they had a historic task to fulfill. On the other hand, Brian saw more and more signs that his military career might have been planned by others. Since he did not believe in fate, the strings must have already been pulled before he started his additional training in Freiburg. Perhaps he had not even joined the American navy voluntarily but had been pushed in that direction without realizing it. Who could have influenced him in this way? Or was it all just coincidence?

Brian was always annoyed that he thought about such things at the worst possible moment. Doubts would not help him one millimeter right now. Surely psychologists could provide an explanation for this phenomenon. One thing was sure; one's own observations could be better explained if one had learned not to permanently talk oneself into believing something. It must have been the fear of an upcoming challenge that had just led him back into the past. It was, as so often, a flight backward, so to speak, into the hiding place of the already known.

Yet the future always lay in the unknown. Even though Brian was considered by some to be a psychic, he didn't really believe in it himself. Of course, there was an extraordinary talent for reading people and predicting their subsequent actions. But when he was right in his suspicions, it was more like he had read about it in a book and not in other people's brains. If he was wrong in his perceptions, he suddenly became average. Namely, one who saw the reason for the failure first everywhere, but not with himself.

Although he knew it, his ego often triumphed over what he had learned. Anna had once told him the same thing. After that, he was miffed for days and thought she was a conceited cow. In the meantime, he admitted that the training in Freiburg had enabled him to resist the temptation to blame others first for things that went wrong. It was a rocky road because this well-known feature of narcissism was like a penetrating virus that kept infecting his body. The study groups often discussed with specialists whether people could change their character traits if they wanted to. Brian then learned in the group that a person's behavior tended to be determined by whether they were accepted by their peers in the living environment. Eventually, he realized that a narcissistic type could not change himself. Brian had needed just such outside influences for his personality development.

Something else still held him captive in his thoughts: *It must be a genetic program code that controls our behavior. And Ravi must have been right that humans are always at the mercy of someone. The program in us is looking for someone who shows us the way. We follow the one who has the most significant attraction to our emotions. It gives security but also makes the mind docile. As it is, this creator must have made an enormous mistake in programming. He should have called in someone more familiar with it.*

What happened to Brian at that moment was what happened to him so often. Just a few hours ago, he had been convinced of doing the right thing with this mission. Ravi had told him that the artifact's recovery in India would allow their god Shiva to return and perhaps reunite the people. Now Brian suddenly had doubts whether this Shiva or Enki or whatever name the people had given it could really be the reason for this action. Other thoughts were also racing around in his head: *If the age of the zodiac sign Aquarius should really dawn, that would fit the prophecies in the lore. The whole thing could be connected with the fact that a particular astronomical constellation makes the return of a deity possible. The only point that doesn't convince me is the supposedly necessary technology. Has this iron column perhaps served an entirely different purpose?*

Monika touched him on the arm. This quickly brought his thoughts to the small table in the officers' mess hall. Everyone stared at him as he said, "Sorry, I wasn't listening for a moment!"

"Gee Brian, what's wrong with you? We need everyone's full attention. I want you to follow everything happening inside and outside the capsule. Do you understand that?"

"Yes, Mr. Brown."

"We are now a diving unit. We need full attention every second. Our lives may depend on it. There is no time for deep thinking now and no time for formalities. Call me Matteo."

The capsule was packed with technology. The occupants wore goggles like those worn by fighter pilots. This kept the most important displays in view at all times. Since the first dive was uncrewed, Fabrice had strapped stuffed wetsuits to the seats. He also attached the goggles for the virtual display to their false heads. For this purpose, he had loaded two small buoys into the hoods. The monitors in the control room could follow the work.

"What's he doing?" asked Monika, and even Lange had to grin when he saw Fabrice drawing faces on the buoys with a grease pencil. He emphasized Monika's femininity with long eyelashes.

"I'm sitting on the left!" Fabrice said after turning to the camera and assuming a victory pose.

Monika answered over the intercom, "On the left may sit whoever wins at arm wrestling!"

"Such childish people!" reacted Matteo. But he didn't think it was wrong that the mood was still quite good.

The crew admired the commander because he was able to rest at the moment he thought it helpful. He hit the hay during the two hours of preparation for the dive. The sounds of the hydraulics pushing the capsule out of the tower woke Lange, and before entering the operations center, he took some coffee from the galley. Norbert had resumed his station, and Lange asked, "How's the little guy today?"

"Thanks for asking. The doctor's pills are doing good. But the little man isn't so steady yet, Cap'n."

"Anyway, the team is happy that the big man can stand again!" Lange said and took another croissant as he walked away.

Braun first tried the controls as the diving capsule hovered over the boat. Although the current of the water was intense, it worked much better than it had days ago when changing from the DaVinci. After only a few minutes, the portal was reached, and the DaVinci II's exterior cameras captured only the cones of headlights disappearing into the darkness.

Braun directed the two technicians who sat in front of the monitors to supervise all incoming information, "Report any noise that is not our own. If reception weakens, stop immediately. We can't lose contact."

"What's that there?" Monika asked, and Matteo focused on the spot she marked with her finger.

"Switch to pilot's view!"

Now, the crew saw everything on their monitors that the rubber pilot in the capsule could see with his special goggles. Fabrice's fake head must have slipped and was hanging to the side.

"Hey Fabrice, just when you're supposed to show some attitude, you cave in!" he had to hear from Monika. Because the dummy's head slipped, the camera image was also a little crooked, and following the natural reflex, the viewers kept their heads tilted. They quickly got used to it, though.

"Cap'n, anything wrong?" asked Zobel, who had looked at the pictures with fascination like everyone else but then saw the look on the commander's face.

"No, no. Everything's okay. Admittedly, though, I'm surprised that the technology works flawlessly."

"You mean because of the technical failures that amateur researchers have reported? We should remember that there were only simple diving robots in this place before us. They had no special protection against electromagnetic interference. Our capsule is shielded quite differently."

"If I'm honest, I was expecting a few problems. After all, there are other dangers than electromagnetism. Let's hope it keeps going this well."

"Or maybe it's just because we're welcome and they're not," was Brian's comment.

"It's possible. Let's hope the trolls in the mountain don't change their minds!" said Fabrice.

"Please don't make derogatory remarks about our hosts. Maybe they can't take a joke," Monika admonished her comrade.

"What's that now?" asked Fabrice, pointing to what was visible in front of the capsule.

"You've got to be kidding!" cursed Matteo. "That's it already?"

Both the sonar radar image and the powerful spotlights showed only solid rock. The capsule had barely entered the cathedral four hundred yards, and already it was over. There was nothing to indicate anything other than bare rock there.

"End of the road!" let Fabrice hear and slammed his fist on the control panel console. He was just able to curb his rage by reducing the speed of the fist before it hit the console. Zobel, whose job was to keep an eye on the crew from a medical perspective, did not miss the diver's outburst. For a brief moment, he thought it wouldn't have been so bad to let Brian have a little meditation session. But the commander had decided against it.

Matteo Braun tried to reassure the others, "Now, wait and see. We let the small laser probe measure every inch of the cave. With that, the computer might be able to figure something out. Somehow there must be an opening. Where else would the USO have come from?"

"Exterior cameras down!" they heard a technician say. "Oh, sorry. It's not the cameras but the headlights. The status indicator shows that they are working. There was just no light coming on."

"I don't understand. What's wrong with the lights?"

"Shall I restart the lamp control once?" came the question from Monika, but before anyone could answer, the surroundings were brightly lit again.

"What was going on?"

"Don't know. Would only be bad if we're out there on our own and suddenly we're in the dark," Monika said.

"Matteo, I'd like to suggest; can't we also scan the rock walls with a long-wave sensor?" asked Peter.

"Why?"

"Visible light will reflect off the surface unless it is transparent. We can penetrate deeper and better detect a hidden door with a long-wave sensor."

"Peter is right. That makes sense," said someone.

"Just activate the sensor and see what happens."

With this method, a completely different picture of the rock surface emerged. Because the long-wave radiation could penetrate the material, they found a spot where the rock was between six and seven feet thick. And there were even more conspicuous features. After a few minutes, they found breaks in the rock wall as if it were composed of regular blocks of stone. The rough surface of the wall, with its protrusions and deep crevices, looked quite natural when viewed superficially.

"Well, if there's a passageway, it must be her. There were huge blocks of stone joined together. And pretty well camouflaged!"

"Could really be some sort of door. But where's the doorknob?"

Lange had withdrawn to think alone. He couldn't get it into his head that he had been sent here without knowing how to open the gate to the cathedral. Did the principals not know either, or did they hope Lange would find a solution with his team?

Then something else occurred to him, but that did not help to calm him down. The torpedoes! Someone had brought the heavy armament on board and kept it secret. At least, it could be assumed that it was supposed to remain confidential. Did someone want him to blow up the stone door using the torpedoes? That would be absolute madness. The detonation would be sensed by all the earthquake sensors in the area. The seismologists would quickly realize where the shaking came from.

Although, if we were fast enough, we could recover the artifact and be gone before the Coast Guard got to us, Lange thought. But he quickly dismissed this thought. No one could know what else was behind the suspected door.

Firing a torpedo at it is irresponsible. Perhaps there are also .... any living creatures behind it?

There was another severe obstacle. He had no access to the torpedoes at this time. The weapons technician Sander found out they lacked the access code for operating the two equipped torpedo tubes. The software faked empty torpedo launchers, and this trick almost succeeded. Then he thought of a possible solution. It was only a slim chance, but it could be a way to trap the supposed traitor.

Lange went to the first officer and said, "Get the capsule back. We have collected enough data. I want to go in with the boat and send the divers with pressure suits to the door. If we can get really close, the divers might be able to see a little more detail."

"You actually want to drive in? But then we're trapped!" said Zobel.

"I don't see any greater risk than anchoring in front of the entrance. Inside, the Coast Guard boats can't see us at all. The roof of the cathedral has already lasted an eternity. It's not about to collapse on us. And we will go in backward. I want the torpedo tubes to point to the open sea in case of an emergency exit."

This rationale seemed logical. The four tubes with the larger diameter were intended for a different type of torpedo and were suitable for an emergency escape. With compressed air, individuals could thus be blown off the boat and reach the surface in a pressure suit without damage. There was one catch, however; there were only four pressure suits on board. At least the weapons engineer understood the real reason for Lange's decision. This boat had torpedo tubes only at the bow. No torpedo could be fired against the rock face if they went backward.

The commander had just given the order to weigh anchor when Peter addressed him, "Cap'n, we might have a problem after all if we go *astern*."

"Every maneuver involves risks," he received tersely as an answer. Apparently, Lange did not want to get involved in a discussion.

As the responsible sonar officer, Peter was obliged to point out additional risks to his commander. He also justified his objection against the commander's refusal, "Due to its design, the propeller produces four times more noise when moving backward than forward. The huge cavity would have an effect like that of a trumpet. I once calculated the noise we would generate as a result..."

Peter sent a graphic to the monitor and explained, "With this sound, we'll chase away every whale from the Arctic Ocean to the North Sea."

Lange was surprised by this effect. He knew that the screw ran louder backward than forwards. However, he had not expected such a sound amplification in the cavity of the cathedral. The collected data from the sonar scanner allowed for very high computational accuracy. Comparable measurements were also carried out by sound engineers during the construction of a concert hall to check their sound quality.

"Did you also calculate what it would look like if we went forward?"

"Of course. Look..."

The result was clear. The "trumpet effect" was only slight when driving forward slowly.

"All right, we're going to go in forward."

A short time later, the two-hundred-foot-long cigar slid into the cathedral between the two side walls of the central opening. While there was a minimum of residual light outside, there was only darkness inside the cathedral.

"Cap'n, we're encountering some strange water vortices ahead!". Zobel pointed to the data from the current measurements sent from the deployed capsule.

"There is a freshwater bubble under the ceiling. At the dividing line between fresh and salt water, these eddies form. But where does freshwater come from here?"

Braun looked at the geological data of the coastal area. He pointed to a spot on the map and explained, "That must be it:

We're about fifty miles west of the San Andreas Fault, which runs along the California coast. With each earthquake, new fissures form in the subsurface, and groundwater can drain them toward the sea. If the cave system behind the door extends into the coastal mountains, there must also be contact with groundwater veins. Fresh water is lighter than seawater. Therefore, it remains on the ceiling in caves and can form such bubbles."

Brian thought that there may be some underground freshwater ocean on earth. He didn't want to again discuss Enki, the god of underground waters.

Even hardened divers have nerves, and Fabrice doesn't seem very balanced. I'd instead not tell ghost stories. The boys would be in a better mood if Lange would let me meditate with them. Monika is an entirely different caliber. Either she's wholly hardened, or she's good at hiding her emotions.

Brian didn't want to miss Monika and Fabrice getting ready to exit. One of the four large torpedo tubes was already prepared for an exit. The twenty-six-inch inside diameter allowed leaving in the deep-sea pressure suit. Monika had already slipped into the leg section while the others helped put on the hull part and got their helmet screwed on. The breathing air should last for more than two hours. For this, a tight-fitting tank sat on their backs. Hoses and valves were attached so they could not be damaged as quickly as in older models. These diving suits were specially designed for navy divers who sometimes had to fight underwater with thrust weapons.

Monika was almost finished while Fabrice was still tinkering with his equipment.

Matteo Braun gave the final instructions, "We'll give you light through the boat's main headlights as long as you're close by. You search along the crevices on the wall for an opening mechanism. Every step will be coordinated with me. Everything clear so far?"

"Roger that!" replied Monika, and Fabrice confirmed, "Aye!".

Shortly after, the two disappeared into the torpedo tube in snow-white pressure suits. Monika insisted on getting out first. "You always have to watch out for the boys. They get cocky easily," she had joked. However, Matteo didn't think Fabrice would be any less careful. Monika was simply used to standing up to any macho man. She also showed that when it came to volunteering for delicate missions.

Once the tube was flooded, there was a quick leak check, and the hatch at the bow opened. The special coating of the deep-sea diving suits reflected the light very strongly. This meant that they were still visible via the onboard camera of the submarine when they reached the rock face.

Of course, it was impossible to move in these stiff suits as divers usually do. The flippers were only good for stabilizing the position. However, the diver could move forward with the attached thrusters. With some practice, the arms were just mobile enough to handle tools or weapons.

The crew in the operations center followed what was happening on several monitors. Via the head camera, they could track where the divers were looking. Brian immediately noticed Monika oriented herself differently and looked at different points than Fabrice. She was obviously more sensitive to the environment, so she first saw the color differences on the rock face. The headlamps emitted a particular light spectrum, making the underwater colors appear more natural.

Monika said, "Look. Any idea why the rock in the middle is brighter than the material further out?"

"If it really is a door, there will be a mechanism. Maybe it was renewed once over time?"

"Could be. Maybe one of the angels came home drunk and rammed the gate?" was Monika's idea.

"Enough of this nonsense. Now concentrate on the places where the rock crevices are. There's bound to be an opening mechanism somewhere," Matteo said.

"Do you really think our angels are rushing through the water at the speed of sound, and then they have a hand crank on the garage door?" Fabrice asked.

"You know, the simplest ideas often get you to your goal the fastest," Monika said, "Look what I found here..."

Monika's helmet camera showed a seven-foot-wide flat spot above a rocky outcrop. This was above the presumed gate. If the color differences were to mark the size, the gate had to be 65 feet wide and 33 feet high. Monika must have been interested in the strange shapes she found on the ledge.

"What is that?" someone asked in the background of the control room, and Zobel replied, "Looks like blue leaf lettuce. It could be deep sea coral or something like that. I've never seen that species before, though."

"Might be an alien vegetable garden," Monika joked.

"Save your humor for later when you run into the homeowners," Fabrice said.

Peter's job during the dive was monitoring the cathedral's entrance. He listened for any sounds in the vicinity. Then he called the commander, "...here it is again!"

Lange was immediately alarmed and looked at the screens while Peter explained, "That sound of the angel again, but this time it's approaching. We're getting a visitor!"

CHAPTER 13

Cathedral dive

Monika was fascinated by how such beautiful creatures could live in this isolation. It was clear to see that the corals grew only above the boundary between fresh and salt water. The boundary layer in the water began just above the suspected door. This suggested freshwater was seeping through the door as it was opened.
"Monika, Fabrice, get back to the boat now. Your trip is over!" they heard Matteo say excitedly.
"What's going on? We haven't even gone around the door yet!"
"No discussion! Back off now!"
Fabrice moved to Monika to check on her. Her hand signal told him that everything was all right. He also urged haste, "Monika, come on, there must be a reason if they call us back. Don't experiment now!"
"I'm just going to cut off another piece of this coral. Swim ahead. I'll get in the tube after you."
Her last words did not reach anyone. The radio traffic was suddenly interrupted. Inside the DaVinci II, more and more alarms were going off. The primary power supply had been shut down due to a malfunction. Lange assumed it was due to a strong electromagnetic field. Only a few vital systems were still functioning. The crew knew that the pressure equalization in the torpedo tubes should still work with the emergency power supply. This should also make it possible for the divers to board.
Because of the interrupted radio communication, Fabrice could not tell Matteo why Monika had stayed behind at the gate. He hoped that the crew had been able to hear the last radio communication even inside the boat. He hovered his control jets directly in front of one of the exterior cameras and asked what to do via hand signals. Matteo then opened the outer flap of the

torpedo tube, but Fabrice shook his head and accelerated with a firm thrust toward Monika. He didn't want to get in without her.

About hundred-and-fifty feet from the boat, the helmet lights went out, and the thrusters also stopped working. Suddenly, only one source of light in the gigantic entrance hall of the cathedral was a shell foamed with gas bubbles. The luminous cover with a diameter of forty feet had just passed the portal between the large columns. Now it was moving slowly toward the gate in the rock wall. Fabrice felt pulsating pressure waves that must have emanated from the object. As it moved past Fabrice, he could see the thing inside the shell. It was clearly triangular with an edge length of about twenty-six feet. The USO had no exterior lights but glowed bright blue in several places. A slightly stronger blast wave hit Fabrice full force and spun him around. He was glad not to be near sharp-edged rock walls at that moment.

As Fabrice turned helplessly in the water, trying to get his bearings, the shape of the approaching object changed. The shell disappeared as if a soap bubble had burst. Another shock wave hit Fabrice, pushing him back another few feet. Now the USO was in full view. It was directly in front of the rock face, where Monika also had to be. Although he should have had other things to worry about, the appearance of this strange underwater vehicle impressed him. The faint light barely illuminated the cathedral, so Fabrice couldn't even make out the outline of his own submarine. The foreign thing, in contrast, left a faint glowing trail that suggested the path it had traveled.

Inside the DaVinci II, the watch crew sat tensely at the few monitors still powered by emergency power. The sensors could just make out the shape of the USO before the central systems failed. Peter spoke aloud what he was thinking, "That thing looks like what pilots in Belgium and Britain documented: just delta-shaped."

Fabrice had no idea what to do. The breathing air treatment system was in emergency mode and would only work for a few more minutes. The control thrusters were not responding either. He wondered whether he should move toward the torpedo hatch with slow arm movements or paddle toward Monika.

Still, the only light came from the triangular object in front of the rock wall. With its dimensions, it had swirled the various layers of water so that the rock face could only be seen in a blur. Instead, Monika's white diving suit reflected the light emitted by the USO for a brief moment. So, she was still at the rocky outcrop where she had found the coral. Now Fabrice saw a short flash, and the whole wall was covered by a glowing blue ring, in which the USO disappeared from one moment to the next. Immediately after that, it was dark, and Fabrice instinctively called for help. There was no sound in his headphones. He was well-trained and had practiced dealing with mishaps in diving hundreds of times. However, having no idea what to do had never happened to him. Now he felt the tightness of this pressure suit as well. Condensation began to collect on his feet, and soon the cold would spread throughout his body. At the moment, he could only ask himself questions, and before he could think of an answer, the next one was already there: *In which direction do I have to paddle to get to the boarding hatch? Monika was right at the gate earlier. Did something happen to her? How long will the emergency supply of breathing air last?*

At least this question could be clarified after he gave the dive computer the command "Show status!". The virtual goggles showed him a few values...

Primary power supply: Without function
Secondary battery: 22 percent
Heating: Emergency operation
Breathing air: Emergency operation–18 minutes remaining

The air pressure in the deep-sea suits was the same as in the submarine. Therefore, the divers could breathe normal compressed air. In the event of a suit leakage, the pressure inside would increase. In such cases, the automatic system supplied the diver with some inert noble gases mixed in with specific breathing gas. Normal breathing air would react chemically under high pressure in the blood, producing toxic effects. Yet, the supply of this particular mixture was only sufficient for a few minutes. At this time, normal pressure had to be restored. Otherwise, the diver would die shortly after.

The suit reported no damage, but it was essential to avoid sharp edges. Yet, this was not easy without any orientation and darkness.

Fabrice decided to wait a few more minutes. His eyes may get a little used to the residual light. He wondered if he should follow his hunch and just paddle in the direction where he thought the sub was. The air should be enough for fifteen minutes. The small emergency supply with the gas mixture would only work if the suit leaked. But since the diver could quickly lose consciousness because of the rapidly rising pressure, it had to be monitored by a second diver. Fabrice suspected no other diver would get out until the boat's power supply was restored.

A metallic sound could be heard. It was clear to Fabrice that it had to come from the DaVinci II. The excellent sound insulation meant only one stable metal connection leading to the outside. That was the last piece of the drive shaft for the propeller. *Of course, they're hitting the drive shaft!* Fabrice thought. He felt able to guess the direction of the sound. Underwater, nevertheless, this was a deceptive perception. The sound was Morse code:

"Fabrice located. Distance fifty-fife yards. Nine yards above deck. Seventeen degrees northeast."

Of course, they give my position. So, I can use the compass to find my way back to the boat.

The news gave him courage. He could determine his position with the three values, but there was another problem; the compass was mounted on his left suit sleeve at about the elbow level.

Great shit! The thing is not illuminated. Super designers!

He couldn't use the compass without light, so he tried to pull his arm as close to his helmet as possible. The residual light from his status indicator may be enough.

Not a chance. The damn thing is too stiff. Such a faulty design!

His helmet heard a warning message: "Breathing air for eight minutes!"

In the leg pocket were small buckling rods, but they were intended only for shallow water depth. These emergency lights withstand water pressure of up to 5 bar. The cathedral was at a depth of almost a thousand feet, with 30 bar pressure. Fabrice wanted to try it anyway. And it had to be quick because after opening the storage compartment, all the rods would be exposed to high pressure. It was not difficult to open the box, but with his stiffened hands, he could only pull out all the sticks at once. They also started leaking immediately because of the pressure. With trembling hands, he bent all of them at once. Although most of the luminous fluid had already been revealed, it still worked. The rods gave off a faint light. Before Fabrice could memorize the details shown on the compass, it was dark again. Even so, he thought to have remembered the position of the compass needle. The boat must be in precisely the opposite direction than he had assumed.

"Breathing air for five minutes!" the friendly computer voice informed him of his remaining life.

Fabrice tried to concentrate. He was shivering all over because the temperature was dropping rapidly. Every movement had to be right now. There would be no second attempt: *What the hell, I have to paddle. It will take me five minutes to get to the boat. Halfway there, I take the crease rods out of the left leg compartment. Then I can recheck the direction.*

The comrade inside the boat continued to tap his Morse code tirelessly. A few things went through Fabrice's mind while moving his arms in circles and his fins as best the suit allowed. As he did so, he felt a thick lump settle in his throat: *Maybe they would catch on if I moved in the wrong direction and informed me about the current position. What could have happened to Monika? Probably the others assume that she is dead. Otherwise, they would have sent her a message, too.*

"Breathing air for four minutes!"

"What is he doing? Why isn't he moving faster?" asked Zobel, looking over Peter's shoulder.

"Can't we try to get him after all? Lucas is ready to go. We can use the second tube to get out while the first one stays flooded to keep Fabrice's entry clear," Peter asked the commander.

"I can't let that happen. Lucas' suit won't work out there either."

"But we don't know that. The electromagnetic pulse occurred when the USO approached. The suit will work."

"If another object approaches, Lucas will meet the same fate. I can't risk that," Lange said, but he wasn't sure about the right decision. Monika was most likely dead. On the other hand, Fabrice still had a slight chance of making it. Then Lucas reported from the torpedo room, where he had been waiting in his pressure suit for the command to get out since the beginning of the whole diving operation. Having a rescue diver on standby was part of the protocol. Lucas' suit was still fully functional because all systems had been turned off at the time of the incident.

Lucas said to Matteo, "I request clearance to exit. I will take a rope with me. It helps to pull myself back if my power supply also fails."

Matteo nodded to Lange, who decided, "Send him out!"

It didn't take a minute, and Lucas was stuck in the second torpedo tube. Before he could get out, the rope's end had to be attached to a hook next to the torpedo hatch.

"Breathing air depleted – emergency supply not available."

Fabrice knew he had a few minutes left with the remaining air in the suit. He wanted to open the flap on his left leg to take out the second package of buckling rods but could only reach it with his left hand. Because it was already stiff and shaky from the cold, it took several seconds. Without being able to see anything, he grabbed the package and wanted to guide it to his right hand with a quick movement. Due to the rapid arm movement, the packet slipped out of his hand. Desperately, he grasped at nothing several times. The chance for a quick look at his compass was gone. There was no light anymore. Because of the stale breathing air in his suit, his ability to concentrate also must have waned.

Nevertheless, he still heard the change in Morse code coming from inside the submarine:

"...Distance ninety feet. Twenty feet above deck. Fifteen degrees northeast."

For a second, a small glimmer of hope appeared in Fabrice because, despite his awkward locomotion, he hardly veered off course. But that was the only ray of hope. Ninety feet was far too much for the remaining air.

I can't do it anymore. Damn, how many times have we practiced emergencies, and now it fails because of the paddle power!

Although it was already challenging to form complete sentences or even pay attention to the Morse code, he suddenly realized that the message had changed, "Lucas is on his way. Hang in there, Fabrice."

Δ

Long March 23

"Could you translate it?"

"The signal is feeble, and some sounds are distorted by reflections. It could be coming from inside the rock formation."

"But nothing else heard from the DaVinci II?"

"No, Commander!"

"Show me!"

Chén read what his sonar technicians had picked up. Someone had been tapping Morse code for several minutes. This was not good news. Since it could only have come from the DaVinci II, they had to be in trouble. Such a position report without encryption would only be sent by sailors in an emergency, and Morse code was something for emergencies.

"No one who wants to remain undetected in the ocean hammers away at a metal object. You can probably hear it all the way to Hawaii. Whatever happened, it's going to mess up our plan. Something must have gone really wrong over there, " Chén said.

He already had an idea of what might have happened. Hobby researchers repeatedly reported malfunctions in electronic components when they tried to approach the formation. Detailed information about this was not available, of course. Chén wondered as these German submarines had the reputation of being particularly well protected against harmful radiation. If the Germans could not continue their mission, that would also mean a change of plans for him. At this point and in this position, he could only communicate with the naval base on Hainan via the "suitcase". However, he preferred to maintain radio silence because Long March 23 was an immobile object at this point and noise from a fixed source was always conspicuous.

Moreover, no one on board had much experience with the new type of sonar converter. Chén knew that with new technology, teething problems were always expected. And teething troubles with an encryption system could mean nasty surprises, should the message signals not go undetected. Of course, the propaganda news from Beijing reported on the latest Chinese technology slightly differently. But as Chén knew very well, that was just propaganda. He preferred to rely on facts for the strategy for the next steps in this mission. As long as they were not in a state of war, down here in the darkness of the ocean, the lives of his sailors had the highest priority, and only then came the Party.

The order to the first officer was, "We are approaching the formation at creep speed. Position us two hundred yards in front of the entrance. There we will have a better view of what is happening inside."

The first officer seemed surprised by this decision, "Commander! The same thing could happen to us as to the Germans!"

"Possibly. But if it is an emergency with the Germans, it would also be good for us to know what went wrong. At our current position, we can't figure that out. We can use our drone at the new location to pay the DaVinci II a visit. Let's do it!"

Δ

Dive inside the cathedral

Lucas was outside, and after the rope was hooked in, he first checked his status displays. All readings were regular. The steering jets brought him close enough to Fabrice to see the reflective suit glowing dimly within two minutes. The helmet lights only reached fifteen yards through the suspended particles in the water. Before he arrived at Fabrice, a queasy feeling spread through his stomach. A terrible sight might await him when he looked into his comrade's helmet in a few seconds.

I wonder if he's still alive. Does his suit have a leak? The water pressure might have pushed the body fluids into the helmet. "Now get a grip!" he finally said aloud to himself, and at that moment, he could hear crackling in the helmet speaker. A second later, Peter's voice was heard, "Hey Lucas. The connection is back up. Can you hear me?"

"Yes. Just reaching our runaway. His breathing air is at zero. Don't know how long it's been. We're coming back now..."

"Understood! We'll get everything ready. Do you see Monika around?"

Lucas had to admit that he hadn't thought about Monika during the last few minutes. His concentration was entirely focused on Fabrice. He, therefore, only said, "No."

Fabrice's immobile body lay face down in the water. The pressure suit automatically assumed this orientation so that an unconscious diver would not choke on his body fluids. At first contact with his hand, Lucas turned the body on its side to look inside the helmet. The first look inside made it clear to Lucas that the internal pressure was still normal. There was no visible tissue destruction. Still, the face looked ghostly. Light gray skin color and almost black lips were reminiscent of a Halloween disguise. This meant oxygen deficiency, although the black lips were only an optical illusion because the artificial light absorbed the blue color of the lips.

The return to the boat became much more manageable because halfway, the boat's headlights came on. Accordingly, the technicians managed to restore the primary power supply. Arriving at the hatch, Lucas first pushed the lifeless Fabrice into the torpedo tube. He then followed and indicated his readiness to ventilate the tube. The time to empty it seemed like an eternity to him.

Why didn't they provide an oxygen connection outside these suits? But he immediately remembered that it would not help Fabrice because even with oxygen, his breathing could not automatically resume. By his estimate, Fabrice was now unconscious for about eight minutes. The chance of survival decreased every second, and the inner hatch was still not open.

When they finally pulled Fabrice out and dragged him directly to where there was enough room for four helpers, Lucas could only marvel at how a well-trained crew made every move. While two sailors stripped off their helmets and suits, two others held the resuscitation equipment ready. Siggi, who as a diver was also trained in emergency measures, wanted to assist the ship's doctor and held out the resuscitation bag to him. Zobel reached out for something else and said, "Give me the laryngeal tube. I can use it to ventilate more effectively."

Lucas was lying a little distance away in his pressure suit and had just managed to open his helmet. What the comrades did to Fabrice could not be seen from his position. He only heard them desperately trying to get Fabrice back, "Go, go, go! You can do it!"

While the others feared for Fabrice's life, Matteo noticed Lucas struggling to get out of the suit. He walked over to him and said, "Are you okay?"

"So far, so good."

"I would like to ask you to go out again with Siggi."

"Monika?"

"Yes. She must be dead by now, but we can't leave her body behind."

"Have you located her yet?"

"No. I'll go into the capsule with Brian first and look for her."

"I see."

Commander Lange coordinated the work to restore the systems. After the power supply was restarted, one control lamp after another indicated that the system was ready for operation again. The improved fuel cell system survived the electromagnetic disturbance well. This made Lange confident that he would survive the subsequent close encounter with a USO.

Sander approached and said, "Captain, I've noticed something strange."

"I'm listening!"

"Just before our systems went down, there were log entries. Look..."

Lange didn't immediately know what his weapons technician was trying to tell him, but when he saw the sequence of log entries, everything became clear to him, "Someone has accessed our onboard computer. It looks like the main power supply has been manually shut down!"

"Not only that. Look here... the system was also turned back on from the outside."

"Then, as the visitor approached, we were targeted and shut down until they left."

"A protective mechanism? The unknowns may have wanted to ensure we couldn't attack them at close range."

"The only thing that worries me is that we are helplessly at the mercy of this goings-on. They seem to do whatever they want with our technology."

"But why the divers, too? They put their lives in danger with it," Lange asked and immediately got the answer from Sander,

"I looked at Fabrice's suit. There was a short circuit in the battery. This was certainly not intended by anyone. More likely an overload due to the strong magnetic field. Look..., the onboard log recorded an increase in magnetic strength until just before the system failure. Such an effect is also observed in quite regular UFO sightings. From this, I conclude that it was not an attack on the diver. The capsule remained undamaged because it is much better shielded from the outside than the diving suits."

The sailors could hear a reassuring shout from the torpedo room, "Hey! We got him! ...Keep breathing, Fabrice...well done!"

Δ

The University of Freiburg, experimental laboratory

The equipment was still busy examining Brian's hair sample. Ashley adjusted their software with the first results, which would later translate Anna's thoughts into sound frequencies. She first wanted to test whether the aura of the tiny hair sample would react to Anna's voice. Ashley even talked about the tissue being trained to read Anna's thoughts telepathically.

"The Russians have already succeeded in doing this," she said, looking at Anna.

"So far, it has only worked on people who have trained it with each other before. Since Brian was one of your meditation students, we might be lucky."

"What are the risks?"

"Several. First, we have to hope that the hairs really are Brian's. Can't imagine if they came from Brian's girlfriend and she hears voices. Not everyone knows that you don't necessarily have to be crazy. We won't know if it worked until the recipient responds."

"Anyway, it's his hair color. And what else can go wrong?"

"Brian might assume it's his own thoughts. It's like a dream. That's when you don't ask if it makes sense right now or not."

"Brian is an experienced medium. He can interpret dreams better than the average person."

"Then let's hope you know him right. Let's get started!"

The apparatus was set up precisely as they had previously used for the tissue from the refrigerator. However, Ashley had placed several hair sections side by side. One sample was left as it was found. Two other pieces had been chemically processed, so the molecules had already been extracted from the cell tissue. Ashley could tell Kai had questions about this and explained,

"The DNA reacts better when it has been previously extracted from the tissue and prepared with a special solution."

"But then why the untreated hair?"

"We only came up with this by chance during experiments. Namely, if a piece of undamaged tissue is nearby, it acts like an amplifier. Maybe the molecular chains 'remember' the owner better when the morphic field is nearby. It is then as if a small piece of Brian's aura is in the same room."

Anna had sat down with a swivel chair right in front of the rehearsals and had to laugh, "Are you making a video recording of this?"

"Yes."

"Jeez, just make my face unrecognizable! I can already see the headline... Celebrity test subject talks with hair of a stranger."

"You're always hiding. How could you be prominent?"

The last remark did not mean seriously, but it hit Anna slightly. Ashley was right. For all the institute's international successes, Anna never made the headlines. There had never been any opportunities in her life to become famous. Since she was a small child, she had lived with the secret of mastering a few things her peers dreamed of when they read their mystery books.

Perhaps a tiny dose of egoism is necessary, she thought briefly before quickly suppressing this thought again. Meanwhile, Kai had attached a microphone to Anna's head and said, "Look, this is how it looks on a radio station. No one will know you're talking to Brian's hair."

He started laughing again, forever at his own joke. Anna met Ashley's gaze and understood that she was also annoyed by Kai.

When she was finally asked to begin, Anna remembered that she hadn't even put her words together. *What do I have to say so that he understands it right away?*

Finally, she did what others knew of her: she trusted her feelings. Calmly, she spoke into the microphone that she should give him a message on behalf of Rear Admiral Breede. The DaVinci II had been equipped with two live torpedoes without permission. This could all be a trap, as the launch of a German torpedo on US territory would trigger a conflict among NATO partners. Chinese principals hunting for the artifact would also be conceivable. She ended her words with, "...Brian, please turn on your mind and make sure the artifact stays where it is."

Ashley looked pleased and said, "Let's look at how the material reacted first."

The microscopes had recorded every change in Brian's DNA with their cameras as Anna spoke. Tensely, they now watched this three-minute sequence. Not very clearly, but they could see Anna sitting in the lab chair. The computer images of the molecules showed her face. But the patterns, also visible around the face, did not make sense to the viewers initially. It just looked beautiful.

Kai was about to make another remark to cheer the others up but held back. He held that out until Anna said, "Look, the original hair has become rougher on the surface and curled up."

Kai muttered, "Looks like Brian's hair is standing on end after your speech."

No one laughed, but Ashley said, "I'll now have the light signals translated back into our language. If we're lucky, we'll hear the same what Brian hears in his head."

The result was disappointing at first. Only noise and crackling, as if you were searching for a transmitter with an old shortwave receiver.

"Wait a minute. The software will take care of it on its own," Ashley tried to dampen the others' disappointment.

"Now! Or am I imagining it?" said Anna enthusiastically.

"Shhh!"

At a slightly higher pitch but still clearly audible as a human voice, they finally heard Anna's words to Brian from the speakers.

"Hey, it seems to be working!"

"You bet. We're now sonicating the DNA molecules with Anna's words continuously. Then we can hope that Brian meditates once in the next few hours to receive it."

CHAPTER 14

DaVinci II

Meanwhile, the diving capsule was back in the tower, prepared for the next trip. With freshly charged batteries, Matteo and Brian drove to where Monika was last seen. It took them ten minutes to cover the two hundred yards. That there must be a massive gate in the rock face was immediately evident after the USO disappeared into it. While Matteo's eyes scanned the area through the portholes, Brian swiveled the exterior cameras and recorded every inch. The computer helped search for conspicuous objects. A lost utensil or a fragment of the pressure suit might be found that way.

"We've reviewed everything several times and only found one piece of freshwater coral."

"Monika will have lost it when she was hit by the blast wave," Matteo said.

"But what if it wasn't a blast wave but...."

"You mean she was pulled through the open gate by the USO?"

"Makes sense, right?"

Brian's mood brightened with a tiny spark of hope, "We don't know what's behind the gate, but maybe she found an air bubble there and is now waiting for rescue?"

"Even with enough breathable air, there would be very little chance that she would still be alive."

"Why?"

"The air pressure down here is as high as the water pressure. At the same time, the oxygen in the body has a toxic effect. And then there's the temperature. At 40 °F without heating, it quickly becomes uncomfortable in the suit."

"But it is not impossible to survive?"

"Let's assume that it would be possible," Matteo said. As a trained diver, however, he knew it would be tantamount to a miracle if Monika were still alive.

Over the long-wave radio, Matteo reported to the control room, "... We're coming back now, then we can take another look at the video footage of the area. We suspect Monika is behind the gate."

Lange replied, "Understood. But you can't go back yet. We have located a sound in front of the cathedral. It's heavily distorted, but it may be coming from X1, who has snuck up on us. We haven't been quiet in the past few hours, which must have made our pursuers curious. You are now heading to the cathedral's entrance to look!"

"Roger that!"

"But be careful and, above all, be quiet."

When the diving capsule arrived at the cathedral exit, it got slightly brighter. Brian looked at his watch. It was 1225 local time, so the sun had to be almost vertical. Some residual blue light reached the ocean floor at a depth of thousand feet.

Matteo searched the area with the passive sonar. It wasn't long before a beautiful silhouette appeared on the radar screen, and he said to Brian, "Look who's come out of hiding. Meet X1."

Brian was amazed, "Why are they standing here like this?"

"They had to know we were in the cathedral, and I don't think they could hear us very well from their old location. I'm sure we also made enough noise to attract the shark."

"Maybe the Chinese shark is here to help, too? They also understand Morse code."

"Do you believe in Santa Claus, Brian?"

"Of course, don't you?"

Matteo looked into Brian's face and was startled. His skin was chalky pale, and his pupils dilated. He had seen this before Zobel had measured the abnormal blood values.

"What's the matter? Aren't you feeling well?" he asked, concerned.

"It's nothing, or it is… I have this inner restlessness again. There's the feeling that I've forgotten something. I used to have a feeling like that before exams. Or maybe it's...a strong energy field. I wonder if it's because of the proximity to X1. Could it be their two nuclear reactors?"

"Absolutely not. Radiation is not emitted there. At most, it could be magnetic fields used by subs for camouflage. But they shouldn't be that strong either."

Matteo radioed Lange and reported Brian's fainting spell.

The commander's reply didn't sound surprised: "Position the capsule a little further out in the open water and wait until I report back! But come back immediately if Wilson's condition worsens."

Brian was a little unsettled: *Is Lange telling me to break the communication blackout? Surely not. He just wants me to ask around!*

The commander, of course, had thought of Brian's story with the angels. If he had these symptoms outside the submarine, perhaps his ability to telepathize would have returned. That would allow him to pick up some of the Chinese conversations.

Lange was right in his assumption. As soon as the diving capsule was out in the open water, Brian felt he was in a large hall full of people. There were noises everywhere.

"Do you also hear that noise, like in a train station concourse?" he asked Matteo, who took off his headphones and listened, "No, I only hear the ventilation and the propulsion."

Everyone was talking, but nothing could be understood.

Brian wanted to put himself into light hypnosis. If he fainted, however, Matteo would panic. That's why he said, "Could be that I step away a little bit. Just let that happen. It's normal!"

It didn't take long for Brian to go into mild self-hypnosis, but he remained conscious. What happened next was something he had never experienced before. Without using any meditation techniques, he heard more and more sounds. Only these seemed to have different sources. As absolutely present, he felt the steady up and down swelling whistling, which he had already identified with Peter as data transmission of the Chinese. And there was more. The whistling was regularly interrupted, and it sounded like two robot voices were talking. Then he heard a different, more human voice, which had just stopped speaking at the beginning of this session. It was not as he remembered it acoustically, but the melody, the way of intonation, and the whole semantics clearly came from Anna.

Brian had his eyes closed, but his lips moved as if he were fantasizing. It was the other way around, though. He tried to form the words that reached him at that moment. The announcement had to be from Anna. He felt it without being able to prove it. Something was strange, though. The message was played over and over again like a canned message. And Anna claimed that she was contacting him on behalf of Breede. While still in a trance, he began to sort out his thoughts: *Something was wrong. Breede warned me emphatically in Rostock that unauthorized persons could use his identity. I should only trust Commander Lange during the mission. But still, the message must be from Anna. Her way of speaking conveys something that no computer can imitate: passion. But why does she know about live torpedoes on board? Why does she fear an international conflict? ...not recover the artifact... This is all very strange. I'll have to discuss it with Lange. Or better not?*

Brian had no idea how much time had passed. He now looked into Matteo's face, eagerly waiting for an explanation, "Did it work? Did you get to hear the Chinese?"

"I don't know, maybe. But I heard something that I need to convey to Lange personally. We should hurry back now," Brian said. But he also realized that it must definitely have something to do with X1: *Of all places, I get this message near it. Was it an attempt by the Chinese to manipulate my mind?*

Matteo refrained from inquiring and ended the conversation jokingly, "Got some state secrets, huh?" Then he steered the diving capsule back into the cathedral.

During the trip back, Brian agonized over new questions that he couldn't answer on his own: *Perhaps the responsibility for the mission's outcome lies with me? What does Anna mean by live torpedoes being on board? Is there a traitor?*

He then realized that no one on board could answer these questions. Nevertheless, he wanted to follow Breede's order and confide in his commander.

The sound of the capsule docking at the tower airlock startled Brian. As he descended the ladder from the airlock into the command center, Lange turned his gaze expectantly to the arrivals. Brian accompanied the commander to his cabin and reported, "I don't know who I was in contact with. It wasn't a real telepathic connection. Someone who felt like Anna told me that the boat was loaded with unauthorized weapons. Is that true, Cap'n?"

Lange was confused. What did this mean? Where would outsiders get such information? "Did this Anna tell you how she knew that?"

"Is it right, then?"

"Yes."

"The training video said submarines do not carry heavy weapons during test runs."

"That's right. I found out on the last leg of our dive. The torpedo control software has been tampered with, and neither Chief Petty Officer Sander nor I have access to the weapons."

"Could someone fire the torpedoes without your order?"

"That's to be assumed. We're working to prevent it."

"I see. And who are WE?"

Instead of answering, Lange asked, "What else did this Anna say?"

"We're all sitting on a powder keg here, only she used different words."

For Commander Lange, the situation now presented itself in a more precise picture: *The torpedoes secretly brought on board are unsuitable for defense against attackers. For that, I, as commander, would have complete access. However, if a mutiny and subsequent escape were planned, the mutineers could use them to shake off their pursuers. Or...*, and then Lange thought of something even more apparent: *This someone might have known that we would come across a locked gate and already given the appropriate crowbar.*

Despite the new findings, Lange decided to stick to the original plan. He also did not want any more confidants for the time being. It did not hurt to take seriously the warning that was delivered to Brian. For the time being, full access to the torpedo control was necessary.

"Wilson. First, not a word about the live weapons to the crew. We must not warn the originator if there is one on board. That increases the likelihood of his making mistakes. I must be faster than him."

"Yessir, Cap'n!"

After the capsule had deposited its occupants via the airlock in the tower of the DaVinci II, it was sent back unmanned to the cathedral's entrance. There it was to remain in standby mode as a silent listening post.

"Commander, please contact the control room," the watch officer called through the intercom, and Lange jumped up the ladder from the basement. The few steps reminded him that he had neglected the fitness training.

"What is going on?"

"Sander really wants to talk to you. He's in the radio room."

"What the hell..." Lange did not utter his curse. Sailors familiar with the armament could not enter the radio room without permission. Why Sander, the weapons technician, was there required an explanation. In fact, he found him outside the locked door of the radio room.

"What's wrong?"

"Something has come up. I haven't found a place where I can show you."

"Then we'll go to my cabin."

"There sits Wilson daydreaming."

"Okay, here then," Lange pointed to the radio room.

The radio operator, whom they had nicknamed Spark, was already waiting for them and began to speak excitedly, "Cap'n, since the capsule has been on its listening post in front of the cathedral, we are getting a permanent signal in. I don't understand it."

"Take it easy and point!"

The tiny radio room was crammed with technology and monitors. Spark pointed his hand at one of the screens, and Lange furrowed his brow as he tried to make something out, "What's that supposed to be, and where did it come from?"

"Good question. According to the readout, it's everywhere. It's like we're at the center of this noise."

"Our boat can't be the source!"

"That's the funny thing. See how the computer interprets the sound..."

It should have a technical cause, and the computer suggested: "Transformer of a substation".

"Pretty dubious analysis, I think," Lange had to admit. "If there was a high-voltage transformer nearby, it would have quickly turned our electronics into scrap metal."

"And we would be grilled!" added Spark.

"You sure know your way around grilling!" said Sander, alluding to an earlier test drive. Spark had accidentally caused a short circuit during a repair, destroying equipment worth two hundred thousand euros. When the radio operator then reported his mishap with a pitch-black face, he was given his nickname by the guard crew.

The commander was concerned about the noise. He instructed his crew, "I want another status report of all systems. And check again with your eyes and ears. Maybe everything didn't restart cleanly after the power failure."

When Lange tried to rush to the operations center afterward, Sander held him by the arm and said, "There's one more thing!"

As the weapons technician radiated serious concern, Lange had an inkling of what was to come, "The software has started an automatic torpedo check."

Lange wondered if the strange noise might have come from this self-test for a moment but quickly dismissed the thought. Such a test lasted only a short time, and everyone knew that noise. Automatic test routines of the torpedoes otherwise only existed when the boat was put into combat readiness. Lange was now getting nervous. Something was out of hand on this boat. If there were weapons on board that he could not control, he would have to abort the mission. His thoughts were racing as he began to think through the possible options. Taking the entire torpedo system out of service wasn't an option either. That would deprive the divers of a quick exit. Only one diver could be slipped through the regular hatches at a time. In a diving accident, rescue via them would not be possible. Continuing his thoughts, the weapons technician interrupted with the next piece of bad news,

"... I can no longer access the software. My access code has been disabled."

Lange now could not keep the problem a secret. He called all officers into the officer's mess and informed them about the operational torpedoes and the loss of control. Brian was also called in.

"If we can believe the logs, the self-test routine must have been automatically or externally started. To solve the problem, I need the expertise of each of you."

The board engineer suggested posting a guard in the torpedo room. Should one of the tubes be activated, the process could be interrupted by an emergency stop switch. This switch was not connected to any of the shipboard computers. A launch could thus be prevented before the outer tube doors opened.

"We'll do it that way!" Lange decided. "However, that's not good enough for me. Lieutenant Nassar, as the ship's engineer, you know the electrical system best. Try to turn off the power without blocking the way through the tubes. Also, two sailors must always remain in the torpedo room, and the fitness equipment is off-limits from now on!"

Prohibiting the fitness equipment was difficult for Lange. It was the only diversion for most sailors.

After a few seconds of silence, Peter Gross asked how the search for Monika would continue. Matteo Braun said with his head down, "You know as well as I do that Monika is dead. We tried the recovery, but a search no longer makes sense if she was pulled through the gate with the USO."

Ronny Zobel disagreed, "But if we have torpedoes on board now, why don't we try to blow up the gate?"

Before Commander Lange answered, he looked Brian in the eye as if to signal him. Then he addressed all the officers at the table, "Maybe I didn't make it clear enough earlier; right now, no one aboard this boat can access weapons control. My access code, which is required to release a torpedo, is no longer valid."

Brian noticed that Lange took a long look at each officer's face. This was too noticeable to remain hidden. It would make them realize that Brian's job was to read each face. However, the commander had cleverly exploited a weakness of the people in his trick. It was not without reason that he specifically addressed the missing password. The "culprit" would unintentionally think of the new password at that moment or even try to remember it. This was a reflex that could not be suppressed by the conscious mind. Even without mind-reading, a trained person like Brian could thus recognize who among those present had something to do with this matter. After a few seconds, Brian knew and was not surprised by the result.

The commander's smartwatch made a shrill sound at short intervals. When he confirmed this by pressing a button, he triggered the battle alert on the boat, and all the sailors rushed to their positions.

Before taking his place in the command room, Lange took the two sailors, Sander and Mueller, aside, "You two go to the torpedo room immediately. And you stay together! If one of the tubes activates on its own, activate the emergency stop switch without consultation!"

"Yessir, Cap'n!"

When Lange entered the command room, the second sonar technician informed him, "The capsule has registered suspicious sounds. X1 has opened its torpedo flaps."

"But they're not going to shoot into the cathedral, are they?" blurted out Zobel. Lange waved it off and looked at the sonar technician's finger, indicating that a USO was approaching far away at high speed.

"How much time until arrival?"

"It's slowing down. I'm guessing eight minutes."

"It looks more like the Chinese have gone into battle readiness because this object is approaching."

"Let's hope you're right."

"We should rather hope that they don't consider it an attack. Can't imagine if they really fired on the USO."

"Maybe we should warn X1?"

"What should we warn about?"

"From the blackout they could face if the USO approaches."

Lange said, "We are not their nanny. Besides, there's no more time for that! Braun shut down the primary power supply immediately. We will remain in emergency mode until further notice! Also, shut down the capsule for twenty minutes!"

"Roger that!"

Lange called Brian into his cab. His intention was to hear what he learned about the officers' body language during the briefing, "Were you able to determine if everyone was telling the truth?"

Brian looked him in the eye and replied, "Yes. And I'm quite sure, too."

"What is it? Come on, talk!"

"Your officers answered the question honestly, Cap'n."

"Are you sure?"

"Yes."

"That's good to hear, but that leaves only two possibilities. Either an automatic program activates the torpedoes at a specific time, or someone is accessing them from outside the boat."

Brian didn't know if the commander had listened carefully to his phrasing because he deliberately said only what he thought about the officers' response. Peter's voice over the intercom prevented him from explaining in more detail what else he had noticed, "Commander, please go to the control room!".

There was a tense silence. Everyone was listening for the arrival of the USO at the cathedral. Twelve minutes had already passed since its discovery.

"What's going on, Lieutenant?" wanted Lange to know when he appeared.

"They should be here by now!" said Peter, but more to himself as he watched all the monitors intently. "I'm afraid we've lost them, or our sensors are being fooled. But I actually called you because of the radio operator. He supposedly heard something."

"Maybe they veered off to avoid the danger from X1?" suggested the first.

"Who's to say they really want to come here, anyway?" the board engineer mused.

Spark reported over the intercom, "The hydrophones are picking up a change in the strange sound."

Peter immediately checked this with his self-developed software. He wanted to know what had changed, and seconds later, he reported to the watch crew, "Other frequencies have been added to the basic sound. It also looks like our boat is vibrating slightly."

"After the soloist, the whole orchestra will now play," Braun murmured to himself, and Zobel added, "Hopefully not a requiem!"

The commander got annoyed with his officers, "Stop that nonsense. Such remarks only unsettle the crew."

While the DaVinci II was in emergency mode, only the most critical systems were functioning. Some workstations in the control room were now shut down. Thus, there was only one space left for double-occupied stations. In addition, the heating was turned off. Lange, therefore, sent most of his crew on free watch. The sleeping bags protected them from hypothermia. Brian and Peter also lay down in their bunks. The permanent tension had taken its toll during the past few days. Only for a few, there was the opportunity to keep the rest times. Therefore, most of them showed signs of exhaustion in the meantime. Hardly any of the officers had slept more than two hours at a time in the last few days.

Brian was now lying on his side but had not drawn his curtain. His gaze lingered on Monika's bed. The sight was unusual because her bed was neat for once, although she never tidied up her things. Before going on duty, she just pulled the sleeping bag straight after stuffing all the clothes underneath. This kind of thing reminded Brian of his mother, who had once used the term pseudo-order for it because he had never voluntarily tidied up as a teenager. Always just enough that the mess was not immediately noticeable, and one of the annoying warnings could still be averted.

A wave of grief flowed through him from his feet to his neck, leaving a feeling of helplessness. Only when his body came to rest and the surroundings offered a little security did feelings that had been repressed until then begin to spread. A lecture by his psychology professor came to his mind, explaining with examples that this effect was part of animal self-protection. Inevitably, he asked himself the question: *What actually predominates in us, animal or human*?

He remembered a book by the German philosopher Gabriel. He claimed that human being is an animal that does not want to be one[29]. Lying on his back, Brian pondered further: *The sentence already contains the reason. A human being differs from animals by his will not want to be one and to be able to think about who or what he actually is. Nevertheless, it becomes clear that we are not yet a wholly developed race. Every animal on this planet provides for the survival of its kind. Only we humans do not! We are not yet intelligent enough to provide for ourselves permanently. There a frightening truth shows up. We are not yet a survivable species! Do the old apocalyptic prophecies contain exactly this message? Would Homo Sapiens become extinct, like all humanoid predecessors, if we do not manage the step to self-preservation?*

Brian stopped these thoughts, even though he knew he was doing what passed for humans: repressing unpleasantness. He lay back on his side. Looking at Monika's bed brought his sadness back. With moist eyes, his field of vision blurred. Then something happened that clearly distinguished him from an animal. Brian could draw a conclusion from the timing of the past few hours. There was something different about Monika's bed. The sleeping bag draped over her things lay there far too neatly. Her sneakers were the only items she always deposited at the foot of the bed, but without covering them. This time, however, the sleeping bag was pulled all over the bed. Also, the hood was not rolled outward as usual. Monika did that so that the fabric could air better.

Did someone tamper with her bed, or am I worrying unnecessarily?

He answered the last question to himself with YES and decided to find his inner peace through meditation. He also felt that the strange restlessness among the crew might also have something to do with the noise. Brian then imagined the pyramid upside down and spinning to keep the buzzing noise away. It worked, and he was deep asleep after a few minutes. So, he didn't get to hear what was happening to the crew in the meantime.

"Still nothing?" Lange asked again. Almost two hours had passed since the USO appeared and disappeared. Since then, they had seen no trace. No explosion sound would have indicated destruction by Chinese torpedoes. Lange, therefore, assumed that the strangers had turned off again.

"What if the Chinese were noticed, and the strangers took another entrance to their base?" Braun asked.

"Possible. But we can't use up our emergency batteries now. Soon it's going to be freezing cold in here. Arrange for normal operation to be restored, and then go to sleep!"

"Understood. What's your plan?"

"When we are rested, you will take the capsule with one of the divers and try again to get through the gate. There must be a way."

"Then the guys will prepare everything in the meantime. Cap'n, do you notice that too?"

"What do you mean?"

"The team is acting strangely. Not just exhausted. It seems like the cohesion is suddenly gone. The guys hardly talk anymore, and when they do, they hiss at each other. I also see the first signs of aggression."

For Lange, this was not news. He had also observed this change in himself. He replied, "You're right, but I don't want to overstate it. We have to take care of each other. I'll talk to the doctor. But for now, let's let him sleep. I'm sure he took a sleeping pill for a reason."

After one of the two power generators in the fuel cell section was running again, the control lights of the onboard systems also jumped back to green one after the other. The watch crew consisted only of the commander, the board engineer and the radio operator. Lange had put on his thick cotton jacket and sat in the swivel chair with his arms folded. He kept his eyes closed, but not without regularly watching the torpedo system's indicator lights. Six of eight tubes indicated operational readiness but were not loaded. For two tubes, the indicators remained red. They were sealed but not functional.

Lange was startled by an announcement, rubbed his eyes and looked at his watch. Matteo reported that the diving capsule was ready for action. Instinctively, his eyes compared the display in the boat with his smart watch and noticed that the blood pressure was much higher than usual. He handed over command to the first and began his inspection walk around the boat. In the torpedo room, he started. The bulkhead was not closed, so weapons technician Eddi Sander and navy diver Siggi Mueller could be heard from a distance. They were discussing whether the commander knew more about the strangers than he was admitting. They seemed to agree that the object should be recovered immediately to get out of the cathedral as quickly as possible.

"We're trapped. The captain knows it, but he's acting like he has a plan. Without this stupid artifact, they won't let us return," Siggi said, and Eddi replied, "Exactly. I also don't know why Matteo wants to take the capsule to the gate."

"The best thing we could do is blow the damn wall with a torpedo."

"The only problem is, we don't know what target they're programmed for, should they activate themselves," Eddi pointed out.

"We are two hundred yards from the gate. The torpedo tubes are aimed directly at the wall. At this short distance, the course cannot be changed at all. A launch will inevitably result in a hit on the gate wall."

"So you wouldn't hit the emergency stop button when it goes off?" Eddi made sure.

"I wonder what kind of game is being played here. They're not telling us the truth, are they?"

Instead of answering, Eddi cursed, "Those damn officers. You don't know who to trust. I can't stand Brian, either. Just that arrogant look when he's had some vision again..."

Lange had heard enough. The two sailors were a risk at the moment. They had even thought about mutiny, a severe alarm signal. Now it was time to wake Zobel. Before he reached the galley, he heard a terrible clang as if the cook had dropped the bowls. When he saw Norbert, everything was clear. He was kicking the bowls lying on the floor with all his might. He flinched when the commander spoke to him from behind, "It'll look weird if you put the dented bowls on the table later."

Lange awaited an explanation from the ship's cook. Instead of an apology for his lack of restraint, Norbert seemed to get even more worked up, "Everyone's just bitching about the cold food. I'm the joke around here. ...I've had it!"

"I see...I'll have a word with the crew." Lange tried a personal approach, although he was seething inside and had little desire to deal with this problem. He was aware, however, that the lack of a proper meal would lead to frustration more quickly than the body odor of his comrades. The cook's insinuation showed signs of bullying. He had to crack down on that. A motivated ship's cook was essential to the commander. He was about to leave but turned around again and said into the galley, "I don't understand why these rascals are getting upset. Your food is usually so delicious that they should be glad to have such good ship's cook!"

"Thank you, Cap'n."

The next stop on his tour was the sleeping section above. Those who were awake got a brief friendly word from the commander. After leaving the quarters, however, Lange knew the mood was worse than he had feared. No one was joking, not a single private word among themselves. He had never experienced that with this crew.

Back in the control room, Zobel was already sitting on the swivel chair and massaging his neck. Lange greeted his second officer and ship's doctor with a gesture that called for him to follow him into the captain's cabin, "Let's talk. We need a change of plans."

"I see similar symptoms in some of them. Under these circumstances, we can't send anyone out!" Zobel stated.

"I know it's going to be hard. But our mission is to get the artifact. To do that, we have to go in."

"But how? We can't wait for days in front of the gate until maybe one of the house's residents opens the door for us."

"If necessary, maybe that, too. Now, don't look so skeptical. Or is there something else?"

"Captain, they didn't send this American with you just because of his visions, did they? As he has indicated, these angels, as he calls them, have often played a role in his life. The headquarters knew that, too, when they sent this greenhorn along."

"You mean I should send him into the capsule with you? Much too dangerous! He can't control the capsule if it would be necessary."

"Whatever you say. Something is preventing the boy from doing what he was sent to do."

"That's possible. Wilson also said that meditation is difficult for him down here. Still, we'll send the pod out without Wilson for now."

"Diving capsule ready to go!" the first's voice could be heard. Before Zobel left the cabin, he said, "I've been thinking about those torpedoes. I can't get it out of my head that someone might have intended these cigars as door openers. They wouldn't be useful for combat action, at least not..."

Lange had understood and finished his second officer's sentence, "...as long as I'm in command, you mean?"

"Well, I just mean."

"I don't really believe in a mutiny. Still, we must prevent someone else from deciding when and where to fire weapons on my boat. And if it all goes wrong, at least I want to have screwed up myself!"

Brian hadn't had such an intense dream in a long time. He felt as if he had slept deeply for hours before it began. It was like his childhood and yet different. At first, he felt safe and was glad not to swim underwater with the angels again. There was air to breathe. Only his feet were in a small puddle. And then he saw the door from his childhood nightmare, yet it looked completely different for the first time: *No, this is not the same door! This one is lighter and smooth, not dark and infinite like before. What does it mean?*

Brian had doubts about whether the pyramid trick was working correctly. It was supposed to ensure him a peaceful sleep and prevent that eerie noise from entering his head. At first, it seemed to work, too. The dream came after an hour of deep sleep, but one crucial detail was missing, compared to his dreaded memories. Still, amid the dream phase, he thought: *Not a single one of those floating creatures can be seen!*

In his usual dream environment, he called out into the endless void: *Brian, where are you?*

He was startled by his own question: *Did I call the angel by my name? What is the matter with me?*

For the first time in his life, Brian suspected that this single angel who kept coming back and befriending him might have been his own ME.

A sting in his chest and an ice-cold shiver down his spine made him wake up. His clothes were soaked through with sweat. The way his senses gathered again made him realize that he had just returned from a deep trance. All the details of the dream were still there. Especially the ending because in it, he was dreaming of an ancient Asian fairy tale that he had first heard while studying Sanskrit.

After years of training, with his brain's help, Brian could go to the place where the memories were stored. Of course, the area was imaginary, and the appearance was from his imagination. Each person imagined this place a little differently. It was rows of fictional books, like an infinite library for Brian. As a child, he had looked at it like a game, memorizing each time the place the book was put back after he had written something in it. Later, when he wanted to "reread" something, he would race to the depository in his mind and find it. It wasn't until adulthood that Brian learned what he had only suspected until then: This place of memories was not only real but also universally shared by all. Every living thing stores its experiences in it. Anyone who took the trouble to learn another person's filing system could also access their memories. If ancient Asian records were to be believed, this art was once among the greatest secrets of the gods. As Brian did, anyone who spent some time studying the origins of Buddhism inevitably learned about the folk tales that were mostly passed down orally. One of these old legends also flowed into the teachings of the *Bon religion*. Of all things, his last dream ended with this story. It was about how people once gained access to this mysterious place of memories:

One day, when the goddess Rhimati visited earth, she liked it so much that she decided to bring her beloved to this place as well. Together they built the seat of their new kingdom on Mount Kailash. Their happiness did not last long because Ahstu, the elder brother and firstborn of the family, came to visit them. He also found favor in this place and believed that his inheritance as the firstborn encompassed all the worlds of the Kingdom of Heaven. Thus, he would also be entitled to rule over the earth. Finally, he appointed himself king. He instructed his younger sister Rhimati to take care of the increase of prosperity in the kingdom. The father promised the throne of the heavenly realm to the elder brother. The birthright of the sister Rhimati was to become the ruler of the knowledge of all deities. As a guardian, she thus possessed the key to the universe's secrets. Equipped with this knowledge and versed in the arts of nature, she created a bird with the head of a toothed predator. She endowed it with magical powers. The bird could sing the sweetest songs, and Ahstu wanted to own such a singing treasure. Rhimati showed all her magnanimity and gave the bird to her brother as a gift. In gratitude, Ahstu granted her to enter Mount Kailash again. In return, Rhimati promised to continue teaching her subjects how to increase the kingdom's wealth.

Impressed by the bird's songs, Ahstu now allowed himself to be taught all the arts. Over time his behavior changed. The newly learned made him forget everything that happened before his arrival on earth. He had also forgotten the claim to his inheritance, and greed suddenly no longer played a role. Thousands of years passed, and nothing was reminded of the old order of the gods.

This is how the new earthlings lived until the bird stopped singing one day. Neither Ahstu nor Rhimati was able to change anything. Without the bird's song, Ahstu fell back into his old habits. He blamed his sister for the bird's failure and, thus, for the waning of his well-being. The subjects caught on to the gods' quarrel and finally stopped serving their old masters, and each began to look after his own happiness.

In anger, Ahstu ordered the bird to accompany him on his sky chariot and to breathe fire until the earth was burned down. In the process, a large part of the earth's inhabitants was also destroyed.

Rhimati and her loved ones fled from Mount Kailash. Before they also left the earth again, the guardian of knowledge made a gift to the remaining people. She took two of the most beautiful and wise specimens and planted her knowledge in their wombs. As a parting gift, she promised to return should they one day succeed in creating a new bird and taming Ahstu with it. Since then, Rhimati would regularly listen to the sounds of the earth to hear from afar what progress the people had made.

Brian was not surprised to remember this Asian fairy tale in his dream. Since his return from India, he has constantly been trying to reconcile the context of the events with his knowledge of ancient religious texts. It was strange, however, how the plot suddenly changed at the end of the dream. Just at the moment when he saw the inside of the dreaded door for the first time in his life, Rhimati crossed his path. Brian took it upon himself to keep looking that way. Whether it was all coincidence or his imagination was just playing tricks on him, he was about to find out. He thought he had found a promising lead: *Hadn't the old monk Ravi told me at parting that I would learn everything else in due time? Was the dream, as so often, a clue? Perhaps I should find out what name this goddess Rhimati has in modern times!*

The more intense Brian got into it, the more complicated the puzzle became. A few big pieces already fit together, but finding the missing answers required asking the right questions: *Could the crop circles possibly be from Rhimati?* Could this be the test for humans? *They are clearly artfully designed images. And these mandalas represent visualized music without a doubt!*

The thoughts seemed to fit together better and better. If the two monks believed that the submarine crew would make it to the artifact's hiding place, there had to be a way in. His intuition and Peter's software should let them clear the last hurdle. At least, that was his plan.

Completely drenched in sweat, he crawled out of his sleeping bag. The heating must have been turned on again. Brian straightened his bed and rolled up his sleeping bag to dry. He wanted to shower quickly, but his gaze lingered on Monika's bed. Under her sleeping bag, the tread of her sneakers was showing, and Brian thought about putting the shoes back on top for a second. They could air out better that way. It took him some effort to touch any of Monika's things. It was a kind of reverence for his comrade but also a little shame because what would the others say if he rummaged around in someone else's bed?

Brian could not move from the spot as if something alien were holding him. His eyes stared unceasingly at the outline of those shoes. *Who had tampered with Monika's bed and why?*

Only now did he see that something else was wrong here. It suddenly seemed to him that not only Monika's clothes, backpack, and odds and ends were stuffed underneath. The bumps looked suspiciously as if... *But that can't be! Or is that...?*

Instinctively, Brian flinched and took a step back so that he hit the bed behind him. Everything began to spin in his head. Then he felt a strange feeling in his stomach and was already looking for a bag to throw up. Fortunately, the sense of having to throw up quickly passed. But not the panic about what he would find under the sleeping bag.

Am I hallucinating, or what's wrong with me? I'll just get someone from the team now! Or better not. For most people, I'm already a freak anyway.

Now his sense of smell also announced itself. A draft with Monika's body odor. More specifically, the scent of her musty sneakers passed his nose. Brian realized that this was all in his head. As before, his thoughts rushed through the shelves of memories in his dream. There he found impressions of Monika. As much as he tried his analytical skills, unlike usual, the memories he tracked down didn't seem to make sense this time. *Or is it just emotions that confuse me so much?*

He gathered all his courage and carefully pulled up the sleeping bag at the foot of the bed. Further and further, until sneakers, a duffel bag and the cotton jacket were visible. With a trembling hand, he pulled the sleeping bag straight again and put the sneakers on top. The left one was heavier, and something hard was stuck in it.

CHAPTER 15

DaVinci II

Matteo and Lucas had boarded the capsule from below through the tower and strapped themselves into their seats. Before closing the hatch, Lange peeked in to wish them success.

"Suppose the door somehow opens. What's in store for us then?" Matteo wanted to hear from his commander.

Lange was annoyed by this question because it radiated uncertainty to his subordinates. At least Lucas had listened with interest. Lange didn't know if he would hit the right tone. In any case, he answered:

"You know, humankind would still be living in wooden huts if they always thought every idea through to the end first. At some point, you just have to start. My main task here on board is to weigh every decision so that the risk for the crew remains calculable. I've been given brave specialists like you two for all other things."

With the last words, the commander pointed to Matteo and Lucas's navy diver insignia on their sleeves. Matteo took the commander's words as a subtle invitation to pinch the ass cheeks together and get on with it. The entire crew lacked sleep, and the fear of what might be behind the door added to that. Such a badge on the arm did not only serve to show one's pride to the outside world. Much more, it supported self-motivation. Those allowed to sew on the badge had passed exams under extreme situations. Examinations which, as a rule, only two out of ten cadets passed. Therefore, the motivating effect of such a symbol in an emergency was only really known to very few people.

Lange went to the control room to supervise undocking the diving capsule. The leak test and safety check had already begun when Zobel addressed his commander, "Please wait a moment before undocking. You should talk to Wilson first."

"This guy just wants me to send him along. I've already turned that down. Tell him I'm busy now."

"I'm afraid that's not possible. Wilson spoke to Lieutenant Gross earlier. Since then, he's completely changed and claims to know that we're all in danger."

"If this is his trick, he'll get three days of cleaning duty!" Lange finally gave in and seconds later was standing in the mess hall.

"Hey Wilson, everything all right with you?"

"It is with me, Cap'n. But I don't know if that applies to the rest of the crew."

"Would be good if you could be a little more specific."

"I noticed an unusual tidiness on Monika's bed."

"That's really remarkable!" Lange tried sarcasm.

"At first, I didn't think anything of it. Before I went on duty, I wanted to put her sneakers on the sleeping bag to air them out, as Monika usually does. One shoe was heavier than the other, and I looked."

"Yeah, so?"

"Look what I found..."

Brian took out a plastic pack. Anna's port stone was inside, but the colorful little bag was missing.

"Two days ago, you showed me this stone," Lange said. "How did it get into Monika's bunk?"

"This is not the stone I found in your cabin, Cap'n." He reached into his pocket and pulled out the colorful little bag with the other engraved stone.

"There are two of them?" asked Lange in wonder.

"No. The stone from Monika's bed must be the original. Since I hold it in my hand, I understand the signal hidden in the strange deep sound," Brian replied. "Someone is playing a game of hiding and seek with us here. That someone probably intended me to find the wrong stone in your cabin, Cap'n."

Lange thought for a moment and said, "It's not sure Monika is behind this. Very strange all the same. It doesn't make sense to me what that's all about. Surely a sneaker is not a good hiding place unless someone wants you to find it!"

"I thought so, too. But my real concern is something else," Brian tried the transition to his actual problem.

"Don't drag it out. Your comrades are waiting in the pod to undock."

"I believe X1 has received a message within the last hour that you may not like."

"You decoded their signal?"

"Lieutenant Gross played a decisive role in that," Brian replied. "Since I have the original stone with me, we can finally do something with the signal from the Chinese. Took us a while to figure out that decoding the signal depends on the temperature of the stone. Peter discovered fluorite crystals' fantastic properties, as they are inside the original stone. At a temperature of 100°F (37.8°C), the crystals have a natural frequency that overlays the Chinese signal. The combination of these vibrations makes the signal readable."

Lange seemed excited, "Then the Chinese encryption system is exposed? How did you actually heat the stone?"

"By carrying it in my back pocket."

"Then you must have a fever, Wilson!"

"No, I mean yes. When I meditate, I can both lower the body temperature and raise it a little bit, depending on the stimulation method."

Peter entered the mess hall and handed the commander a handwritten note. It was the decoded message addressed to X1:

"Have empty bird's nest destroyed by German weapon!"

"Whoever brought the port stone on board must have known we needed it badly down here," Zobel said.

"But now it's also feared that the Chinese tampered with our weapons software. To me, things become clearer now: they want us to steal the artifact, and then they will use our torpedoes to destroy the hiding place."

"Why destroy an empty hiding place? And anyway, what if they don't mean the cathedral at all by bird's nest?"

"But?"

"Don't know, could be anything."

Brian raised his head and said, "I think I know the bird's nest. The first burning projectiles were called 'dragon eggs' by the

Chinese. According to mythology, dragons lay their eggs in nests."

"What a load of crap!" slipped out Peter.

"You can say that again! The torpedoes are not supposed to be fired at all. Someone wants them to explode while they're still in the tubes."

"Wait a minute!" said Lange.

"It says here... 'Have empty bird's nest destroyed by German weapon!'... Our boat would be empty only after we evacuated the crew."

"Let's hope you're right, Cap'n," Brian said. "Maybe that's what the Chinese called the artifact's hiding place. Figuratively speaking, after all, we're about to steal the egg from the dragon's nest."

Lange said, "We just don't know, and speculating doesn't make it better. While the capsule is out, we have to watch out for the torpedoes. Nassar has determined that power cannot be cut without disabling the two empty tubes for egress. Also, the torpedo control system does not receive power from the system until the launch command is given. So until we come up with something better, the only thing left to do is to use the emergency shutdown switches in case the software takes on a life of its own and issues a launch command. Lieutenant Nassar will watch as a third person in the torpedo room until further notice."

"Roger that!"

The diving capsule slowly slid out of the tower a few minutes later. Matteo steered manually. Brian sat in the control room at the second sonar technician's place and listened with his headphones for news from X1.

The dive to the gate was unspectacular. In the meantime, they had already covered every square foot several times and searched it with high-resolution cameras. The computer compared the images with the photos taken during the previous dive. The result was a sensation. Undetectable to the human eye, the rock on the surface of the gateway was not the same. Although the outer shape was identical, there were microscopic deviations. A spectral camera adapted for the navy produced the images needed for this. This made it possible to determine the material composition of foreign objects.

Lange went to Nassar in the torpedo room and wanted to know from him, "Any idea what this means?"

"Glad you need me for better tasks than watching out for two red switches, too."

"Complaints are the responsibility of the second officer today, but Zobel is currently participating in a study on earplugs," Lange blocked the complaint in his casual way.

"What is it now? Do you have any ideas?"

Nassar nodded and explained, "If I had to design a door to open at this water pressure, I would build some kind of membrane that would only let through what was supposed to get through."

"Can you explain that in more detail?"

"It does look like the rock dissolved or deformed for the moment of passage and then re-solidified. Perhaps the rock dissolved between the marked edges, and only at the moment the USO passed through the wall."

"And how does that happen?"

"The lattice structure of a material can be destroyed by vibrations. So we could destroy the wall with powerful sound waves, just like the Israelites used their trumpets to tear down the walls of Jericho back then."

Sander seemed amused by the idea, "It's just a pity we don't have appropriate trombones on board. We were only given two torpedoes in the baggage compartment." At the same time, he put the word baggage compartment in quotation marks with his fingers as if his contribution would otherwise not be understood.

The commander wanted to bring more objectivity back into the discussion, "The story with the destroyed wall doesn't explain how the gate could close again after the passage of the USO."

Brian had overheard what Lange wanted to know from the board engineer a few minutes earlier and followed him into the torpedo room. He had overheard the last exchange of words and said, "I thought of something else. That's why Lieutenant Nassar has the right idea. Sound waves might actually be the door opener we're looking for. Because it reminds me of the meditation methods of Buddhist monks. During a trip through China, I visited the great Buddha statue of Leshan. It is supposed to protect people from the waters of the three rivers that converge at this spot. The sculpture was carved directly into a mountain. I asked one of the monks present how the Buddha got into the mountain. At that time, I thought that I had mistranslated my question and that the monk answered something completely different for this reason. As if it were a matter of course, he answered me: 'If our prayer can penetrate the mountain, then a living being can also pass through.' I nodded to him, but he seemed to have noticed my skepticism. He offered to join me in the prayer of his brothers. Then, he said, I would also find that I could penetrate the mountain."

"So?"

"I declined with thanks. Still, something kept me from going. I watched a dozen monks chanting the typical 'Om' while sitting in front of the Buddha."

Lange's face was transfixed, "You don't seriously mean they would come through the gate with prayer?"

"You're right. That won't be enough. We would have to pray, or rather sing, all together!"

Up to then, Eddi and Siggi had hardly contributed anything relevant to the discussion. Now, however, they were infected by the commander's shaking head. The whole thing seemed so bizarre to them by now that they would probably have invested a high bet that Brian's mind had succumbed to the stress the crew was subjected to in this confined space underwater.

Avi Nassar's reaction was quite different as he nodded in agreement with a thoughtful expression, "Gee, Wilson! You always come at the right time!"

In a hushed tone, Eddi said, "I'd like to know if his female acquaintances feel the same way."

Only Siggi laughed at this, while Avi began to explain his theory, "Every substance is held together by the interacting forces of the particles. And what is held together by a defined state can also be separated by a defined state."

Lange looked interested but seemed to grow impatient, "Please explain it less verbosely!"

"With that, I just want to say... Minerals have a molecular lattice structure, so vibrations can particularly change their properties. That's why I believe the gate liquefied quickly while the USO passed through it. This is a purely physical process and should also be possible for us."

Brian also interfered again, "I know, this may sound a bit strange now, but in Freiburg, there is a teaching Anna Stein who has already demonstrated something like this practically."

In his words, a switch in Brian's head must have flipped again. He stared into space and did not move.

"What is it?" wanted Avi to know.

"Anna had us listen to a tone before the experiment. She used a kind of tuning fork for this. When she turned the sound louder and louder with the help of an amplifier, a piece of sandstone lying on the table suddenly became transparent and took on the consistency of jello."

"She turned the mineral into liquid glass?"

"Sort of."

Lange was wide awake, looking at one of the two filled torpedo tubes. Brian guessed what he was thinking, "You mean the torpedoes might not contain explosives, but some kind of music box?"

"Could be. But without a matching coin, there's no music!"

Again, in a severe tone, Brian said, "Cap'n, I don't believe in coincidences. Things keep happening in my life that make me think someone is thinking the same thing as me simultaneously."

"Huh?"

"I mean, the ideas don't come by chance. It's like someone is steering me and giving me the right thoughts at the right moment."

"You know I'm skeptical about this, but at least your explanation for the door mechanism sounds plausible."

"How can we take advantage of your theory?" Lange asked.

"Well, the stone in my pocket is called a port stone by its owner. Certainly not without reason. Besides, it acts like an amplifier of brain waves. You should let me go with the capsule. If the gate doesn't open despite the port stone, you and the rest of the crew will take over the job of the jukebox."

"You mean we should sit here and chant 'Om'?"

"Yes."

"Who's going to teach this to the team if you're not there, Wilson?"

"Lieutenant Gross has determined the pitch in which to sing. It is a simple C sharp at 136 hertz, which the computer could preset."

"Isn't it enough to just turn up the speakers?" asked Nassar.

"I don't know. There must be enough people with brains tuned in to each other. And there's something else we should discuss with the doc."

The commander returned to headquarters to inform Zobel and the other officers of the changed plan. The news that the "chanting" portion of the crew would most likely fall into a light trance while chanting "Om" together left mixed expressions on their faces. Brian expected protest from the doctor because Zobel knew the effects of the body's drug, DMT. Even simple meditation exercises would be expected to cause side effects. He would then have to deal with a crew under drugs. But the protest did not materialize. On the contrary, he agreed with the commander that someone would take over his watch during the next few hours. Zobel wanted to take complete care of the crew.

Brian observed with amazement that the ship's doctor made the same preparations as he knew from the introductory courses in Freiburg. There, a classically trained psychotherapist was always present at the beginning. This made him curious, "I assume you are familiar with the possible side effects?"

"Sure. After I joined the navy, I continued my education in psychotherapy and psychology. That was a prerequisite for participating in such special missions," Zobel said as a matter of course.

"I see."

"Really? Many soldiers might be unfit for duty before they are sent to the war zone."

It didn't escape Zobel's notice that Brian understood him. Nevertheless, he wanted to explain it in more detail, "Today's recruits have learned to shoot at people and to see the most serious injuries. That's why they would actually need psychotherapy before their first deployment."

"You mean because of..."

"Yes, but it's not just violence in video games that you get used to. Brainwashing takes place in the subconscious. If I were a dictator, I would freely hand out the games to my people. This way, even the youngest could be brought onto my ideological course. The enemy image could thus be shat into the brain of even the last unspoiled."

For a moment, Brian was startled by the choice of words. But he also sensed the pressure on the second officer as he worried about the sailors' state of mind. He suspected that Zobel was referring specifically to the autocrats in Russia and China and said, "But we in the West are not much brighter. After all, our country's billion-dollar video game market has emerged. These are the best conditions for everyone to turn into a psychopath.

Nevertheless, there has been a development. In the past, only the socially worse off were at risk. Today, there are rows and rows of psychopaths in the top echelons of the financial world," Brian said.

"Certainly not only in the financial world. It is not for nothing that all modern armies are equipped with more and more psychotherapists. That was the reason I was recruited into the navy after medical school. And you know what, Wilson? Maybe it's slated for people like you to provide therapy for us shrinks later when we eventually go nuts, too. My point is, I don't think the Asian mind healing thing is so bad."

Brian was relieved. Zobel's words took away his feeling of being a freak on the team, "Okay, let me get people together. But please, let's just take volunteers. Would be good if I could talk to everyone briefly beforehand."

"The commander won't mind, but why do you want to talk to everyone individually?"

"Not every person vibrates in the same spectrum. Those who are not inwardly convinced will only disturb others while meditating."

Δ

Hainan Island, Sanya Naval Base, 1915 local time, One day after Anna's contact attempt

"Have a good evening, Vice Admiral!" the watch commander said, and Ji nodded to him in response as he left the staff building through the main entrance. At this time, only two cars were left in the executive parking lot. It was raining cats and dogs, so Ji gave his driver a hand signal to pick him up at the door. Instead of driving forward, he looked at the silver SUV parked next to him. The license plate number and the car's color set all alarm bells ringing for the head of the South Sea Fleet. The unknown vehicle was from the mainland. Police and state security used these Chinese SUV models in white or silver.

His driver was still standing rooted to the spot. Ji had seen through the scene. He had no choice but to walk through the rain toward the car. Just before he reached it, a man in civilian clothes got out of the silver SUV and came toward him. He gestured to get into the second car, "Your driver has been informed that you will be riding with us, Vice Admiral Ji."

"Where are we going?"

"We will take you home, where you and your wife will not be allowed to leave the house until further notice."

Ji realized that there was no point in asking any more questions. He was sitting in this car with three officials from the Sixth Bureau of the Ministry of State Security. This unit was responsible for espionage matters and thus had authority within the military. Since the navy provided telephone and Internet access to his house, he was virtually cut off from the outside world. Regardless, none of that would matter to the success of the mission in the Pacific. The rest was now out of his hands. His principals, who for more than ninety percent of the world's population did not exist, would no longer protect him. However, he had achieved his most important goal, to do everything possible to stop the triumph of Western imperialism in the world.

Δ

Freiburg, 7:30,
Two days after Anna's contact attempt

The vibration on her wrist became stronger and stronger. Slowly one eye opened, and Anna realized what was going on. The smartwatch told her that the schedule's relentless rigors applied this Monday again. The computer considered that she hadn't gone to bed until an hour after midnight and had set the alarm clock thirty minutes later. According to the programming, a minimum rest period of six hours was observed.

Sergei had made an agreement with his staff. The institute's central mail and appointment system ensured rest periods for the scientific team. This required a change in thinking because now people were warned at work or home when their bodies needed rest. This system must have been developed by programmers with less practical experience. After all, a colleague had told of unpleasant side effects that he had experienced. He wanted to end the day with a romantic evening. After he and his female acquaintance reached the climax of the evening, their fun was spoiled by the female voice of a connected cloud service, "Your physical strain requires a higher oxygen saturation! I recommend ventilating the room and paying attention to the rest time!"

Sergei had scheduled a meeting at the Institute early on the previous Sunday. Previously, he had been contacted by the foreign minister. Not only in Brussels and Berlin were some people getting more and more nervous. Rear Admiral Breede had informed Friedemann and Ambassador Koning that there had been no contact with DaVinci II for four days. The original schedule had thus become obsolete.

Meanwhile, the US side had contacted China through diplomatic channels to inquire about the whereabouts of the nuclear-sub Long March 23. Satellite surveillance had located it off US coastal waters. The official Chinese response, of course, was outrage and that it was a hoax. Behind the scenes, however, diplomats had been sitting together for twelve hours to address the issue. Friedemann was informed by her contact in the Order that the Chinese leadership indeed had no current information on the current whereabouts of their sub. At this point, they could not tell if the commander acted on his own initiative. In any case, they said Long March 23 was not operating in this sea area on behalf of the Chinese navy. Every effort would be made to recover the boat and clarify the circumstances. After the initial excitement, the Communist leadership assured that no nuclear weapons were on board, nor were any hostile acts intended against any other country.

Anna did not have to be at the institute until 10 o'clock for the next meeting. Because of the current events, Mailly was worried about Anna's safety. Like last night, she was to use the institute's driving service again. These driverless cabs for short trips had all-around camera surveillance.

More and more unrest arose because Anna was the only option to contact the DaVinci II. Most insiders doubted that the first attempt had been successful two days ago. Anna herself was optimistic about having reached Brian. She simply felt it. Still, it remained unclear whether his influence on the commander would be enough to dissuade him from his plan. In the previous evening's conversation, Rear Admiral Breede had assured her that Wilson would not be influenced by anyone. Sergei still had Breede's words in his ear, "Unfortunately, I must admit that I did not think through the consequences in detail. I gave Brian Wilson the order to take instructions exclusively from his commander Lange. This Wilson cannot know whether a message sent in my name is genuine."

Anna answered him, "I am convinced that he recognized me and could weigh the truth of the words exactly. If anyone has learned to recognize lies, it is Brian Wilson, even if he could not personally perceive my voice!"

Sergei trusted her. However, he also knew how many white spots still existed on the map of the human psyche. One fact spoke in favor of Brian being able to recognize the truth himself. There was a kind of soul mate between people trained as mediums in Freiburg. Students in Anna's training groups were characterized by being able to penetrate deeply into the subtle world with their minds. There were, as Sergei called it, senses of the higher levels. Anna had specialized in this in her self-created training plans.

The participants invited by Sergei arrived on time in the bug-proof meeting room. Anna had taken the stairs and found walking exhausting. She was sweating unusually heavily and could already detect a smell coming from her armpits. She initially assessed the feeling of weakness only as overexertion during the last few days. Right at the door, she met Mailly, who at first looked startled, but then jokingly asked, "You didn't have any men over yesterday, did you?"

"You should know me better. I only get involved with men when I've sedated them first," Anna tried to counter. "Then they are less demanding. But to reassure you, I had my prescribed sleep, as the employee-friendly app confirmed to me," she added, still with the undertone typical for Anna.

Mailly did not want to get on her nerves any further, so she refrained from saying that the reddened eyes indicated inflammation in the body. Anna would soon learn the reasons for this from a completely different source.

Fifteen minutes late, Sergei appeared, "I'm sorry, but events are overflowing at the moment. News from the Foreign Ministry is coming in regularly. And what we just heard from China cannot reassure us at all."

Sergei was standing right next to Anna. That's why he didn't see that she had closed her eyes for a few seconds while everyone else was hanging on Sergei's lips.

"What we discuss here is strictly confidential. Hence, no one outside this room is allowed to know what the German Ministry of Defense will task us with."

"What about Ashley?" Gregor wanted to know.

"We will decide that later," Sergei said before going to the presentation screen and continuing, "According to current information from allied intelligence agencies, a coup attempt was foiled in China last night. This was probably unexpected by most because the system just seemed to stabilize again in recent months. The Communist Party proved how firmly in the saddle it was by removing key people from their posts almost simultaneously across the country that night. We do not know what role the diplomatic contacts of NATO partners or the Security Council played. But the fact is that the authorities in China struck after they had to admit to the West that they had lost a nuclear submarine. In fact, it is probably the same object that the German DaVinci II has been tracking for a few days. At the moment, both subs have disappeared."

"Do we know yet from which side the coup was organized?" Mailly wanted to know.

"I don't know. Friedemann didn't comment on that. But one thing is interesting and could be a clue. One of the first detainees was the commander of the South Sea Fleet. This guy was in charge of the navy's most secret projects and the Chinese submarine fleet in the Indo-Pacific. This leads us to believe that this missing submarine may have something to do with the coup attempt."

"So, we don't know if this vice admiral was a spy either, do we?"

"That is also uncertain. But as Friedemann said, such an approach does not correspond to the methods of Western intelligence services. Everything points to a domestic affair. It remained so until the NATO Council knocked on Beijing's door about the submarine. After that, the Chinese leadership probably felt compelled to strike. As it looks, they had prepared this counterattack for a long time. Anyway, for Germany, it is an embarrassing situation."

While Anna sat slumped in her swivel chair, looking off into space somewhere, Gregor slid onto the edge of his chair and was listening tensely, "Roland Breede is responsible for the DaVinci mission in the navy. He works closely with the Foreign Minister and has confirmed that NATO has been alerted. Friedemann, meanwhile, is on his way to New York and is expected at the Security Council. The earliest the media will be briefed is 20:00 today. Until then, as has been indicated, what we hear will remain in this room."

Of course, Mailly already suspected what was now expected of Anna. Otherwise, she would not have been invited to this meeting. Finally, Sergei addressed it directly, "Anna, we will need your help again. We don't know if Brian informed his commander about the content of your message, and we don't know how Lange reacted to it. We must somehow succeed in getting to this captain. Currently, no one knows anything about the intentions of the Chinese submarine commander. He may not yet know that the supreme commander of the submarine fleet has been deposed. Possibly, the German-American conflict was intended to serve as the starting signal for the coup in Beijing. Friedemann fears that Chinese propaganda blames foreign forces for the internal attack. We must also assume that religious groups in Tibet will be accused of supporting the coup. I do not need to tell you what this means for our institute. We are that institution in Germany which maintains the closest contact with Buddhist and other religious leaders, especially in Tibet and India."

When Anna heard her name, she was startled but could not follow the rest of the words. She stood up and said, "Please excuse me. I have to go to the bathroom for a minute."

Seconds later, she had disappeared through the door.

"If there are no more questions, I would like to end the meeting anyway," Sergei said and, without words, saw Mailly leave the room to check on Anna. Finally, only Gregor was present, "Oh Gregor, please make sure that Anna can resume her contact attempt in Ashley's lab. I hope my words didn't hurt her too much."

"Maybe she feels more for this Wilson guy than we think?"

When Mailly entered the ladies' room, Anna was not there. The men's room was also empty. She tried her cell phone, but no one answered. Panic set in because she might have collapsed and been lying helpless somewhere.

CHAPTER 16

Cathedral, diving capsule

"What are those shadows there?" Lucas asked as he pressed his head against the porthole. Brian tried to make out something, but the view through the window was blocked.

Matteo was busy with the controls and had to keep an eye on all the instruments while his right hand operated the control lever.

"Lucas, please take over the lighting so we can get pictures through the exterior cameras as well."

"I did, and I noticed shadows *aft*. Should be about fifteen yards away."

"Please don't do anything stupid now. We need all headlights in the direction of travel. The capsule has no collision warning. You'll have to take care of that."

"It's okay!"

While Lucas concentrated on the control panel, Brian looked through the rear porthole. He associated the word shadow with the winged creatures from his dreams. The hairs on his neck stood up, and his whole body tensed like a gazelle that could smell the lurking predator nearby. He said nothing to the others about this fear. When the brief fright wore off, curiosity took over. Brian pressed his face against the glass and shielded the light inside the capsule with his hands. Hoping his eyes would adjust to the residual light in the cathedral, he waited. His pulse was still high, and the window was fogging up. He wanted to wipe using his sleeve, but the thermal suit was unsuitable. Lucas noticed and said, "There's a vent switch under the window. That helps with fogging. Used to get upset when my old man kept turning off the vent in the brand-new car, thinking it would warm up the engine faster."

"Old people just. But old habits at least keep old prejudices young. But thanks, it's working already."

"Are you still looking for the shadows, or what's back there?"

"I thought...oh, must have been my imagination...hey look, there it is again! This time clearly. Two black and white objects always keep the same distance behind us!"

Matteo looked at the passive radar and saw two dots that he had thought was a sonar reflection all along, "If it was just one dot, I would think it was a drone that X1 sent us."

"Lucas, check with the guys and see if they can see it more clearly. It's too far away for our cameras."

"Aye!"

"Peter, can you see what's following us at a steady distance?" reported Lucas to the control room.

"There's nothing there except a few suspended particles that have been stirred up. The computer sees it as normal reflections. My guess is that it's being pulled along by the suction of the capsule."

Matteo reported to the control room, "I'm stopping the capsule now. Then we'll see if the floating particles continue to follow us."

The engines of the propulsion propellers fell silent. The light current turned the capsule very slowly clockwise. As a result, Brian's rear window now pointed to the side.

"Lucas, can you turn the top headlight *aft*, please?"

"You can do it yourself. Here's the switch," Lucas pointed with his hand to the control panel on the ceiling. Brian fiddled for a while, a narrow strip of light occasionally grazing a rock protruding from the floor. He pressed his head against the porthole again, trying to see details. As if from nowhere, a black something appeared and bumped against the window from outside. For a brief moment, something white also flashed. The impact caused the capsule to tilt slightly to the side. The control room also immediately noticed the sound, "Did you bump into anything?"

Lucas spoke in a slightly raised voice, "No! Something rammed us. It must have been an animal."

"Hey, Central! There's something wrong here. These aren't floating particles. You must be seeing something!" Matteo now shouted into his microphone.

Peter made different adjustments and extended the measurement to other wavelengths. Then he found something, "According to the shape, they are medium-sized dolphins. But we can rule that out."

"Why?"

"Dolphins only dive to depths of 980 feet in exceptional cases and only when hunting. After fifteen minutes at the latest, they must surface to breathe. But the two objects do not look like they are hurrying to the top."

"Matteo suspects that X1 has sent a drone. What do you think?"

"You mean they send two drones at once because one doesn't trust the other?" asked Peter.

"Shh!" someone hissed behind Peter, saying, "I was admonished that we should behave ourselves and not be so loud. The Second is sitting in the gallery with our new recreation group, intoning the Hail Mary."

Brian turned on his microphone and butted in, "Gee Peter, don't make fun of that. I hope they're only singing the 136-hertz note. The Hail Mary is more for tenors and men without... well, you know."

Brian's last words fell silent because he realized what nonsense he had just told. And now it was clear to him why. Fear and insecurity sometimes make words just bubble out. At such moments, everyone instinctively tried to distract themselves with something. Lange must have also recognized the situation and intervened harshly, "Stop this nonsense! Now, what about the two objects behind the capsule?"

Peter replied, "They have moved away and are making small circles ten yards away. So, if they are supposed to be Chinese drones, they are disguised as dolphins. However, the detection software confirms biological signatures."

"What does that mean?"

"The temperature profile at the surface corresponds to a marine mammal. We measure a body temperature of 95.5 degrees. Correction: 95.9. Wait a minute! The temperature seems to be rising, and equally so for both. There are inaccuracies because dolphins, like other whales, have thick layers of fat. I can only measure at the warmest zone, the eyes."

"Okay, what species are we talking about?" Lange wanted to know.

Peter said, "The photo scan says they are black dolphins. The top is jet black, and the bottom is almost white."

"That explains the bright reflections in the headlights," Brian said.

"But that makes it even stranger. This species is only found in colder waters in the South Pacific. And as I said, it's been twenty minutes now, and they're still not trying to breathe."

"So it's clear then; it must be drones that are biologically camouflaged," Lange concluded.

"But there's something else wrong!" Brian contradicted.

"Okay. Why don't you just ask them?" Lucas said, and judging by his tone, he meant it.

"I think they have already answered without question," Brian returned, "I'm quite sure of it. We're supposed to follow them."

"What? Where to?" asked Matteo.

Lange's voice could be heard from the control room, "Just follow them. It looks like they are moving toward the gate now."

Matteo nodded, "Ok, having an escort is not bad either."

Lange addressed Brian again, "Wilson, our singing club is already in top form. I think you've made a good selection."

As the diving capsule moved toward the gate, the two dolphins sat down directly in front of it. One of the front cameras was pointed at each one. Their movements seemed natural, and even the typical playfulness of these marine mammals could be seen. It was about fifty yards to the gate wall when the dolphins suddenly swam away. The cameras could only follow the path a little way.

"What was that? Where did they go?" asked Matteo, and Peter reported from the control room, "I had them on sonar. Since they swam before you, the computer also identified them again as black dolphins."

"I get it, but where did they go?"

"Disappeared to the top. I have no more signal... Wait..., there they are again! Somewhere in the ceiling of the cathedral, they have reappeared."

"Gee! Maybe they have a way to breathe there?"

"Possibly. It's not so important now. Just follow them," Lange announced from the control room. He had no idea what these dolphins were all about. This was one of the few situations as commander where his intuition had more influence on the decision than his expertise. The reason was simple. He trusted that Brian was right.

Δ

Long March 23

"How long have they been out now?"

"Looks like the diving robot stopped. That was thirty minutes after undocking. There are other echoes, but they may be reflections from their propulsion propellers," the second board engineer replied.

"Are they not moving anymore? Could they have noticed our drone?" the navigator wanted to know. Commander Chén replied, "That's unlikely. We would have noticed their passive sonar scan immediately at this distance."

Security Officer Ning confirmed his commander's comment, "This drone is the quietest killing machine on this planet!"

"I can't agree with that," Chén countered. "Poison murders in the courts of Chinese emperors are still considered the quietest and most mysterious methods of getting rid of unloved people."

No one dared to oppose this comparison. Chén was known for his metaphor, which he could skillfully combine with similes without directly criticizing anyone. Remarkably little has been said about historical poisonings in the Chinese public sphere. Since the dissident murders of recent years, poison attacks seemed to have become a new taboo subject.

"Commander! We should bring our drone closer. If the Germans manage to open the gate, we can slip through with them. We won't have a better chance to get inside."

"What do you want us to do inside, Mr. Ning? Our mission is clear. Robbing the nest is not one of them."

"Maybe, but we'll never know what's behind it unless we're there."

Ning did not seem to be alone in this opinion. The other officers in the command room also turned their eyes to the commander, who sensed the mood emanating from them. He concentrated on using his deep and clear voice at an average volume, "It remains so. For now, we just observe. Did everyone understand this order?" The tone of voice and his charisma had an effect. The discussion ended after an "Understood" was heard from everyone present, and the captain finished recording the ship's log.

Before this meeting, the radio operator informed the commander that the quarter-hourly signal from the naval base had been absent for two hours, "Mr. Ning was with me earlier because of that." he said. "He wanted to check with the base. I refused initially because you had ordered radio silence, after all."

For Chén, Ning's attempt to defy his instructions was an alarm signal. From now on, he had to pay even closer attention to these security officers. Ning was the alpha male, while Weng seemed more of the silent follower. Both were dangerous. Ning, however, would not shy away from actively influencing the crew.

"It's all right. I'll take care of it," Chén replied. It was clear to him that something must have happened that would impact the entire mission. The signals sent every quarter hour contained only brief coded information about whether everything was all right at the home base. There was no return signal of this type to keep the whereabouts of Long March 23 secret. The instruction for action in the absence of the signal was known only to Chén, and it was unambiguous. Six hours after the absence of the sign, it could no longer be assumed that there was a technical problem. In this case, the plan might have been blown, and Chén had to complete the mission alone. The only issues he had were with the two officers of the security service, whose internal work instructions on board were known to no one but themselves. Sometimes these control bodies had an extraordinary plan B, which meant being vigilant. Moreover, Chén did not know if Ning and Weng carried weapons other than their service pistol. Besides the commander, they were the only ones whose luggage was not checked.

Whatever the absence of the signal meant, radio contact with the home base would be dangerous at the moment. The Chinese naval stations would immediately have the opportunity to take control of his boat. They could also issue action orders to security officers that would get in the way of his own plan. If something went wrong at the naval base on Hainan, Chén wanted to keep the news a secret as long as possible.

There was something that worried Chén even more. Ning and Weng, along with the commander and first officer, had access to secret technical equipment in the radio room. One of them was the remote access to the DaVinci II's onboard computer. Its torpedo system, which was still inactive then, could be controlled remotely.

Δ

Cathedral, diving capsule

"Slow down!" yelled Peter as he saw the capsule accelerate ten yards from the rock face.

"I'm already giving full thrust backward, but it's reacting very slowly," Matteo replied after his right hand had already pressed down the small lever on the control stick for the second time with his thumb. He had been dreaming at a moment when it mattered. The capsule was rocking, and the strong acceleration had mixed the freshwater floating above the gate with the salt water. Now the wall was only a blur. The capsule lurched, and the back of Brian's hand was slammed against the apparatus. Instinctively, he pressed his other hand on the hurting spot. While doing so, he noticed that not only did the diving capsule vibrate, but he was also shaking. *Here we go*, he thought, and asked the control room, "Everything all right with our singing circle?"

Lange replied, "Everything's okay. I just hope their voices don't break down."

"I think it's starting. We can't let them go limp now!" Brian said, sounding as if his tongue was numb.

Peter reported, "The dolphins have disappeared from the monitor again. Can you see them through the window?"

"No, everything is still blurry here. The water eddies don't allow any visibility." Lucas replied, and then there was the expected blue light ring around the capsule. Everything vibrated, and the last thing they heard from the DaVinci II was Lange's words, "...check in with the long-wave signal on the way back."

For a moment, it seemed to Brian that the sounds in the capsule fell silent. He had a theoretical explanation for this phenomenon. On the other hand, looking at the glass window next to him caused his heartbeat to stop for a moment. It seemed as if all the panes on the outside had become opaque. He became even more agitated when he remembered the reason. The rock they were passing through at that moment was made of minerals. The mighty sound waves changed the aggregate state of the material and made it permeable to solid bodies. Unfortunately, glass was also made of minerals. If they were to liquefy now, they might be unable to withstand the water pressure!

$$\Delta$$

Long March 23

"What does that mean?" wanted to know Ning, interrupting the conversation of the watch officers.

"There are only two possibilities; either the drone was destroyed, or it disappeared through the gate together with the German diving capsule," the board engineer replied.

"In any case, none of it can be found."

Ning looked into the face of the navigator, who was personally piloting the drone until it disappeared but did not participate in this discussion. On the contrary, he quickly turned back to what was happening on his monitor.

Ning asked the board engineer, "You mean the capsule is inside the mountain now?"

"Yes. And from the looks of it, they had no trouble getting in at all."

"Well, we can't see inside the capsule. So, I wouldn't bet on it!" Weng said, and the board engineer turned to him, "Why so pessimistic? We should give the Germans some credit, too."

Chén interrupted the conversation in the command room with an order, "Prepare the rendezvous! Before the capsule reappears, we sit next to the DaVinci II. We'll take care of our drone later."

Then he turned to Ning and indicated that he wanted to speak to him privately. They went into the adjacent officers' mess, where there was a direct passage to the radio room. When all the doors were closed, Chén said, "Your solo operation with the drone will have consequences. I gave orders not to send it through the gate with them."

"Then it must have been a misunderstanding, commander!"

"If this had been a misunderstanding, I would have to question your fitness for duty due to conspicuous forgetfulness. My order was clear, and your confirmation can be read in the ship's log. By contrast, you omitted to record your order to the navigator in the ship's log. The navigator had to make it up for you. This was also a gross violation of the service regulations! In addition, you undermined my authority in a manner recognizable to all officers. Since you are an experienced officer, one could assume intent. What do you intend to do, Captain Lieutenant Ning?"

With a squeezed-out apology, Ning wanted to save the situation. He was well aware of his misconduct but occasionally forgot that his uniform had only been wearing the insignia of a lieutenant captain for two weeks. Without the help and loyalty of the officers on board, no one could perform his duties aboard this nuclear submarine. Even those who could not stand this Chén still had to get along with him.

Δ

Diving capsule

Lucas panicked as the inside of the capsule was flooded with blue light. What if Matteo didn't have a plan for how they would find their way back to the boat, either? Lucas didn't want to rely on this esoteric Brian either. Sure, that guy could do wondrous things with his mind –and maybe with the minds of others– but he would probably be useless for steering a diving capsule through solid rock.

Even a look at Matteo's face could not dispel Lucas' skepticism. His mouth was agape as if he wanted to scream. He held the control stick firmly with both hands and had no control over the vehicle. Now the capsule was no longer moved under its own power. That it was moving, however, was clearly perceptible. Everything they touched vibrated like an electric toothbrush. Every designer would try to avoid such vibrations because that was the last thing a complex technical system should be confronted with.

"Hey, Matteo! Are you okay?" Lucas asked, but all that came out of his throat was an unintelligible croak. The fact that he couldn't understand himself with words made things even scarier. He turned to Brian for help, who recognized the panic on Lucas' face and typed something into the console, "Air molecules and vocal cords resonate –impedes the propagation of sound."

Lucas nodded as a sign that he had understood. Brian's confident answer reassured him that he had grasped the proverbial straw before drowning. *Either this madman is entirely clueless and radiates optimism even in the face of death, or he really understands what's going on. And now the windows are also fogged up outside,* Lucas thought. Matteo's demeanor as the first officer at the moment instead radiated uncertainty.

The vibrations subsided, and Matteo's face relaxed. He knew the design of this capsule and also its weak points. In the past, there had been problems with the cable entries.

Brian had another problem at that moment. He kept staring at the window next to him. The strongly curved glass became increasingly blurred on the outside. He didn't say anything because that wouldn't help anyone. Instead, he simply closed his eyes and waited for the big bang.

Instead of vibrations, the capsule began to rock again. Matteo said in a normal voice and without much excitement, "We are sinking."

"What?" But Matteo reassured, "Don't panic. We guessed correctly that there is freshwater behind the wall, and that has a lower density than salt water. I must therefore increase the buoyancy."

A soft hiss was heard as compressed air flowed into the ballast tanks. The capsule righted itself slightly, but before it began to rise, a hard thud was heard, and the submersible stopped.

"We've sunk to the bottom." Lucas said, and Matteo ordered, "Damage control!"

Brian wanted to get involved but didn't have a checklist for it. Only the condition of the window glass caught his eye. They were transparent again. Brian's fear had not come to pass.

As expected, only the long-wave control signal from the sub penetrated the rock face. They were now on their own.

"Try adjusting the exterior headlights for all-around visibility," Matteo said, and Brian was disappointed because he had hoped to see something he already knew from his dreams. Instead, the visibility was only about two yards because the impact swirled mud from the ground.

"No damage. Primary energy is 87 percent. Should be enough for about seven hours," Lucas said, and then his voice grew more excited as he pointed his index finger at something lying on the ground in front of the capsule, "Look there!"

"It looks strange. Not like... can that..." Lucas tried to ask.

All three of them had their hearts up to their necks. What would they find? The fact that Monika had disappeared since the USO appeared had pushed the crew into the background. The recovery of a body was not part of their mission. That would require the external intervention of a diver, but the capsule had no pressure lock to the outside. Only one grappling arm was present, but they might need it to recover the artifact.

361

All three pressed their heads to the front window, and Brian said, "It doesn't look like a pressure suit. More like a mini-submarine."

"Our energy is limited. If there is still time after we return, we will look. Now we have to find a way through the cave," Matteo said and began to put the capsule in motion.

Lucas's mood had suddenly improved, "We should look for a signpost that says TO THE ARTIFACT."

"Times good that you have already found your humor again."

The capsule hovered very slowly, and Matteo switched on the sonar scanner. He wanted to use it to create a 3D map of the surroundings. The cursory glance over an otherwise little-noticed display left him amazed. The outside thermometer showed 79°F.

"Wow, how can it be so warm down here?"

"I suspect thermal water. We're only 56 miles from the San Andreas Fault. There are plenty of hot springs here," Matteo explained.

The 3D map on the primary monitor showed more and more details. They were in an elongated cavity about a hundred feet high. Hovering a few feet behind the wall, they had come through a few minutes ago. However, the wall was absolutely smooth and looked nothing like the natural rock on the other side. The opposite end of the cavity was not visible, so they had to go further.

"We will not waste time and look," Matteo said and began to steer in that direction.

The farther they got from the gate, the more precise the water became. The end of the elongated room was still not visible, but it appeared like an ascending passage with a square cross-section. Height and width hardly changed. Only the irregular indentations on either side were noticeable.

"Where might these passages lead?" asked Lucas, looking at Brian. He was suddenly acting strangely. His face looked like he had a fever again. Brian guessed what Lucas was about to ask and beat him to it, "I'm fine. I just feel like someone's trying to contact me telepathically again."

"You can do that here, so deep in the mountains?"

"You know what, I've been here before on vacation when I was a kid. Up on the coast, though. There, the valleys of the Santa Monica Mountains reach all the way to the ocean. That's kind of weird, isn't it?"

"What's weird?"

"That Monika just got her resting place here," Brian replied, and it was quiet for a while until the sonar scanner disturbed the silence. Its range was about two hundred yards, and in front of them, it detected an obstacle.

"Either the hallway makes a bend, or that's where it ends."

"If we don't find anything, we'll have no choice but to search the side corridors."

"Maybe Lucas' idea with the signpost wasn't so stupid," Matteo said, staring at the images from the outside cameras. There was something on the ceiling above them that didn't seem natural.

"I'm going to pull over closer. There's something ..."

As the image became more apparent, it was obvious that the ceiling at the cave had been polished smooth.

"I guess this is where the novice drivers regularly scraped the ceiling, huh?" joked Lucas.

When Matteo drove even closer, a measuring device struck out immensely. It was the magnetic field strength meter.

"Along the strip, there is an anomaly!" Matteo said.

"We shouldn't get too close, but I'll follow the strip now. It's bound to lead somewhere."

Brian suggested, "Maybe the USOs will get direction this way. Then it might actually be our guide."

The "signpost" eventually led to the right into a side corridor. After less than fifty yards, however, it was over. Only solid rock remained. Lucas used the long-wave scanner to see if there was a cavity anywhere. Nothing.

"End of the road!"

Before frustration could arise, they bathed in bright blue light again. Something gripped the capsule, and the vibrations were back. The windows also became cloudy before anything could be seen outside.

"Are we being lifted up? It feels like we're in a rickety elevator," Lucas said.

Then there was silence. Lucas whispered to Brian in the back, as if it made sense to be quiet, "What's going on? The sensors are going crazy!"

"It's no wonder. We're on dry land," Matteo said, and sure enough, drops of water were running down the windows outside.

"We can't get out, though. The capsule is standing on the hatch. This thing is not meant for shore leave!" Lucas said while trying to make out anything through the window.

"Look!" he pointed outside. Brian leaned forward to see something, but Matteo pointed the outside camera at two moving objects.

"They are humans, aren't they? Anyway, they're wearing quite comfortable-looking overalls."

"I'm sure you can ask them about it right now," Lucas replied, but Brian said from behind, "They're not humans but *Manujas*."

"How would you know?"

"They've already answered your question. I'm afraid I'm the only one who understands them right now. But maybe they speak one of our acoustic languages."

When the two figures reached the capsule, one looked through the porthole and made something like a welcoming hand gesture. Brian explained, "He says his name is Shet-Ahma. They intend to help us out of the pod."

His companion briefly looked at the construction of the diving capsule and then ran off somewhere. In the meantime, Shet-Ahma held his hands to the capsule and closed his eyes. Then he said telepathically to Brian, "*You are carrying something that I know well. It once belonged to a good friend.*"

"*Then you can only mean this...*" said Brian, holding Anna's port stone to the window.

"*Right. I can barely feel it, but it must still have enough power to open the front gate. Since you know how to use this stone, you'll also have a reason to be here.*"

Before Brian answered, he explained the conversation with the stranger to his comrades. Then he turned his thoughts back to

Shet-Ahma, *"To be honest, I don't know much about the stone. It was stolen from my master. Maybe to get to this place."*

"I see."

Meanwhile, Shet-Ahma's companion was back. He pulled a flat cart behind him. To be more precise, the carriage drove behind on its own. Arriving at the capsule, he was introduced by Shet-Ahma, *"This is Thriot. He is currently my only student. At the moment, however, it seems more like I could learn something from him."*

"Please don't overdo it with the praise, Master," Thriot countered and meanwhile, the flat "hand cart" drove up to the capsule. The air began to vibrate slightly, and a few seconds later, the diving capsule hovered three feet above the ground.

"The hatch is exposed. I think we can open it now." Matteo said after Brian nodded at him. To move better, they peeled out of their stiff protective suits. But better mobility brought one disadvantage. There were no shoes, so they had to crawl through the hatch in their sports socks.

Matteo was the first to get out and was unaware of the event's significance. He simply walked up to the *Manujas* and extended his hand in greeting. Brian thought it was funny how Matteo oozed across the gravel floor in his sports compression socks. Shet-Ahma took Matteo's hand and indicated a bow. Lucas and Brian came closer and greeted the two hosts with a matter-of-factness as if they had just dropped by for coffee.

Shet-Ahma said in fluent English, "I suppose this language is all right for you?"

"I'd love to!" replied Matteo, introducing himself with his full name and military rank, as he might have seen in a movie once. Lucas and Brian left it at their first names.

"All right, First Lieutenant at Sea Matteo Braun. I assume you are leading this group. Please follow us to the living quarters.

The walk led over rough scree. While Brian and Lucas coped well with it, Matteo looked as if he were walking over red-hot coals. Thriot didn't miss that, saying, "The ground is about to get better. We're sorry you're in pain because of it."

Δ

Long March 23

"We can't wait any longer now. Send out the second drone. And I want to read the dossier on this Brian Wilson," Commander Chén ordered.

"Yes, sir!" the second navigation officer confirmed.

Chén had previously looked at the files of the German crew. Some of them had the note "Research not completed". It was typical that officers such as Captain Lieutenant Lange had briefly described resumes. This man fascinated Chén. He had been studying him since it became clear that Lange would be the commander of this mission.

In his file, there were no references to his private environment. Not even a note as to whether he had a wife and children. Chinese security agencies usually handled this quite differently. In any case, it was challenging to find Lange's weaknesses. This man left practically no traces in the social networks. Not even high-ranking politicians managed to do something like that. Almost always, a family member or acquaintance unknowingly posted something compromising. Seemingly trivial comments, photos with background images to show off, something of that nature. Not so with Lange. There was something wrong here. There must be more if this man's life was cleaned up like this.

For Chén, it was maddening to have an adversary he didn't know much about. It limited the use of his country's most powerful and advanced weapon: *social psychology*. Not that it would have much influence on the mission's outcome, but Chén would have liked to know if this Lange ticked like he did. The situation would be different in a real battle because every enemy move must be anticipated. But if everything went according to plan, it wouldn't come to that.

Now he still wanted to look at Brian Wilson's file.

This small underwater drone was called Xión Fēng in Chinese, and its mission identifier was XF2. One of its tasks was to search for its missing sister drone, XF1. If it could not be reactivated, it had to be destroyed. Another task was to dock undetected with the DaVinci II. A special drill could penetrate the outer protective shell on the fuselage and attach a Chinese interface to the Germans' onboard electronics. One detail was fascinating. For the first time, they could test in practice how good the new German encryption system really was.

The navigator, Lieutenant Lin, sat at his place in the command center and controlled the XF2. The image from the front camera was displayed on several monitors. Directly on the wall with the gate, they heard a faint long-wave signal from XF1. So, the drone had to be right behind it. A command was issued to attempt its restart. If successful, the lost drone could attach itself to the German capsule to return together. The monitor showed warnings concerning XF1, "Automatic self-destruct active in case of enemy contact."

This message did not worry Lin further because he thought it was a standard message. However, he overlooked an additional note stating that the self-destruct mechanism was not the usual routine. Mr. Ning had already given the drone the order to self-destruct immediately in the event of an unwanted enemy approach. XF1 would thus trigger the explosion entirely autonomously. As it would turn out later, this was not such a good idea with a device that might be damaged.

Only when Commander Chén looked at the incoming data himself came across this detail. Unlike Ning, he knew every technical innovation on board. He was annoyed that this security officer was convinced he had even commissioned the drone's mission configuration on his authority. Ning believed that the right ideological attitude would enable any heroic deed in an emergency. So now Chén also had to iron out the mistakes of leaders who suffered from dangerous overconfidence.

Δ

DaVinci II

"What does that mean?" Peter wanted to know, and Avi answered in an uncertain voice, "Something is wrong with the motion sensors. Judging by the data, the dolphins should be back. But the cameras aren't catching anything. Can't you hear any sounds?"

"So far, just ambient noise. I'll take a look at the last half hour in the log," Peter said, and while he was checking all the noise logs in fast forward, his eyes fell on a tiny rash, "This happened twenty minutes ago. The sound is so quiet, as if it were a swirl of water. We don't pay any attention to something like that."

"Can you locate it?" wanted Avi to know.

"Three feet behind the front hatch."

As a board engineer, Avi knew every inch of the boat. This type of boat had a weak point where the noise had occurred. There is a place where all cable connections to the torpedo room go through a single hole. The construction of the bulkhead did not allow any other solution. If this place were damaged, the complete technology in the forward part of the submarine would be cut off. This also affected the pumps for the ballast tanks, which were needed for surfacing.

"Very strange, isn't it?"

Avi suggested waking the commander, "Something's wrong. That's one of the most vulnerable points on our hull, and there's a noticeable noise everywhere."

Peter asked, "Don't you think we should check what's behind it first?"

Avi shook his head vehemently, "This vulnerability is top secret. Besides me, there shouldn't be many who know about it. And of all places, we hear conspicuous noises."

"I wouldn't necessarily call it conspicuous yet," Peter placated, not wanting to wake the commander for a trifle. However, the decision was taken away from them when an alarm light appeared, indicating a blockage in the tower airlock. That was the only airlock the diving capsule could dock with.

"The tower airlock interlock indicates a malfunction. Now it's getting dicey. You have to inform the captain!" Avi spoke to Peter, the officer on watch at that moment.

Lange had gone to sleep after the diving capsule with its three occupants disappeared through the gate. He did not expect their return until two hours later and wanted to use the time to catch up on sleep. The plan was that the "singing choir" would not return to action until the capsule was on its way back. They were to announce themselves with their long wave transmitter when they wanted to pass the gate again from the inside.

The quiet prematurely ended with Peter's voice on the loudspeaker, "Commander, you are needed in the control room!"

The news of the power interruption at the tower lock caused Lange's adrenaline level to rise exponentially. When he felt his pulse, his mind forced him to take countermeasures. He tried not to appear agitated, either by frantic movements or by his facial expressions. Zobel watched him closely and immediately recognized that a catastrophe must have occurred. Nevertheless, Lange spoke calmly, "Suppose there is no indication of the cause in the ship's log, right?"

"Right, Cap'n."

Lange exuded aplomb and conveyed to the sailors that he was still in control of the situation. In reality, he was desperate. This power disturbance at the lock could not be a coincidence. And it happened after the most sensitive part of the outer skin began to make noticeable noises. Someone may have wanted to prevent them from taking the artifact aboard. The lives of the occupants apparently played no role in this action.

Keeping these thoughts to himself, however, Lange still hoped to find the cause or get the three occupants back into the boat via the torpedo tubes. But then he would have to leave the capsule behind, and the changeover at this depth without pressure suits was very dangerous for the divers. And then there was Wilson, who had no training in deep diving. An alternative would be to bring the DaVinci II to the surface. This would allow the three to enter via the forward hatch. Yet, this would happen in full view of the US Coast Guard.

Without much hope of success, Lange assigned Lieutenant Gross to find the cause of the circuit shutdown at the lock. He hoped the fellow was smart enough. Of course, Lange knew that the Chinese could also be behind it. Perhaps he had underestimated the captain of X1.

Lange thought who was behind it must have had access to the secret design documents. As often as he went over the crew in his mind, no resume matched a traitor. He thought back to the officers' meeting the day before. Wilson was supposed to find out who knew anything about the changed access code for the torpedo facility. The question was whether this Wilson was right when he found out that everyone had answered truthfully. Then it occurred to him that Wilson's answer didn't include everyone present at all because he had said: "All the officers answered your question truthfully, Cap'n".

That, in fact, excluded two people at the table: Brian Wilson, who was not an officer, and he, the captain, who had asked the question. Inevitably, the thought occurred to him: *was this intentional, and what does this Wilson really know? And what if not only the Order had sent him on this mission, but someone else was taking advantage of his abilities?*

Lange saw once again what problems the organizational structure of this Order caused. Since no one knew exactly who had what background knowledge, no one played with open cards. And without trust, conflict situations were difficult to resolve. In any case, one thing was clear to Lange: *Wilson is not a member of the Order. He was merely trained to be sent on a single mission, this one. I wonder if he already suspects this himself, and that's why he gave me this cryptic answer yesterday.*

These thoughts led Commander Lange to another problem. If Wilson learned that everyone was taking advantage of him, he might start acting alone.

Δ

Diving capsule

Brian's head throbbed. It was not a typical headache because he had never experienced anything like it. The pyramid trick didn't help either because he couldn't concentrate on it. Matteo and Lucas didn't seem to have any problems. Brian suspected that it was due to his physique, which was more sensitive to vibrations than other people.

A few minutes earlier, they were led by Thriot to this room, where a coat of thick fabric and a pair of cloth shoes were ready for each of them. Lucas and Matteo's shoes were much too big, but Brian's feet with shoe size 13 fit perfectly.

When Shet-Ahma entered the room, Brian's headache subsided somewhat. Shet-Ahma must have noticed the discomfort because he said, "Please forgive me. These rooms amplify our brain waves with crystalline mineral material. This is due to the presence of beings from a higher vibrational dimension. Since you are an aggressive race, these beings want to hide their existence, and I will not explain more about this. I am afraid you will not be able to stay here for long."

"Um, of course," Matteo stuttered. "Maybe we should explain why we're here first."

"We would appreciate that. I think it's common for people to ask permission before guests enter someone else's house."

Matteo was surprised by these words and said, "You call this your house?"

"Well, whatever is meant by a house."

"I had actually assumed that you were the guests on our planet," said Matteo, who apparently did not think it necessary to respect his hosts.

"We will not be able to discuss this with you because we have been trying to do so with the representatives of the United Nations for years. Maybe this much: Thriot and I are Manujas. We represent a race that lived on and with this planet long before modern man. Only your ignorance is the reason that you consider us strangers here."

371

As Brian listened, he felt ashamed of Matteo's statement. It was not lost on Shet-Ahma that Brian did not share his comrade's opinion. Brian also managed to telepathically convey the reason for their coming. There was no concrete term for the artifact, so he called it the missing part of an iron pillar. And before Matteo would bring it up in his awkward way, Brian mentioned that they would ask for it to be handed over. Matteo started to say something, but Thriot beat him to it, "We are pleased to hear that people are interested in the artifact. It was entrusted to us for safekeeping, and you are here to change that. You should have good reasons for that."

All eyes were now on Thriot. It was clear to Matteo and Lucas that Brian had already revealed the intention of their visit.

"We also have the question of who is sending you and what it will be used for."

Matteo couldn't help but blurt out, "As far as I am informed, the artifact was given to you by Tibetan monks for safekeeping. It is mankind's property, and the German naval command sent us to return it. I assume that is sufficient justification."

What he heard then angered Brian even more, and he turned to Matteo to tell him quietly, "Making demands won't do any good. Please let me do the negotiating."

Lucas found the situation embarrassing, and to distract from it, he asked, "Where did the two dolphins go that accompanied us to the gate of this cave?"

"There, you have met two lovely helpers. These animals are our eyes and ears in the sea when we are not flying boats ourselves. They are special breedings."

"Don't they have to come to the surface to breathe?"

"Yes, they do, but there are enough air supplies in the caves. They have learned to use them for longer dives. The chemical composition in their blood is adjusted for long dives at that depth."

The keyword air supply must have triggered a signal in Brian: *Monika!* At that exact moment, he thought Matteo also realized that there might have been a chance of survival for their comrade.

Thriot understood what the guests were thinking and said, "I see, you were assuming the death of your companion. Sorry, we should have immediately mentioned that we found her."

"How is she? Can we see her?"

"In your terms, I'm afraid it's not easy to explain. When our unmanned patrol boat passed the entrance gate, your comrade was thrown through the gate with the blast wave. Her suit ruptured, and she suffered oxygen poisoning and tissue injuries. The flying boat's sensors detected the incident and recovered your companion. We have no technology here to heal such injuries. Therefore, she is now in a transit condition."

"What does transit condition mean?" asked Lucas.

"Well, maybe you just look at it for yourselves," Shet-Ahma replied, and Brian sensed a kind of embarrassment from him for the first time. Perhaps he was not used to delivering bad news of this kind.

On a round platform on the floor was a pedestal to which a square glass plate was attached. A holographic image appeared above it. No matter how hard the three guests tried, they could see nothing in the moving play of light and shadow. Then Thriot said, "I must interrupt you. There's a problem in the sector behind the gate."

Shet-Ahma made a hand gesture. Thereupon, an image was projected above the glass plate. Directly behind the gate through which they had entered the cave interior, a vehicle about six feet long was circling, which looked like a cigar-shaped mini-submarine.

Matteo said, "We found this device lying on the ground after we passed through the gate. It seems to have a malfunction. Look, it has trouble staying level and has collided with the wall several times."

No sovereignty insignia was visible, only Chinese writing. Thriot understood the guests could not read the characters and said, "This means DRAGON FIRE. What worries us is this... Shet-Ahma made a hand gesture, and after that, a detail of the nose was magnified, "I know this technique."

He pointed with his hand to a spot on the front of the object, "This one is widespread in weapons of humans. Small cylinders

373

are screwed over such fasteners, containing the explosive charge detonators."

Matteo said, "Yes, it looks similar to a Russian underwater drone we regularly see during theoretical diving training. Judging by the writing, China now also has such mini-subs. If the drone were fully intact, we could disarm it. That's what Lucas and I have been trained to do. But the problem lies elsewhere. The explosive is not used as a weapon but to self-destruct. Any attempt at tampering will detonate the device."

Thriot said, "That was my guess, too. And that's why we can't just take it out of service. Normally, we dematerialize important components or interrupt the power supply with a wave pulse. But now we have to think of something else."

Matteo hoped that the Manujas had not yet run out of ideas. But he was interested in something else first, "I don't want to push, but I'd like to know where Monika is now."

Shet-Ahma swiveled his head to look at each person's face individually. Then he said in a severe tone, "Of course. As you wish. I'm just surprised you came here as a group, whereas now you act more as individuals. This behavior seems to be becoming more and more pronounced among you humans. I hope you understand we are concerned about what you have come here to do."

Matteo understood the criticism and was ashamed that he had already spoken in his name several times. The two Manujas usually spoke of WE when they expressed an opinion. They probably agreed much more often before either of them said anything. Brian didn't try to apologize either, secretly hoping that Shet-Ahma sensed his sentiments. And there it was with him again, this habit of looking at things from the first-person perspective.

Thriot then explained that an unmanned boat had set out to look at the Chinese drone, "In the meantime, let's go see Monika!" he said as if they were now in for an ordinary sick call. The image projection above the pedestal still didn't reveal anything right.

"I see," Thriot said. "I forgot that humans process images in their heads differently than we do."

Thriot meant that people are used to simply mirroring perceived images in the brain. What the projector showed, however, were multiple projections superimposed on each other. In response to questioning looks from his visitors, he said, "The multiple projections allow images to be mapped from entangled quantum spaces. In other words, if an image is taken from a great distance and we want to see it here without delay, this is only possible if the transmitter and receiver are connected via an existing time-independent field. You, humans, know something like this under the name *Higgs field*, which is omnipresent in the universe. By the way, humans can also see in this way. Your brain can be reprogrammed accordingly by training."

After a few hand movements, the image became visible. What they saw made them feel like actors in a movie. The camera perspective showed a container about ten feet long without a lid, which looked as if it was made of marble. One could not see the person lying inside. The entire body was covered with an opaque gel.

"Is she alive, and where is what we see here?"

"Some of her organs are not functioning at the moment. The regeneration will take days. She has multiple cell damage, but her spirit is preserved and can be reunited with the body later if Monika wants it."

"How..."

"Of course, I understand that you are interested in where she is. Please understand that we have to keep this to ourselves. It is a place where we still feel safe on this planet."

Thriot added, "We propose to ask Monika how she would like to return to the people after her recovery. By your standards, she would be clinically dead at the moment."

Matteo was puzzled, "If I understood correctly, her spirit is no longer connected to the body. But where did it go?"

"We have a method of storing what you call spirit or soul in the place of all memories. However, when I call it place, I mean this Higgs field. Thus, the spirit of a living being is not in a single place but everywhere. Therefore, beings who plan an ascent into higher energy levels do not go to a new place. Only their material body disappears. If I call it so, the soul can, in principle, also return to a newly created body or even to a foreign organism. There are also some living beings with two souls, as you may know."

Lucas spoke quietly to himself, "Crazy! Monika is in heaven and can come back!"

Thriot seemed to get into the topic and enthusiastically explained, "The human brain is capable of many things. Unfortunately, some things have become more difficult since there have been various reprogramming by your gods in the past."

At the word reprogram, Brian sensed an inner excitement in Shet-Ahma, who looked Thriot in the eye. Brian could pick up snippets of their conversation, *"Now that wasn't so clever of you! We shouldn't make people uncomfortable."*

Thriot replied, *"I know. Forgive me. But I suspect this Brian Wilson knows exactly what the artifact was once used for. People will have to learn sooner or later anyway that the intelligence of Manujas and humans is the result of regular reprogramming."*

"Right, there are people who suspect it. To know it is something entirely different. Experience shows that the future owner of the artifact would appoint himself or herself a superhuman or even a god if she or he does not already feel as such. Their collective consciousness is not developed enough to make a joint decision about the next evolutionary stage of humanity."

Thriot seemed convinced by this, for he asked, *"What do you propose?"*

"We're going to take Brian Wilson aside. He seems to know the most about people's past. I'd like to get his opinion first."

After the last words, Brian suspected that the two Manujas had intentionally included him in their telepathic exchange. This was immediately confirmed when Shet-Ahma smiled at him and asked in spoken language, "I hope your comrades will understand if we continue our conversation without them."

Shet-Ahma told the others that they had chosen Brian to discuss the artifact. Matteo was smart enough not to get into a discussion about this. He nodded in agreement.

Δ

Beijing, 22:45, small meeting room of the Communist Party of China Politburo

President Xi had called the Politburo Standing Committee for a special meeting two hours earlier. It has always been difficult for outsiders to find out how this board worked or what decision-making powers the individual members had. This was true even for its chairmanship. Western intelligence agencies suspected that Xi held it. But there was no official information about it.

At this hour, it was dead quiet on the sixth floor. Every sound was swallowed by the red carpet. Premier Li walked down the long hallway and stopped at the door to the conference room. His hand hesitated to push down the brightly polished door handle. The security guard standing a few feet away was about to ask if he could help, but Li finally pulled the door open forcefully and entered the room.

President Xi looked up briefly from his smartphone and nodded. For Premier Li, it was the signal to open the meeting:

"It has been a long day for everyone. Nevertheless, before sending the information to the Central Committee and the commissions, we must decide today. As chairman of the Central Military Commission, President Xi has put the People's Liberation Army on high alert. The coup attempt has been thwarted. The task of the Central Disciplinary Commission will now be to search for infiltrations in all ministries and agencies. So much for the afternoon's decisions. There is one more issue that we need to take care of. By now, the head of the South Sea Fleet, Vice Admiral Ji, has sent the nuclear submarine Long March 23 on an unauthorized mission. The submarine, which had just been commissioned, was to test communications with the new global satellite system. This was a top-secret project, and we missed that individual military leaders were influenced..."

Li faltered and searched for a suitable word, "...were influenced by a foreign power. We don't know yet..."

President Xi interrupted him, saying, "We need to address things clearly to avoid misunderstanding. It can be suspected that a splinter group of the Anabhu has gained access to our most secret military projects. Vice Admiral Ji must be involved in this conspiracy. This is likely related to the coup attempt. So, the Disciplinary Commission's search will focus on the Vice Admiral's environment first!"

Then Li continued his speech, "We have sent the nuclear submarine Long March 21 to search for Long March 23, with which there has been no contact since it came near the US Pacific coast. Following this meeting, we will officially notify Americans and NATO that the People's Republic of China does not intend hostile actions. The US Coast Guard will also be asked to assist us in the search for Long March 23. We will be forced to extremes if we cannot dissuade Commander Chén from his intention or remotely bring the boat into our territorial waters."

"What was this Ji really up to?"

President Xi responded, "We can only assume that someone appealed to his patriotic duty and influenced him to return to the Chinese people what was stolen by Buddhist enemies of the state in the last century. Unfortunately, we are falling on deaf ears in the World Security Council in this regard. The majority in the Council has decided that the artifact will remain in the custody of the Guardians. We have to accept that for the moment. But most importantly, we must now do everything we can to ensure that none of our nuclear subs are drawn into an international conflict."

"You mean Long March 23 should be sunk if necessary?"

"No. Sinking is not an option. We still hope that the crew can be incapacitated. Commander Chén is as fanatical as Ji and will do anything to get possession of the artifact. Nevertheless, the matter is not hopeless. Our great scientists have improved this boat class so that it can be remotely controlled in emergencies since the last modernization."

"What is the role of the two officers of the Tenth Division?"

"We have to assume that the two were chosen by Vice Admiral Ji to look after the crew's discipline, including the commander. However, Ji will never let them in on his real plans. I think they are reliable."

Δ

DaVinci II

"Cap'n, access to the system configuration is now completely blocked. It appears that the onboard computer has independently started an emergency program."

"I don't know of any such emergency shutdown program!" Lange answered his board engineer Nassar over the intercom. He was still watching the emergency stop switches in the torpedo room. Perched on a toolbox with a notebook on his lap, he could do at least some of his routine work.

"The program is used by the submarine manufacturer. It must be removed before delivery to customers. Apparently, someone found a way to hide this utility in the system. Now it has been activated and interferes with our security features."

Lange nodded, "It all fits together." Without saying it, he thought he still could not rule out having a mole in his crew. However, the traitor could also be among the manufacturer's personnel in Kiel, and then he would wrongly suspect his comrades. In his mind, Lange went through the crew again. He inwardly refused to deepen his suspicions; *few are familiar with the military's top-secret computer systems. One of them worked directly at the shipyard... But that can't be. I must be mistaken!*

Peter suddenly stood next to Lange and said, "We can't rule out the possibility that the Chinese have attached an electronic interface to our outer skin. At this point, they would have access to the onboard controls. That strange noise earlier might have been the rubber hull being tapped."

"Then we'll have to check it out. If the lock doesn't work again within the next hour, I'll get out and check," Lange said.

"But Siggi Mueller could go out! He's bored in the torpedo room and would like to do something," Peter suggested.

"No. Boatswain Mueller has to evacuate the capsule in an emergency. I'll take the suit from Fabrice, whose batteries have been replaced. For this dive, my training is sufficient."

Repairing the airlock in the tower proved impossible. Whenever Avi managed to supply power to individual units, they automatically locked. Without access to the programming, this blockage could not be changed. There was still an emergency opening mechanism from the outside, but it was only intended for evacuation with the help of a rescue device. It was not suitable for docking the capsule. Lange finally decided to go outside. Twenty minutes later, Siggi flooded the torpedo tube the commander was in to get out.

"Can you see the picture of my camera?"

"We see and hear you, Cap'n!" Avi confirmed from the control room.

While Lange shimmied with his stiff pressure suit over the bow to the top of the hull, a thought flashed through his mind; *so far, we haven't had any problems with the hydraulics on the torpedo tubes. What if their control system should also stop working later? Then they won't even be able to bring me back!*

CHAPTER 17

In the cathedral

As the cone of light from his helmet lamp grazed the area behind the forward hatch, Lange felt he was not alone. The helmet speaker provided reassuring signals, informing the diver that the systems were functioning correctly. The technology's status messages were developed in conjunction with psychologists because sounds provided a sense of security. Divers who didn't want that could also turn off the beeping and whirring.

Lange felt he was hearing something in the depths that shouldn't be there. Then it occurred to him that it might be the sound they had been listening to for quite a while. Only he heard it out there in the original. It was rising and falling as if the source was approaching once and then moving away again. It occurred to him what natural reasons there might be for this: Sharks circled their prey in this way before they attacked. But human hearing could not detect a shark at all. Just as this realization reassured him, his headlamp caught sight of something dark passing about five yards away. *Another drone disguised as a dolphin?*

He asked over the voice radio, "Did the dolphins show up on the sonar screen again?"

The DaVinci II recorded the image from Lange's helmet camera. Nassar rewound a bit and saw the shadow as well.

"The sensors aren't picking up anything, Cap'n," he heard Peter's voice.

Avi added, "I looked at the helmet cam video again. It's moving too smoothly for an animal. Could be more like a drone."

"No matter what is lurking around. It would be good to know that it has no teeth!"

"The only signals the sensors pick up are a few reflections from suspended particles."

"How do these suspended particles move?"

It didn't take long for him to respond. Not three feet above him, a cylindrical object floated away.

"That thing is clearly a drone! I could even see the little screw tunnel on the tail. Why the hell don't you see this thing on the screen? So close, our collision sensors must even detect it!"

The board engineer then reported back, "We can confirm your suspicions. The video recording evidently shows a drone. And in the meantime, we also know why we can't see anything in the control room. The sensors are deactivated. We are practically blind. So, we can't even navigate safely out of the cathedral!"

Shit, Lange coursed and decided to look behind the front hatch to see if there was anything conspicuous. After all, that was the reason for being out here. He was now directly above the hatch and could see someone drilled a six-inch hole in the rubber cover at the suspected location. In it was a slightly lighter plug. With the stiff gloves of his suit, he could do nothing at all. The foreign part had been screwed into the rubber casing. It would be impossible to remove it without a suitable tool. At least one thing was sure: this foreign object caused the problems. Someone had used it to gain access to the onboard controls. While Lange was thinking about which tool he could use to unscrew the plug, the drone approached from the side. Only at the last moment did he realize it was an attack and tried to dodge. It was too late. A heavy blow hit him on the right side. The suit bounced a bit off the impact, but he was thrown several feet away from the boat. Then he remembered that his helmet camera could be set to 360°. That way, he hoped to see the next attack more quickly. His right arm was paralyzed by the pain. Therefore, the adjustment could only be made by voice input.

Shortly after, the board engineer spoke up, "What's going on with you? Why did you move away from the boat?"

"Wasn't on purpose! I'm being attacked. You were right, Nassar. There is something like a bug behind the front hatch. And our uninvited guest probably wants to prevent me from tampering with it. I think that's very rude!"

The drone hovered over the bug when Lange had brought himself back to the fuselage with his control jets. He didn't like the term because an electronic bug was usually only used for eavesdropping. But this thing could also actively access the onboard network. In any case, the drone guarded this wiretap like a fish guards its clutch of eggs.

Lange did not dare to contact the control room. He suspected the drone might be listening in, thus foiling his plan. He knew of similar Russian-designed mini-submarines. Perhaps the Chinese had replicated the original 1:1. Then there would be a self-destruct mechanism. Its detonator was screwed into the head. But disarming it was out of the question because without a suitable tool, it would be certain death. But there was something much more interesting about the Russian-made drones. The military counterintelligence services obtained some details of secret weaponry by getting service manuals for handling them. These were less protected than the design documents because less qualified personnel also had to be trained in handling the weapons. The regulation said the drone had to be de-energized immediately upon its return. There was a switch for that. Of course, the whole thing was just theory and did not mean that the Chinese drone was identical in construction to its Russian equivalent.

It's worth a try, Lange considered and wanted to approach the drone with a trick. If the internal pressure in the suit needed to be regulated, there was a little release valve on the chest. He opened this slightly and was immediately surrounded by an envelope of tiny air bubbles. Hoping to fool the drone, he approached it from the front.

Δ

Long March 23

"What is that guy doing?" asked Commander Chén as he looked at the screen with a couple of officers. They could follow the camera footage from XF2.

"The diver has opened his pressure valve. He probably thinks he can use it to camouflage himself, Commander. How naive!"

Chén moved closer to the screen, trying to make out details, "Or he's desperate, and this is his last act."

Then Chén recognized what he had hoped to see: the face of this Richard Lange. His helmet was now only three feet away from the drone.

"Let him come even closer. I want to see the face closely!" Chén ordered his technician. If the drone hadn't switched to manual control minutes ago, it probably would have rammed Lange again. Being rammed several times could mean his death.

"Commander, we can't let him get any closer. He could shut down the drone."

"That's impossible. Germans can't know this type of drone. The fact that we have such weapons is not even known in the Pentagon."

The bubbles suddenly became so dense that Lange could no longer be seen.

"What's going on?" asked Navigator Lin, who was in charge of drone operations.

When the bubbles cleared, there was no diver to be seen either and eventually, the drone camera image disappeared utterly.

Δ

In the cathedral

Bloody hell cursed Lange realizing his mistake. He had managed to shut down the drone after lying on its back under the protection of the water bubbles. Thus, he could activate the switch for the power interruption just as the Russian service regulations stipulated.

At first, he had still expressed with gloating, "That's what you get for just recreating everything!" But the good feeling was over when a small green light came on and a time display of 180 seconds began to count down. The self-destruction mechanism had activated.

He had to assume that the explosion would not only destroy the drone but also cause damage to the submarine. *This monster must get out of here*, but that was all he could initially think of. Then Lange clutched the drone with both hands and switched on the propulsion jets of his pressure suit with his eyes. The navy divers, of course, had much more practice with propulsion. In addition, the weight of his "luggage" made it difficult to change direction. Therefore, on the first attempt, he bumped into the tower. Fortunately, he bounced off, heading toward the cathedral entrance with the disliked firebird. The joy of the successful maneuver lasted only a short time because the counting-down clock showed only 65 seconds left. He decided to let go at 30 seconds and head back. Then the drone should be one hundred yards, maybe a little more, away from the boat.

Addressing the crew, he shouted into the microphone, "Control center! Battle alert! Prepare for a blast wave in 50 seconds."

"Roger that!" he heard Nassar's voice.

Lange had no idea how strong the blast wave of the detonation would be. He knew nothing about the type and quantity of the explosive. Now it was up to him to let go at the right time.

The green number got relentlessly smaller: 32, 31, 30... *let go now,* he thought, but his right arm was stuck. The glove's locking ring must have jammed during the crash. It was stuck right between two parts of the drone's cover that had bent.

How hard can I pull on the sleeve without it tearing?

Lange considered loosening the ring on the sleeve and returning without the glove. The risk of a damaged glove was very high for combat divers. Therefore, the suit had special protection. When water enters the glove at high pressure, a sealing sleeve inside will be pressed around the forearm, preventing the pressure from rising in the rest of the suit. No diver has yet been able to test whether this mechanism works at a water pressure of 30 bar.

What the heck; the hand is then ruined, but still better than being torn to pieces.

18, 17, 16... *it's about time!*

He hung on the drone's right side and released the glove's fastener with his left hand. To accomplish this, two safety clips had to be opened. He was sure the latch was open, yet he couldn't twist the glove off. *Wrong direction of rotation? ...can't be!*

7, 6, 5 seconds to self-destruct. Lange pulled and shook as hard as he could. *Bloody hell, it's not going to work like that!*

Then he concentrated solely on turning the shutter and finally succeeded. The glove was off.

Expecting terrible pain, he squeezed his eyes shut. The pain didn't come, but the clock was already at 000 seconds.

Instead of turning in the other direction and returning to the DaVinci II as quickly as possible, Lange continued to squint his eyes and waited for the detonation. During these last seconds, it became hushed in the control room because they had heard everything. Now they waited for the shock wave of the explosion.

The blast wave failed to materialize, but instead, Nassar spoke up, "Captain! Can you hear us?"

"I don't know why, but I hear you!" said Lange, already on his way back while his gloveless right hand was exposed to the massive water pressure.

"I hate to admit it, but Spark must have had the most brilliant idea today!" said the board engineer.

Twelve minutes later, the boys pulled their commander out of the torpedo tube. Zobel was already standing by with the emergency kit. Only under normal air pressure did Lange begin to feel the pain in his right forearm. Zobel knew this kind of injury from high water pressure. He injected a strong painkiller before they got Lange out of the suit.

While the hand and forearm were being treated, Nassar recounted what had happened, "Spark kept bugging Lieutenant Gross to analyze all the sounds we had heard for hours. Gross then looked at the long-wave carrier signal emanating from X1. Because of the low bandwidth, this signal contains very little data. That was the reason why none of us took it seriously. Except for the radio operator. He then finally found a pattern in it."

"Please don't make it too exciting. I still want to see the end!" moaned Lange.

"The Chinese send simple commands to their drones in this way. Spark was able to figure out four different sequences. One of them was probably responsible for turning off the self-destruct mode. He then sent that signal to the drone."

All eyes now turned to Spark, who stood proudly and sheepishly at the entrance to the control room.

Peter asked, "How did you know which sequence would be the right one?"

"I didn't know that, but the captain always says that you shouldn't wait forever for your luck. You just have to make up your mind sometimes!"

Peter's mouth remained open until he heard Avi say, "We should play the lottery with our radio operator!"

Δ

Hiding place of the Manujas

"You wonder about our living atmosphere?" Thriot asked as he escorted Brian into a small room.

"You can say that. Humans usually decorate rooms to make them more homelike."

"We don't attach so much importance to these things. That could be because we can always be where we feel most comfortable in our minds. Material things only matter if they are important for survival. Our senses are most stimulated by original works of art."

"Original?"

"Nature is always the original. We prefer to live out our artistic creativity in spiritual togetherness."

"I don't know if I have the leisure to deal with that right now. We were sent here on a mission, and I would like to repeat my request to hand over the artifact."

"Did they actually tell you what the artifact was needed for?"

"All I know is that, in the broadest sense, it's supposed to reunite the religions that are at odds. It is to help send the spiritual leaders on a common path."

Thriot pointed to a square mat lying on the polished floor. He sat down on it with his legs crossed and offered Brian to do the same.

Shet-Ahma returned and said, "Our other two guests are interested in the data archive. We will ask them to join us later to hear our decision."

Brian didn't know whether to explain his request in more detail or wait to see what the Manujas would offer him. When the pause became too long, he discovered about himself, "It can't be a coincidence that in the last few years, I have met more and more people who have a common cause. Only after returning from India did I realize that someone had chosen me for this mission long ago and trained me purposefully. You will understand that I feel as if I am not a self-determined being. Do you know what I mean?"

"Please let us explain what we think about self-determination. We know different definitions for it. In our opinion, a living being can only determine its own life to a limited extent. With you humans, there is the word fate. You can believe in fate, but we do not. The career of an adolescent is always preconceived by someone. This can be the whole society, for example, by organizing education. In your case, a smaller group within your community decided to give you an exceptional education. It seems they had good reasons for doing so because only a few people have reached the spiritual maturity to recover the ancient knowledge of your ancestors."

Brian pondered, as he listened, whether Shet-Ahma might not have understood what he meant by self-determination.

The answer came without him asking again:

"Yes, I know you didn't get to choose many things in your life. Also, being here today was not your choice. Therein hides the philosophical part of your question: Is it good for an individual to decide every detail of his fate for himself?"

"Uh..." Brian tried to answer the question, but Shet-Ahma was getting at something else. He nodded at him, "Exactly. This is not a question anyone should answer lightly. In every country, the subjects must recognize for themselves when their leaders override the majority's will out of self-interest. We Manujas had not understood why people on earth always fall into the same cycle because your historians had described it before people established a uniform calendar."

"You mean our philosophers of antiquity?"

"Yes. In particular, I mean the established *constitutional forms*. We Manujas have also realized very late in our history that we have been manipulated for millennia. Manipulated to subordinate ourselves to the imperiousness of autocrats."

"What got you out of trouble?" wanted Brian to know.

"A cure, but at the same time, it can be a poison: democracy."

"Poison?"

"Yes. We also once lived in similar forms of society to yours. However, it was mostly a mixed form of monarchy and democracy. Democracy, in particular, thrives on the fact that the actions of the people's elected representatives are controlled. Whenever self-control was abolished, the system disintegrated. It poisoned itself in the process. This point in time has always been the alarm signal, but rarely have we heard it."

"I see. You're telling me that our people face a similar problem, right?"

"We fear that this process is in full swing right now. Countries, where people's freedom with a healthy degree of self-determination was already part of everyday life are suddenly electing selfish rulers as their leaders again. Purposefully selected lies are repeated by these leaders until the first subjects believe them. Once this has happened, the process of decomposing the system begins. This works all the better the fewer personal contacts people have. The biological tools for distinguishing truth from lies are blinded by media impressions and the constant repetition of false statements. What once ensured survival for our primitive ancestors can be the undoing of modern society. Regular experiences once changed the behavior of the whole group. They learned from each other. The more individuals had the same experience, the stronger the learning effect. This is how the brain still works today. However, if the new learning is a lie, it is difficult to program it back. Negative brain manipulation can only be corrected again by curative manipulation."

"You talk about manipulation. Are we humans being manipulated by a higher power? That sounds fantastic to me. Who would that be?"

"A powerful person must always be given power first. It doesn't matter whether he comes from within the ranks or from far away. It always works the same way."

"Was that the answer to my question? Who exactly is the higher power?" Brian asked impatiently because he could no longer see what his host was actually getting at.

"You are impatient, and I understand that. That's why I'm trying to express myself differently... The power over a group is always held by the one who knows the secret of the truth."

"The secret of the truth?"

"Defining truth is complicated. I can try my version: A true fact can be explained logically with facts. But our brain is also creative and intuitive. That lets us make assumptions. How right you are with your guess depends on how many facts are already known. So, if you want to get followers, teach them to take wishes for facts. Then you just have to make sure they have the right desires. As we have observed, it has become increasingly popular to win elections this way, too."

Brian's mood suddenly improved because all the words he had heard made sense. Again, he addressed both hosts, "Perhaps I am just beginning to see the connections. If the artifact can manipulate large crowds of people, how must I imagine this manipulation?"

"We know about your experiences in India. The monks have announced your arrival to us. Since you are here, we also feel how much it bothers you. With your permission, we will shed some light on the whole matter: The artifact is a crystal that does nothing but generates vibrations. Strictly speaking, we are talking about three frequency levels. I'll try to explain it very briefly:

In the first stage, a constant low frequency is generated. This corresponds to the natural electromagnetic fundamental vibration of this planet. You humans also call this the *Schumann frequency*. Natural catastrophes like earthquakes or cosmic impacts can change this vibration of the earth, which can also upset the life and harmony of the whole planet. As long as the crystal works, it always balances the ground. It is like a pacemaker for the earth.

In the second stage, a higher frequency is generated. Some of the megalithic structures on earth have been built for this purpose. Very well-known are the stone rows in Carnac, France. They amplify the signal of the vibrating crystal and create resonances in the atmosphere. Two things happen if the brain of humanoids is permanently exposed to these vibrations. First, certain parts of the genetic material can be altered. Individual genes can be specifically switched on or off. One can also say that the brain becomes receptive to certain information and no longer accepts others. The individual can be implanted with wishes. Everyone can imagine what happens then. Unfortunately, Manujas realized one day that our species was also trained with such a method long ago.

The third stage of the crystal served to correct wrong developments. If something goes wrong during the reprogramming, memories can be erased in this way. By simple reprogramming, access to the acquired collective memory is interrupted. These beings then forget everything their culture once produced. Human lore states that such a thing has happened at least twice during the last twelve thousand years."

Although Brian had already imagined some of what he had heard, he was shocked. He didn't want to be the one to send such a message to mankind. There was really only one option. This whole story had to remain secret until someone would come up with a plan to gently bring the truth to light. A society that could not cope with different cultures, diseases and religious disputes would find such information challenging. Chaos would be preprogrammed.

Shet-Ahma must have sensed precisely what thoughts were going through Brian's mind. He asked the crucial question, "Do you want us to hand over the artifact to you?"

Brian was desperate, "If I return without the crystal, others will come. Over and over again."

Shet-Ahma said, "Most of the human representatives I could talk to about this agree with you. Since the hiding place will soon cease to be a secret, we must find a new one. But because the crystal guarantees life for all living beings, it must remain on the planet. Now you know what task Thriot and I are doing here."

"I am afraid that this hiding place is already in great danger. The DaVinci II has heavy weapons on board that could destroy it all. I also don't know the objectives of the Chinese submarine commander that followed us here."

"Then a ruse might help," Thriot suggested. Glancing at Shet-Ahma, he asked, "Shall I explain, master?"

The master answered with only an approving head movement.

"The monks who protected the artifact in Tibet for a time created a copy of the original to fool thieves. We suggest you take this copy with you. It will take a while for it to be noticed. What is it, do you agree?"

"Anyone who knows me will realize I'm hiding something."

"You would have that problem anyway because the current job would never be something for the general public. You're going to have to master that."

"I am a Marine and have taken an oath. Moreover, I trust the people who sent me on this journey. None of them seem to have selfish goals."

Shet-Ahma elaborated more, "It's not that difficult to understand. Just as we must serve as guardians of the Manujas, there are also guardians among mankind. They organize themselves into religious communities that operate worldwide. Their task is to preserve the remaining knowledge of your ancestors from destruction. Only then can it still be used by future generations. They will make themselves known to those they deem worthy. In our opinion, you should trust what they do. We also believe that they are acting rightfully. But you should also consider: Your principals know that another group is currently trying to abuse the myth surrounding the god Shiva. There it probably concerns a kind of vigilante justice, with which parts of mankind are to be wiped out because of their depravity. Maybe one of them considers himself a god and wants to make the prophecies from the holy scriptures come true. The fear of these fanatics must have moved your principals to move the artifact to a new safe place. Unfortunately, the identity of these fanatics is not really clear. Anyway, if you take the copy, we will continue to watch over the original here for now."

"That's all understandable. Nevertheless, I don't want to disappoint these people precisely because they have given me such a great responsibility!"

With a gentle smile, Shet-Ahma nodded, "It remains your choice."

"But where did the legend about this god Shiva come from?"

"As with all legends, the origin, in this case, is difficult to determine. Besides, we Manujas have our own myths about Shiva himself. These are only many thousand years older. But, interestingly, the events are always similar. Only the names have changed over time. We called our creators the Old Masters. Where they came from and why they disappeared again is not yet completely clear even to us. Remember, this planet's great extinction during the Flood was not only for humans. We Manujas were also affected. This also led to the loss of a large part of our culture. In this way, the creator of Shiva, who is probably also the creator of the said iron pillar, always manages to hide his own identity."

"Could the Anabhu be behind this?"

"The Anabhu are also only a creation, but even older than we Manujas. They are likewise in search of their origins and biological models. Basically, they fear the artifact because it can be dangerous to humans. They need your race for genetic replenishment."

Thriot was probably not as patient as his master. He asked straightforwardly, "We would like you to answer now. Do you agree with the proposal to take the copy instead of the original?"

Brian lowered his head as he replied, "I was given an order, and you just said I should trust what my bosses do. How am I supposed to live with this conflict?"

After hearing this, Thriot got up and left the other two alone. After a few minutes, Shet-Ahma said, "Thriot will come back with two containers. You can then choose. We will accept your decision no matter what it is."

Before Matteo and Lucas were brought into the room, Brian asked to speak with Monika alone. He wanted to be able to report back to the team later on how she was really doing. The coupling with Monika's thoughts took a while, and Brian suspected that Shet-Ahma had helped in the process. Although Monika was still amid a near-death experience, her words seemed quite orderly. Her first question was how the comrades were doing. She didn't say anything about herself at first. It wasn't until Brian specifically asked her if she would return to the crew after recovery that she seemed to consider the possibility. Monika simply replied, *"Probably so. But don't worry about me. Maybe I'll enjoy this security for a while. Actually, it's a similar feeling of freedom as diving in the sea, only here you're not so alone."*

On the way back to the diving capsule, the three visitors were accompanied only by Shet-Ahma. Brian noticed that walking was difficult for him, so he asked, "I heard from your stories that you have personally met many generations of your people. I hope this question is not impolite, but I am still interested in how old you are."

"That's not impolite at all. Age plays a far more important role for humans than us Manujas. You should know that we do not measure it by years but by how often we are reborn as beings with the same soul. If my research is correct, I was born in 410342, according to our time calculation. That was about 41000 earth years ago. As standing next to you, the body is only 421 years old. Thus, you see that it is difficult to answer your question."

"Thanks, it still helps me understand some things better. It's just... if... maybe you know..."

"I understand. You've had dreams and visions involving Enki, the Sumerian god of underground waters. Did you want to ask about that?"

"I had thought maybe..."

"I am not Enki, but he and his brother Enlil were part of our mythology from when I was first trained. They only bore different names in each culture. It is possible that this Enki also bore the name Shiva during a later visit to earth. As you have learned today, much of our lore has also been erased. Like your historians, our scholars are also trying to fill these gaps. My advice is, don't spend too much time looking for the gods. Sometimes, it is good that part of any truth is made of wishes. This is how we keep alive the myths that are part of our cultures, after all. What kind of world would it be if there were no more magical fantasies?"

Diving capsule

Before the capsule approached the cathedral gate, they searched every corner for the Chinese drone.

"The thing must have run out of power. And it doesn't look much better with our batteries. We still have eight percent left. So, there's no time left to search," Matteo said. Thriot had explained to him before they left that as long as they had Anna's port stone with them, the portal would open by itself when they approached.

A few minutes later, the capsule was again enveloped in that glowing blue bubble that accompanied every portal passage. When the onboard instruments finally confirmed that they were back in the cathedral, the DaVinci II's signal appeared on their screen. Matteo emitted a grunt, and while Brian was still clueless, Lucas also realized what was wrong there. Right next to their boat was a massive object, about twice the size of the DaVinci II. Matteo carefully steered the capsule toward the tower where they were going to dock. The familiar position lights were missing. In fact, the DaVinci II was utterly dark, which could in no way be normal. A short moment later, one of the mysteries was solved. The onboard computer had now identified the alien object as X1. So, the Chinese lay right next to the German submarine.

"DaVinci II, can you hear us?" Lucas tried over the regular frequency, but there was an answer they didn't expect:

"This is Chén Li, commander of Long March 23. We received a distress call from your submarine. Due to an accident, your submersible cannot dock there. Power has failed on key systems. We are offering you assistance. Please follow the light signals to our lock number 2. A grapple arm will take over your capsule there."

"Do you believe that?" wanted Lucas to know after he turned off his microphone.

"We don't have the time for long deliberations. I guess we have no other choice. Without electricity, we can't dock."

The diving capsule fit comfortably into the giant airlock of Long March 23. Hanging on a chain, they were pulled into a hangar after the lock-in. There were not only such drones as they had already seen but also two small submersibles.

The capsule was lashed down with several belts and now hung quietly at about three feet. A technician wearing an orange vest indicated with a hand signal that the crew could get out.

"Well, they still have to work on friendly facial expressions here," Lucas said, pressing his face against the glass.

"You look like a sad sack yourself. Why don't you be the first to laugh? Maybe that will work."

Indeed. The Chinese man waved back when Lucas waved and forced a smile.

"Gee, guys, we'll go down in naval history as ambassadors of international understanding," were Brian's words, who let the other two go first as they disembarked. There were good reasons for his reticence. He first wanted to stow away the metal case Thriot had handed him. Inside was the translucent crystal artifact 24 inches long and 8 inches in diameter. Matteo had stored the case in the wall compartment of the first aid kit. Brian tried to cover the case with a life jacket, but he was also worried about the port stone. Should the Chinese snatch it, Anna would never get her property back. He decided to leave the stone in his pocket and got out. The three were then taken by two marines to a staircase leading up two floors to a briefing room. They were offered to use the washroom and help themselves to a small buffet.

"The circumstances of our meeting are probably very unusual, but I am pleased to offer you my hospitality. Welcome to Long March 23," they were greeted by Commander Chén in fluent English. He even showed some humor when he said, "I'm sure you'll forgive me for not offering you a tour of my boat."

Matteo introduced himself as the leader of the group. Brian could feel Chén's eyes on him again and again. He seemed to know exactly who he was dealing with, which didn't reassure Brian.

An officer entered the room and reported to his commander that the capsule was now connected to a charger. Matteo formally thanked him for his hospitality and used all the pleasantries he could think of in English. Finally, he mentioned what was expected in international maritime law. Still, he would have little chance of success, "I hope you understand that we cannot give you access to the inside of the diving capsule."

"Now forget about your service regulations, my dear Mr. Braun. They didn't help you either when the technology of your fantastic camouflage submarine failed and made it impossible for you to return."

The disrespectful choice of words indicated that Chén deliberately wanted to appear arrogant. Brian suspected a tactic behind it. The guy wants to make us angry because that quickly leads to rash statements. Also, an old adage applies in such cases: In anger, a person loses his mind.

Brian would have chosen a different tactic in the commander's place. In his experience, it was always good to first gain the trust of an interlocutor and show him some appreciation. If he doesn't achieve that, the doors remain closed from the start. But here they were among military men, different rules applied and – as Brian feared – other methods of getting someone to talk.

"I'm sorry, I can't use the commonly known Chinese diplomacy in this case. We just don't have enough time for it. My boat will leave this place again in thirty minutes. Either with you or without you. After thirty minutes, your batteries will be sufficiently charged for a return trip. If you follow our instructions, the technology in the DaVinci, pardon me, the DaVinci II will also be working again. Excluding the torpedoes, of course," Chén added with a grin.

"What do you want from us?" asked Matteo.

"Just hand over the item given to you behind the gate, and we will be able to congratulate each other in a year on the anniversary of this successful mission."

The cynicism didn't seem genuine to Brian. He had also noticed that Chén always turned his back on him while he spoke. So, the man knew very well that Brian was a trained medium.

"What happens if we refuse to hand over anything to you?"

"In that case, we will take it, and on top of that, it will be a long uncomfortable journey for you. You three will be charged in my country with stealing an ancient Chinese cultural object."

"I see."

"My men will be back here in twenty minutes, and then I hope you will join them in going to your dive pod. What happens there is your decision. Bon appétit!" were his last words before he left the room.

The air had cooled in the meantime, not only because of Chén's speech. The thermometer on Brian's sleeve showed only 55°F.

"The pigs are blowing ice-cold air in here. I guess that's supposed to be a taste of what we can expect on a trip to China together," Lucas said.

Matteo looked into space for a while. His despair could not be overlooked. Brian tried to convince him, "Let's hand over the suitcase. We have to assume that otherwise, they will let the crew die. No one will ever know it was the Chinese. I could never live with that guilt."

Matteo had probably already thought similarly and agreed.

When they arrived at the diving capsule later, Chén was waiting for them a few steps away on an aluminum box. Behind him were two officers, apparently accompanying their commander. Matteo got in without saying anything and took out the case with the crystal. He was surprised that everything seemed to be in its place. So, no one had searched the capsule. He placed the case at the commander's feet and said, "Now, please also keep your promise to turn the DaVinci II's systems back on."

Chén nodded, "Of course. And thank you for choosing this option. Even if it doesn't seem very likely to you at the moment. I can assure you that the contents of this suitcase are in the best hands."

He did not get an answer to that.

The launching of the capsule seemed like an eternity to Brian. While he looked out the window, strapped into his seat, the last expression on the commander's face stayed with him. He hadn't turned away this time, and somehow Brian was convinced that his previous words were sincere.

Three hours later, the DaVinci II was ready for operation again. All systems were checked twice. Only the torpedo system remained out of service.

Long March 23, alias X1, had long since ceased to be seen or heard when Lange ordered to leave US coastal waters in stealth mode.

Δ

Pacific, Long March 23,
1,130 nautical miles northeast of Hawaii, shortly before midnight

"Commander, we have a malfunction with all navigation equipment. Sonar and long wave radio are completely down."

"Was there any contact before?"

"Nothing."

"Give the order to surface!" replied Chén to the first officer. Somehow, Chén had already suspected that such an incident would occur. Since the suitcase with the artifact had been on board, the two security officers, Ning and Weng, had behaved differently. They stopped doing their patrols and instead retreated to their cabin. According to the log, Ning had appeared in the radio room only once, shortly after they had left American coastal waters.

Mr. Lin had drops of sweat on his forehead. As the first navigator, he was responsible for most of the systems, none of which were working. He knew the technology on this submarine down to the last detail. The log showed that the onboard computer had taken control of some systems while the crew had limited access. The sequence of equipment failure corresponded precisely to the algorithm for switching to remote control. So, another sub or mission control at the naval headquarters had taken command. During training, Lin was given only one possible reason: To get the crew and technology out of a dangerous zone and thus protect them from enemy attack. That it could be an exercise was ruled out because the commander would be in the operations center. The crew received a radio message from the approaching submarine Long March 21 that they wanted to moor alongside. Some sailors prepared the rendezvous after climbing onto the deck via the main hatch.

A short time later, four naval officers from the second boat entered Long March 23's operations center and reported to Commander Chén.

Ning's satisfaction was evident. He stood next to Chén while the latter received the information that he was under arrest until further notice and was not allowed to leave his cabin.

Δ

DaVinci II

"I wonder if we'll ever understand what really happened in the last two weeks," Zobel said as he took the medication to his commander's cabin.

"Do you think it would have gone better if we had known about everything from the beginning?" asked Lange.

"Probably not. But if you ask me, Matteo Braun's report also lacks a bit of truth."

"The military always works the same way as politics. Everyone gets the report that is meant for them. Even I, as commander, have no idea what the guards told this Wilson guy when they insisted on talking to him alone. He must have trusted them, and our principals already knew that. Turned around, the Guardians, as they call themselves according to Braun's report, will also have realized that this Wilson would not harm anyone for his own benefit. I don't know if it's just because he can't lie. In any case, we should accept that he wants to keep his mouth shut."

Zobel suspected that Lange was suffering from the side effects of the painkillers. Nevertheless, he still asked, "What are you personally taking home?"

"The realization of having a fantastic team, even though I'm a huge asshole myself."

"Hey hey hey. I'm sure that's too much self-criticism," Zobel placated.

"I don't think so. That Brian Wilson was supposed to find out which of my officers wasn't telling the truth. He then flatly claimed that he and I were the only ones faking it to the others. That was really a strong play, but he was right!"

"Isn't it a lie to pretend to others?" Zobel wondered.

"Good question, but maybe sometimes there's no other way."

EPILOG

Freiburg

During lunch, Anna received the news of the DaVinci II's appearance from Mailly. Rear Admiral Breede had previously informed Sergei, who immediately wanted to call Anna. Thus, she deliberately left her mobile in the office to concentrate on her colleagues. Otherwise, her fingers and head would have been busy checking the news. Of course, it hadn't escaped her attention that she had been driving crazy for days.

When Mailly whispered something in her ear, she shot out of the cafeteria to the elevator like a rocket. The elevator seemed to respond particularly slowly today. Even hammering on the call button didn't help. Finally, she took the three flights of stairs to the top. She opened the institute app with trembling fingers, and everything seemed to conspire against her again. An error message disappeared only after she restarted the app. Then, finally, the hoped-for news: Brian was online. So the submarine had to be on the surface, and there was cellular connectivity.

She decided not to call immediately but to send a message, "Are you okay?"

It took less than ten seconds before the answer came, "I'm okay. Thanks for everything! Can I get through?"

By that, he meant contacting Anna telepathically, and she had to grin. The "getting through" was an expression that she used as a synonym for thought transmission.

With Anna's port stone in hand and squeezed into his tight sleeping niche, he was through seconds later, *"Hey, I'm so glad your warning reached me in time. I don't know if I would have made a different decision otherwise."*

Instead of telling him how pleased she was to hear his voice, Anna immediately raged, *"Tell me, why do you just disappear from the scene? Do you know how much effort we had to go through here to get to you?"*

"No, but I'd love for you to tell me about it over a beer at your local StuSie bar around the corner!"

"Uh..."

"Before you make an excuse... I have a present for you too! Well, actually, it's already yours."

"Are you talking ... but of course, you couldn't have connected so quickly without the stone. How did it get into your hands?"

"The only way I can tell that story is over a delicious beer in your bar."

"Don't talk nonsense, or I'll fail you in your next classes!"

"Okay, convinced me," Brian conveyed while the corners of his mouth almost reached his ears. Anna felt this warm aura even without seeing him. But then the port stone couldn't keep her waiting, *"So how did you get my stone?"*

"Someone must have stolen it from your apartment on behalf of the navy. Or maybe they just wanted to borrow it and thought you wouldn't even notice for a few days. It doesn't matter. In any case, I haven't found anything specific about the people behind it. Only from Monika do I know..."

"Who is Monika?"

"Oh yeah, she's, was, I mean, she's a navy diver on our crew."

"So what, she's not anymore?"

Brian told about Monika's diving accident and that her spirit is still separated from the damaged body.

"... Anyway, Monika could tell me a few things about it. But they didn't tell her much either. She was told to keep the stone and a copy of it until we were at our destination. She was told that the copy was to find out who on board would be able to tell the original from the fake. So, the thieves must have known the secret of the port stone. They probably wanted to prevent the wrong person from being sent to the guards. However, Monika did not complete her mission to the end."

"When will you be back in Europe?"

"If all goes according to plan, next Friday."

"See you then!" Anna said goodbye.

"Wait a minute!"

"Yes?"

"I just wanted to... oh, nothing. See you!"

Δ

Hainan Island, Sanya Military Base

The arrival of Long March 23 occurred four days after the rendezvous northeast of Hawaii. Unlike usual, the 410-feet-long nuclear submarine was received without a military ceremony. A silver SUV was parked in front of the barrier to the wharf. The security officers, Ning and Weng, had a strange-looking suitcase and boarded the car. The SUV's destination was the Electronic Intelligence Service building near the base.

Chinese material scientists examined the brought object and found that the cylindrical object was a natural quartz crystal. According to the chemical signature, the mineral came from Madagascar. A crystal of this size and perfection was rarely found. So, everything pointed to the fact that it was a genuine artifact. They needed more time to examine the wrought iron frame that enclosed the crystal. The iron had an engraved inscription, just as the legend said. The characters were similar to the runes known from northern Europe. Three linguists and an expert in anthropological linguistics finally agreed on the following translation of the inscription:

WHEN THIS VOICE IS HEARD, THE PEACE OF MIND WILL BE DISTURBED

Despite the success, the experts' joy did not last long. Metallurgical analysis of the iron showed that the ore had been mined in Asia and forged about ninety years earlier. Thus, the material did not match the original iron pillar once made from the Chinga meteorite.

Captain Lieutenant Ning oversaw the artifact investigation and was disappointed for different reasons than the scientists. Since the artifact turned out to be a fake, Ning would probably have to keep dreaming of a promotion.

Δ

Freiburg, StuSie bar in the student housing estate

The setting sun illuminated the flat building with the charm of the prefabricated seventies structure. A few young people were standing in front of the entrance to the bar, smoking. Although autumn drew close and the surrounding trees had almost shed their leaves, no one wore a jacket.

Anna had left the institute late and was now on her way to her meeting place. She couldn't help but smile when she thought of Ashley, who had left the institute with her that evening. She had been picked up by a man whom Ashley kissed for a long time as a greeting. This reminded Anna of the incident in Ashley's lab when they discussed how stupid newly in love sometimes acted. Kai had laughed his head off at the thought of what it would be like to give the cook a few drops of love potion for the soup. Now Anna felt like she had caught it from Ashley. That flip in her stomach, the constant glances at her smartphone, the sudden need to dress a little prettier and even use makeup. It couldn't be because of that stupid guy, could it? Ashley's theory about this kind of manipulation of the brain fascinated Anna.

When she saw Brian walking through the adjacent park towards her, the rational side of her brain stirred once again for a short moment that evening: *I must absolutely prevent any guys from manipulating the brains of us people for their own purposes out of imperiousness. The one thing which works all by itself, only by the biology of two bodies, is perhaps the only reasonable manipulation in this world!*

AUTHOR'S MESSAGE

As in this book, each freely invented story is true in a particular way. Since I do not have the privilege to be able to fall back on cosmic (or divine) helpers, the nourishment plan of my imagination consists only of my own experiences and experiences transmitted to me by others. Consequently, I also have to make particular efforts to distinguish the lie from the truth.

Finally, I was convinced by the argument that we humans need powerful telescopes for the vastness of the cosmos, but only functioning senses for our own coexistence. I would like to briefly introduce two representatives of this thesis:

> *Human dignity comes from the ability to think about oneself. [...] Thinking is a sixth sense that we should train.*[29]
>
> Markus Gabriel (philosopher), Germany 2020

> *Everything that ever happened to you, you experienced right within you. Light and darkness, pain and pleasure, agony and ecstasy – all happened within you. [...] All human experience is one hundred percent self-created.*
>
> Sadhguru on Inner Engineering, India 2020

Δ

Because I have been asked about this repeatedly, I am happy to comply with the request to highlight a few of the most essential facts and fiction from this book. I don't want to list everything, but I'd like to show that the borders of the fictional world are not always clearly recognizable. If you want more details, you can find them in the references at the end of the book.

What do you think is based on facts? Be surprised!

The Maritime Operations Centre (*MOC*) is the naval command center in Rostock (Germany). In addition to air and sea rescue departments, there are also units for NATO special operations.[12] Nevertheless, the described episode from the planning phase of the object is fictitious.

The islands of the Mediterranean are full of prehistoric sites, and new surprises await archaeologists every day. The *cart ruts* on Malta and Gozo have always captured people's imagination.[3] Even if their true purpose is still in the dark, the solution described by Tony in the book (a transportation system based on levitation) would be theoretically feasible today. Also, the phenomenon of the negative mass (sonic mass), which can be observed in connection with the *phonons,* is not an invention of the author.[24]

The megalithic complex *Whispering Knights* (also Whispering Stones) exists and is located near the English village of Long Compton. It belongs to the Neolithic complex Rollright Stones, which borders the counties of Oxfordshire and Warwickshire. The ultrasonic effects that visitors regularly report have already been studied and documented using scientific methods.[1],[8]

Religious sources and inserted quotations from them are not invented, even if they do not represent the complete context of the source text. Also, the painting Madonna with St. John's Boy, on which a flying object can be seen, exists in Florence (Italy). Respecting people who follow a religion, I want to clarify that I do not intend to denigrate or misrepresent religious content. However, the zeitgeist of modern society allows me to present my interpretations without considering old dogmas.

Anna has a vision in which she finds herself in the Yad Vashem Holocaust Memorial (Israel)[25.2]. In the process, an anti-Semitic theme is broached that is so real we don't even want to imagine it. Using the example of the forged *Protocols of the Wise Men of Zion*[25.1], Sergei, the institute's director, sees himself confirmed in his mission to lead young people out of a mendacious world through education.

The *ARHGAP11B* humanization gene has resulted in a unique point mutation that actually (and only) in humans led to a rapid increase in brain size and pronounced wrinkling of the neocortex. What triggered this unique mutation has not been elucidated to date. Even the current knowledge about evolution does not provide an explanation for this.[15.1],[15.2]

Fragments of the stainless iron pillar shown to Brian on his journey exist. They are displayed in Dhar, India, in the so-called Pillar Mosque (Lat Masjid). The missing part of the technical-looking object causing such a commotion in the story, in fact, disappeared at some point.[27]

The internal structure of the Leonardo DaVinci II largely corresponds to the submarine class 212 built in a German shipyard in Kiel. This submarine class is one of the most modern and secretive maritime weapon systems. Many technical features, such as the propulsion system, are not accessible to the public. The latter prompted me to rely exclusively on fuel cells for power generation. The supercavitation drive in this type of boat is not real. Nevertheless, supercavitation torpedoes and rocket propulsion are already in use. However, research was still underway in 2021 on such a propulsion system for submarines used in the DaVinci twins.[32]

There is no evidence of a hermetically sealed underground meeting room at UN headquarters in New York City. Floor plans and blueprints of this building are not accessible to everyone for understandable reasons. The room and its technology are, therefore, fictional. What is not made up is the *metamaterial*[42], with which the fictitious room is equipped.

Both Anabhu and Manujas, which significantly impact the lives of people in the novel, come from the author's imagination. However, civilizations that were older and more technically advanced than we humans are part of oral and written traditions, myths and legends on all continents. The imagination of many book-and-screenplay writers has been mainly stimulated by the unanswered question of how humans managed to build so precisely without modern tools. If engineers (and not only ideologists and archaeologists) are asked, it becomes clear that history still has significant knowledge gaps.

The topic of gods and extraterrestrials brings us to the question of what *Enki*, the Sumerian god of knowledge and subterranean waters, might be all about. Although water oceans have already been detected on various icy moons, the discovery of vast water deposits in the earth's outer mantle is even more spectacular. While the existence of living things inside the earth is pure speculation, scientists from various countries have demonstrated, and published in Nature in 2014, that the mantle mineral ringwoodite contains more water in total than all the oceans. With this knowledge, calculating the earth's mantle density leads to satisfactory results.[50]

In Freiburg in southern Germany, the research of border areas of psychology and phenomena of extrasensory perception has a long tradition. The Institute for Frontier Areas of Psychology and Psych hygiene is financed by a foundation and private funds. In 2021 Prof. Dr. Schmidt took over its management. However, the author invented what was described in the book about this institute's working methods and persons.

The destination of the DaVinci II on its adventure voyage is a stone underwater formation off the coast of California, clearly visible on satellite images.[17] It is located in a marine natural reservoir where special permits are required to dive. Information on the water depth where the object is situated ranges from 1000 to 1600 feet. Amateur researchers and other curious people have not managed to approach this strange structure until today. Thanks to such secrecy, our curiosity and imagination constantly receive new food.

Some persons like Prof. Fyodorov, Rear Admiral Breede and Isabel Friedemann are associated with a secret organization in the course of the plot, which they only call the Order. This secret society is, of course, a fictional part of the book. It is not the author's intention to spread conspiracy theories about this.

But what about China's activities in the Pacific and elsewhere along their new Silk Road? The Chinese People's Liberation Army's South Sea Fleet is coordinated from the Sanya naval base on Hainan Island, as described. Chinese nuclear submarines operating in the South Pacific are also based there. For years, tensions have been rising throughout the Pacific region. According to the North Atlantic Alliance, China is flouting territorial regulations under international law and has begun developing uninhabited islands as military bases. Littoral states feel threatened by this, which regularly escalates in UN meetings. However, due to China's veto power in the Security Council, this has hardly had any consequences. Since 2021, Germany has also supported the navies of Australia, Singapore, Japan and the USA in military patrols to protect the free trade routes in the Indo-Pacific region.[2]

From the author's point of view, the dynamic development of Chinese technology was ridiculed for too long and often regarded merely as stolen copies of Western technologies. The seriousness of this misjudgment can already be seen today in its effects. Just as in the Mediterranean region, countries in other parts of the world have become economically dependent on China and thus politically blackmailable. What communism failed to achieve in the twentieth century could now become an export hit for China. The Chinese confidently portray their state order as superior, and their rapid economic growth initially seems to prove them right. However, the bill that the Chinese people will have to pay for this path has not yet been issued. The fact is that even within China, countercurrents are already emerging that dislike the autocratic course.

This book also draws parallels with the cultural past. It may be that the creation of a new world religion is unrealistic. But is what is happening in autocratically ruled countries like China anything new? What is new is probably only the technology and how the masses are manipulated. Is there perhaps something going on those Greek scholars like Polybios already recognized with their *Cycle of Constitutions*[48]?

Wherever social forms were replaced in the past, there were corresponding adjustments in religions (with and without gods). Thus, religious leaders always had to adapt their methods to give a new orientation to their followers. Do we still have to care about that today? I mean, yes! With the help of modern media, self-appointed prophets quickly spread their ideas or conspiracy theories. But...

The Age of Enlightenment (in the 17th and 18th centuries) also brought ordinary people from superstition to the sciences through education. This means that the chances for generations

Z and Alpha in the new enlightenment era are good: They will no longer be guided by prejudices and be diverted from the truth. With every advance in education, charlatans and "gods in cloaks of invisibility" will have a more challenging time simply replacing facts with assumptions or wishes.

---- Δ ----

Finally, a note on my own behalf. Your opinion is important to me, and it helps other readers if there are real reviews in the online bookstore. That's why I'm happy about every review of this book.

PERSONS IN THE BOOK

Anna	Anna Stein, research associate at the Institute of Psychology at the Faculty of Business, Economics and Behavioral Sciences at the University of Freiburg
Ashley	Dr. Ashley D. Harrison, Human Geneticist at the University of Freiburg, Germany
Spark (nickname)	Radio operator on the DaVinci II
BROWN, Matteo	Lieutenant at Sea Matteo Braun, First officer on the DaVinci II
BREEDE, Roland	Rear Admiral Roland Breede, Head of Special Operations at the Maritime Operations Centre (MOC) in Rostock, Germany.
Brian	Chief Warrant Officer (CWO) Brian Wilson is an American naval officer. A specialist in languages and communications as well as computational linguistics, the German-American was assigned to the Maritime Operations Center (MOC) in Rostock.
CERRAH, Pablo	Pablo Cerrah is one of the Commissioners in the European Commission, responsible for Foreign Affairs and Security Policy, at the same time Chairman in the Foreign Affairs Council in the EU
CHÉN Li	Captain Chén Li (Chinese naval rank: Hai Jun Shang Xiao), submarine commander
Christina	Civilian employee in the Maritime Operations Centre (MOC) in Rostock
Ela	Egyptian high priestess

Fabrice	Chief Petty Officer Fabrice Richter, navy diver
FRIEDEMANN, Isabel	German Foreign Minister
Gregor	Research Associate, University of Freiburg
GROSS, Peter	Lieutenant at Sea Peter Gross, sonar specialist on the DaVinci II
JI Fang	Vice Admiral Ji Fang (Chinese naval rank: Hai Jun Zhong Jiang), head of the Chinese Southern Ocean Fleet.
Kai	Kai Lohr, scientist at the University of Freiburg, sonar researcher specializing in hypersonics
Kanja	Buddhist monk in India
Kilian	Former student in Freiburg, Germany, lives with partner Paula north of Oxford, England
KONING, Rudi	NATO-Ambassador Rudi Koning, Permanent Representative of Germany to the North Atlantic Council
LANGE, Richard	Lt. Captain Richard Lange, submarine commander of the German navy
LIN Yong	Lt. Seaman Lin Yong (Chinese naval rank: Hai Jun Shao Wei), navigator on the Chinese nuclear submarine Long March 23
Lucas	Boatswain Lucas Raziewsky, navy diver
Mailly	Scientific assistant of Sergei at the Institute in Freiburg
Monika	Chief Petty Officer Monika Breitner, navy diver

NASSAR, Avi	Lieutenant Avi Nassar, boarding engineer on the DaVinci II
NING Gui	Captain Lieutenant Ning Gui (Chinese naval rank: Hai Jun Shang Weng) is one of the two security officers aboard the submarine Long March 23. He belongs to the Tenth Department of the Chinese Ministry of State Security.
Norbert	Ship's cook (also called smut or smutje in the German navy)
Olaf	Employee in the Maritime Operations Centre (MOC) in Rostock
Paula	Partner of Kilian, German-speaking correspondent in Great Britain
POT, Sigfried	Lieutenant at Sea Sigfried Pot heads a military investigation committee
Ravi	Buddhist monk in India
Renaldo	Employee at the Institute in Freiburg
SANDER, Eddi	Chief petty officer Eddi Sander, Weapons technician / torpedo specialist
Sean	Boatswain Sean Keller (marine), German-American, friend of Brian
Sergei	Prof. Dr. habil. Sergei Sergeyevich Fyodorov, Professor at the University of Freiburg, former member of a Russian Masonic Lodge
Shet-Ahma	Diplomatic representative of the **Manujas** to the United Nations Security Council
Siggi	Boatswain Siggi Mueller, navy diver
Thriot	A disciple of Shet-Ahma and born **Manuja**. He stays on earth to study the origin and history of his race at original sites.

WENG Zemin	First Lieutenant Weng Zemin (Chinese naval rank: Hai Jun Zhong Wei) is one of two security officers aboard the Chinese submarine Long March 23. He belongs to the Tenth Department of the Chinese Ministry of State Security.
XI Jinping	General Secretary of the Communist Party of China, President of the People's Republic of China, Chairman of the Central Military Commission, (presumably) Chairman of the Standing Committee of the Politburo of the Comm. Party of China
Dr. ZHOU	Senior neurologist at Oxford University Hospital.
ZOBEL, Ronny	Lieutenant at Sea Ronny Zobel, Second Officer on the DaVinci II with double function as Technical Officer and Ship's Doctor

GLOSSARY

Achala: Name of the planet earth, which is used by the **Manujas**, a part of its inhabitants.

Aft: In sailor language, for the rear of a seagoing vessel.

Aka: A subtle world exists for the **Manujas** beside their material world. In mythology, everybody is said to be surrounded by an aura (**morphic field**). Living or nonliving nature is permeated by the aka and is connected to each individual aura. The Manujas believe one can travel between the subtle and materialized worlds. This is a secret knowledge of the **old masters**.

Alpha waves (see also theta waves): Electromagnetic waves (8-13 Hz), which include radio waves. In the brain, they indicate a relaxed state of wakefulness or the state before falling asleep.

Anabhu: Alien race (Sanskrit: the disobedient). A species believed to be an upper group of the **Grays** or **Greys**. Splinter groups of the Anabhu are known to regularly violate the Galactic Code. Therefore, this part of the Anabhu is occasionally called The Dark Ones or Dark Greys.

Angkor Wat: Most famous temple complex in Angkor, Cambodia. According to satellite images, it is part of a vast complex of about 1000 temples around Angkor. It was most likely built in the 10th century on the remains of a much older city. The orientation was according to the cardinal points. The north pole must have been located elsewhere during the construction of underlying ruins, which are still undated. [35], [36]

Ankh (Anch): The Ankh, also Anch symbol (Latin: Crux ansata), is an ancient Egyptian symbol that stands for continued life in the afterlife. It is often depicted as a ritual tool. As a hieroglyph, the symbol stands (according to modern interpretation) for physical life and creation. The symbol consists of a T (TAU) with an attached half lemniscate. [34]

☥

The T marks the three-dimensional space, and the lemniscate is the elevation of the vibrational state. It represents the key to spiritual ascension into the subtle world.

ARHGAP11B: (see *Human Genesis Gene*)

Bon religion: Before Buddhism became known in Tibet, the Bon (Bön) religion was predominant until the 8th century. Its roots include shamanistic rituals. Swastika-Bön (the origin of the swastika symbol) goes back to the mythical teacher Buddha Shenrab Miwoche (lifetime around 18,000 BC). [44]

Bridge (also **rubber bridge** or **contract bridge**): This is a card game for four people. Two players form a team and sit opposite each other.

Cargo cult: This term originates from encounters between Melanesians living in isolation and Europeans. People recreated objects brought by Europeans with their material and included them in ritual acts. All over the world, such imitations of things appear, which even modern people could not have shown to the natives (space suits, Vimana temple towers in the form of the spaceships of Indian gods, etc.).

Cart ruts: Cart or grinding marks on the islands of Malta and Gozo (English cart rut phenomenon) are furrows in the rock that date from prehistoric times. The background of their formation is controversial. [3]

Constitutional cycle (according to Polybius): The historian Polybius defined this cycle in the 2nd century BC as a constant alternation of six constitutional types. Three legitimate/good forms (monarchy, aristocracy and democracy) are regularly replaced by three forms of decay: monarchy by tyranny, aristocracy by oligarchy, and democracy by ochlocracy. The system's destruction always occurs through the moral decay of the rulers, which expresses itself in greed, arrogance, injustice and imperiousness. [52]

Deepfake: Deepfakes are, for example, realistic-looking photos and video or audio recordings that have been altered and falsified using artificial intelligence techniques. By now, some software can also fake autonomously in artificial neural networks. A dangerous area of application could be the denigration of public figures. [18]

Dingli: Dingli is a locality on the southwest coast in the Western District of Malta. [4] Nearby are enigmatic structures in the rocks, also known as **cart ruts**. There is a small military radar station on the Dingli cliffs there.

DMT (dimethyltryptamine): A tryptamine alkaloid with hallucinogenic properties. It is found in animals and plants and resembles to the neurotransmitter serotonin. Indigenous peoples in the Amazon basin use it for ritual purposes. [37] It enables our brain to create novel thought structures and sensations. In addition, Dr. Rick Strassmann suspects this substance is secreted by the human pineal gland during certain spiritual rituals and at birth and death. [38]

Enki: (Akkadian: Ea) In Sumerian mythology, Enki is the wisdom god and ruler of the freshwater ocean Abzu (Enki's residential city). He is considered the creator of humans and various hybrid beings. These gods are sometimes depicted with wings and sometimes with a habitat of water. This fits the rule over the land, water and air, including living creatures. [45.1]

Left: Enki, god of wisdom and underground waters.
Right: Sumerian scroll seal. On the left is the goddess Inanna. In the center is the sun god Utu, on his right Enki and his vizier on the far right. [45.2]

Falun Gong: A Chinese form of meditation, concentration and movement to exercise the body and mind. Ancient martial arts are also included. Probably also because of its Buddhist origin and the moral philosophy conveyed, this form of spirituality is classified by the Chinese Communist Party as dangerous to the state. [46]

Falun Gong symbol

Generation Alpha: This generation (born around 2005 to 2025) is considered the successor to **Generation Z**. They have grown up entirely with the technologies of the early 21st century. Digitally networked from birth, these people have different access to global knowledge than all previous generations. However, this circumstance also harbors dangers for their personality development, which they can only avert themselves. [19]

Generation Z: Generation Z (born around 1995-2005) is the name given to the successor generation to Generation Y, also known as Millennials.[18] These generations are characterized by excellent scientific and political education, particularly evident in new ways of thinking about and dealing with the environment and the economy. Because of their strong impact on shaping public opinion, conservative political organizations have had to adapt quickly to this generation to survive politically.

Gobekli Tepe: Prehistoric Stone Age site in Anatolia (Turkey). [39]

Greys / The Greys / Dark Greys: "The Greys" is a name used by modern humans for a special kind of aliens. They are also called **Anabhu** (translation from Sanskrit: the disobedient). There seem to be different groups of this species. Representatives of pre-astronautics do not exclude that they could be humanoid/hybrid robots (part machine, part biological). In the book, a part of this species does not always adhere to the Galactic Code, which has earned them the name Dark Greys.

Higgs field: According to the thesis of the Scottish physicist Higgs, the entire universe is filled with a kind of "quantum syrup", the Higgs field. If elementary particles move through this viscous medium, they are slowed down and thus get their mass. Put simply, matter acquires all the properties we know through interaction with this field. [49]

Human Genesis Gene (ARHGAP11B): This gene is a duplication of the ARHGAP11A gene and has only been found in humans. A point mutation led to the folding of the cerebral cortex. It appeared in humans about 5 million years ago and enabled rapid brain growth. 11B enabled social intelligence, which meant that individuals learned from each other and could store what they learned in groups. At this point, biological evolution stopped and was replaced by social development.
[15.1], [15.2]

Janmashtami: (also Krishna Jayanti) is an important festival in Hinduism. It falls on the eighth day of the month of Shravan (in the modern calendar, in July or August). It celebrates the birth of the god Krishna, who Hindus believe lived on earth as a divine child around 1400 BC. [28]

Kesa: monk's robe (garment) expressing membership in a Buddhist Order.

Kha: Being from the subtle world, **aka** (see also **mentor**). If there is a spiritual connection between Manuja and Kha, the Kha gets the name affix of his worldly protégé. Kha can be invoked through meditation. Manujas and Kha (as mentors) live in a cultural and spiritual symbiosis. A direct mental connection to the Kha can only be established by those who have reached a similarly high level of consciousness.

Linga (Lingam): Hindus see in it the creative and the destructive power of Shiva. Today, usually made of polished stone, the figure is shaped like an upright cylinder (also considered a phallus). The iron pillar of Dhar (India) has a forged iron top in the shape of a lingam. The origin and original meaning are unknown.

Mandala: The word mandala means circle or circular and has magical or religious meaning in Hinduism and Buddhism, but also in other religions. The various shapes show diagrams that depict the universe. The center of the universe is called Bindu (point, drop, essence, number zero). In Sanskrit, it also means divine seed. From a point, everything can originate (even the Big Bang).

Manuja: Humanoid race. Striking external features: Long skull, long arms and legs, large feet and ears, fair skin. Intelligence and communication skills seem to be more advanced than in humans.
In modern times, the word comes from Sanskrit, meaning "born of Manu". Manuja can also tell "son of man" or "noble man" in another context. [5]

Master: Among the Manujas and many other races, a designation for teachers. Often these are also coordinators for meditation.

Mentor: Term for an experienced person who makes his knowledge and experience available to others. People have borrowed this term from Greek mythology and Homer's Odyssey. [7]
For Manujas, mentors are spirit beings from the **aka** (see also **Kha**). Manujas and mentors live in a cultural and spiritual symbiosis. Kha can establish a direct mental connection with other beings only if they have reached a similarly high level of consciousness. Alternatively, a medium may be interposed. Also, in modern times it is suspected that Kha try to communicate with people unilaterally, for example, via crop circles.

Merkaba (Merkabah / Mer-Ka-Ba [23]**):** Merkaba literature often refers to God's Throne Chariot, which is usually shaped like a Merkaba. The symbol illustrates two tetrahedrons whose tips are inserted into each other. This throne chariot is most accurately described in the vision of Ezekiel (Ezek 1,4), whose writings are included in the Jewish Tanakh and the Christian Old Testament. NASA engineer Josef F. Blumrich analyzed Ezekiel's text and built a model of this throne chariot. The result was a realistic-looking spaceship. The temple described by Ezekiel was later reconstructed by Hans Herbert Beier (an engineer) as a take-off and landing site. [19], [20], [21]

In the 21st century, more and more crop circles with various representations of such Merkabas appear worldwide. [22]

Mesolithic: Middle Stone Age, 9000-7000 BC.

Metamaterial: These are artificially produced substances that do not occur in nature. They have fantastic optical, electrical and magnetic properties. They can even be used to make "invisible cloaks". [42]

MOC / Maritime Operations Centre: Naval command center with operational management tasks in Rostock on the German Baltic coast. The MOC includes the German-Polish submarine command cell and the SAR control center (Search and Rescue). Units such as the MOC are part of the NATO communications structures but also operate worldwide in civil air and sea rescue. [12]

Morphic field (also morphogenetic field or shaping field): A field that contains information about structures of the material world. According to Rupert Sheldrake, it is a field that is responsible as "form-giving causation" for the development of structures in biology, physics, chemistry, and society. Such form-giving fields can't be detected directly with measuring instruments of the material world. However, due to their interaction with matter, their effects on matter, including living beings, are measurable. One method of indirect detection is Kirlian photography. [9]

Neocortex: The outer and, from the point of view of evolution, the youngest part of the cerebral cortex. Unique to humans is the conspicuously strong folding, which allows for a larger surface area and a higher number of interconnected cells in the skull. It is scientifically confirmed that this part enables higher cognitive abilities. The intense folding arose only in humans. Virtually overnight, a gene called ARHGAP11B caused this change and, thus, human evolution. [14], [15.1]

Paleolithic (Old Stone Age): Begins with the oldest human finds about 2.3 million years ago and ends between 10000 and 9000 BC.

Port stone: In the book, the port stone is depicted as a ritually used artifact. The mostly palm-sized and engraved natural stones or crystals amplify the energy signature of living beings. They can help in meditation to connect to the subtle world and communicate with beings there. The idea is inspired by similar objects commonly found in South America.

Protocols of the Wise Men of Zion: A writing based on forgeries. It was created by unknown editors at the beginning of the 20th century and later became an influential programmatic document of anti-Semitic conspiracy thinking. These so-called Protocols purport to be a secret document of a meeting of Jewish world conspirators. Although the writing was exposed as a forgery in the London Times as early as 1921, it spread worldwide and is still cited today as evidence of a Jewish world conspiracy. [25.1]

Shaping field: (see *morphic field*)

Social psychology: As a subfield, this science deals with human behavior and perception. Among other things, it describes the influencing of thoughts and feelings. Targeted manipulation is one way of abuse, for example, when our social world is divided into "we" and "others". Conspiracy theorists use this to create and solidify enemy images (e.g., with fear). This attempts to convince individuals or groups of a self-designed reality that many find difficult to escape. [47.1], [47.2]

Sonic mass/phonons: Sound waves can transfer mass. The phonons (quantum units of acoustic waves) react to gravity. Thus, sound waves have an influence on gravity. Exotic phenomena can be observed in experiments. Objects were held in suspension via a tractor beam. The mass of the sound waves reacts exactly inversely to the gravity of the usual mass. Thus, levitating objects are no longer fiction. [24]

Schumann frequency (also Schumann resonance): This phenomenon is named after Otto Schumann. Electromagnetic waves of specific frequencies form standing waves along the earth's circumference. These waves cause resonance with everything on the planet. Research is underway to determine how prolonged disturbances of these resonances affect the bio-rhythms of humans. [16]

Shiva: In **Indian mythology**, Shiva is one of the three primary Hindu gods who form a **Trimurti** (Trinity). Shiva is considered the destroyer, Brahma the creator and Vishnu the preserver. The female power of Shiva is Shaki, who appears as his wife, Parvati, among others. On close inspection, one can see male and female features in the statue. The four arms also embody dualism and the union of two sexes in one deity.

Shiva statue in a temple in Bengaluru (India) [26]

Stress injury: A term commonly used in the navy for particular stress to the point of a nervous breakdown. Often occurs in stressful situations in confined spaces, as is common in submarines.

Swastika: Swastika (swastika) comes from Sanskrit and means something like "bringing luck". It already appeared in the Bon religion, a predecessor religion of Buddhism. In Chinese and Tibetan, it is used both left-handed 卍 and right-handed 卐. The four arms symbolize the masculine and feminine and the eternal cycle of birth and death. [43.1]

Statue with a beard and swastika, made from the iron of the Chinga meteorite, stolen during a Nazi expedition in Tibet in the 1930s [43.2]

Theta waves: Theta waves in the brain (4-7 hertz) are the waves of the subconscious and occur especially during relaxation and falling asleep. They also happen in dreams (REM sleep), meditation and hypnosis. They stimulate the cooperation of different brain regions and enhance memory and recall. They occur more intensely when we are creatively or spiritually active. Theta waves alone remain unconscious. Only when **alpha waves** (8-13 Hertz) are added can we consciously perceive their contents (actively dream) or remember them. [10] Sleep research has proven that dreams and memories can be generated or manipulated by stimulation from the outside. [40]

Transdimensional: In terms of spatial extension, transdimensional communication refers to places outside the three-dimensional (material) world. A believer's prayer can be seen as an attempt at transdimensional communication.

USO (Unidentified Submarine Object): While an object of unknown origin observed in the airspace is called a UFO, it is called a USO if it can also move underwater.

Vedas (also Veda or Weda): The Vedas is a **Sanskrit** term most often translated as "knowledge" or "sacred teaching". It is an initially oral tradition and was later written down a collection of religious texts in Hinduism. In India, the Vedas are also revered in the sense of secular knowledge. In 2008, the Vedas were included by UNESCO in the Intangible Cultural Heritage of Humanity list. [13]

Wave genetics: Controversial theory of the Russian Pjotr Garjajev (Prof. Peter Gariaev). According to this theory, DNA contains the blueprint of life and must also be understood as a coded language. The chemistry of the genes is the "keyhole" in the door to the quantum world. The consciousness and the memory of humans are also supposed to be located there. This seems to be connected with the **morphic fields**. The aura of living and dead matter can be made visible in the so-called Kirlian photography. The aura of living beings is said to contain form and hereditary information. [33]

Whispering Knights (also **Whispering Stones**): These stones are part of the "Rollright Stones" complex. The associated monuments are found south of Long Compton in Warwickshire, across the border in Oxfordshire in England. Knowledge of the original extent of the complex, its purpose, and the builders had not yet been thoroughly researched. [1], [8]

Zen (also Zen Buddhism): The culmination of Zen Buddhism is experiencing the present moment, practiced in meditative immersion. [30] Zen also includes that wanting makes you unhappy. For Western cultures, it is astonishing that this teaching seems contradictory in many places, yet it only conveys to resolve these contradictions. This could be the key to discarding prejudices and not simply believing the convenient answers.

Sources and Websites

On the Internet, you can quickly find interesting information on many topics. In this respect, I appreciate Wikipedia, too. However, I recommend interested readers also check the sources given there.

1	Hausdorf, Hartwig: **Die Botschaft der Megalithen**, F.A. Herbig Verlagsbuchhandlung GmbH, Munich, 2015
2	https://www.bundeswehr.de/de/organisation/marine/aktuelles/indo-pacific-deployment-2021 (**German navy in the Indo-Pacific**) 2021
3	Bötig/Borowski/Strüber, MALTA-GOZO-COMINO, Karl Baedeker Verlag, Ostfildern, 2016 (**Phenomenon in Malta: cart ruts / track ruts / grinding ruts**)
4	https://commons.wikimedia.org/wiki/Category:Dingli (**Place in Malta: Dingli**) 2021
5	https://wiki.yoga-vidya.de/Manuja (**Manuja and its meaning in Sanskrit**) 2020
6	Rösler, Veit: **ATAXIT-Trigonometrie – Die Geheimnisse von Isis Maria Stella Maris – Das Universum in der Königskammer**, 2. Auflage, BoD, Norderstedt, 2017
7	https://de.wikipedia.org/wiki/Mentor_(Mythology) (**Mentor in mythology**) 2020
8	https://www.rollrightstones.co.uk/stones/whispering-knights https://de.wikipedia.org/wiki/Rollright_Stones (**Whispering Knights / Whispering Stones**) 2020
9	Sheldrake, Rupert: **Das schöpferische Universum**, Ullstein Taschenbuch, Berlin, 2010
10	https://www.hirnwellen-und-bewusstsein.de/hirnwellen_1.html --- https://www.researchgate.net/publication/225217097_Neurobiologie_der_Hypnose (**Alpha waves / Theta waves of the brain**) 2021
11	Image credit: Rubin Museum of Art - New York (Licensing: public domain in China, copyright expired), photo post-processed: Karsten Lehmann (**Tibetan mandala of** the Naropa tradition with the tantric female deity Vajrayogini) 2021
12	https://de.wikipedia.org/wiki/Marinekommando (**MOC / Maritime Operations Centre**) 2021
13	https://de.wikipedia.org/wiki/Veda (**Indian Vedas**) 2021
14	https://www.mpg.de/12628279/groesseres-gehirn (**Neocortex**) 2021
15.1	Marta Florio, Mareike Albert, Elena Taverna, Takashi Namba, Holger Brandl, Eric Lewitus, Christiane Haffner, Alex Sykes, Fong Kuan Wong, Jula Peters, E. Guhr, Sylvia Klemroth, Kay Prüfer, Janet Kelso, Ronald Naumann, Ina Nüsslein, Andreas Dahl, Robert Lachmann, Svante Pääbo, Wieland B. Huttner: **Human-specific gene ARHGAP11B promotes basal progenitor amplification and neocortex expansion**, 2015. (**ARHGAP11B Gene**)
15.2	https://de.wikipedia.org/wiki/Wieland_B._Huttner (**human-origin gene / point mutation**) 2021
16	https://de.wikipedia.org/wiki/Schumann-Resonanz (**Schumann frequency / Schumann resonance**) 2021

17	Image Credits: Google Earth Landsat/Copernicus, Data SIO, NOAA, U.S. Navy, NGA, GEBCO, Data CSUMB SFML, CA OPC, Data LDEI-Columbia, NSF, N ... (33° 53',49"N 119° 10' 25'' W) 7 km **(Underwater Structure Coast California/USA)** 2021
18	https://de.m.wikipedia.org/wiki/Generation_Z **(Future Children "Generation Z")** 2021
19	https://www.wuv.de/marketing/wer_ist_eigentlich_diese_generation_alpha **("Generation Alpha" in the 21st century)** 2021
18	https://de.m.wikipedia.org/wiki/Deepfake **(Deepfakes)** 2021
19	https://de.m.wikipedia.org/wiki/Merkaba **(Merkaba and sources of ancient chronicles)** 2021
20	https://wiki.yoga-vidya.de/Merkabah **(Merkaba/Merkabah)** 2021
21	https://de.m.wikipedia.org/wiki/Ezechiel **(Ezekiel also Ezekiel, Israeli prophet)** 2021
22	https://www.thebongiovannifamily.it/213-notizie/6780--die-merkaba-der-goetterwagen.html **(Merkaba - Crop Circles/God Chariot/Vimana)** 2021
23	Melchizedek, Drunvalo: **The Flower of Life, Volume 2**, KOHA Verlag GmbH, Dorfen, 2019 **(Merkaba / Mer-Ka-Ba, Light Body, Chakra and Scale)** 2019
24	https://www.scinexx.de/news/technik/haben-schallwellen-eine-masse/ **(Phonons, sound waves with mass and gravity)** 2021
25.1	Jeffrey L. Sammons: Einführung. In: Ders. (Hrsg.): **Die Protokolle der Weisen von Zion**. Die Grundlage des modernen Antisemitismus. Eine Fälschung. Text und Kommentar. 6. Auflage. Wallstein, Göttingen 2011 --- https://de.m.wikipedia.org/wiki/Protokolle_der_Weisen_von_Zion **(The Protocols of the Wise Men of Zion)** 2021
25.2	https://www.yadvashem.org/de.html **(Yad Vashem Holocaust Museum)** 2021
26	https://de.m.wikipedia.org/wiki/Shiva **(Indian deity Shiva)** **Image credit: : Creative Commons Attribution-ShareAlike 4.0 International (CC BY-SA 4.0)**, 2021
27	Hausdorf, Hartwig: **Nicht von dieser Welt - Dinge, die es nicht geben dürfte**, F.A. Herbig Verlagsbuchhandlung GmbH, Stuttgart, 2015 **(Iron pillar of Dhar / India)** 2021
28	https://de.m.wikipedia.org/wiki/Janmashtami **(Janmashtami holidays)** 2021
29	Gabriel, Markus: **Der Sinn des Denkens**, Ullstein Verlag, Berlin, 2018
30	https://de.m.wikipedia.org/wiki/Zen **(Zen, Zen Buddhism)** 2021
31	Photo: Sculpture (Temple of Philae), Karsten Lehmann
32	https://physik.cosmos-indirekt.de/Physik-Schule/Superkavitation https://de.m.wikipedia.org/wiki/Superkavitation **(propulsion with supercavitation long since a reality)** 2021
33	https://wavegenetics.org/de/ http://www.max-zander.org/wellengenetik-einfach-erklaert-das-wahre-potential-der-dna/ **(Wave Genetics)** 2021
34	https://de.wikipedia.org/wiki/Anch# **(Ankh or Anch symbol / Ancient Egyptian hieroglyph)** 2021
35	https://de.m.wikipedia.org/wiki/Angkor_Wat **(Angkor Wat Temple Complex)** 2021
36	https://m.youtube.com/watch?v=K2b5yMJVr4g (Klitzke, Axel, **Geheimnisse von Angkor Wat**, Video) 2019 http://www.hores.org/

37	Rumpl, Lukas Johannes, Diplomarbeit „**Effekte des endogenen Dimethyltryptamins (DMT)** auf biopsychologische Parameter und therapeutische Implikationen", Medizinische Universität Graz, 2018
38	Strassman, Rick: **DMT: The Spirit Molecule**, Park Street Press, 2000 https://www.zentrum-der-gesundheit.de/bibliothek/koerper/koerperfunktionen/zirbeldruese **(DMT, dimethyltryptamine, pineal gland)** 2021
39	https://www.unesco.de/kultur-und-natur/welterbe/welterbe-weltweit/unesco-welterbe-goebekli-tepe **(Göbekli Tepe)** 2021
40	https://www.welt.de/gesundheit/psychologie/article127929142/So-lassen-sich-kuenftig-ihre-Traeume-beeinflussen.html **(Research: Actively influencing dreams)** 2014
41	http://www.newyork.citysam.de/hauptsitz-der-vereinten-nationen.htm **(UN Headquarters in New York)** 2021
42	https://www.weltderphysik.de/gebiet/materie/metamaterialien/ **(Metamaterial)** 2021
43.1	https://vedanta-yoga.de/indische-mythologie/swastika-hakenkreuz-hinduismus/ https://de.m.wikipedia.org/wiki/Swastika **(Swastika / Swastika)** 2021
43.2	https://www.spiegel.de/fotostrecke/raetselhafte-statue-buddha-mit-bart-und-swastika-fotostrecke-157696.html **(Statue with beard and swastika from Tibet)** 2021
44	https://de.wikipedia.org/wiki/B%C3%B6n **(Bon Religion)** 2019
45.1	https://de.m.wikipedia.org/wiki/Enki **(Sumerian god Enki/Ea)** 2021
45.2	Image credit: British Museum Collection (public domain), *Open Government License of The Controller of Her Majesty's Stationery Office (OGL3)* 2021.
46	https://de.m.wikipedia.org/wiki/Falun_Gong **(Persecution of Falun Gong followers in China)** 2021
47.1	https://de.m.wikipedia.org/wiki/Sozialpsychologie 2021
47.2	Kessler / Fritsche: **Sozialpsychologie**, Springer Verlag, 1st ed. 2018 **(Enemy Images in Social Psychology)** 2018.
48	https://de.m.wikipedia.org/wiki/Verfassungskreislauf **(Cycle of Constitutions - Plato/Aristotle/Polybios)** 2021
49	https://www.weltmaschine.de/physik/higgs/ **(Higgs field)** 2021
50	https://www.wissenschaft.de/astronomie-physik/wasserreservoir-tief-im-erdinneren/ **(water reservoir in the earth's interior)** 2021
51	Photo (edited): Traces in the rock (Malta/Gozo islands), Academic dictionaries and enceclopedias. https://de-academic.com/dic.nsf/dewiki/1249698 2017
52	https://de.wikipedia.org/wiki/Verfassungskreislauf **(Cycle of Constitutions in Polybios)** 2021
53	Source (graphic edited by Karsten Lehmann): Andreas Mohorte/Engadget/World Economic Forum, Geneva 2018.
54	Photo (edited): Saumy Nagayach / Tripoto - Madhya Pradesh Travel Guide, 2020

Special Thanks

Valuable support I received in uncounted hours before this book could be finished. Whether the discussions about content, criticism, or suggestions for wording, I am very grateful to all contributors because they had an indispensable part in it.

The topic of human genetics may have given me decisive inspiration. The starting point was the publications by Prof. Dr. Wieland B. Huttner and his team at the Max Planck Institute of Molecular Cell Biology and Genetics in Dresden. In these papers, the scientists described that an unusual gene mutation was significantly involved in the erratic growth of the human brain. Huttner didn't write anything about targeted human development. But the idea was enough to give the targeted sociological formation of man a place in my fictional story.

Special thank goes to my wife, Ines, because she again had a lot of patience while I discussed my ideas. Helpful was not only the encouraging words but especially her honest criticism, especially since she was usually the first to be confronted with my drafts.

I want to thank our daughters Maja and Carolin because they took a lot of time for the manuscript. Whether critically questioned details, generation-typical formulations or even sociological aspects, they were always able to surprise me and provide textual clarification.

This time, too, I had help with formulating anatomical and medical facts. In this regard, I received valuable advice from my brother, Dr. med. Lutz Lehmann. He made it easier for me to balance academic aspects and literary freedom. I always value conversations with him very much.

The incredible support of Elke Harms has contributed significantly to the success of this project. This concerns her help with correcting and proofreading and the exciting discussions during our regular dog walking, where she gave me valuable suggestions.

I still have a guilty conscience that I have not sufficiently appreciated someone. In conclusion, thank all test readers and those who supported me with research or organizational matters for their help.

The Author

Karsten Lehmann, born in 1965 in Dresden, studied mechanical engineering and automotive engineering. He then moved into software development and was an IT manager for many years. In his books, characters travel through time and into the frontiers of science to follow the traces of ancient civilizations. In doing so, he clarifies how digitization is changing lives and behaviors. Lehmann confronts us with the targeted manipulation of our psyche in everyday life.

Since the 1980s, the author has been investigating early human history and ancient building structures. Like other contemporaries, he has encountered a paradox. Some of the oldest cultural legacies seem more perfect than recent ones. The search for the secrets of this prehistoric era also runs through his adventurous stories. It is fascinating to see what is still waiting to be discovered. But Lehmann has already found one thing: enough adventure for his novel heroes.